The PRINCESS of BURUNDI

THOMAS DUNNE BOOKS

ST. MARTIN'S MINOTAUR 🙢 NEW YORK

The PRINCESS of BURUNDI

Kjell Eriksson

Translated from the Swedish
by Ebba Segerberg

THOMAS DUNNE BOOKS.
An imprint of St. Martin's Press.

THE PRINCESS OF BURUNDI. Copyright © 2006 by Kjell Eriksson. Translation © 2006 by Ebba Segerberg. All rights reserved. Printed in the United States of America. No part of this book may be used or reproduced in any manner whatsoever without written permission except in the case of brief quotations embodied in critical articles or reviews. For information, address St. Martin's Press, 175 Fifth Avenue, New York, N.Y. 10010.

www.minotaurbooks.com

Book design by Irene Vallye

Library of Congress Cataloging-in-Publication Data

Eriksson, Kjell, 1953–
    [Prinsessan av Burundi. English]
    The princess of Burundi / Kjell Eriksson ; translated from the Swedish by Ebba Segerberg.
        p. cm.
    ISBN 0-312-32767-6
    EAN 978-0-312-32767-5
    I. Segerberg, Ebba. II. Title.

PT 9876.21.J39P7513 2006
839.73'8—dc22
                                                                    2005050965

10   9   8   7   6   5   4   3   2

One

The plate trembled, knocking over the glass. The milk flowed out over the waxed tablecloth like a white flower.

Typical—we have almost no milk left, she thought. She quickly righted the glass and wiped up the milk with a dishrag.

"When is Dad coming home?"

She twirled around. Justus was leaning up against the doorpost.

"I don't know," she said, throwing the dishrag into the sink.

"What's for dinner?"

He had a book in his hand, his index finger tucked in to mark the page he was reading. She wanted to ask him what it was, but then she thought of something and walked over to the window.

"Stew," she said absently. She looked out at the parking lot. It had started to snow again.

Maybe he was working. She knew he had talked to Micke. He always needed extra workers for his snow-removal crew, and it had been coming down for days now. John wasn't afraid of heights, either.

Berit smiled at the memory of how he had climbed the drainpipe to her balcony long ago. It was only on the second floor, but still. He could have broken his neck if he had fallen. *Just like his father,* she thought, and her smile faded.

She had been furious with him, but he had just laughed. Then he had scooped her up in a tight embrace, with a strength you would never have thought John's slender body was capable of.

Later—clearly flattered—she liked to tell the story of his climb and his persistence. It was their earliest and most important shared memory.

Snow removal. A small tractor drove across the parking lot and pushed even more snow up over the heavily laden bushes by the edge of the lot. Harry was the driver. She recognized him by his red cap.

Harry was the one who had set Justus to work, giving him a summer job when no one else was hiring. Lawn mowing, clearing out trash, weeding. Justus complained, but he had been bursting with pride at his first paycheck.

Berit's gaze followed the snowplow. Snow was falling thickly. The orange signal light revolved on the roof of the tractor. Darkness settled in over the buildings and the parking lot. The light was flung to the far corners of the grounds. Harry was certainly busy. How many hours had he had to work the past few days?

"This weather's going to send me to the Canary Islands," he had shouted to her the other day when they met outside the front door.

He had leaned on his shovel and asked her about Justus. He always did. She turned and meant to say hello from Harry but Justus had already gone.

"What are you doing?" she cried out into the apartment.

"Nothing," Justus yelled back.

Berit assumed he was sitting in front of the computer. Ever since August, when John had dragged home the boxes, Justus had sat glued to the screen.

"The kid has to have a computer. He'll be left behind otherwise," John had said when she complained at the extravagance.

"How much did it cost?"

"I got it cheap," he had told her, and quickly showed her the receipt from the electronics store when he caught her look. That accusing look, the one he knew so well.

She looked around the kitchen but there was nothing else to be done. Dinner was ready. She went back to the window. He had said he would be back around four and it was close to six now. He usually called if he was delayed, but that had been mostly when he was doing a lot of overtime at the workshop. He had never liked to work late, but his boss, Sagge—Agne Sagander—had a way of asking that made it hard to say no. It always sounded as if the order in question were going to make or break the company.

He had grown more quiet after he was fired. John had never been one to talk much, of course—Berit was the one who supplied the conversation—but he became even less talkative after he was let go.

He had cheered up only this fall. Berit was convinced that it had to do with the fish, the new aquarium he had been talking about for years and that had become a reality at last.

He had needed all that work with the fish tank, had spent a couple of weeks in September on it. Harry had given him a hand with the final assembly. He and Gunilla had come to the grand opening. Berit had thought it silly to inaugurate a fish tank but the party had been a success.

Their closest neighbor, Stellan, had looked in, as had John's mom, and Lennart had been sober and cheerful. Stellan, who was normally quite reserved, had put an arm around Berit and said something about how cute she looked. John had just smiled, though he usually was sensitive about things like this, especially when he had had a drink or two. But there was no reason to be jealous of Stellan.

Harry had finished clearing the parking lot. The flashing orange signal flung new cascades of light across the path to the laundry facilities and communal rooms. Snow removal. Berit had only a vague idea of what this task involved. Did they still climb up on the roof like in the old days? She could remember the bundled-up men from her childhood with their big shovels and ropes slung in great loops over their shoulders. She could even recall the warning signs they posted in the courtyard and on the street.

Was he over at Lennart's? Brother Tuck, as John called him. She didn't like it. It reminded her of the bad old days. She never knew what to make of it: Lennart's loquacious self-assurance and John's pressed silence.

Berit was only sixteen when the three of them met. First she got to know John, then Lennart. The brothers appeared inseparable. Lennart, tossing his long black hair off his face, unpredictable in his movements, always on the go, picking nervously, chattering. John, blond, thin-lipped, and with a gentleness about him that had immediately appealed to her. A scar across his left eye created an unexpected contrast with the pale skin in his slightly androgynous face. The scar was from a motorcycle accident. Lennart had been driving.

Berit had been unable to understand how John and Lennart could be brothers. They were so different, both in appearance and in manner. Once she had gone so far as to ask Aina, their mother, about it. It had been toward the end of the crayfish party, but she had only smiled and joked about it.

It didn't take long for Berit to figure out that the brothers didn't always make their money in traditional ways. John worked at the workshop off and on, but it seemed to Berit that this was more to keep up appearances, especially with regard to Albin, his father.

John had a criminal bent. Not because he was evil or greedy, but simply because a conventional lifestyle didn't seem to be quite enough for him. It was something he had in common with many of the people around him, teenagers who appeared well adjusted on the surface but who drifted around the eastern parts of Uppsala most evenings and nights in anxious herds. They picked pockets, snatched purses, stole mopeds and cars, broke into basements, and smashed shopwindows as the spirit moved them.

A few, like John and Lennart, were permanent fixtures. Others came and went, most of them dropping out after six months or a year.

Some took classes at the Boland School in order to become painters, concrete workers, mechanics, or whatever other professions were open to working-class youths in the early seventies. Others took jobs straight out of middle school. None of them continued with more formal academic subjects at the high school level. They had neither the will nor the grades for that.

Most of them lived at home with their parents, who were not always the ideal people to prevent substance abuse, theft, and other illegal activities. They had enough of their own problems and often stood by, quite powerless to do anything to stop their offspring. They were awkward and embarrassed when dealing with the welfare workers, psychologists, and other social officials, confused by the bureaucratic language, their own inadequacies, and their intense sense of shame.

"If I hadn't had them, it would all have gone to hell," John had said once.

It was only when he was getting regular work at the factory that he started to move away from life on the streets and the gangs. Regular work, a new sense of being appreciated, decent wages, and then Berit.

Lennart delivered groceries by day and hung out at the pool hall in Sivia at night. John was there too. He was the better player of the two, though that hardly bothered Lennart, who spent most of his time on the flipper machines down below.

That was where Berit met them. She had come with a girl named Anna-Lena, who was in love with a boy who frequented the place.

She fell in love with John at first sight. He snuck around the pool table with the cue in his hand and played with intense concentration, something that appealed to Berit. He rarely said anything.

His hands were slender. She studied his fingers splayed on the green mat, his gaze focused along the stick, serious. It was the seriousness she noticed. And eyelashes. His gaze, the intense gaze.

She wasn't sure what made her start thinking about the pool hall. It had been years since she had been there. It was probably because she had been thinking about Brother Tuck, and about how John was probably with him. She didn't want to call. They were probably drinking. Sometimes John felt he had to have a real session with Lennart. It didn't happen very often nowadays, but when his mind was made up nothing could stop him. Not even Justus. The boy knew it, knew his father deep under the skin, and his protests were never particularly loud or long-lived.

Once, when Justus was about twelve, John let himself be talked out of it and came home. Justus had called his uncle himself and demanded to speak to his father. Berit was not allowed to listen; Justus had locked himself in the bathroom with the portable phone. John came home after half an hour. Staggering, but he came home.

It was as if these occasional evenings with his brother functioned as a temporary return to his former existence. These drinking sessions kept the brothers close. Berit had no idea what they talked about. Old times, their childhood in Almtuna, or something else?

They didn't have much common ground. They cleaved to each other because of their shared past. Berit sometimes felt something akin to jealousy when confronted with this world that was largely foreign to her. Their childhood, the early years, appeared to be the only source of joy when they were talking. Even Lennart's voice, normally void of emotion, grew warm.

And Berit stood outside all of this. Her life with John didn't count, or so it seemed to her. She entered his life when everything turned, when his childhood reached a definitive end. She wasn't there in the early, light-filled days, the happy years that would be remembered and retold.

"When is he coming?"

"Soon," she replied, shouting.

She was grateful that Justus was in his bedroom.

"He's probably clearing snow somewhere. I've never seen anything like it."

She expected him to say something else, but he didn't. She wanted to hear his voice, but he didn't say anything. *What is he doing, thinking?* Did she dare leave the kitchen and go to his room? But the half-darkness of the kitchen was all she could handle. No light, no quick flickering characters on a computer screen, no questioning looks from Justus.

"Maybe you can help Harry," she shouted. "Make a little extra."

No response.

"He'll probably need some help with the basement stairs."

"I don't give a shit about his snow."

Justus had suddenly reappeared in the doorway.

"It's not just his snow," Berit said gently.

Justus snorted and stretched out a hand to the light switch.

"No, don't turn it on!"

She regretted it the instant she said it.

"It's just that it's cozy with a little darkness. I'll light some candles instead."

She felt his gaze from the doorway.

"You should make a little money," she said.

"I don't need any. And Dad has money, anyway."

"Of course, but not a lot. You've been talking about buying a camera."

Justus gave her a dismissive look. Was it a look of triumph?

"No harm in asking him, though, is there?" she continued.

"Nag, nag, nag," he said and turned on his heel, in that way that only he could, and went back to his room.

She heard him slam his door and the creaking of the bed when he threw himself on it. She walked back over to the window. Harry and his tractor had disappeared. A number of lights were on in the building across the way. She could see families around the dinner table. A bluish TV light flickered in a few others.

A shadow moved next to the parking garages and she almost shouted with joy, but as she kept watching no John appeared. Had she only imagined it? If you walked down between the rows of garages you eventually came out by the garbage cans, but there was no one there. No John. Berit stared out into the darkness. Suddenly she glimpsed the figure again. She had seen someone for a moment, a man in green, but it wasn't John.

Who was it? Why had he waited before emerging by the garbage cans? It occurred to her that maybe it was Harry's brother, who used to help him with the snow removal. No John. The short moment of relief was replaced by loneliness.

The potatoes on the stove were still lukewarm. She turned the burner with the stew to its lowest setting. *He'll be here soon,* she told herself, and cupped her hands around the pot.

She called Lennart at half past seven. He answered on the fifth ring and sounded sober. He hadn't heard from John in several days.

"He'll turn up," he said lightly, but she could hear the concern in his voice.

Berit could imagine him restlessly shuffling back and forth in the hall.

"I'll make a couple of calls," he said. "He's probably just having a few beers with someone."

Berit hated him for those words. *A few beers.* She hung up.

She called John's mother, but did not mention that he was more than a few hours late. She had called in the hope that he had looked in on her and been detained. They chatted for a while as Berit walked around the apartment.

Lennart called at a quarter past eight.

"Why'd you hang up on me?" he started, and she could hear that he had a few drinks in him. That's when she knew.

"Where can he be?" Now her desperation broke out.

Justus came out of his room.

"I'm hungry," he said.

She gestured to him to calm down and finished talking to Lennart.

"Do you have any idea where Daddy can be?" she asked.

She knew she shouldn't be letting it get the upper hand, but the anxiety made her tremble. Justus made an awkward movement with his hand.

"I've no idea, but he'll be here soon," he said.

Berit started to cry.

"Mom, he'll be here!"

"Yes, he'll be back soon," she said and tried to smile, but it was mostly a grimace. "I just get so worked up when he doesn't call and let me know. The potatoes are ruined."

"Can't we eat in the meantime?"

She was suddenly furious. Because she interpreted Justus's words as somehow disloyal, or because of an intimation that something terrible had happened?

They sat down at the kitchen table. Harry and his tractor reappeared in the courtyard, and Berit was about to say something again about snow removal but stopped when she saw his face.

The potatoes were pasty and the meat tender but lukewarm. Justus cleared the table in silence. She watched his mechanical movements. The jeans, which were two sizes too big, hung from his thin thighs and nonexistent butt. His fashion and music tastes had been changing lately, from a penchant for soft English pop, which Berit had often been able to appreciate, to a noisy, jerky rap music that sounded only discordant and angry to her ears. His taste in clothing had changed accordingly.

She looked at the clock on the wall. Nine. Now she knew it would be late. Very late.

Two

He was watching the bus driver. She was all over the place, first pulling too close to the car in front and driving much too fast, then slamming on the brakes.

"Women drivers," he mumbled.

The bus was half full. An immigrant was sitting directly in front of him, probably a Kurd or an Iranian. Sometimes it seemed to him as if half of all the people he saw were *svartskallar,* the derogatory term for dark-haired foreigners. Gunilla sat three seats away. He smiled to himself when he saw her neck. She had been one of the prettiest girls in the class with her long blond wavy hair and shining eyes. Those silky tendrils had given her a fairy-like appearance, especially when she laughed. Now her hair had lost all its former luster.

The bus approached the roundabout at high speed, and the resulting sharp deceleration forced a passenger near the door to lose his balance and lunge forward. His shoulder bag swung around, hitting Gunilla in the head, and she turned. *She looks the same, but different,* he thought when he saw her startled and somewhat annoyed expression.

He had seen her in this posture countless times, her body half-turned and her head craning around. But at school there had often been something indolent and teasing about her, as if she were inviting the gaze of others, though not Vincent. She had never invited him to do anything, had hardly even registered his presence.

"You gave me nothing," Vincent mumbled.

He felt sick to his stomach.

Get off so I don't have to see you anymore, he thought. The Iranian had a bad case of dandruff. The bus careened on. Gunilla had gained weight. Her girlish languor had been replaced by a heavyset fatigue.

Get off! Vincent Hahn bored his eyes into her head. When the bus passed the building that in his day had been Uno Lantz's junk store but now housed modern offices, he had an idea. *Sick, so fucking sick,* he thought. *But damned good.*

He laughed out loud. The Iranian turned and smiled.

"You have dandruff," Vincent said.

The Iranian nodded and his smile widened.

"Dandruff," Vincent said more loudly. Gunilla and a handful of the other passengers turned around. Vincent lowered his head. He was sweating. He got off at the next stop and remained standing in one place after the bus continued down Kungsgatan. He looked down at his feet. He always got off too early. *My poor feet,* he thought. *My poor feet. Poor me.*

His feet led him down Bangårdsgatan to the river and then down toward Nybro bridge. He stopped there, his arms hanging passively at his sides. Only his eyes moved. Everyone seemed to be in a hurry. Only Vincent Hahn could take his time. He stared down into the black water. It was December 17, 2001. *How cold it is,* he thought as the sweat on his back started to freeze.

"The poor Talibans," he said. "Poor everyone."

The foot traffic behind him grew heavier. More and more people were walking over the bridge. He lifted his head and looked toward the Spegeln movie theater. A large collection of people had gathered on the street outside. Was it a protest of some sort or had there been an accident? A woman laughed loudly. He realized that the theater was simply showing a popular movie. Laughter. As people moved across the street it looked like a laughing demonstration.

The cathedral clock struck six and he checked his wristwatch. Vincent smiled triumphantly at the clock tower, which was fifty-five seconds too fast. The cold and the chilly breeze from the river finally drove him to cross the street and make his way to the central square, Stora Torget.

"It was so bad I didn't dare . . ." he heard someone say, and he turned around to catch the rest. He would have liked to find out what it was. What was it that had been so bad?

He stopped and stared at the back of the person he thought had uttered those words. *Soon it will be even worse,* he wanted to shout. *Much, much worse.*

Three

Ola Haver was listening to his wife, an amused smile on his face.

"Who are you laughing at?"

"No one," Haver said defensively.

Rebecka Haver snorted.

"Go on, please. I'd like to hear the rest," he said, and stretched out his hand for the salt shaker.

She shot him a look as if she were deciding whether or not to go on telling him about the situation at her workplace.

"He's a threat to public health," she said, pointing at the photograph in the county-administration newsletter.

"Surely that's taking it a bit far."

Rebecka shook her head while she again tapped her finger on the bearded county-politician's face. *I wouldn't want to be under that finger,* Haver thought.

"This is about everyone in our community, the aged, the weak, the ones who neither dare nor have the ability to speak up for themselves."

He had heard this particular line of reasoning before and was starting to get sick of it. He salted his food a second time.

"Too much salt isn't good for you," Rebecka said.

He looked at her, put down the salt shaker, grasped his spoon, and ate the rest of his overly hard-boiled egg in silence.

Haver stood up, cleared the table, and put his coffee cup, saucer, and egg cup in the dishwasher, hastily wiped down the kitchen counter, and turned off the light over the stove. After these habitual actions he usually checked the temperature on the outside thermometer but this morning he remained standing in the middle of the kitchen. Something stopped him from moving over to the window, as if he were restrained by an invisible hand. Rebecka looked up briefly but went back to her reading. Then he knew. After checking the thermometer he would bend down and kiss his wife on the top of her head, say something about how much he liked her. The same routine every morning.

This time he hesitated, or rather it was his body that hesitated, that refused to take those two paces to the window. This discovery confused him.

Rebecka had stopped reading and was watching him with a kind of professional attentiveness, ingrained after many years of hospital rounds. He made a gesture as if to close the door to the dishwasher, but it was already shut.

"How are you feeling?"

"Fine," he said. "I was just thinking."

"Do you have a headache?"

He made a sweeping motion with his hand as if to brush this aside. During the fall he had suffered recurrent attacks of blinding pain in his forehead. It had been several weeks since the last attack. Had she noticed the reason for his hesitation? He didn't think so.

"Our division is getting a new guy today," he said. "From Gothenburg."

"Strip him of his gun," Rebecka said tartly.

He didn't bother to reply; suddenly he was in a hurry. He left the kitchen and disappeared into the next room, which they used as an office.

"I'm going to be late," he said, from halfway inside the closet. He threw on a sweat suit, shoes, and a sweater that Rebecka had made for him. He pulled out a bag from the clothing store Kapp Ahl from under some boxes, shut the door to the closet, and quickly walked out through the kitchen.

"I'm going to be late," he repeated, and hesitated in the hallway for a few seconds before he opened the front door and stepped out into the chilly December morning. He took a few deep breaths, setting off with his head down.

December. The time of darkness. For Rebecka—or so it seemed—the darkness was heavier than it had been in years. Haver couldn't remember her ever having been so low. He had been watching her strained attempts to put on a good face, but under the frail exterior her seasonal depression, or whatever it was, tugged at the thin membrane of control stretched over her pressed features.

A few snowflakes fluttered down. He met Josefsson from apartment 3, who was out with his poodle. This neighbor, who admired police officers and was always full of effusive praise for members of his profession, smiled and said a few words about the winter that was now upon them. Josefsson's enthusiastic cheeriness always rubbed him the wrong way. Haver mumbled something about having to work.

He thought about Rebecka. She should start working again. She needed to have people around, the stress of the ward, regular contact with patients and colleagues. Their small evening talks when she and Haver would tell each other what had happened at work that day had been replaced by a sullen atmosphere and a tense anticipation of what would happen next. They needed something new, an injection of new energy. Since child number two, Sara, their relationship had lost much of its spice.

Haver now felt as if the routines at work were mirrored by a kind of somnambulism at home. There was a time when he had felt a physical joy at the thought of coming home, a longing for Rebecka, just to be close to her.

Was she the only one who had changed? Haver had thought about this. Sammy "Rasbo" Nilsson, a colleague in the Homicide Division, said it was a sign of his age.

"The two of you have entered into a middle-age crisis, the time when couples realize that life isn't going to get any better," he had said, smiling.

"Bullshit," Haver had cut him off. Now he wasn't so sure. He loved Rebecka, had done so from the very first. Did she love him? He had discovered a new, critical expression on her face, as if she were looking at him with new eyes. Sure, he worked a lot more now that Ann Lindell was on maternity leave, but there had been times when he had worked at least as much and back then it had never bothered her.

The cell phone rang.

"Hello, it's me," said Chief Ottosson. "You can forget about target practice today. We have a body."

Haver froze. Josefsson's poodle barked in the distance. It had probably met up with the female Labrador from apartment 5.

"Where?"

"In Libro. A jogger found it."

"A jogger?"

The sun was barely peeking over the horizon. Were there really people up and running this early, in this weather?

"Forensics is on its way," said Ottosson.

He sounded tired and distant, as if he were almost bored, as if a jogger coming across a dead body were a routine occurrence.

"Homicide?"

"Most likely," said Ottosson, but he corrected himself immediately. "Definitely. The body is mutilated." Haver now heard the note of hopelessness in the chief's voice.

It was not tiredness but despair at the human capacity for evil that made the thoroughly nice Ottosson sound so distracted.

"Where is Libro?"

"Right where you drive out of town, on the right-hand side after the county storage facility."

Haver thought hard as he was unlocking the car door, trying to recall what the rest of Börjegatan looked like.

"The car-inspection facility?"

"Farther. It's where the county dumps its snow."

"Okay, I know where that is. Who else?"

"Fredriksson and Bea."

They finished the conversation. He had told Rebecka he would be late and he would be, for sure, but now for a completely different reason from the one he had imagined fifteen minutes ago. The local police-union meeting would be replaced with a strategy session at work or some such business. The union would have to wait, as would his scheduled practice session at the shooting range.

John Harald Jonsson had bled copiously. The originally light-colored jacket was now deeply stained with blood. Death had probably come as a relief. He was missing three fingers from his right hand, severed at the second joint. Burn marks and blue-black contusions on his neck and face bore witness to his suffering.

Forensic technician Eskil Ryde was standing a few meters from the body, staring in a northerly direction. Haver thought he looked like Sean Connery with his stern features, stubble, and receding hairline. He was gazing out over the Uppsala plains as if expecting to find answers out there. Actually he was watching a Viggen fighter jet.

Beatrice and Fredriksson were crouched down. The wind was blowing from the west. A colleague in uniform was putting up police tape. There was an indefinably sweet smell in the air that made Haver turn around.

Fredriksson looked up and nodded at Haver.

"Little John," he said.

Haver had also recognized the murdered man immediately. A few years ago he had cross-examined him in a case involving his brother, Lennart, who had named John as his alibi witness. A nice guy, as far as Haver could recall, a former small-time thief who had never resorted to violence. Not surprisingly, John had corroborated his brother's claims. He was lying, of course, Haver had always been convinced of that, but even so he had never been able to disprove Lennart Jonsson's alibi.

They had talked about fish, Haver remembered. Little John had a passion for tropical fish and from there it wasn't too great a step to fishing.

"What a fucking sight," Beatrice sighed, getting to her feet with effort.

Ottosson's car pulled up by the side of the road. The three police officers watched their chief talk to some of the curious onlookers who had already gathered by highway 272, about fifty meters away. He gestured with his hand to show that they couldn't park their cars along this stretch of road.

"Where is the jogger?" Haver asked, looking around.

"In the emergency room," Bea said. "When he ran out onto the road to flag down a car he slipped badly. He may have broken his arm."

"Has anyone questioned him?"

"Yes; he lives in Luthagen and runs here every morning."

"What was he doing out here in the snow?"

"He likes to run on the bicycle trail, apparently. But first he does some stretches and moves in from the road. At least that was his explanation."

"Did he see anything?"

"No, nothing."

"He's probably been here all night," the forensic technician said, indicating the body.

"Tire tracks?"

"All over," Beatrice said.

"It's a dump, for Pete's sake," Fredriksson said.

"Got it," Haver said.

He took a closer look at Little John. He was severely bruised, the victim of someone who was extremely thorough or enraged, or both. The burn marks—most likely from a cigarette—were deep. Haver bent over and studied Little John's wrists. Dark red marks bore witness to them having been tightly bound.

The stumps on his hands where the fingers had been removed were blackened. The cuts were neatly made, probably with a very sharp knife or scissors. Maybe pliers.

Ottosson came jogging over and Haver went up to meet him.

"Little John," he said simply, and the chief nodded.

He looked unexpectedly alert. Perhaps it was the brisk temperature.

"I heard he had been mutilated."

"What did Little John know that was so important?"

"What do you mean?"

"I think he was tortured," Haver said, then suddenly he thought of the murdered man's tropical fish. *Piranhas.* He shivered.

Ottosson sniffed. A sudden gust made them look up. Haver's thoughtful mood from the morning remained. He felt unenterprising and unprofessional.

"A protracted struggle," he said.

Ottosson took out a checkered handkerchief and blew his nose loudly.

"Damned wind," he said. "Found anything?"

"No. He was probably brought here by car."

"It's open," Ottosson stated, nodding in the direction of the raised barrier. "I come by this way fairly often and I never see anyone turn in here, other than in the winter when the county trucks dump snow here."

Haver knew that Ottosson had a cabin near the city and thought he had heard that it was on Gysingevägen somewhere.

Ottosson suddenly turned around and spotted Fredriksson and the forensic technician, who were talking next to the body. Bea had left the pair and was wandering around nearby.

"Why did you come out here?" Haver shouted at his back.

Ottosson didn't usually turn up so quickly at the scene of a crime.

"I booked Little John when he was sixteen. It was his first contact with us."

"How old did he get?"

"He was forty-two," Ottosson said and continued to his car.

Four

She was taken by surprise. She had looked back at the sound of something she thought was a scream. Ann Lindell turned around. A woman's scream.

When she turned back again he was right in front of her, Santa Claus, with an overabundant beard and a macabre face mask.

"Good grief, you scared me to half to death."

"Merry Christmas," the Santa said, trying to sound like a Walt Disney character.

Go to hell, she thought, but smiled.

"No, thank you," she said, as if the Santa had been trying to sell her something, which had probably been his intention because he left her in order to turn his attention to a couple with three children.

She walked into the supermarket. *He would do more good shoveling the sidewalk,* she thought. *Then at least you'd be able to get in.* She stamped hard to get the snow off her feet and took out her shopping list. It was long and she was already exhausted.

Candles were first on the list, then an endless number of various food items. She didn't want to be doing this, but she had no choice. It was the first time her parents were coming to Uppsala for Christmas. Granted, her mother had promised to bring a few Christmas dishes with her, but the list was still daunting.

She was sweating by the time she reached the vegetable aisle.

"Do you have any cabbage?" she asked a passing employee, who gestured vaguely.

"Thank you," Lindell said pointedly. "Thanks for the detailed directions."

A hand appeared on her arm. She turned around and saw Asta Lundin.

"Ann, it's certainly been a long time," she said.

She kept her hand where it was, and Ann Lindell felt the pressure on her arm. The past flickered in front of her eyes. Asta was the widow of Tomato-Anton, a labor-union buddy who had been friends with Edvard Risberg. Ann had met her a few times through Edvard. They had had coffee in her kitchen and Edvard had later helped her when she moved into town.

"Asta," she said simply, unable to think.

"I see you have a little one," Asta said, nodding to the carrier on Ann's back.

"His name is Erik," Ann said.

"Is everything all right?"

She wanted to cry. Asta's hair stood like a halo around her thin face. She recalled Edvard's saying that Tomato-Anton and Asta were some of the best people he had ever met.

"Yes, everything's fine," Ann said, but her expression betrayed her.

"There's a lot that has to go in the shopping cart," Asta said. "What a chore."

Ann wanted to ask about Edvard. She hadn't talked to him in a year and a half, ever since that evening at the Östhammar hospital when she told him she was pregnant with another man's child. She hadn't heard anything about him through anyone. It was as if he had been erased from her life. Was he still living on Gräsö island, renting the flat above Viola's? What was he doing? Was he in touch with his teenage boys? And—this is when she started to lose it—was he seeing anyone new?

"You look good," Asta said. "Pink cheeked and healthy."

"Thanks. How about you?"

"My sister's coming up for the holidays."

"How nice. My parents are coming up too, they want to see how Erik has grown. Have you . . ." Ann started, but couldn't bring herself to finish.

"I understand. Our Edvard," Asta said, putting her hand back on Ann's arm.

Ann remembered what Edvard had told her about Asta and Anton, how physically affectionate they had been, how much they had hugged and kissed each other. For Edvard, the Lundins had embodied the principle of fidelity in their relationship to each other and in their lives.

"Maybe you don't hear much from Gräsö," Asta said.

"Is he still there?"

"The same place. Viola is a little frail these days, I think she had a stroke in the fall, but she's back on her feet again."

"That's good," Ann said flatly.

"Should we have a cup?" Asta asked.

They sat down at a small table and drank some of the complimentary coffee from paper cups. Erik whined a little, so Ann took off the baby carrier and unzipped his little coat.

"He looks nice and healthy," Asta said.

There was so much Ann wanted to ask about, but she held back. It felt strange to sit there with this old woman, as if they had known each other for a long time, and yet they hadn't. She felt ashamed. She had betrayed Edvard and by extension his closest friends. She had hurt him, caused him pain, she knew that, but she saw no bitterness in Asta, or anger.

"Edvard is doing well," Asta said. "He came by about a month ago. He looks in on me from time to time."

So he's been in town, Ann thought. *Maybe we've passed each other on the street, maybe he saw me?*

"He keeps busy with work," Asta continued. "He works on as before. They've all been workaholics, that family. I knew his father and his grandfather before him."

Ann nodded. She remembered Albert Risberg, the old man who lived upstairs at Ramnäs farm, where Edvard was working when they first met.

"He's become a real Roslagen boy."

Asta paused, took a sip of her coffee, and looked at Ann.

"I'm sorry things turned out the way they did," she said. "It really is too bad."

"I can't say it's been the best time of my life," said Ann.

"Edvard isn't a strong man. Anton often said that to me."

Ann didn't want to hear any more, and it was as if Asta could tell, because she interrupted herself.

"Life doesn't always turn out the way you expect," she said with a crooked smile.

"Has he . . . ?"

"No, he lives alone," Asta said.

"You're reading my thoughts," said Ann.

"Your thoughts are an open book, my dear. Do you still love him?"

Ann nodded. She didn't want to cry, not in a supermarket with crowds of people. She would let the tears come when she was alone. Of course she still loved him.

"These things take time," Asta said. "Life will get better again, you'll see."

These things take time, Ann repeated to herself. Had Asta talked to Edvard? *Perhaps he wants to meet with me—to forgive?* She wanted to ask Asta what she had meant but feared the answer.

"Maybe," she said and stood up. "I have to keep shopping. Thanks for the chat."

Asta didn't say anything. She stayed at the table and was still there when Ann walked by a little later on her way to the deli counter. That gray hair, her thin hands on the table. Ann sensed that she was thinking about Anton.

Five

He felt drawn to the moss peeking out from under the snow. If it had been summer he would have stretched out on it for a little while, taken a short rest. He breathed deeply. Once, twice. She had turned on a lamp in the living room. He was able to catch a few brief glimpses of her.

"I am a forest warrior," he said aloud.

It was an appealing thought, that he was a creature from outside, approaching the warm windows from the moss and the darkness.

Suddenly a light went on in the bedroom. She was naked from the waist up except for a light-colored bra. She opened the closet, took out a sweater, and pulled it on in a motion so quick that he swore. He wanted to see her. How he had dreamed about those breasts!

She remained in the bedroom, turning this way and that in front of the mirror, making some adjustments. She walked closer to the mirror and leaned forward. He had to do the same in order to keep watching her. The distance from the window to the tree he was hidden behind was around five meters. He sniffed the trunk. A smell of moisture, nothing else.

She turned off the light and left the room. He waited for ten minutes before gingerly approaching the patio and crouching down behind the railing. What was his plan? Indecision caused him to hesitate. He'd thought he had it all figured out, but now that he was here, so close to one of his tormentors, it no longer seemed appealing.

Vincent Hahn felt himself going back twenty-five, thirty years. There had been moments of greatness even then, moments when had he decided to turn the tables. These intentions, however, inevitably crumbled in the face of reality. She still had the power to unnerve him, a fact that infuriated him but did nothing to help him throw off these feelings of inferiority and passivity.

Six

A knife, Haver thought. *What kind of person kills with a knife?* Lacerations to the chest and arms, severed fingers, burn marks—all pointed to a case of torture. He scrawled a few lines on his notepad before he rolled his chair up to the computer and started to write a report. After he had entered the preliminary data, there was a knock on the door. Fredriksson looked in.

"Little John," Fredriksson said.

"I've accessed all our material on him."

"It's damned cold out there."

Fredriksson still looked frozen.

"His brother is still active from time to time," he said and sat down.

Haver pushed his chair back and looked at his colleague. He wanted to finish the report but realized that Fredriksson wanted to talk.

"It must have been a while."

"On the contrary. Lennart Albert Jonsson was charged with larceny with aggravating circumstances as recently as last spring."

"Any consequences?"

"The charges were dropped," Fredriksson said. "The witnesses backed down."

"Under threat?"

"I assume so."

"I guess we'll have to take a look at this brother."

"The remarkable thing is that John managed to stay out of trouble for as many years as he did," Fredriksson said.

He stood up and leaned against a filing cabinet and looked unusually re-laxed, as if a murder case were just what he needed before Christmas.

"I assume you know he's married. I've met the wife. A real looker. They have a boy, Justus."

"How the hell do you remember all these things?"

"There was something I liked about that family. Little John's wife was something else. A real dame, no doubt about it. Attractive, of course, but not just that. There was something more there."

Haver waited for him to continue, for an elaboration of the "something more," but Fredriksson seemed to have moved on.

"So *looker* and *dame* are synonyms?"

"Guess so," Fredriksson said, smiling.

"Bea is over there right now," said Haver.

He was happy to have gotten out of it, even though he should have been there. The first meeting with close family members could yield important information.

He remembered the wife of a suicide they had handled. The man had blown himself up behind a barn in the Hagby area, and when Haver and a female colleague, Mia Rosén, had knocked on the door of the newly wid-owed woman's house in order to relay the sad news, she had started to laugh. She laughed nonstop for at least half a minute, until Rosén shook her. The woman managed to regain a modicum of control over herself and mumbled something of an apology but could not conceal her pleasure over her husband's death.

It turned out that the man had been severely intoxicated with a blood alcohol level so high that they could not rule out the possibility that some-one else had strapped the explosives to his body. There were car tire tracks on a thin and muddy tractor trail behind the barn. A car had pulled up to and then reversed away from the location, most likely a blue car, which they had determined from collision damage to a young pine tree by the side of the road.

When they questioned the woman a few days later there was a man in the house. He owned a red Audi.

Fredriksson interrupted Haver's thought process.

"Who kills with a knife?" he asked, picking up on Haver's earlier thoughts about Little John.

"A drunk involved in a fistfight that escalates into murder or gang violence."

"Or a calculating bastard who doesn't want to make a lot of noise," Fredriksson said.

"He was slashed and tortured before he was killed."

"What do we make of the fingers?"

"Blackmail was the first thing I thought of," Haver said. "I know, I watch too much TV," he said when he met Fredriksson's gaze.

"I think Little John may have had some information that was very valuable to someone else," he continued and rolled his chair out from under the table.

"John was a quiet, stubborn kind of guy," Fredriksson said.

He took a few steps toward the window but turned quickly and looked at Haver.

"Heard anything from Ann?"

"A few weeks ago. She sends her regards."

"From a few weeks ago, thank you. You're quite the messenger. How is she?"

"Being a stay-at-home mom isn't really her thing."

"How about the kid?"

"He's fine, I think. We talked about work mainly. I think Ann was involved in charging Little John's brother once."

Fredriksson left Haver, who was still thinking about John's wife. He was curious to hear what Bea had to report. If he knew her, Bea would take her time in getting back to the office. She had the best touch in handling families, friendly without being intrusive or overly emotional, thorough without being finicky. She could take a long time in building up the necessary trust, but consequently often uncovered information that her colleagues missed.

Haver called Ryde on his cell phone. As he had expected, the forensic technician was still out in Libro.

"Anything interesting?"

"Not much other than that it's started to snow again."

"Call me if you find anything exciting," Haver said, feeling somewhat impatient. Ryde should have found something by now. Something small. Haver wanted fast results.

Please let it go well, he thought, in the hope that the first homicide investigation he was heading would lead to a swift arrest. He was by no means inexperienced. He had worked with Lindell on several cases and believed himself up to the admittedly challenging task, but he also felt bodily twinges of insecurity and impatience.

He grabbed the phone again, called the DA, and thereafter tried to track down a certain Andreas Lundemark, who was in charge of the Libro snow dump. Haver wanted to establish how that operation was managed. A large number of truck drivers had been out there, to which tracks in the giant mounds of snow bore testament. Someone might have seen something. Everyone would have to be questioned.

He tracked down Lundemark's cell phone number with the help of Information, but when he dialed the number no one answered. Haver left a message.

He hung up and knew he had to do the right thing. He sat with John's and his brother's files in front of him. He leafed through the papers. A not insubstantial narrative, particularly in Lennart's case. Haver made a note of the names that cropped up in the various investigations, fifty-two names in all. Every last one would have to be questioned. Most important was the group in Lennart's file designated as his "closest associates," a number of thieves, fencers, drinking buddies, and others whom Lennart was thought to know.

Haver found himself getting lost in thought, his mind drifting back to Rebecka. He was a good investigator but came up short on the home front. He couldn't really see what was bothering her. She had been home on maternity leave once before and that time everything had been fine. Should he simply ask her? Sit down with her after the kids had gone to bed and essentially interrogate her? Not leave anything to chance, be systematic and try to ignore the fact that he might be the guilty party?

"Tonight," he said aloud and stood up; but he knew as he did so that he was lying to himself. He would never have the energy to talk to her after coming home from the first day of a homicide investigation. And when exactly would he go home?

"I mustn't forget to call," he mumbled.

Beatrice stood for a while in the entrance hall, reading the names of the residents. There were two Anderssons, one Ramirez, and an Oto. Where did Oto come from? West Africa, Malaysia, or some other far-off land? There was also a J. and B. and Justus Jonsson, two floors up.

She was alone in her errand, which pleased her. Delivering the news of a death was probably the hardest task. Beatrice was simply distracted by her colleagues in such situations. Dealing with her own emotions was hard enough, and she was happy not to have to support a colleague who would perhaps start shooting off at the mouth or go completely silent and inject a greater sense of anxiety.

The woodwork around the door had been newly replaced and still smelled of paint. She tried to imagine that she was there to visit a good friend, perhaps someone she hadn't seen for a long time. Full of excitement and anticipation.

She stroked the pale green bumpy wall. The smell of paint mixed with the smells of cooking. Fried onions. *Oto is making his national dish,* she thought, *in honor of my visit. Oto, how nice to see you again. Oh, fried onions! My favorite!*

She took a step but stopped. Her cell phone vibrated. She checked to see who it was. Ola.

"We've just received a missing-persons report," he said. "Berit Jonsson called in to say she hasn't seen her husband since last night."

"I'm in the stairwell," Bea said.

"We told her we'd be sending someone over."

"And would that be me?"

"That would be you," Ola Haver said with great seriousness.

Damn it all to hell, she thought. *She knows we're coming. She thinks I'm here to ask her about John's disappearance, and instead I'll deliver the news of his death.*

She remembered a colleague who had been called to the scene of an accident. An older man, hit by car, death was instantaneous. The colleague had recognized the man from his home village. He had been acquainted with the man's parents and had stayed in touch with both the man and his wife when they moved into the city.

He took it upon himself to deliver the news of the man's death. The man's wife was delighted to see him, pulling him into the apartment with words about coffee and how her husband would soon be home, he was just out somewhere momentarily, and then they would all be able to have a bite and catch up.

Beatrice climbed the stairs one after the other. John, Berit, and Justus Jonsson. The doorbell played a muffled melody, a kind she disliked. She took a step back. The door opened almost immediately.

"Beatrice Andersson, from the police," she said and put out her hand.

Berit Jonsson took it. Her hand was small, warm, and damp.

"That didn't take long," she said and cleared her throat. "Please come in."

The entryway was narrow and dark. A heap of shoes and boots lay right inside the door. Beatrice removed her coat and reached for a hanger while Berit stood passively beside her. She turned around and tried a smile but couldn't quite pull it off.

Berit's face was void of expression. She returned Beatrice's gaze with neutral eyes and they walked into the kitchen without a word. Berit gestured toward a kitchen chair with her hand but remained standing at the kitchen counter. She was about thirty-five. Her hair, sloppily gathered into a ponytail, had once been blond and was now dyed a reddish brown. A shade probably called "mahogany," Berit guessed. Her left eye was slightly walleyed. She wasn't wearing any makeup, and there was something naked about her face. She was very tired. She gripped the counter behind her back with her hands.

"You must be Berit. I also saw the name Justus downstairs. Is that your son?"

Berit Jonsson nodded.

"Mine and John's."

"Is he at home?"

She shook her head.

"You have reported John as missing," Beatrice said, then hesitated for a moment before continuing, even though she had quietly planned it out.

"He should have come home yesterday afternoon, at four, but he never did."

She wobbled over the "never did," freeing one of her hands from the counter and rubbing it over her face.

Beatrice thought she was beautiful even in her present state with all her worry, the large black circles under her eyes and her stiff, exhausted features.

"I'm sorry to have to tell you this, but John is dead. We found him this morning."

The words settled like a chill over the kitchen. Berit's hand hovered by her face as if she wanted to take cover, not hear, not see, but Beatrice saw how the realization crept over her. Berit lowered her arm, bringing it forward in an open position, palm up, as if begging for something. Her eyelids fluttered, the pupils grew larger, and she swallowed.

Beatrice stood up and took Berit's hand again and now it was ice-cold.

"I'm very sorry," she repeated.

Berit scrutinized her face as if to determine if there was any trace of uncertainty in it. She pulled her hand away and put it in front of her mouth, and Beatrice waited for the scream, but it never came.

Beatrice swallowed. She saw Little John's battered, beaten, and burned body, in her mind's eye, dumped in a bank of snow that was dirty from the city's streets.

Berit shook her head, gently at first, almost imperceptibly, then more forcefully. She opened her mouth very slowly and a strand of saliva ran out of the corner of her mouth. Beatrice's words were taking root, burrowing into her consciousness. She stiffened, not moving a muscle, unreachable during the time that the message about her John sank in, that he was never going to come home again, never hug her, never walk into the kitchen, never do anything again.

She made no resistance when Beatrice put her arms around her shoulders, led her away to the chair by the window, and sat down across from her. She caught herself quickly taking note of what was on the table: an azalea that needed water and was starting to wilt, the morning paper, an Advent candleholder with three candles that had burned halfway to the bottom, and—farthest in by the wall—a knife and fork crossed over an empty plate.

Beatrice leaned in across the table and grabbed Berit's hand again and gave it a squeeze. Then came a single tear that traced its way down her cheek.

"Can we call anyone?"

Berit turned her face toward Beatrice, meeting her gaze.

"How?" she asked hoarsely, in a whisper.

"He was murdered," Beatrice said in a low voice, as if she were adjusting the volume to match Berit's.

The look she got reminded her of a sheep slaughter she had witnessed as a child. The victim was a female sheep. The animal was taken from the pen, braying, and led out into the yard. She was wild but let herself be calmed by Beatrice's uncle.

It was the look the sheep gave Beatrice at that moment, that tenth of a second before it happened. The white of the eye glimmered, the expression full of hurt, no suggestion of fear, more as if posing a question. It was as if there weren't room enough in the world for her despair, although the pen was so spacious, the pastures so rich.

"Murdered," Berit mumbled.

"Can we call anyone? Do you have any siblings?"

Berit shook her head.

"Parents?"

Another shake.

"Justus," she said. "I have to get a hold of Justus."

"Where is he?"

"At Danne's."

"Close by?"

"Salabacksgatan."

I can't do this, Beatrice thought, but she knew at the same time that as far as she was concerned, the worst was over. The words had been said. She would do everything she could to assuage the woman's pain and give her the answers she was looking for. A feeling of reverence gripped her. It was a feeling familiar to her from before. Beatrice was far from religious, but she could sense what people sought in the religious messages and rituals. There was so much in her police work that intersected with the big questions, myths, and dreams.

She had noticed that the police often had to play the role of confessional priests, people to whom one could unburden oneself. Even the uniformed police officer, who technically represented authority, power, and the bad conscience of the citizen, could receive these confidences. That had been her experience on the beat. Or was it her personality that had invited these many instances of quiet, breathtaking intimacy? She didn't know, but she cherished these moments. She had told herself she would never become cynical.

The front door was suddenly thrown open.

"Justus," Berit gasped.

But it was a man who rushed into the kitchen. He caught sight of Beatrice and halted abruptly.

"Are you a minister or something?"

"No," Beatrice said and stood up.

The man was panting, his gaze aggressive.

"Who the hell are you, then?"

"A police officer."

"They've killed my brother."

He waved his right arm in front of Beatrice.

"Lennart," Berit whispered.

He stopped short in his fierce attack, looking at her as if he had only at that moment registered her presence. He lowered his arms and his whole body deflated like a balloon pierced with a needle.

"Berit," he said and took a step toward her.

"Bastard," she said and spat in his face.

He took her outburst with calm, wiping his face with his sleeve. Beatrice glimpsed a tear under the arm of his jacket where the bloodred lining peeked out.

"Was that really necessary?" he asked, and Beatrice could read only confusion and grief in his face.

"It was your fault," Berit said with teeth so tightly clenched that it was hard to understand how she could utter any sounds, let alone speak. Her voice shot up into a falsetto register. "It's your fucking fault my John is dead! You always dragged him into your shit. Always you!"

Lennart shook his head. His face was lined and black stubble covered a surprising amount of it. Beatrice would never have been able to guess that the man in front of her had been Little John's brother.

"I don't know anything about this," he said. "I promise."

Beatrice decided spontaneously to believe him.

"How did you find out that your brother was dead?"

"Your blabbering friends," he said curtly and looked away. "The whole town knows," he continued, turned to the window. "If you start shouting over the police radio that Little John is dead, then everyone will hear it."

Unbelievable, Beatrice thought. *The name of a murdered person announced unscrambled on the radio.*

"My brother, my little brother," Lennart Jonsson sobbed, leaned up against the windowsill, his face pressed against the pane.

"I'm going to kill those bastards, you know. I'm going to find the one who did this and torture him to death."

Beatrice wondered what details of the murder had also been broadcast. Berit had sunk down on the chair again and sat lifelessly with her gaze fixed on some place where Beatrice was unable to follow.

"Will you be staying with her for a bit?" she asked. "She could do with the company."

It was hard to know if her brother-in-law was the best companion for her, but Beatrice told herself there was a logic to it. A brother and a wife, linked for always with their shared life, the memories, grief.

Lennart turned and nodded in a conciliatory manner. A drop of Berit's saliva was still caught on his stubbly chin.

She got the address of Justus's friend and that of John and Lennart's mother, went out into the hall, and called Haver and told him to make sure the mother was notified.

Lennart was downing a beer when she returned to the kitchen. *Maybe just the thing*, she thought.

"Berit," she said, "do you know where John was going last night?"

Berit shook her head.

"Was he running an errand? Was there someone he was going to meet?"

Berit didn't say anything.

"I have to ask."

"I don't know."

"He didn't say anything when he left?"

Berit lowered her head and looked like she was trying to remember the day before. Beatrice could imagine how she was going through those last few minutes before John had walked out the door and disappeared from her life for good. How many times was she going to relive that day?

"He was his usual self," she said finally. "I think he said something about the pet store. He was going to buy a pump he had ordered."

"Which store?"

"I don't know. He went to all of them."

She started to cry.

"He had a hell of a fine aquarium," Lennart said. "They wrote about it in the papers."

Silence fell.

"I thought maybe he was helping with the snow removal. He also talked about trying to get a job at the sheet-metal shop of someone he knew."

"Micke?" Lennart asked.

Berit looked at her brother-in-law and nodded.

Micke, Beatrice thought. *Now we're getting all the names.*

Haver, Beatrice, Wende, Berglund, Fredriksson, Riis, Peter Lundin— no relation to Asta and Anton—and Ottosson had gathered around an enormous box of gingerbread cookies. Fredriksson helped himself to a generous portion and piled the cookies up in front of his cup. Eleven in all, Beatrice noted.

"Think they'll make a good boy out of you?" she asked, referring to the old folk saying. Fredriksson nodded absently. Ottosson, who must have considered himself good enough already, declined the offer of gingerbread when the tin came his way.

"Go on, take one," Riis said.

"No, thank you," the chief said.

"Little John bled to death," Haver said suddenly. "Someone, or perhaps more than one, stabbed him with a knife or some such sharp object. Blood loss is the official cause of death."

The group around the table digested this piece of information. Haver paused. He imagined his colleagues creating an inner picture of Little John's final moments.

"In the stages leading up to his death he was subjected to repeated blows to the head and chest," Haver continued. "In addition, he has burn marks, probably caused by cigarettes, on his arms and genitals."

"So we're looking for a sadistic smoker," Riis said.

"Aren't all smokers sadists?" Lundin asked.

Haver gave him a look and continued.

"He probably died sometime between four and eight P.M. yesterday. The exact time of death is difficult to establish because of the preserving effect of the cold on the body."

"Any trace of alcohol or drugs in his blood?" Ottosson asked.

"He was clean. The only things they found were the beginnings of an ulcer and a liver that could have been in better shape."

"Alcoholic?"

"No, you couldn't call him that, but he put his liver to work," Haver said and looked suddenly very tired.

"Can his death have been a mistake?" Beatrice said. "The fact that he bled to death after so many small wounds indicates an ongoing assault. If your intention is to murder someone, surely you would aim to kill the first time."

This is absurd, Haver thought.

"Torture," he said. "Torture is what it is."

"He was a tough bastard," Ottosson said. "I don't think he was an easy one to break."

"You can't predict that about someone," Fredriksson said and had his eighth cookie. "It's one thing to sound tough from behind a desk when you're being questioned about a theft, it's quite another to keep a stiff upper lip when you're being tortured to death."

Ottosson wasn't one to belabor a point, but this time he defended his statement.

"Little John was stubborn and brave. He never gave in even though he was small."

"But surely you never tortured him?" Riis said.

Ottosson had told them that he had questioned Little John on several occasions. He had been there when John had been brought in the first time at the age of sixteen and he had seen him from time to time during the following five or six years.

"Do we think this is part of some old business or something new?" Ottosson continued. "For my part, I have trouble believing that John would have gotten himself mixed up in something new. You've met his wife and kid, Bea, and John seemed to have been getting along well, at least these past ten years. Why would he jeopardize all that now?"

Bea nodded and indicated that Ottosson should keep going. She liked hearing what he had to say. He had a long history that stretched out before she had joined the force or even started school. He was a wise man. He hardly ever lectured them in overly long harangues, and just now she wanted him to keep talking, but he stopped and snatched Fredriksson's last gingerbread cookie, giving Beatrice a mischievous look.

"His wife seems all right and the boy too. That is to say, he's been unemployed for a while and that probably caused a few problems but hadn't led to anything serious. Some partying from time to time, his wife said, but no serious drinking. She may have been putting a good face on things but I think he was keeping to the straight and narrow. He spent a lot of time on his fish tank—it's the biggest I've seen. Four meters by one meter, at least. It takes up a whole wall."

"Talk about water damage if that thing started to leak," Riis said.

Ottosson shot him a look as if to say, *Enough of your stupid comments.* Riis gave him a wry smile.

"It seems to have been his main interest," Beatrice said. "He belonged to a tropical fish society, was active on the board, and had dreams of owning his own tropical fish store one day."

Ottosson nodded.

"What about the brother?" Haver asked. "He doesn't seem completely aboveboard. Could he have gotten John involved in something?"

"I don't think so," Beatrice said. "Not consciously anyway. Lennart seemed genuinely surprised. Of course you would be shocked if your brother was murdered, but there isn't anything that indicates he even sensed that John had been pulled into any kind of trouble."

"He didn't look too bright," Ottosson said. "Do you think he was simply unaware of something he had caused, that it would have these kinds of consequences?"

Beatrice looked doubtful.

"Maybe he's just putting two and two together now," Ottosson said.

Morenius, who was the head of KUT, the criminal information service, walked into the room. He threw a sizable folder on the table, sat down, and sighed heavily.

"Sorry I'm late but there's a lot going on right now." He underscored this with a new sigh.

"Have some coffee," Ottosson said. "It'll pick you up."

Morenius laughed and reached for the insulated coffee jug.

"Cookies?" Ottosson said.

"Lennart Jonsson is a steady client with us and several other departments," Morenius started. "He has fourteen counts of traffic violations, three counts of drunk driving, sixteen counts of theft—three of which with aggravated circumstances—one count of assault and probably twenty others unknown to us, one attempted swindle, one count of drug possession, but now it's too far back in time, three counts of unlawful threats and disturbance in court proceedings. The list goes on. In addition, he has ten financial penalties and a debt of thirty thousand. He receives social welfare and has filed a claim for early retirement."

"What the hell for?" Lundin broke in.

Morenius looked exhausted after reciting his lengthy list but took a sip of coffee and continued.

"Apparently he has an old injury," he said. "He fell from some scaffolding about five years ago and has basically been unable to work since then."

"But he has worked?"

"Mostly construction, but even for Ragnsell's and as a bouncer for a short time. There have been periods where he's lived a pretty normal life."

"Is Lennart our key to the whole thing?"

Ottosson's question hung in the air. Fredriksson helped himself to a new heap of cookies and kept chewing. Riis looked bored. Lundin looked down at his hands, and everyone expected him to get up and go to the bathroom to wash them. His germophobia was a running joke. The need for paper towels had risen considerably since Lundin had started working.

Haver started to talk about his mapping of the Jonsson family's circle of friends and acquaintances.

Beatrice listened at first but then her thoughts returned to her visit with Berit Jonsson. She tried to catch hold of something that had nagged at her then, something that came up when they were talking about her son. Was it something Berit had said? A look, or a change of expression? A kind of concern?

Ottosson interrupted her train of thought.

"Hold on, Bea. I just asked you a question. Did Berit say anything about John's finances? Did the family have a hard time after he lost his job?"

"Not that I know of. It didn't look as if they were suffering unduly. Berit works part-time as an in-home attendant for social services, and John probably got his unemployment benefit."

"We'll run the routine checks," Ottosson said. "Can you handle that, Riis?"

Riis nodded. It was the kind of assignment that appealed to him.

"I'm planning to go back there tomorrow, talk to Berit and the boy, and search John's belongings," Beatrice said. "Does that sound okay?"

"Sounds fine," Haver said. "Checking the pet stores didn't give us anything, but we'll keep at it. There must be other stores with some of this equipment, or people selling it out of their homes. Someone will have to check the tropical fish societies. We need to determine all of John's activities that day."

Ottosson ended with some general remarks that no one paid any attention to, though they all waited politely until he was done. Framing these meetings in the right way was important to Ottosson. He wanted them to have a cozy, personable feel.

It was quarter past eight in the evening. The assignment tasks were complete.

Seven

Mikael Andersson phoned the police at ten thirty. The call center—that is to say Fredriksson, since everyone else was in Eriksberg dealing with an assault—handled the matter.

Fredriksson had been enjoying his evening in the office. It was nice and quiet, and he finally had time to sort through some papers. He employed a to-him-brilliant system of eight piles, the largest of which was destined for that most comprehensive of archives: the wastebasket. He thought about how the advent of computers had triggered all that talk of the paperless office. Well, that certainly hadn't become a reality at the Uppsala police station.

Not that he had anything against paper. His inner bureaucrat reveled in the folders, ledgers, and binders. Most of his colleagues, especially the younger ones, stored a lot of information on the computer. But not Fredriksson. He wanted to have rustling papers and binders to leaf through. The hole punch and stapler occupied a central place on his desk.

If the call interrupted him, the tone of his voice did not betray it.

"I knew Little John," said the voice on the other end. "You know, the guy who was murdered."

"What is your name?"

"Micke Andersson. I just found out. I've been working and I left my cell phone at home. I do snow removal and . . ."

"Okay," Fredriksson said calmly. "You come home and find a message on your cell phone that John is dead. Who left the message?"

"John's brother."

"Lennart Jonsson?"

"He only had one brother."

"You knew John?"

"We knew each other our whole lives. What happened? Do you know anything?"

"A little, but perhaps you know something we don't?"

"I saw John yesterday and he was the same as always."

"When was that?"

"Around five, maybe."

"Where?"

"At my place. John had been to the liquor store and stopped by."

Fredriksson made notes and continued. Little John had turned up at Mikael Andersson's apartment on Väderkvarnsgatan. Mikael had just come home from his job at the sheet metal shop. He had just stepped out of the shower and thought the time was around five o'clock. John had been to the state liquor store at Kvarnen. He seemed happy, not troubled. He had been carrying two green plastic bags.

They had discussed a number of things. John had spoken about his fish tank, but he had not mentioned buying a new pump. Mikael had talked about work, about an evening shift he thought he was going to do. A couple of rooftops needed to be cleared of snow.

"Did he have anything on his mind? Did he ask anything in particular?"

"No, he was just stopping in on his way home, as I understood it. I asked him if he wanted to help with the snow removal. The company often takes on extra hands, but he didn't seemed interested."

"He didn't want any extra work?"

"Well, he didn't say no outright, but he didn't pick up on it."

"And that surprised you."

"Little John wasn't the type to sit around. I think I expected him to jump at the offer."

"Did he need the money?"

"Who doesn't?"

"I mean, for Christmas or something."

"He didn't say anything about that. And he had enough to buy Aquavit, didn't he?"

John had stayed about half an hour, or three-quarters of an hour. Mikael Andersson had left his place to shovel snow at the apartments on Sysslomansgatan at a quarter past six. He was under the impression that John was on his way home.

"One more thing. He asked to use the phone but then he changed his mind. He never called."

"Did he say whom he was going to call?"

"No. Home, maybe. He said he was late."

Mikael Andersson put the receiver down and felt around for the pack of cigarettes he usually kept in his breast pocket until he remembered that he had quit two months ago. Instead he poured himself a glass of red wine even though he knew it would make him even more tempted to smoke. John had always teased him about preferring his "chick drink" and at first he had felt ashamed, but by now it was accepted as a fact of life.

He had lived with a woman called Minna for four years. One day she had left, never to return. She never even came back for her furniture or personal belongings. Micke waited for two months, then he packed it all up himself and drove out to Ragnsell's dump in Kvarnbo. He filled half a container with her junk.

She was the one who had taught him to drink wine. "The only good thing I can say about her," he would say. "I maybe could have understood it if I had hit her or been a bastard," he told his friends who wondered why Minna had left, "but to up and leave like that, I don't understand."

He sat down in the living room in the same armchair as yesterday when Little John had sat across from him. He hadn't taken off his coat. John, whom he had known his entire life. His best friend. *My only friend, actually,* he thought, and couldn't help sniffling.

He drank some of the wine and it calmed him. Rioja. He rotated the bottle toward him and studied the label before refilling the glass. Now that half hour with John seemed incredibly important. He wanted to recall everything, every gesture, laugh, and look. They had laughed, hadn't they?

He drank up and closed his eyes. *We had a good time, didn't we, John?* He had been standing there with those plastic bags in his hands and said something about the holidays. Mikael was suddenly convinced that John had left the bags behind, and he walked out into the hall to check if they had been left there under the hat shelf. But he saw only his sneakers and wet work boots, which he should dry out before the morning.

He walked thoughtfully out into the kitchen. What had John said? Mikael looked at the clock on the wall. Could he call Berit? He was sure she was awake. Maybe he should go over there? He didn't want to talk to Lennart. He would just rant and rave and carry on.

The horse-racing schedule was on the kitchen table. *I'll bet we win ten mil' now that you're dead*, he thought, sweeping the schedule and tip sheets onto the floor. *We who never won anything but played anyway. Week after week, year after year, in the hopes of the big win. The rush. Happiness.*

"We didn't know what we were doing," he said aloud. "We didn't know shit about the horses."

If they had been tropical-fish races we would have cleaned house, he thought as he picked all the papers from the floor. Minna had taught him something besides drinking wine: If you let things start piling up on the floor you know you're on your way out.

He rested his head against the windowpane, mumbled his friend's name, and looked at the snow falling outside. He normally liked Christmas and all the preparations, but he knew this view from his kitchen window of his neighbors' holiday decorations would hereafter always be connected with the memory of John's death.

Lennart Jonsson was making his way through the snow. A car honked angrily at him as he crossed Vaksalagatan. Lennart waved his fist in the air. The red lights disappeared toward the east. He was gripped by a feeling of unfairness. Others got to ride in cars while he had to walk, jumping over the mounds of plowed snow, crossing here and there to find cleared footpaths.

If he looked up and west he saw Christmas lights stretching in toward the center of town like a row of pearls. The snow crunched under his boots. A woman had once told him she wanted to eat that sound that shoes made on the snow when it was very cold. He always remembered her words when he walked in crunchy snow. What had she meant? He liked it, but didn't really understand.

A car with a Christmas tree on the roof drove by on Salabacksgatan. Apart from that there was no one. He stopped, letting his head hang down as if he were drunk, and realized he was crying. Most of all he wanted to lie down in the snow and die like his brother. His only brother. Dead. Murdered. The desire for revenge tore through his body like a red-hot iron, and he knew the pain after John's death would let up only when his murderer was dead.

Missing John was something he would have to live with. He pulled up the zipper on his down jacket. He was wearing only a T-shirt underneath. He walked along the street with a gait so foreign to him that he noticed it physically. He who normally rushed around without a thought was now proceeding with deliberation, scrutinizing the buildings around him, noticing details like the overflowing garbage can at the bus stop and the snow-covered walker, things to which he would normally never even have given a second thought.

It was as if his brother's death had sharpened his senses. He had only a few beers in him, John's beers. He had stayed with Berit until Justus had gone to sleep. Now he was sober, alert as never before, watching his neighborhood slowly being covered by a white shroud.

The snow crunched under his feet and he wanted to eat not only the sound but the whole city, the whole damn place; he wanted to tear the whole place down.

At Brantings square he was only a few blocks from home, but he stopped when he was halfway across. A tractor was working its way methodically through the masses of snow, plowing the parking spaces, entrances, and exits.

Was John already dead when he was dumped in Libro? Lennart didn't know, he had forgotten to ask. John got cold easily. His thin frame was not built for this weather. With his slender hands he should have been a pianist. Instead he became a welder and an expert in tropical fish. Uncle Eugene used to joke about how John should go on the *Double or Nothing* show on TV since he knew everything about those fish down to the last fin and stripe of color.

Lennart watched the tractor, and when it passed close to him he held up his hand in greeting. The driver waved back. A young man, about twenty.

He pressed a little harder on the gas when he saw that Lennart was still there, put it in reverse with a confidently careless hand movement, came to an abrupt stop, adjusted his position, changed gears again, and spun around, preparing to take on the last sliver of snow.

Lennart was suddenly tempted to wave the driver down and exchange a few words with him, maybe say a few things about Little John. He wanted to talk to someone who understood the importance of hands.

He kept thinking about his brother in discrete body parts. Hands, the careful laugh, especially when he was among strangers—no one could claim that John had a dominating personality. That wiry body, its surprising strength.

John had been good at marbles too. As a kid John was always the one who went home with a bag full of marbles and new toy soldiers in his pocket, especially mastering those difficult ten- and twelve-step games. Only Teodor, the janitor, could beat him. He came by sometimes, borrowed a marble, and sent it flying in a wide arc, taking down a soldier. Being helped in this way was cheating, strictly speaking, but no one complained. Teodor treated them all the same, and each hoped that maybe next time he would be the one to get the favor.

Teodor laughed a lot, maybe because he sometimes had a beer or two, but mainly because he was a man who showed his feelings. He loved women, had a fear of heights, and was afraid of the dark. Apart from these important characteristics, he was most known for his expertise and efficiency in matters of building maintenance. Few could rival him in that area, especially when gripped by his famous temper.

Sometimes Lennart thought: *If we had had teachers like that, with that strength and those weaknesses that Teodor has, then we would all have become professors of something.* Teodor himself was a professor of being able to sweep a set of basement stairs without raising the dust, of doing three things at once, of keeping the grounds so clean that he made picking up garbage seem like an art form, of grooming the gravel paths and flower beds so well that they looked good for two, three weeks at a time.

We could have learned all this at school, Lennart thought while watching the tractor. *Do you believe me, John? You were the only one who cared—no, that's wrong; Mom and Dad did too, of course. Dad. With his damned stutter. His damned rooftops. All that metal crap.*

Teodor didn't have a big tractor, just shovels to start with and then a strong old Belos with a detachable snowplow hitched to the front. John and Lennart had helped shovel basement stairs, and once, in the mid-1960s—an unbelievably snowy winter—Teodor had sent them up on the roof, fifteen meters above the ground. They were the sons of a roofer. Ropes around their middles and small shovels in their hands. Teodor sticking his head up through the trapdoor, directing, holding the ends of the ropes. The boys sliding on the slippery slate, sending the snow down and over the edge. Svensson was down below, directing pedestrians.

One time Lennart had looked over the edge and waved to Svensson. He had waved back. Had he been sober? Maybe. Teodor in the trapdoor, terrified of looking down. To the west were Uppsala castle and the twin spires of the cathedral. To the east, Vaksala church with its pointy tower reaching like a needle toward the sky. More snow in the air. A beating heart under the winter jacket.

When it was time to crawl back up and then down through the trapdoor, Teodor laughed with relief. They went down to the boiler room, where the yard waste was burning in a huge furnace. They warmed themselves there. The air was hot and dry, with a slightly sour smell, but good. It was a smell Lennart had not come across since.

In a space next to the furnace there was a Ping-Pong table and sometimes they would play a round. John was the nimbler of the two. Lennart was the one who wanted to take care of matters with a smash.

Sometimes Teodor gave them soda, serving himself a beer. John always drank Zingo. Lennart smiled at the memory. So long ago. He hadn't thought about the boiler room for ages, but now he reconstructed the various spaces, smells, piled crates with glass bottles and newspapers. So long ago. Professor Teodor had been dead for a few years.

Lennart bowed his head like a graveside mourner. He was freezing but wanted to dwell in his memories. Once he got home, life's fundamental shittiness would no doubt reassert itself. Then he would have a drink, if not several.

The driver of the tractor glanced at him as he drove past. Lennart didn't care what he thought. It was a long time since he had cared. *He can go ahead and think I'm crazy.*

One time they had surprised Teodor. It was for his birthday, an even year, one of the parents must have told them. He was scared of the dark and the assembled kids heard his voice in the distance through the winding basement passage. He sang to calm his nerves. "Seven lonely nights I've been waiting for you . . ." came echoing toward them, amplified by the narrow passage, the many dark corners and nooks. When he rounded the bike storage the neighborhood kids started to sing and Teodor stiffened with fear until he understood. He listened to their rendition of "Happy Birthday" with tears in his eyes. These were his kids, he had seen them grow up, rascals he had lectured and played Ping-Pong with, the ones whose soccer ball he nabbed when they played on the soft, wet grass, and the ones he juggled with in the boiler room.

Ten boys and a janitor in a basement. So long ago. John and his childhood. Back then before the future was set. Lennart took a deep breath. The cold air filled his lungs and he shivered. Had it always been fated that his brother would die young? It should have been he. He who had driven drunk so many times, drunk bad liquor, and hung out with drifters just living for the day. Not John, who had Berit and Justus, his fish, and those hands that had welded so many flawless seams.

He started to walk. It was no longer snowing so heavily, and a few stars could be seen between the clouds. The plow had now moved on to the south end of the square. It had stopped, and Lennart saw the young man pull out a Thermos, screw the cap off, and pour out some coffee.

When he passed the tractor he nodded and stopped as if on impulse. He walked over and knocked softly on the door. The guy in the tractor lowered the window about halfway.

"Hey there," Lennart said. "Looks like you have quite a job."

The young man nodded.

"You're probably wondering what I'm doing here in the middle of the night."

He stepped up onto the tractor so that his head was more on the same level as the driver's. He felt the warmth of the cabin streaming toward him.

"My brother died yesterday. I'm a little down, as you can probably understand."

"Damn," the young man said and put his cup down on the dashboard.

"How old are you?"

"Twenty-three."

Lennart didn't know how to continue, but he knew he wanted to keep talking.

"How old was your brother?"

"He was older than you, but still. My little brother, you know."

He looked down at his shoes, which were soaking wet.

"My little brother," he repeated quietly.

Lennart looked at the guy for a short moment before nodding.

"I only have one cup."

"That's okay."

He took the steaming mug from him. There was sugar in it but that didn't matter. He drank some and then looked at the guy again.

"I was just looking in on my brother's wife," he said. "They have a kid about fourteen."

"Was he sick, then?"

"No, murdered."

The young man opened his eyes wide.

"Out in Libro, if you know where that is. Yeah, of course you do. That's where the county dumps its snow."

"That was your brother?"

Lennart drank the last of the coffee and handed back the mug.

"Tastes fucking good to drink something hot."

But he shivered as if the cold had penetrated his core. The young man screwed the cap back on and shoved the Thermos into a bag behind his seat. The gesture reminded Lennart of something and he felt a sting of envy.

"Got to get home," he said.

The young man looked out over the square.

"It'll stop soon," he said, "but it's supposed to get colder."

Lennart hesitated on the step.

"Take care of yourself," he said. "Thanks for the coffee."

He walked home slowly. The sweet taste in his mouth made him long for a beer. He picked up the pace. Through a window he saw a woman busying herself in the kitchen. She looked up and wiped the back of her hand against her brow as he was walking past. The next moment she went back to arranging Christmas decorations in the window.

It was almost two when Lennart came home. He turned on only the light over the stove, took some beers from the counter, and sat down at the kitchen table.

John had been dead for thirty hours. A murderer was still at large. For every second that ticked by, Lennart's desire to kill the man who had murdered his brother grew.

He would check with the police to find out what they knew, if they were willing to say anything. He looked at the clock again. He should have started immediately, should have started making calls. For every minute, the injustice that his brother's murderer was able to move and breathe freely was growing.

He got himself a pencil and piece of paper, chewed on the end of the pencil for a while, then scrawled the names of eight men. They were all men his own age, small-time crooks like himself. A few druggies, a blackmailer, moonshiners, and a dealer—all old friends from the Norrtälje institution.

The gang, he thought when he looked over the list, *the ones that law-abiding folk went out of their way to avoid on the street, that they pretended not to see.*

He was going to stay sober and clear-minded. He would have all the time in the world to drink himself to death later.

Lennart opened a beer but had only a few sips before he left it on the table and walked into the living room. He had a one-bedroom apartment. He was proud of the fact that he had managed to keep his crib all these years. Sure, the neighbors had complained from time to time, and sometimes the rental agreement hung in the balance.

There were some photographs on a shelf. He took down one of them and looked at it for a long time. Uncle Eugene, John, and himself on a fishing trip. He couldn't remember who had taken the picture. John held up a pike and looked happy, while he himself was serious. Not unhappy, but serious. Eugene looked content as always.

More fun than a barrel of monkeys, Aina had said about her brother. Lennart would remember that Saturday for a long time, his mother with one hand on Eugene's neck and the other on Albin's. They were sitting at the kitchen table. She had put out some cold cuts, Eugene was talking away in his usual manner, and she was on her way to the pantry when she paused and touched the two men she loved most. Her hands rested there for maybe ten seconds while she made that comment after something her brother had said. Lennart remembered looking at his father, who appeared relaxed like he always did after a shot and a beer. He seemed not to notice her hand, at least he didn't remark on it, pull away, or look embarrassed.

How old had he himself been when the picture was taken? Maybe fourteen. It was about then that things had changed. No more fishing trips. Lennart felt as if there were a tug-of-war inside him all the time. From time to time he could feel happy and at peace, like when they were up on the roof, he, John, and Teodor, after they had finished with the snow. Or when he was with Albin at the metalwork shop, the few times he was allowed there. There, Albin's stutter was of no consequence. Nor was his tiredness. When Lennart was little he thought his father was tired from the stuttering, it looked so exhausting when the words wouldn't come. But that tiredness was gone at the shop. He moved in a different way.

Lennart suddenly remembered how Albin's face would sometimes contract as if suffering from a cramp. Was it pain or exhaustion? Was that why he fell? They had told him it was icy. Or had he jumped headfirst? No, his colleague had seen him slip, heard the cry or scream. Was he stuttering then as he fell helplessly? Was it a stuttering cry that echoed against the massive brick walls of the cathedral?

He must have screamed so loudly that it reached the archbishop. The top dog had to be notified so he would have time to prepare a place for Albin high above the roofs and spires he had clambered on. *He must be welding something up there in heaven,* Lennart thought. What else would he be doing? He needed to have something to do with his hands, hated being idle. Golden rooftops up there, or copper at the very least.

He suddenly missed the old man, as if his grief for John pulled the one for his father along with it.

"Only a little while longer," he said aloud and struggled with his emotions.

He sat in the dark apartment, one hour, two, maybe three, nursing his grief. His lips and cheeks grew stiff and his back ached. He stayed up and seemed to relive the good times with John.

He pushed all the bad times away. Sure, he had wondered about the connections, been asked questions in school, at the child psychologist's, at the police, in jail, at social services, at the unemployment center. They had all asked him about stuff. He had tried to find the threads. Now they converged at a snow dump in Libro, a place no one had ever thought about.

He knew there were no clear-cut answers. Life was a mixture of coincidence and hopes that often ran out in the sand. He had stopped wondering about it all a long time ago. He had chosen his path. And if he was the one who was in sole control of this decision—he had stopped asking himself about that a long time ago. That it had all gone wrong, gone to hell, too many times, he knew that. He didn't blame anyone or anything anymore. Life was what it was.

The other life, the righteous life, was there like a reflector that gleamed momentarily as it caught the light. Of course he had tried. There was a time during the eighties when he had worked for a construction company. He had shoveled gravel and mulch, packed lunches, and developed muscles like never before in his life.

He had met people who had known Albin and slowly he developed another image of his father. Old construction workers talked admiringly of the knowledgeable old roofer, praise that Lennart absorbed. The collective memories of Albin's great skill seemed to extend to his son a little.

Sure, there had been good times. And then John. His little bro. Dead. Murdered.

Berit cracked the door for the third time in half an hour, looking at Justus's ruffled hair and the naked face that still bore traces of tears.

She closed the door but remained standing there with her hand on the doorknob. *How is this going to go?* she asked herself. The feeling of unreality lay like a mask over her face. Her legs were as heavy as if they were set in plaster casts and her arms felt like foreign outcroppings on a body that was hers and yet not. She moved, talked, and experienced her surroundings with full possession of all her senses but as if at a great distance from herself.

Justus had broken down. For several hours he had been shaking and crying and screaming. She had forced herself to be calm. Then he had eventually calmed down and, as if with the wave of a hand, sunk down into a corner of the sofa. Something strange came over his young face.

They had immediately become very hungry. Berit quickly cooked some macaroni, which they ate with cold Falu sausage and ketchup.

"Does it hurt to die?" That had been one of his questions.

How was she supposed to answer? She knew from that female police officer that John had been assaulted, but she didn't want to hear any details. *It hurts, Justus,* she had thought, but in order to comfort him she told him that John had most likely not suffered.

He didn't believe her. Why should he?

Her hand on the doorknob. Closed eyes.

"My John," she whispered.

She had been sweating, but now she was cold and walked with stiff legs to the living room to get the blanket. She stood passively in the middle of the room, wrapped in the blanket, unable to do anything now that Justus had fallen asleep. Before, he had needed her. Now the minutes were ticking away and John became more and more dead. More distant.

She walked over to the window. The smell of the hyacinths almost choked her and she wanted to smash the window to get some air, fresh air.

It was snowing again. Suddenly she saw a movement. A man disappeared in between the buildings on the other side of the street. It was only a split second, but Berit was convinced that she had seen the figure before, the same dark green clothing and a cap. She stared down at the corner of the building where he had disappeared, but now all that could be seen were some footprints in the snow. She wondered if it was the same man she had seen while she was waiting for John. Then she had thought it was Harry's brother who was helping him with the snow removal, but now she wasn't sure.

Was it John appearing to her? Did he want to tell her something?

Ola Haver came home shortly before nine.

"I saw it on the news," Rebecka said to him first thing.

She gave him a look over her shoulder. He hung his coat in the closet and felt the fatigue settle over him. From the kitchen he heard the continuous hacking of a knife against the cutting board.

He walked into the kitchen. Rebecka had her back to him and he felt drawn to her like metal shavings to a magnet.

"Hi," he said and buried his face in her hair.

He felt her smile. She kept slicing and cutting.

"Do you know that in Spain women spend four hours working in the home a day and the men only forty-five minutes?"

"Have you been talking to Monica?"

"No, I read it in the paper. I had time for that in between the vacuuming, breast-feeding, and laundry," she said with a laugh.

"Should I do something?" he said and put his arms around her body, grabbing her hands so that she had to stop cutting.

"It was a study involving several European countries," she said, freeing herself from his grasp.

"How did Sweden do?"

"Better," she said curtly.

He knew she wanted him to leave her alone so she could finish the herring salad or whatever it was, but he had trouble letting go of her body. He wanted to press up against her back and bottom.

"Was it bad?"

"The usual. Hell, in other words, but Bea had the worst of it."

"Informing the family members?"

"What else is going on? How are the kids?"

"Was he married?"

"Yes," Haver said.

"Children?"

"A boy, fourteen."

Rebecka tipped up the end of the cutting board, pulling the knife over the board to scrape the last pieces into the frying pan. He looked at the knife in her hand. The stone in her ring, the one he had bought in London, gleamed ruby red.

"I'm making something new," she said, and he knew she was talking about the food.

He straightened up and went to shower off.

Eight

Justus Jonsson got up out of his bed at twenty to four in the morning. He had woken up with a start, driven by a single thought. His dad's voice: *You know what you have to do, boy.*

Why hadn't he thought of it before? He tiptoed to the door, opened it, and saw the light on in the hall. He listened, but the apartment was quiet. The door to his parents' bedroom was slightly ajar. He peeked in and saw to his surprise that the bed was empty. He was confused for a few seconds—had she left? But then he saw that the covers were missing and then he understood.

She was sleeping on the sofa. He walked over and stood so close that he could hear her breathing and then, reassured, returned to the bedroom. The closet door squeaked softly as he opened it. With the most careful movements he could muster he carried a chair over so that he could reach the top shelf, all the way at the back.

That's where John had kept the boxes of aquarium equipment, spare parts to the pumps, filters, a jar of pebbles, plastic bags, and the like. Behind all this Justus located what he was looking for and carefully teased out the box. His mother coughed and he stopped, waiting for half a minute before he dared to get down, put the box on the bed, put the chair back, and gently shut the closet door.

The box was heavier than he had expected. He tucked it under one arm, looked out into the hall, and listened. He was sweating. The floor was cold. The clock out in the living room struck four.

Justus had saved his father. That's how he felt. A wave of warmth pulsed through him. *It's our secret*, he thought. *No one will find out, I promise.*

He crept in under the covers, pulled his legs up, and put his hands together. He prayed that John would see him, hear him, touch him. One last time. He would have given anything to feel the touch of his father's hand again.

On the other side of the city, Ola Haver was getting up. Was it the headache that had woken him or one of the kids? Rebecka was sleeping heavily. She always woke up at the slightest sound from the little ones, so he suspected it was the pain behind his brow that had cut his sleep short.

He took a couple of painkillers, washed them down with a glass of milk, and remained standing at the kitchen counter. *I should be sleeping*, he thought. He looked at the time: half past four. Had the paper arrived? At that moment he heard the door to the apartment building slam shut and he took that as a sign.

He waited at the front door and picked the paper up when it was pushed through the mail slot. It struck him that he had never seen the delivery person, but he sensed it was a man. That's what the steps in the stairwell sounded like. A person who serves us every morning and whom we would sorely miss if he stayed home one day. No face, just a pair of feet and a hand to push the paper through the mail slot.

Haver unfolded the newspaper and turned on the kitchen lamp. The picture from Libro was the first thing he saw. The story had not changed. Liselotte Rask, the public relations manager, confirmed the facts of the brutal murder and added that the police had recovered certain traces at the site. Haver smiled. *Yes*, he thought, *my shoe prints, Ottosson's, and Bea's.*

The picture of the victim didn't do him justice, but in comparison to how his body had looked it was a glamour shot. *People just can't imagine,*

Haver thought. *They don't know what we have to see. Not even Rebecka understands—but how could she?*

Haver pushed the paper aside. He thought about how he should organize the day. He took a look at the list of tasks he had assigned himself the night before.

Bea was going to search John's apartment in Gränby. Sammy would maybe accompany her. He was good with kids. And Haver thought John's son would probably like dealing with a male police officer.

John's brother had to be questioned, and they would have to question the wife again. Bea hadn't managed to get much out of her during their conversation yesterday.

According to Berit Jonsson, her husband had taken the bus downtown. Which bus? They could probably find the driver. He or she would perhaps recall at which stop John had gotten off. The pet-store line of inquiry also had to be pursued to see if he had bought a pump and in that case where and when. They had to do everything possible to try to re-create John's steps on his last afternoon.

Haver dismissed all thoughts of the murder investigation, pulled the paper back over, and read it thoroughly. He had plenty of time and his headache was getting better. He assuaged his hunger with a banana and some yogurt.

He wasn't tired exactly, but tense in preparation for the day's activities. If they could establish the movements of John's last days relatively quickly, their chances of solving the case increased dramatically.

It was no accident, nor was it a murder committed in haste, he was convinced of that. The murderer or murderers would be found in John's circle of acquaintances. It shouldn't be too hard to establish a cast of characters.

The motive? Money, Bea had said. Drugs, was Riis's suggestion, although Ottosson had dismissed this, saying that John Jonsson had never been a dealer. The chief had gone as far as to claim that John had hated drugs.

Haver leaned toward the theory that it was money. An old debt that had not been repaid, a lender who went out of control, who perhaps had been provoked. He would ask Sammy to compile a list of known lenders. Haver knew of some already, above all Sundin from Gävle, who sometimes made guest appearances in Uppsala, also the brothers Häll and the "Gym Coach," a bodybuilder who had a background in karate. Were there others? Sammy would know.

Debt. It must have been a substantial sum to motivate murder, Haver mused. *What exactly constitutes a "substantial sum"? One hundred thousand? Half a million?*

It struck him suddenly that the murderer was perhaps also reading the morning paper at this precise moment. In contrast to the newspaper reporters and the police, the killer knew the whole story. Consumed by this thought, Haver got up and walked to the window. It was snowing. The lights were on in a couple of windows on the other side of the street. Perhaps he was there, in one of the apartments on the other side?

Haver snorted at these musings but couldn't rid himself of the thought that the murderer was also awake right now. The thought both appealed to him and appalled him. He liked it, because it meant that the murderer was unable to sleep in peace, did not feel secure, and was worried by the words that the police "had recovered certain clues." He was thinking, probably for the hundredth time, of how he had transported the dead or dying man to Libro. Had he dropped something or left tracks? There was perhaps some small detail that he had missed, a mistake that he sensed, that was now depriving him of sleep in the wee hours. But he disliked thinking of how the murderer was free to read the paper, drink his coffee and wander out into the morning, sit in the car or perhaps even board a plane, only to disappear from reach.

"Stay where you are," Haver mumbled.

"Did you say something?"

Rebecka appeared in the doorway. He hadn't heard her get up. She had the green nightgown on. Her hair was messy and she looked tired. He guessed that she had been up nursing the little one.

"I was just talking to myself," he said. "I'm reading about the murder."

Rebecka yawned and went to the bathroom. Haver cleared his things up in the kitchen, refilled the coffeemaker and switched it on. He felt torn again. The peace and quiet of the morning was over and so was the possibility of quiet reflection, but at the same time he loved having her there with him, not least in the early morning.

It was something left over from childhood. In his home, the mornings had always been unusually peaceful, a pleasurable time for family members to be together. They had been an unusual family in that they had all been morning people, almost to the point where they tried to compete over who could appear the most cheerful and friendly.

Haver had tried to re-create this with Rebecka, even though she often bordered on a state of complete exhaustion in the mornings. He would make her coffee, toast, and, before she had gotten pregnant, a boiled egg and roe spread. Now she couldn't stand the smell of either egg or roe.

He ate his eggs with a feeling of guilt, but he couldn't bring himself to completely exclude them from his morning ritual.

Rebecka returned from the bathroom. She smiled and ruffled his hair.

"You're a mess," she said.

He grabbed her, pulling her close, and hugged her, with his nose pressed against her stomach. He knew she was reading the paper over his head, but he drew in her smell and for a short while forgot all about the black headlines.

Nine

Modig took the call at seven thirty five A.M. He was working the night shift and was still on duty. His colleague Tunander had had a car accident on his way to work and wouldn't be in until eight.

Not that it troubled Modig unduly. No one was waiting for him at home and he was still feeling unusually alert. His vacation was due to start soon. He had taken off more days than usual and booked a trip to Mexico departing on December 23. When the call came he was wondering what the food would be like. His experiences with so-called Mexican food in Sweden had not filled him with great expectations.

"Someone has strangled Ansgar!" a woman said, clearly distraught.

Modig had little patience with people who panted or even breathed audibly on the phone.

"Please calm yourself," he said.

"But he's dead!"

"Who's dead?"

"Ansgar! I already told you."

"What's your name?"

"Gunilla Karlsson."

She wasn't breathing as heavily now.

"Where do you live?"

The woman managed to tell him her address with some difficulty, and Modig wrote it down in his usual scrawl.

"Tell me exactly what happened."

"I walked out onto the patio and there he was, hanging on the fence."

"Ansgar?"

"Yes. I saw at once that he was dead. And he's not even mine. How am I ever going to explain this? Malin is going to be devastated."

"Who is Ansgar?"

"My neighbor's rabbit."

Modig couldn't help smiling. He made a sign to Tunander, who had just walked in, and wrote "dead rabbit" on the pad of paper so that he could read it.

"And you found him on your patio?"

"I was looking after him. They're away on a trip and I was going to look after Ansgar while they were gone. I was supposed to give him food and water every morning."

"Did someone string him up or did he get caught on the fence?"

"He has a rope around his neck. He was murdered."

Does killing a rabbit qualify as murder? Modig wondered as he wrote "murdered" on the pad of paper.

"When did you see him last?"

Tunander left the room chuckling.

"Last night as I was checking on him. Oh, dear God," she said, and Modig knew she was thinking of her neighbor, Malin.

"Do you have any idea who would be likely to strangle a rabbit?" Modig asked and was suddenly hit by a wave of fatigue.

The woman started to tell him about the care of the rabbit in great detail. Modig stared into space. He heard voices of other officers coming from the area of the building called the Sea.

"We'll see what we can do," Modig said kindly.

"Will someone come out? I have to go in to work. Should I let Ansgar hang there?"

Modig thought for a moment.

"Let him stay where he is," he said finally.

Tunander came back with a cup of coffee.

"How can you name a rabbit Ansgar?" Modig asked when he hung up.

"What kind was it?" Tunander asked.

"What kind?"

"There are all kinds of different breeds. Didn't you know that?"

He sat down.

"How did it go?"

"Just some dents," Tunander said and was immediately serious! "Some bitch drove right into me."

He shook his head. Modig got up.

"Anything to report?" Tunander asked.

"It's been quiet. A few calls about Little John."

"Anything of substance?"

"Maybe. I don't know," Modig said absently.

He felt exhausted. Mexico was definitely the right decision.

"He was white," he said.

"Who?"

"Ansgar," Modig said and heaved himself out of his chair.

Modig left the building, not to return for another fourteen days, just as a meeting concerning the case of John Jonsson was called to order in the large conference room. The assembled group consisted of the usual people from the Violent Crimes Division, Morenius from the Crime Information Service, forensic specialist Ryde, Julle and Aronsson from the Patrol Division, and Rask, who headed the public relations team. A total of twenty or so individuals in all.

Ottosson presided over the meeting. He was getting better at it. Haver glanced at him. He was sitting on Ottosson's left side, where Lindell normally sat. It was as if Ottosson sensed what he was thinking about, because at that precise moment he put his hand on Haver's arm, looked at him, and smiled, just like he always did with Ann Lindell.

The touch lasted only a fraction of a second, but the smile was warm and the nod Ottosson gave him filled Haver with joy. He looked around to see if anyone had registered this gesture of collegiality or even friendship. Berglund, who sat across from Haver, smiled slightly.

Haver was surprisingly tense. He was usually dispirited by the sight of so many people gathered around the table, which could only mean that some atrocious act of violence had been committed. Not that he was sick of his work, but he—like his colleagues—realized that a murder investigation drained resources from the other cases. Some people would go free as a result of the fact that they were all sitting there. That was just the way it was. *Violence begets violence, as the saying goes,* he thought, and that was literally true in this context. Maybe it would be a case of wife-beating or a downtown brawl that would suffer and only encourage the perpetrators to continue.

The chief talked about sending "the right signals." A murder investigation signaled an escalation of crime. Haver had always known this, but the insight struck him with new force this morning, perhaps because Sammy Nilsson had been complaining as they were walking into the conference room. He was taking part in a new project involving street crime, started after a number of "incidents"—as the chief put it—three assault cases involving youth gangs, the last on the evening of the Santa Lucia celebration.

Now Sammy was forced to leave this work in order to assist in the Little John case. Haver had seen the dejection in his colleague's face and he understood it completely. Sammy was their youth man, more so than anyone else on the squad. Assisted by colleagues from Drug Enforcement, he had made large inroads in dissolving the gangs, talking sense into the young men who descended upon the town and outlying suburbs like a pack of wild animals. Those were Sammy's own words.

"They're like a pack of animals driven from their hunting grounds," he had said, without specifying exactly where these hunting grounds were located, or who it was who was driving them. Haver had the impression that it was the gangs who were driving other, more peaceful citizens from the streets.

Ottosson asked for silence and almost immediately everyone around the table stopped talking. The chief paused for a few seconds while the whole room sank into stillness. It was as if he wanted to hold a moment of silence for Little John. Everyone was aware of the fact that Ottosson had known the deceased over the course of his entire adult life. Perhaps that was why everyone, as if in wordless agreement, stopped their chatter and their rustling of papers. A few looked at Ottosson, others stared down at the table.

"Little John is dead," Ottosson began. "There are probably those of us who don't think that's much of a loss."

He paused again, and Haver, who again cast a quick glance at his boss, sensed his doubt as to how he should continue—or was he wondering how his words were going to affect the assembled officers? Ottosson was always concerned about maintaining an upbeat atmosphere, and Haver expected that he would be very careful not to say anything that might have a negative impact.

"That would be a pity, however," Ottosson said in a forceful voice. "Little John was once a young kid who took a wrong turn, a hell of a wrong turn. Many of you know his big brother, Lennart, and there you have part of the reason why. I have the advantage of having met their parents, Albin and Aina. Fine, decent people."

How is he going to pull this off? Haver thought, feeling an almost physical discomfort. *Fine people* was a phrase Ottosson sometimes used, a note of approval that implied more than adherence to a lawful lifestyle.

Haver looked at Bea, who had spoken to John's mother to test her reaction, but she sat with her head lowered.

"I know they tried to steer their boys right, but it may have been beyond their power. We know very little of what determines a person's course of action," Ottosson said thoughtfully.

Bea lifted her head at this outburst of philosophical speculation. Ottosson looked around with slight embarrassment, as if he had committed an indiscretion, and to Haver's relief he abandoned the subject.

"Ola," he said in a different and more familiar tone of voice. "Please run through an account of the events to date."

Haver started by giving them greetings from Ann Lindell, which he immediately realized was a mistake. He tried to repair this error by quickly establishing the perimeters of the murder case. He hastily sketched out the contours of the case, which he said he hoped his colleagues would flesh out with the results of the forensic investigation, the distilled results of any questioning that had taken place. Other issues they needed to address were: Had the initial investigation of the crime site yielded anything? Had there been any results from going door to door? What were the results of the autopsy? Had the initial investigation of the crime site yielded anything?

Haver proceeded through the points on his list in a systematic fashion. No one interrupted him, and when he finished there was an unusual silence in the room.

Did I forget something? Haver wondered and quickly consulted his notepad.

"Excellent," Ottosson said and smiled.

"Over to you, Ryde."

The forensic specialist spoke in his usual morning drawl. The snow dump in Libro had yielded a number of interesting objects, although of course many of these had nothing to do with the murder: empty cigarette packs, toys, car tires, orange traffic cones, the sidewalk advertisement from a local café, two plastic balls, a dead kitten, three ice scrapers, and so on. The most remarkable object recovered so far was a stuffed bird, a herring gull, according to Hugosson, a technician who was also an avid bird-watcher.

Two of the objects seemed significant: a length of green nylon rope, about eight millimeters in diameter, and a bloodstained work glove. Results of the blood analysis were not in yet. It could turn out to belong to John, but it could also have come from any one of the many trucks that frequented the dump. Ryde speculated that a driver could have injured himself, stained the glove with blood, and then tossed it or dropped it accidentally. It was a lined winter glove of the label Windsor Elite.

However, the length of rope, barely fifty centimeters, could be directly connected with John. The pattern of the rope fit the marks left on his wrists, and furthermore—and this clinched it—some of John's hairs had become entangled in the rope's fibers. The rope, which could have been bought at any gas station or corner store, had been recovered three meters from the body.

They had found a number of tire tracks. Most of these belonged to heavy vehicles with wide tires. Trucks, according to Ryde's personal opinion. Also tracks from another piece of machinery, probably the Cat that the county had brought in to clear the snow.

But one set of tracks was of greater interest. These belonged to a car and had been found close to John's body. The prints had been somewhat unclear since the ceaseless snow had partially covered them, but because of the relatively sudden swing from mild to cold weather during the night of the murder, one part of the tracks had frozen and the technicians had been able to reconstruct the pattern and the width.

Ryde spread out a series of photocopies on the table.

"Two hundred twenty millimeters wide, a radial tire, with studs, probably from a van or jeep. This is no rusty Ascona," he added drily.

"Could the car belong to a county official?" Fredriksson asked, touching one of the black photocopies as if he could feel the pattern with his fingers.

"Sure," Ryde said. "I'm only giving you what we have. You draw the conclusions."

"Excellent," Ottosson repeated.

The meeting continued with Riis giving the results of his investigation into the Jonsson family finances. Much of this was preliminary, as all of the data was not yet in, but for Riis the picture was clear: A low-income family who could not afford much in the way of excesses.

John's unemployment had hit them hard. There had been more purchases made with monthly payment arrangements and there had been three incidents of failure to make loan repayments during the past two years.

They did not currently receive any housing assistance. The mortgage payment on their condo was reasonable, in Riis's opinion. There were no incidents recorded with the local housing authorities or from their neighbors.

They only had one credit card, an IKEA card with a balance of around seven thousand kronor. Neither Berit nor John had any private retirement savings or shares or other assets. John had an account with the Föreningssparbanken, where his unemployment benefit was deposited. Berit received her salary in a private account at Nordbanken. She grossed approximately twelve thousand a month.

John had only one small life-insurance policy, through the trade union, and it was probably not worth very much, according to Riis, who concluded his report with a sigh.

"No excesses and worsening finances the past two years, in other words," Haver summarized.

"There was one more thing," Riis said. "In October, John received a deposit into his account of ten thousand kronor. It was an electronic deposit that I have not been able to follow up on yet. I'll do so later this morning," Riis added in a for-him unusually defensive tone, as if he was expecting to be criticized for not having all the facts at his disposal.

Haver considered the information; it was clearly the most interesting thing to have come to light so far.

"Ten thousand," he said, looking like he was thinking about what he would do with ten thousand kronor. "We can only speculate at this point as to where it came from, but it sounds a little fishy."

Fredriksson coughed slightly.

"Yes," said Haver, who knew him well.

"We now know what John did late yesterday afternoon," Fredriksson said casually. "He was stocking up on booze at the liqour store and then he dropped in on a friend, Mikael Andersson, who lives on Väderkvarnsgatan. He called last night and is coming to the station in half an hour."

"What time was John there?"

"He dropped in around five and stayed for half an hour, maybe forty-five minutes." Fredriksson went through the rest of Mikael Andersson's account.

"Okay," Haver said. "Now we can start tracing him. Mikael Andersson lives on Väderkvarnsgatan, which is a block or so from the main square. How would he get home?"

"Bus," Bea said. "You don't walk all the way up to Gränby when you have two big bags of bottles. I wouldn't, at any rate."

"I think the number three goes from Vaksalagatan," said Lundin, whose contributions at morning meetings were getting increasingly sporadic. Haver sensed that his increasing germophobia and obsession with cleanliness were to blame.

"We'll have to check in with the appropriate bus drivers," Haver said.

"Maybe we should post a guy at the bus stop at around the time we think John took the bus and have him show people a picture of John and . . ."

"Good idea," Haver said. "A lot of people take the same bus on a regular basis. Lundin?"

Lundin looked up with surprise.

"That time of day is tricky for me," he said.

"I'll do it," Berglund said and gave Haver a dark look. He hated seeing Lundin's pained and confused expressions.

"The brother—that's where we should plunge the knife, isn't it?" said Sammy, who had been quiet until now. He sat at the opposite end of the table, so Haver hadn't even noticed him.

Ottosson drummed his fingers on the table.

"He is a bottom-feeder," he said. "A particularly nasty bottom-feeder."

In Ottosson's world there were "decent people" and "bottom-feeders." The latter had lost some of its force since so many bottom-feeders swam around the city. Many in schools, as Sammy pointed out repeatedly through his work on street violence.

Beatrice thought of John's hobby and imagined his brother, Lennart, swimming around in the fish tank as a "particularly nasty bottom-feeder."

"Me and Ann were the last ones to take him in," Sammy said. "I wouldn't have anything against reeling in this particular barracuda."

Enough with the metaphors, Haver thought.

"We'll have him in for questioning. It sounds reasonable to let you do the first round," he said, nodding to Sammy Nilsson.

The meeting ended after another fifteen minutes of speculation and planning. Liselotte Rask remained behind with Ottosson and Haver to discuss how much information to release to the public.

Sammy Nilsson thought about Lennart Jonsson and tried to remember how he and Ann Lindell had dealt with him. For the most part it was Ann who had managed to connect with him. Lennart Jonsson was a professional. He didn't get intimidated or tricked into saying too much. He gave them only the bare minimum. He was helpful when it suited him, and closed as a clam if need be.

Sammy recalled the mixed feelings that this notorious criminal had inspired in him. It had been a mixture of helplessness, anger, and fatigue. He had been forced to realize that while Lennart Jonsson most probably was guilty of everything he stood accused of, they had not been able to pin enough on him to get a conviction. The feeling of helplessness stemmed from knowing they could have broken down his defenses if they had had more time. And if they had managed that, Lennart would have cooperated. He knew enough to know when further resistance was futile. That was part of his professionalism, to acknowledge when the game was up and then be willing to cooperate with the police. Sammy had the feeling that Lennart Jonsson didn't like to play games. If you got away with it, fine, if not, bad luck.

Sammy decided to drive out to Lennart's apartment right away. He thought about calling Ann and discussing the situation with her but held off. She was on maternity leave and deserved to be left in peace.

He was relieved to leave the station. The last few incidents of street crime had resulted in a good deal of desk time, with reports to write and all kinds of calls to make to the necessary authorities and school personnel. Teenage criminals were among the most depressing things Sammy knew. Not that he didn't like teenagers. He coached a soccer team a few nights a week. He knew how fun kids could be despite their rowdy behavior.

He always thought of the boys on his team when he was confronted with trouble on the street, many of those guys only three or so years older than his soccer players. Two different worlds.

The kids on the team were the well-adjusted sort who came from a relatively affluent suburb. These were children whose parents were involved in their lives, driving them to practices and meets, and who knew the other parents, from neighborhood associations and PTA meetings.

The boys Sammy met through his profession were of a whole different category. They came from one of the large housing districts on the outskirts of the city, an area many Uppsala inhabitants had never even seen, existing for the majority only as a name that often figured in headlines.

A few of the boys did sports. Sammy had seen a few of them at the UIF boxing association, boys with talent who had come in from the street and were now directing their energies at the punching bag.

If we just had the time, he thought, and would often say, *we could manage these kids as well.* All they lacked was time and resources. Sammy Nilsson had not grown cynical, something he saw in several colleagues. He still defended the gang members, upholding the possibility of life without crime and drugs, but it was a position that claimed a high price to maintain, and he wondered how long he would be able to hold out. The year before, it had been even harder for him to hold on to his positive outlook.

It had also become harder to discuss this with his colleagues. All too often Sammy's speeches about the importance of good neighborhoods and schools were met only with dismissive comments. It was self-evident, it was written on every wall, they seemed to say, but who had time to bike around Stenhagen and Gottsunda, playing the nice police officer, offering the friendly ear?

When he talked to school counselors, curators, preschool teachers, and social workers, they breathed the same air of defeat. Every day the papers announced budget cuts in the public sector: health care, education, and social services.

Sammy Nilsson and his colleagues were forced to take up the slack.

Lennart Jonsson was woken up by someone banging on the door. The ringer had stopped working over half a year ago. He knew what it was all about. In some ways he was surprised that it had taken so long for the police to turn up.

He opened the door, but immediately turned around and walked back into the apartment.

"Just have to take a whiz," he yelled.

Sammy Nilsson stepped inside. The air was stale, musty. He waited in the hall. He heard the sound of the toilet being flushed. Next to the mirror there were three framed prints by Carl Larsson. Sammy sensed that Lennart had not chosen them himself. Two coats hung on hooks under the hat shelf. If you overlooked the pungent grocery bags filled with empty beer cans by the door, the sparsely furnished entrance hall looked not unlike the waiting room of Sammy's dentist, which was located in a 1950s downtown apartment building.

Lennart came out of the bathroom, dressed in jeans and a T-shirt, half untucked. He was barefoot and his black hair stood on end. Their eyes met. For a moment Sammy felt as if he were visiting an old friend, and he had the impression that Lennart was thinking the same thing.

"I'm sorry about your brother."

Lennart nodded, breaking eye contact. When he raised his eyes his expression had changed.

"Should we sit down?"

Lennart nodded again and gestured toward the kitchen, letting Sammy go first.

"What do you think?" Sammy said as a way to begin.

Lennart snorted. He removed a beer from the table.

"You were the one who knew him best. Who wanted to see Little John dead?"

"I don't know," Lennart said. "What do you know?"

"We're trying to establish a clear picture of John's life, what he was doing these past few months, this past week, the day before yesterday. You know the story. We're still gathering pieces of the puzzle."

"I've been thinking," Lennart said. "But I haven't been able to come up with anyone who would've wanted to knock off my bro. He was clean—had been for years."

He gave Sammy a look as if to say: *And don't you try to pin some shit on him now.*

Sammy Nilsson went through the usual questions. Lennart gave short answers. Once, he interrupted himself, walked over to the kitchen counter to get a banana, and consumed it in seconds. He then offered a banana to Sammy, who took one but set it down on the table.

"There's one guy who spent a lot of time with John. Micke Andersson," Lennart said. "Have you talked to him?"

"We have," Sammy said, but without mentioning that Micke had contacted the police the night before.

"There aren't a lot of us," Lennart said, and Sammy assumed he was talking about John's limited circle of friends.

He fetched another banana and ate it just as quickly.

"Some kind of banana diet?" Sammy asked.

Lennart shook his head. He looked thoughtful. Sammy restrained himself from asking further questions.

"The way I live, the people who are closest to you are the most important. Others can rat on you, betray you, but not a brother. Not John. We've always helped each other out."

"For better and for worse, perhaps?"

Lennart snorted again.

"There are some things you'll never get," he said. "Why would I trust anyone else?"

No; why would he? Sammy thought.

"Sometimes you have to," he said.

Lennart smiled faintly.

"Who's the 'you' of 'there are some things you'll never get'?" Sammy asked.

"All of you," Lennart said.

Sammy looked at him. He had heard enough. He knew what would follow—a harangue about the downtrodden members of society.

"When I played Ping-Pong in high school and won a match against the teacher he threw his racket at me. He had just hit a worthless serve, and when I bent over to pick up the ball he threw his racket at me with full force. It caught me behind the ear. Do you want to see the scar?"

Sammy shook his head.

"I was in a remedial class and Ping-Pong was the only thing I was good at. We used to play two, three hours a day."

"Getting back to John for a moment," Sammy said. "How were things at home?"

"What?"

"For him, I mean. With Berit."

"Berit's all right."

"I'm sure she is, but how were things between the two of them?"

"Who's been saying stuff?"

"No one."

"Glad to hear it," Lennart said.

The way Sammy saw it, Lennart had armed himself with nonchalance and arrogance. Sammy Nilsson knew he was likely to collapse without it, but nonetheless it irritated him.

"I'm trying to solve your brother's murder," he said.

"No shit."

Sammy left the apartment, hurried down the stairs, and just outside the front door happened to kick an empty can into a flower bed. It landed in a heap of paper trash.

He called Ottosson from the car in order to see if anything new had turned up, but the chief didn't have much to report. Sixten Wende had started charting movements at the snow dump in Libro. Now they had a preliminary list of all the drivers who usually trucked snow in. More names would probably be added. Wende had taken on the task of calling every last one of them.

Peter Lundin had checked into the tire-track patterns that had been recovered in Libro. So far they had not matched them to a car belonging to a county official. Andreas Lundemark, the only official who had any business at the dump, drove a Volvo with completely different tire prints.

"But it could be anybody, for that matter," Ottosson said. "Someone out with their dog or on a romantic assignation."

Sammy heard someone talking to Ottosson in the background.

"I'll give you a call later," Sammy said hastily. "I need to check into a few things."

Ten

Haver stood by the car. He decided not to think about all the interrogations and background checks that had to be done, but to concentrate on the matter at hand. He had felt this before, the sense that the quantity of things to be done overshadowed the most obvious.

Take a systematic approach, he told himself, but immediately became unsure about how he should proceed.

Sagander's Mechanical Workshop was located between a tire company and a business specializing in the installation of aluminum doors. It was the kind of building you didn't notice unless you worked in the area.

A fence about two meters in height ran the perimeter of the yard, in which Haver picked out a couple of containers, a few pallets filled with metal scraps, and a flatbed truck piled high with scrapped pipes. A couple of bathtubs were propped up against the wall.

Haver noted that there were three cars parked in front of the building: a Mazda, an old rusty VW Golf, and a fairly new Volvo.

As he walked into the yard the clouds parted and the sun peeked out unexpectedly. Haver looked up. A crane on a nearby lot swung around and lowered its load. The crane operator paused and watched the men working below. One of them used his arm to signal to the operator, who was barely visible in the small cabin about ten meters off the ground. The crane swung around a few meters. The man made a new sign and shouted something to his colleague, who laughed and shouted something in return.

Haver's father had been a construction worker and sometimes as a boy Haver had accompanied his father to work. This was most often on small jobs, but sometimes it had been on big residential sites swarming with people, materials, machines, and sounds.

He watched the construction workers and carpenters at work with a tug of longing, envy, even. But above all he felt a warmth well up inside him, both from the sun and from watching the workers in their coordinated efforts. Even their work clothes—jackets lined in loud colors—brought a silly smile to his face.

One of the workers caught sight of him and Haver raised his hand. The man copied his movement and continued to work.

A screeching noise from inside the workshop broke the spell. Haver returned to reality—the black asphalt breaking through the dirty snow, a mess of scrap, wood shavings, rust, loose pieces of cardboard, and the depressing aluminum facade with its windows completely covered in dust.

He sighed heavily and avoided the muckiest areas of the yard. The metal door was unlocked. Haver stepped inside and was greeted by the sound of metal, sparks from a welder, and welding smoke. An older man was carefully polishing a large stainless steel drum with an angle grinder. He took half a step back, pushed the safety glasses onto his forehead, and scrutinized his work.

He must have seen Haver out of the corner of his eye, but took no notice of him. A somewhat younger man, also dressed in blue overalls, looked up from his welding. The man with the angle grinder continued his work. Haver waited some three or four meters away, looking around and trying to imagine Little John at work.

Then he caught sight of a third figure in the dim, far end of the shop, where a man threw a metal pipe onto a workbench, pulled out a measuring stick, and somewhat carelessly measured the end of the pipe, shaking his head and finally tossing it aside. He was about fifty years of age, his hair gathered into a ponytail. He looked up, taking stock of Haver, then disappeared behind a pipe-storage unit.

In a small office tucked into one side of the room Haver saw an older man bent over a folder. Haver sensed that it was Sagander himself. He made his way over to the office, nodding to the angle grinder, meeting the young welder's gaze, and then knocking on the glass door.

The man, who was not dressed in work clothes, pushed his glasses up onto his head and indicated for him to step inside, which Haver did. The office smelled of sweat. He introduced himself and made to take out his identification, but the man waved it away.

"I thought you'd come," he said in a voice hoarse from whiskey. He pushed against the desk and rolled his chair out onto the floor.

"We read about Little John. Please have a seat."

He was in his sixties, fairly short, perhaps 175 centimeters tall, with graying hair and ruddy skin. His eyes were spaced far apart and he had a big nose. Haver thought people with big noses looked strong-willed, and in Sagander's case this was supported by his manner of speaking to and looking at his visitor.

He gave the impression of being a person who wanted results, fast.

"I understand John used to work here," Haver said. "It must be terrible to read about it in the papers."

"Not as terrible as it must have been for John," the man said.

"Are you the boss?"

The man nodded.

"Agne Sagander," he said quickly.

"How long did John work here?"

"Almost all his working life, short as it was. He wasn't more than a boy when he started."

"Why did he stop working here?"

"There wasn't enough work to go around, that's all."

Haver sensed a streak of irritation, as if Haver wasn't quick enough for him.

"Was he good at his job?"

"Yes, very."

"But you let him go?"

"As I said, we have no control over the market."

"Looks like it's full steam ahead out there," Haver said.

"Now is now. That's not how things were back then."

Haver was quiet. Sagander waited, but after a few seconds he rolled his chair over to the desk and closed the folder that lay open. Haver decided to plunge ahead.

"Who killed him?"

Sagander froze with his enormous hand suspended above the folder.

"How the hell would I know something like that?" he said. "Ask his good-for-nothing brother."

"You know Lennart?"

Sagander made a noise that Haver interpreted as yes, but that also gave an idea of what he thought of John's brother.

"Maybe he also worked for you?"

"Oh no," Sagander said, and rolled out across the floor again.

"When did you last see John?"

Sagander put his hand up to his nose. *He can't keep still for a second,* Haver thought.

"It's been a while. Sometime last summer."

"Did he come here?"

"Yes."

"What did he want?"

"To talk, to visit."

"Was there anything in particular?"

Sagander shook his head.

"Is there anything else you could say about John, apart from work? If you know anyone who knew him . . ." Haver didn't know how he should put the question.

"Anyone who might have wanted to kill him, you mean?"

"Something like that, yes."

"No. Can't think of anyone. This is a workplace."

"Can you think of anything that happened that might appear in a different light, in hindsight? Something you might connect with the crime?"

"No."

"Did he ever ask for an advance on his salary?"

"There's a question for you. It happened, not very often. Now and then."

"Was he irresponsible with money?"

"I wouldn't say that."

"Drugs?"

"No luck there. A little vodka from time to time but nothing that inter-fered with his work. Maybe when he was younger, but that's a common story."

Sagander looked searchingly at Haver.

"You don't have much, do you?"

"Would you mind if I talked with your men? They've probably worked with John."

"All three, in fact. Of course. Talk as much as you'd like."

Sagander had returned to his desk and reopened the folder by the time it took Haver to get up and leave the stuffy office. As Haver was closing the door the phone rang and Sagander grabbed the receiver with irritation.

"The shop," Haver heard him say, as if there were only one metalwork shop in the whole town.

Erki Karjalainen, the man with the angle grinder, looked as if he had been waiting for Haver, because as soon as Haver stepped out of the office he signaled that he wanted to speak with him. Haver walked over to him.

"You're from the police, aren't you?" the man asked in a Swedish-Finnish dialect.

"That's right. It must be written on my forehead."

The Finn smiled.

"It's a terrible thing," he said, and Haver saw that he meant it. He discerned a mere suggestion of shakiness in the man's face that betrayed his emotion.

"John was a good guy," he continued, and his accent became more distinct. "A devil of a welder."

These were the kind of men who beat the Russians, Haver thought.

"And nice."

He looked over at the office.

"A good friend."

Haver was touched by his simple words. He nodded. Karjalainen turned his head and looked at the welder. *Is he as good as Little John was?* Haver wondered.

"Kurre is good but John was better," the Finn said, as if he had read

Haver's mind. "It's a disgrace that he had to quit. There were still a few jobs and we knew things were going to get better."

"Did they get along?"

A thoughtful expression came over Erki Karjalainen's face, and when he spoke, his words no longer had the succinct assurance of his earlier answers.

"There was something that wasn't right between them," he said. "I think Sagge used the lack of work as an excuse to get rid of John."

"What was wrong?"

Erki took out a pack of cigarettes. He smoked Chesterfields, something that surprised Haver. He thought they had gone out of business.

"Let's step out," Erki said. "Do you smoke?"

Haver shook his head and followed him out into the yard. The clouds had filled the patch of blue sky and the construction workers were taking a break.

"They're building offices," Erki said.

He inhaled a few times. Haver studied his face in the daylight. He had a narrow, lined face that was marked by hard work. His dark hair was slicked back. Bushy eyebrows and thin lips. Nicotine-stained teeth in poor condition. He reminded Haver of an out-of-work Italian actor from the 1950s. He sucked deeply on the cigarette and spoke with puffs of smoke punctuating his speech.

"Sagge's a good guy, but sometimes he can be a hard-ass too. We have to put in a lot of overtime and John didn't like that. He had a family, and the older his boy got, the less John liked to work late."

"And Sagge took his revenge by firing him, you mean."

"Revenge," Erki repeated, as if testing the word. "Maybe that's taking it a bit far. Sagge is a stubborn bastard, and stubborn bastards sometimes do crazy things, against their better judgment."

"Like firing a good welder to make a point?"

"Yup. I think he regrets it, but he'd never say anything like that."

"Did you ever see John after he stopped working here?"

Erki nodded and lit a new Chesterfield with the remains of the first.

"He came by sometimes but he never talked to Sagge."

"But with you he did?"

"With me he did."

The Finn smiled sorrowfully and looked even more like a character in a Fellini film.

Before Haver left the workshop he talked to the other two employees,

Kurt Davidsson and Harry Mattzon. Neither of them was particularly talk-ative, but they strengthened the image of John as a skillful welder and pleas-ant colleague. They did not, however, appear to take his death as much to heart as Erki did.

The long-haired Mattzon said something that struck Haver as strange.

"I saw John on the street here last summer. It was the last week of my holiday. I was down here getting a car-roof box I keep at work. My brother was going to borrow it. When I swung out onto the street I saw John com-ing down this way."

"In a car?"

"Of course."

"He doesn't own a car," Haver said.

"I know. That's why I remember it. I thought he had bought one."

"What kind was it?"

"An old white Volvo 242 from the mid-seventies."

Haver couldn't help smiling.

"Was he alone?"

"I don't know."

"When was this?"

"Must have been the first week of August. Sunday, I think. My brother was going away and I had promised to get him the roof box, but had for-gotten to take it home so I had to come down here on a Sunday."

"Had he been here at the workshop?"

"It's hard to say," Mattzon said, taking a few steps to the door and put-ting his hand on the handle. Haver realized that the man had burned him-self. There were bright red blisters on the knuckles of the left hand. A few blisters had burst and revealed the inflamed flesh beneath.

"Maybe he came down to meet someone here?"

"Like who? Everything was closed, shut down for the summer. Sagander was in Africa, on safari," Mattzon said and opened the door.

"You should see to that hand," Haver said. "It looks bad."

Mattzon peeked into the workshop, then looked at Haver. He didn't bother checking his hand.

"At least I'm alive," he said and returned to his work.

Haver caught sight of Sagander in his office before the door shut. He took out his cell phone and called Sammy Nilsson but he didn't answer. Haver looked down at his watch. Lunchtime.

Eleven

Vincent Hahn woke up at half past nine. Today was bingo day. Even though he was in a hurry he stole a few moments by Julia's side and caressed her firm buttocks. He would put new panties on her tonight. He'd steal some from Lindex, his favorite place. A dark pair, most likely, but not black.

The mannequin's rigid posture sometimes bothered him, making it appear as if she were watching him. When it was too much he would tip her onto the floor and let her lie there for a day or two. That took her down a peg.

It had been a bad night. Vincent Hahn did not count true remorse among his arsenal of emotions, but it was the sound that had bothered him and haunted him in the early hours.

He always ate yogurt in the mornings, two helpings. Yogurt was pure.

The bus was thirty seconds late but the driver only smiled when it was pointed out to him. He was known to all the drivers of this route. During his first year in the area he had compiled statistics regarding the various drivers, their punctuality, if they were polite or not, and how they drove. He had sent an analysis of these results, ingeniously displayed, to the Uppsala public transport authorities.

The reply had infuriated him. During the following few weeks he made various plans for his revenge, but, as had been the case so many times before, they came to nothing.

Now he felt stronger and more prepared to follow through. He didn't know why it was different this time, just that he felt more equipped to deal with it. Now he had not only the justification but the endurance.

He had started last night. A rabbit. Rodents should not be kept in residential areas. He knew that many people agreed with him and that they would silently thank him. He knew this because of the letter he had written to the housing authorities.

Maybe Julia had made the difference? He had acquired her last spring. He had long thought he wanted to share his life with someone, and when he found her in the Dumpster he knew he had found his companion.

She had been dirty and he had spent a whole day cleaning her off and repairing a tear in her groin. Someone had been violent with her. He had saved her from that. Now he guarded her, changed her underwear, and gave her love.

He got off at the bus terminal and walked up Bangårdsgatan to the bingo hall. He always looked around before going in. Once he was inside, some of the tension lifted.

Twelve

The headlines in the morning paper screamed: MURDER. Her first impulse once she had finished reading was to call Ottosson. The morning fatigue vanished. This was her job.

Some got a kick out of the sports pages and the latest results, some preferred the massive texts in the arts-and-culture section, and others read the cartoons or the home-and-garden inserts. None of this interested Ann Lindell, but a murder in her hometown made her heart beat faster. She was excited not by the violence itself or the fact that a person had been brutally slaughtered, but by the fact that it meant she had work to do.

She studied the text carefully and tried to read between the lines. Haver's and Ryde's brief comments didn't yield much, but she knew enough to assume they didn't have much to work with at this point.

She pushed the paper away. She had been home for nine months now. The baby, Erik, was growing incredibly slowly. She often called him "my poor boy." She didn't mean anything by this other than that she felt sorry for him because he had been born to a single parent, and a police officer at that.

She thought she was not a particularly good mother. Not that the little one was suffering—he got all the care and attention he could want—but Ann continually felt impatient over the time it was taking. Why couldn't he hurry up and grow so that she could go back to work?

She had mentioned it to Beatrice, saying that she felt like she was being disloyal to him, but Bea had just laughed.

"I've felt the same thing," she said. "We all love our kids, but we want so much. The kids are everything to us, and yet they aren't our life, so to speak. Some women love to putter around at home but I almost went crazy that first year. Sitting around the playground shooting the breeze with other moms was not my thing."

Ann was only partly comforted by her colleague's words. Guilt gnawed at her. She felt as if she were copying other mothers, especially her own, in almost everything she did. It was as if she weren't a mother for real.

She had never lived this close to another human being, never poured almost all her strength into caring for another. It was tiring but also filled her with a sense of power and pride. She was continually surprised at the direction her life had taken, over the change in herself.

She lived in two worlds, one where she pretended to be a good mother while the dual feelings of impatience and guilt coursed through her, and another where she proudly pushed her stroller through the streets of Uppsala, filled with a gentle happiness.

She didn't think much about Erik's father. That was a surprise. During her pregnancy, especially in the last few months, she had toyed with the idea of looking him up. Not to get him to leave his family—she had already found out that he was married and had two children—and not to extract any kind of allowance, not even to get him to admit paternity. *Then why?* she asked herself. She couldn't give herself an answer, and now that the baby was here she didn't care about him any longer.

Ann's parents had pressed her for information, but she had resisted their attempts to extract the name of the father. It was of no significance to her or her parents, after all, as she would never live with him.

She would have to reconsider the matter when her boy was older. As a matter of principle she had always thought every child had a right to know his father. But now she was no longer so sure. He wasn't needed. What she denied in herself was the slumbering half-hope that there would one day be a man who would take on the role of a stand-in.

She often hated herself for her somewhat dismissive attitude but used rationalizations to deny the needs she had felt the past few years when her thoughts of Edvard had confused and weakened her.

Things are as they are. Be a good mom just as you've been a good cop. Period. You don't need a man, she told herself, fully conscious of the fact that she was engaged in an act of self-deception. The art of survival, Beatrice had called it, the one time they had talked with unusual candor about Ann's situation.

She was grateful for Beatrice. She would never have thought that her colleague would one day come to mean so much to her. Beatrice had always seemed like an iron lady with principles to boot. Ann had tentatively sought her out, eager for the friendship but dreading her judgment.

She often felt like a wandering sheep, driven hither and thither by her violent feelings for Edvard, her—in her own opinion—adolescent desire to have a man in her life, and her vacillating emotions toward the child.

But Beatrice had not judged her. Quite the opposite: the feeling of rivalry that had once existed between the two officers had dissipated and Beatrice had become a close friend, something that Ann had missed ever since she had left Ödeshög. Sometimes she imagined that it had to do with the fact that Beatrice no longer had to compete with her, now that Ann was incapacitated, away from her post, bound to the little bunting.

Ottosson, their chief, had always treated Ann as his favorite, supporting her and showing her small favors, although always in private since he was careful not to jeopardize the group camaraderie. But Beatrice must have sensed it anyway, perhaps feeling unjustly ignored.

Whatever the case, Ann was happy over Beatrice's interest in her as a personal friend. It was an unfamiliar feeling. From talking exclusively about work, they now shared so much more as friends.

She called Ottosson. She knew she would not be able to contain herself, so she called right away.

Ottosson chuckled delightedly at the sound of her voice. Lindell felt that he could see through her. He filled her in on the case, and, as she had suspected, they did not have much to go on. She had never heard of Little John before, but she knew Lennart. She didn't think it such a good idea that Sammy was the one assigned to question him. Those two had never really hit it off, but she didn't say anything about her reservations. She remembered the notorious small-time crook as arrogant.

As she listened to Ottosson's report she was filled with an overwhelming desire to be back at work. She heard in his voice that he was stressed, but he still took the time to talk to her. Lindell sat at her kitchen table. Out of habit she had grabbed a pad and started making notes.

She could see it all in her mind, the morning meeting, the colleagues bent over their desks with a phone in their hands or in front of a computer screen. Haver's receptive face, Sammy's slightly careless style, Fredriksson staring into space while he unconsciously pulled on his nose with his fingertips. Lundin in the toilet, no doubt soaping up his hands, Wende searching the database, Beatrice gritting her teeth and methodically working her way through the list of names and addresses, and Ryde, the sullen forensic specialist, pondering and wise behind his mask of gruffness.

She wanted to be back there again, soon. The little one whimpered. She unconsciously put a hand to her breast and stood up. *What was the reason for the murder?* she wondered. *Drugs? Debts? Jealousy?* She threw a last glance at her notes and then walked slowly to Erik's room.

He lay on his back, looking either at a spot on the ceiling or at the colorful bells that hung above the crib. Ann looked at him. Her little one, her poor boy. His eyes fixed on her and he let out a soft whimper.

When she picked him up his face came to rest against her throat. The special blend of sweet and sour smells that rose from the chubby body, now resting warm and heavy against her chest, made her hug him gently and coo at him.

Ann carefully laid him in her unmade double bed, unbuttoned her blouse and the nursing bra, and lay down beside him. He knew what was coming and his arms worked with furious anticipation.

The little one sucked eagerly while Ann adjusted herself into a comfortable position. She stroked his soft hair and closed her eyes, thinking about Lennart Jonsson and his brother.

Thirteen

Mikael Andersson sat down in the visitor's chair. Fredriksson gathered a few folders together into a pile.

"I'm glad you could stop by," he said.

"Of course," Mikael said.

"You may be the last person to have seen Little John alive," Fredriksson began.

"Except the killer."

"Except the killer, yes. Had you known him long?"

"My whole life. We grew up in the same neighborhood, went to school together, and hung out after that."

"Why did you continue to associate with him?"

"He was my friend," Mikael said and looked at Fredriksson.

"Did you get along well?"

Mikael nodded. Fredriksson thought that the man in front of him in no way corresponded to the image he had formed of him when they talked on the phone. Mikael Andersson was short, only around 165 centimeters Fredriksson guessed, and solidly built, fat actually. Fredriksson knew he installed metal roofing but had trouble imagining him moving around on a rooftop.

"What did you do together?"

"We'd get together, bet on horses, play a little bandy sometimes."

"Sirius isn't up to much these days," Fredriksson said.

"Right. What else do you want to know?"

"You must know Berit and Lennart."

"Sure."

"So, tell me about them."

"Lennart is a whole chapter, but you must know all about him. Berit's a brick. They've always been together."

Micke leaned forward, elbows on his knees, and interlaced his fingers before he continued. Fredriksson noted the changes in his face as a wave of red washed over the pugdy cheeks and throat.

"She's all right," he said. "It won't be easy for her now that John's gone. And the kid too. I don't get it. He seemed the same as always. Have you got any leads?"

"Nothing too promising," Fredriksson admitted.

"I think he was picked up by someone who later killed him. I just don't know who that would be."

"Someone offered him a ride?"

"But who would that be?"

"You can't think of anyone who had an ax to grind with John?"

"No, nothing that would have made them want to kill him. John knew how to toe the line."

"How was he doing financially?"

"He wasn't rolling in money, but they managed. Things got worse after he stopped working for Sagge."

"Why did he stop?"

"There wasn't enough work, they said."

"Who's 'they'?"

"Sagge and his wife. She's the one who calls the shots."

Fredriksson pinched his nose.

"Someone picked him up, you said. Did John have any business out in Libro? Was there some company out there he needed to visit, or a friend?"

"Not that I know of. He didn't have too many friends."

"Did you ever see John with drugs?"

Mikael Andersson shot a quick glance at Fredriksson. He inhaled deeply and breathed out through his nose. Fredriksson had the impression that Micke was trying to decide whether or not to tell the truth.

"A long time ago, maybe. But that was all over and done with."

"How long ago are we talking about?"

Micke made a gesture as if to say: *God only knows, it must have been years ago.*

"When we were young," he said finally. "Twenty years ago."

"He never mentioned drugs after that?"

"Talk is one thing, but I never saw John with any drugs the past few years."

Fredriksson leaned back, put his hands behind his head, and looked at him. The police officer's face revealed nothing. He sat there for half a minute, then slowly put his hands back down, leaned back over the desk, and wrote a few lines in his notebook.

"Tell me about John," he said. "What kind of person was he?"

"He was quiet, just like his dad. His dad stuttered badly, but not John. He was a good friend. He didn't have a lot of friends at school. It was just me and a couple of other guys. He'd always been interested in fish. I don't know where that came from. Maybe it was his uncle, Eugene, who started the whole thing. We used to go fishing with him. He had a cabin out towards Faringe."

Mikael paused. Fredriksson sensed that he was trying to go back ten, twenty years in time.

"He was happy there, in the dinghy," he continued. "It was a little lake. A cold bastard of a lake, with the forest growing right down to the shoreline."

"What did you catch?"

"Perch and pike, mostly. John sometimes talked about going back there again, but we never did, like with so many things. When we sat in the boat it was like being kids again. We could row from shore to shore without effort. The only break in the forest was the clearing where Eugene's house was. It was a converted shed with a storage locker made out of sugar crates fastened together. The lake was like a sealed room. John oftened talked about those trips. In late winter Eugene would take us wood-grousing. We walked in the darkness over the swaying ice until we came to a felling area where he had made a shelter out of twigs and branches. We curled up in there. John always liked little places like that. The small lake and the tiny shelter."

"He also worked for a small company," Fredriksson added.

Mikael nodded.

"He wasn't really a troublemaker, not even when he was younger. As long as we stuck to Ymer and Frodegatan, everything was fine. When we were little you could get almost anything in Almtuna, our suburb. There were five grocery stores within ten minutes' walk. Now there isn't even a place called Almtuna. Have you seen that sign, over by the Vaksala school?"

Fredriksson shook his head.

"It says 'Fålhagen.' All the old names are disappearing. I don't know who makes those decisions, that no place should retain the old names. Eriksdal and Erikslund are also gone. Even Stabby is called 'Outer Luthagen.' "

"I've moved here recently," said Fredriksson, who was not familiar with all the old areas and districts of Uppsala.

"I think they do it to confuse us."

" 'Luthagen' probably sounds better than 'Stabby' in the real estate ads."

"Maybe," Mikael said, "it's about the money, then. I think about the old days more now. Must be age."

"And what do you see?" said Fredriksson, who found he was enjoying the discussion.

"The yards. Kids. There were a lot of us. John and Lennart and others." Mikael stopped and his face took on a sad and starved expression.

"It was a long time ago, but it feels so close," he said. "When did it all go to hell?"

"For John and Lennart, you mean?"

"Not only them. You know their old man worked on the railroad. His dad too. He helped build Port Arthur, which was supposed to be employee housing for rail folk. But we lived up on Frodegatan. I felt a real connection with them back then—not anymore. That's what gets me. I take a walk through the old neighborhoods sometimes. For John and Lennart I think it all started back when Lennart was twelve and me and John were nine. We had been playing bandy in Fålhagen. There was a big field out there that was hosed down every winter. Lennart had swiped a wallet in the dressing room from a guy named Håkan. I sometimes ran into him downtown. Lennart took out the wallet as we were teetering home on our skates. Nineteen kronor. We were scared shitless, but Lennart just laughed."

"It was the needle that became a bowl of silver," Fredriksson injected, referring to the old folk tale.

Mikael nodded and continued. Fredriksson leaned over and checked to make sure the miniature tape recorder on his desk was still going.

"Nineteen kronor. I didn't want any of it, I was too scared, so Lennart and John divvied it up between them. Lennart was always fair with his brother. That was the problem for John—having a big brother who always shared. Did it start then? I don't know."

"Lennart and John were close?"

Mikael nodded.

"Did Lennart drag John into something?"

"It sounds plausible, of course, but I don't think so. Lennart always protected his brother."

"Maybe he involved him in something without being aware of it."

Mikael looked doubtful.

"What could it have been, though? Lennart was a small-time guy."

"Maybe he was on to something big this time," Fredriksson said. "But okay, let's leave it. I also wanted to ask you what you thought of John and Berit's relationship. Were they happy together?"

Mikael snorted.

"Happiness?" he said. "That's quite a word, but all right, I guess it applies to them."

"No hanky-panky on the side?"

"Not in John's case, I wouldn't think. You know, they met when they were sixteen. I was actually there the first time they met; it was at a pool hall in Sivia. We hung out there almost all the time. One day Berit came by with a girlfriend. She fell for him immediately. He wasn't like the rest of us, loud and all that. John was quiet, thoughtful. He could throw anyone off their stride, he was so quiet."

"So you're saying John and Berit have been faithful to each other for over twenty years."

"When you put it like that it sounds crazy, but that's how I saw it. I never heard him talk about other broads, and we talked about most things."

There was a careful knock at the door and it opened. Riis looked in.

"I have a note for you, Allan," he said, while looking the visitor up and down.

Fredriksson leaned over the desk and took the folded note, opened it, and read the short message from his colleague.

"I see," he said and looked at Mikael. "You said that John and Berit hadn't been in such good shape financially."

"The last little while, yes."

"Was that why you deposited ten thousand kronor into his account on the third of October?"

Mikael flushed a deep red again. He cleared his throat and Fredriksson again glimpsed an expression of fear in his eyes. Perhaps not fear exactly, more like anxiety. He knew it didn't mean anything. Most people, especially those sitting in front of a desk at the police station, reacted that way on the subject of money. They could talk calmly about any number of unpleasant things, but invariably they grew nervous at the mention of money.

"No, not really. Things weren't so good for me back in September. John stepped in with the ten thousand and I was paying him back."

"Tell me what happened."

"Like I said, I was short on cash and John offered to help out."

" 'Help out.' Ten thousand is pretty good for a man who's unemployed."

"I know, but he said it was no problem."

"May I ask why you were short on cash? Were you in the habit of borrowing money from John?"

"It's happened before, but not very often."

"Why, then?"

"I'd been gambling. Roulette. That's all."

"And lost?"

"That's how it goes, isn't it?"

"Where was this?"

"A place called Baren Baren, if you know where that is."

Fredriksson nodded.

"But then you got some money?"

"I was paid my salary. That was enough to take care of the loan. And then I lived cheap for the rest of October."

"It was not the case, then, that you had borrowed more and the ten thousand was a first installment?"

"No, it wasn't anything like that," Mikael assured him.

"Did John say anything about how he was able to produce so much money without blinking an eye?"

"No."

"It was not the case that you were supposed to perform a service for the money, but that you changed your mind and returned the cash?"

"No. What would that have been?"

"I don't know," Fredriksson said and carefully refolded the note. "When were you at Baren Baren?"

"I was there a lot."

"John too?"

"Sometimes."

"Did he gamble?"

"Yes, but never large amounts."

"You wouldn't call him a gambler?"

"No, not really. He was pretty careful."

Fredriksson was silent for a moment.

"I know how it sounds, but I swear I'm telling you the truth."

"It's pretty normal for a friend to help out a friend," Fredriksson said quietly, "but as you can understand, the picture changes when one of the two is murdered."

With that, he ended the session.

Mikael tried to look relaxed but the air of openness at the beginning of the conversation had dissipated. He followed Fredriksson out without saying a word, and when they reached the last door, which the police officer held open for him, Mikael again assured him that it had all happened exactly as he'd said.

Fredriksson believed him, or rather, wanted to.

Fourteen

At three thirty Vincent Hahn stepped out onto the street, an extra two hundred kronor in his pocket. As always, it was like stepping out into a new world. People were new. The street that ran from the railway station down to the river had changed its character during the few hours he had spent inside the bingo hall. It looked more dignified, like a stately boulevard in a foreign country. The people around him seemed different from the ones he had left for the bingo hall's warm retreat.

The feeling stayed with him for a minute or two, then the hostile voices returned, the shoves, and the looks. The linden trees no longer lined the street like leafy pillars but terrifying statues, black and cold, suggestive of funerals and death. He knew where this feeling came from, but did everything to suppress it, to avoid images of the graveyard where his parents lay buried.

Vincent Hahn was a bad man, and he knew it. If his mother and father could be brought back to life they would be horrified to see that their youngest child had become a misanthrope, a person who was suspicious of everyone and everything and who—and this was the worst—saw it as his task to revenge himself on those around him for their wrongdoings.

There could not be punishment enough for them. Hadn't he suffered? But who cared? Everything simply kept going as if he didn't exist. *I'm here!* he wanted to shout out to everyone on Bangårdsgatan, but he didn't, and no one even so much as slowed down to pass him as they hurried on their way.

Air, he thought, *I'm nothing but air to you. But this air will poison you, my breath will annihilate you, envelop you in death.* He had made his decision. Now there was no fear, no hesitation.

He laughed out loud, checked his watch, and knew that he would begin this very evening. It was wonderful to finally have a plan, a meaning. A couple of retirees emerged from the bingo hall. Vincent nodded to them. To him they symbolized defeat. He didn't want to stay with this thought because it led to both his source of strength and his weakness. The thoughts, memories. Until now they had held him down as an insignificant creature. He nodded to the old couple, loyal companions from the solitary community of the bingo hall, victims like himself. In some way he was sure they would understand. Living, but dead.

His bingo win made him strong, almost overconfident. He decided to go to a café. It would have to be the Güntherska. He could maintain his sense of control from the sofa in the corner.

Fifteen

The photograph in the evening paper was of a young John Jonsson. Gunilla Karlsson recognized him immediately, as she would have even if they had used a recent picture of him. She had bumped into him just a few months ago, unexpectedly, at the grocery store. And on top of that she had had Justus in preschool. Actually not in her room, but he was a boy who stood out. It was mostly Berit who dropped him off and picked him up, but sometimes John turned up in the afternoon, straight from work. He had a nice smell. She had wondered what it was for a long time before she had the courage to ask. He had been completely at a loss until he realized she meant the smell of welding smoke. He had exused himself, looked extremely embarrassed, and mumbled something about not having had time to shower. Gunilla had been equally embarrassed and assured him that she liked the smell. There they were, with Justus between them busy putting on his warm things, both blushing furiously and looking at each other. Then they had burst into laughter.

After that time he often smiled at her. He told her about the body shop and offered their services in case the preschool needed any repairs. She had thanked him but said she didn't think they needed to have anything welded. "But please feel free to stop by more often," she had added, "we're short on men around here."

He had looked at her in the old way, which she remembered so well from their days at school, and felt warm inside. He liked her words—that's what his look told her—but Gunilla also read something else there, a spark of attraction.

She would have wanted to kiss him, not passionately, just a peck on the cheek to draw in more of that welding smoke that had penetrated all his pores. It was a fleeting impulse that lasted no more than a second, but it returned to her every time they met.

They stood there for a short while, close to each other, and it was as if time had stopped. It occurred to her that John was one of the few people she saw regularly and who had met both her parents while they were still active. Now they were both in homes, unreachable.

She had also met John's parents, the stuttering Albin and Aina, who used to leave terse notes in the communal laundry facilities urging her neighbors to clean up better after themselves.

A long time ago she had been in love with John. Back in junior high, maybe seventh grade. She had been part of the group that hung out on "the hill," an empty lot next to Vaksala square. John and Lennart used to go there, as well as thirty or so other teenagers from Petterslund, Almtuna, and Kvarngärdet.

A builder who had gone bankrupt stored leftover lumber and parts at the top of the hill and the youngsters had arranged these in an ingenious series of tunnels and rooms. Gunilla had gone mostly for John's sake and had been frightened by the heavy smell of paint thinner, trichloroethylene, and other chemicals that hung in the air.

The paint sniffing came and went in waves. At certain times no one was doing anything but then there would be an outbreak that would last for a few months or more. It was mainly a summer and fall activity. The police made occasional raids but no one really took the substance abuse seriously.

Gunilla had often thought about the number of brain cells that must have died on the hill. She was glad she had managed to break away from the group even though it meant she had lost contact with John.

And now he was dead. She read the article, but composed an internal text about his background and life. It struck her how little information there really was about John in the paper, even though the article was three pages long. The reporter had made things easy for himself, had dug out a list of John's sins and also connected the murder with a crime that had taken place a few weeks earlier when a drug dealer was knifed down in central Uppsala. "A city of violence and terror," she read. "The standard image of a sleepy, idyllic university town with its lively student life and dignified academic traditions is increasingly being replaced by images of violence. The popular children's series of Pelle Svanslös and his innocuous feline adventures feels remote when we study the number of reported crimes and the unsettling realization of how many of these crimes remain unsolved. The police, plagued by internal conflicts and budget cuts, seem at a loss."

"A sleepy, idyllic university town," Gunilla sniffed. Uppsala had never been that, at least not for her. Even though she had been born and raised here she had never visited any one of the historic student organizations or even watched the graduating class don their caps on the last day of April and listened to them singing spring songs on the slopes of the castle grounds. It had never been an idyll for her. Nor for John.

But what would John have had to do with a drug dealer? She knew he and his brother had been involved in their share of shady dealings but she doubted that it had ever involved drugs. John just wasn't the type.

She pushed the newspaper away, stood up, and walked to the window. The snow had stopped falling but a strong westerly wind blew it onto the roof of the garages. Her closest neighbor was walking up to the building with bags of groceries.

She walked past the mirror in the hall, stopped, and looked at herself. She had gained weight. Again. While she stood there she suddenly thought of the rabbit. How could she have forgotten? She walked quickly to the patio door, opened it, and saw Ansgar hanging from the railing, just as she had left him this morning, but now his abdomen had been slit. The internal organs that spilled out had a grayish cast.

There was also something white in the cut. She walked closer and looked at the stiff corpse with disgust. The rabbit's wide-open eyes seemed to be staring accusingly at her. It was a note. She drew it out carefully. It was bloodstained and she shivered as she unfolded the tiny piece of paper, no bigger than a bus ticket.

The handwriting was almost illegible and looked as if it had been done in haste: "Pets are not appropriate in densely populated areas." No signature.

What a mean-spirited thing to do, she thought. How would she explain this to Malin, the girl next door? She looked back at the rabbit. Incredible, to kill a rabbit. It had to be a very sick person.

Should she notify the police again? Had they been here? Probably not. They had more pressing matters to attend to than a dead rabbit.

She thought of John again and started to cry. People could be so awful. Had the note been there this morning, or had the person who strangled Ansgar returned later? She looked around. The forest that encroached on the buildings was starting to grow dark. The light from the windows was reflected on the tall trunks of the pine trees. The wind sighed in the treetops. Granite boulders lay scattered about like large animals.

Gunilla went back into the apartment. Her feet were wet and she was cold. She pulled the patio door shut and closed the blinds. Her initial fear was starting to give way to anger, and she hesitated as she stood there. Then she decided to get in touch with the head of the building association. He was a curmudgeon, but he needed to be notified about this. Perhaps he had received complaints about pet owners in the area. Maybe there had been another incident that could be connected to Ansgar's death?

She found his number in the phone book, dialed the number—which was confusingly like her own—but no one answered. She thought about going over to the neighbors to see if they had heard anyone sneaking around outside but she didn't feel like leaving her apartment. Maybe he was still out there.

Malin and her parents were away and wouldn't be back until the weekend was over. The neighbors on the other side were recent arrivals. They were an older couple who had sold their house in Bergsbrunna. Gunilla had spoken only briefly with the woman.

The news at six didn't mention John's murder. She changed the channel to check the local news program on channel 4, but the top stories were over and the weather was of no interest to her. Not now.

Calm down, she told herself.

It was the work of a madman, a sick human being. Mentally, she ran through the list of other occupants. Was there anyone capable of strangling and disemboweling a rabbit? No. Her neighbor Cattis could be difficult and she certainly had opinions on everyone and everything, but she was hardly so far gone as to do this.

The wind had picked up and Gunilla thought she could hear the rabbit's body rhythmically smacking against the railing. She knew she should cut him down but didn't want to go out onto the patio again. And if she called the police again, what would they do? They must have enough on their hands with John's murder without investigating the death of a pet rabbit.

She heard Magnus Härenstam's voice on the television as she gently pushed open the door and at the same time turned on the outside light. It didn't turn on and she tried again with the same result. A branch of the bird-cherry shrub that Martin had planted was dashed against the plastic roof. *Why did he plant it so close?* she had time to think before she noticed that the rabbit was gone. As it was white, it took a while before she spotted it again. Had it been blown down onto the snow or had someone taken it down?

She looked out toward the trees, holding her breath and crouching down slightly so that she would not be as visible to the outside. The pine trees swayed in the wind. The bird-cherry branch scraped against the roof. She took a few hesitant steps, wearing only thin stockings. Ansgar couldn't stay down there, people would think she had done it. Malin would never forgive her.

She was terrified, but strangely not very surprised, when a hand covered her mouth and another encircled her waist. She tried to bite her attacker but couldn't open her mouth.

"Rabbits are disgusting," a voice hissed in her ear, a voice she recognized but was unable to place.

The man's breath stank of decay. Gunilla tried to kick back with her legs like a frightened horse but had no strength. The man only chuckled, as if her show of resistance amused him.

"Let's go in," he said smoothly.

Gunilla desperately tried to place the voice. She had been so stupid. He must have been hiding behind the door.

He dragged her back into the apartment without allowing her to see him. He turned off the light by pressing his back against the button, then dragged her farther into the room and gave her a shove so that she fell into the sofa.

"Hi, Gunilla," he said. "I just wanted to drop in for a visit."

His voice was so familiar. She studied his face, which was narrow, with two deep lines that ran down his cheeks, a black beard, almost bald on top, and with a smile on his lips that frightened and confused her.

"I'm talking to you."

"What?" Gunilla said.

She had seen his lips move but had no idea what he had said.

"Do you remember me?"

Gunilla nodded. Suddenly she knew who he was. She started to shake.

"What do you want?"

The man laughed. He had bad teeth, disintegrating and covered in tartar.

"Did you kill the rabbit?"

Vincent Hahn's features stiffened in a mask, a laughing mask.

"I want to see your breasts," he said.

She flinched as if he had struck her.

"Don't touch me!" she sobbed.

"That's what you said before, but now I'm the one who decides."

He didn't look so strong, she thought. His shoulders and wrists were thin, but she knew how easily one could underestimate a person. Even mere children could be moved by rage to incredible feats of strength, which their bodies did not seem capable of. They had talked about self-defense at the daycare, once, when one of her colleagues had completed a course. She knew she had a chance to escape if only the opportunity arose. No one was invincible.

"If you show me your breasts I'll leave."

He looked tired. Maybe he was on medication.

"Then I'll leave," he repeated, and leaned forward so that his sour breath wafted over her again. She had to fight against revealing her disgust.

What was the right thing to say?

"Take off your sweater."

"It's certainly been a long time."

"Or I'll lay you on the ground."

She stood up. Suddenly she felt sorry for the man in front of her. At school he had always been the one the other students looked down on or treated as an outsider, someone who never fit in. But he had not been completely without friends, and he actually seemed to manage his schoolwork well. A few years ago, when she was leafing through her yearbook, she had seen a picture of Vincent's thin figure. She had thought at that time that it was strange how Vincent seemed to have gone through high school virtually unchanged—lanky, acne-ridden, and to all appearances unaffected by the usual emotional and hormonal storms that descended on everyone else, especially the boys. He had simply been there, attentive to the teachers, sometimes with an air of superiority toward the other students, but often ingratiating, wanting to please.

"I need to have a drink," she said. "I'm so scared. Would you like some wine?"

He looked back at her with a total lack of expression. She wondered if he had even understood what she had said.

"Would you like some wine?"

He grabbed her when she tried to walk past. Her arm hurt. He pulled her over but she managed to keep her balance.

"Let me go. I'm only getting some wine. Then you can see my breasts."

Don't show your fear, she thought, as the image of the strangled rabbit with his slit belly made her whimper softly. She pulled off her sweater and saw Vincent sway at the sight of her upper body.

"Okay, one glass," he said and smiled.

He followed her closely. She could feel his body heat behind her back. He was breathing heavily. The wine bottle clinked against the stand and it was as if the noise startled him, because suddenly he grabbed her shoulder, the way Martin did when her neck and shoulders were tight, but this grasp was much harder and turned her around.

"You remember me, don't you?"

"Of course," she said. "But you've changed a lot."

"So have you."

Gunilla freed herself from his hand and reached for the corkscrew hanging above the counter. Vincent Hahn stood right next to her, his sour, foul-smelling breath filling the entire kitchen, and she was struck by the thought that she would never be able to get it clean again.

"Do you like red wine?" she asked and raised the bottle.

The blow came from nowhere, startling both her and Vincent. Everything happened like a reflex action, the instinctive self-defense of an animal.

The bottle struck him on the side of the head and she finished the attack by thrusting the corkscrew into his chest.

Wine was spilling everywhere. Vincent's face was twisted with pain and surprise. He teetered, fumbling with his hand against the kitchen table, grabbing the back of the chair, then gliding down onto the floor and pulling the chair along with him. Wine and blood mingled together.

Gunilla stood rooted to the spot for a few seconds, paralyzed, still with the broken bottle in one hand and the corkscrew in her left, leaning over, tense, prepared to attack again, but the man at her feet hardly moved. The pool of blood spread out like a dark rose over the linoleum. The raw smell of the blood mixed with the heavy scent of the Rioja.

"You bastard," she said and pointed the broken bottle at his face, but then she suddenly dropped the sharp-edged weapon and fled from the kitchen, pulled open the front door, and ran out into the dark night.

The cold outside was intense. She slipped in the snow but ran on. Her cries filled the whole yard and the neighbors said later that it had sounded like a terrified, wounded animal.

Åke Bolinder, who lived in the tower block and had just taken his dog off its leash, was the first on the scene. He came running around the corner of the laundry building to see a woman sink to the ground. He immediately recognized her, not because he knew her particularly well, but because he had seen her at the association meetings and occasionally in the grocery store.

When he reached her he smelled the wine that came from her body and noted the tightly gripped corkscrew in her hand. He commanded his dog to sit and leaned over her, not sure of what to do next. He looked up at the wide-open door to her apartment.

Bolinder was a peace-loving man in his fifties, well-groomed and unmarried. He stared at Gunilla's breasts, at the black bra that stood in stark contrast to the white snow, kneeled down and pulled away a little of the hair that had fallen over her face. *What if she throws up?* he thought and prepared to jump back. But her expression was almost calm. In the distance he could hear the footsteps of someone running, a balcony door opened, and someone shouted something he didn't quite catch.

The dog, who was still obediently sitting a few meters away, growled. Bolinder looked up and followed the dog's gaze. In the door frame there was now a man, his face distorted with pain and hate. Bolinder could hear the rasping sounds of his exhalations, which formed small white puffs of vapor in the cold night. Blood was dripping from his beard.

Jupiter, the German shepherd, started to bark. Bolinder stood up.

"What is it?" Bolinder asked and at that moment Jupiter attacked. Bolinder didn't know if his usually so gentle dog had been roused to action because of the note of fear in his master's voice or the fact that the man in the doorway took half a step forward. The dog's lunge came without warning.

The man in the doorway lost his balance but managed to pull the door shut at the last moment. Bolinder saw Jupiter jump up, heard the sounds of his heavy body come into contact with the hard door and then saw him be thrown back onto the ground.

The dog was back on his feet again immediately and barked loudly. His first somewhat tentative attempts had turned into full-throttle barking. Bolinder called his dog over but Jupiter took no notice of him. Gunilla moved slightly and Bolinder leaned down over her again. She opened her eyes and flinched when she saw her neighbor, pulling herself up onto one elbow and staring at the apartment and the barking dog.

"He tried to rape me," she said.

Suddenly she became aware of her almost naked upper body, sat up, and crossed her arms over her chest. Bolinder took off his coat and gently placed it over her shoulders.

Despite the pain and the unexpected turn of events, he had had the presence of mind to grab a towel from the bathroom and wipe the blood from his head. He pressed it against his forehead, which was throbbing, then carefully felt the outline of the cut with his fingers. He didn't think there was a fracture, but it was an ugly wound. The bottle had caught him right above the brow, which is where the copious amounts of blood had come from. The corkscrew had penetrated his shirt and a few centimeters of his flesh but been stopped by bone and had not hurt him significantly.

Vincent Hahn was bewildered rather than confused by what had happened. He had thought he had her where he wanted her, but she had tricked him. Now he had to escape. He heard furious barking and raised voices outside. He threw the bloody towel onto the floor, picked up a clean one, pressed it against his head, and disappeared out into the night the same way he had come.

He ran. Dizziness threatened to overcome him but he kept on running. He knew the forest well and where the paths led. If he chose the nearest one he could be home in five or six minutes, but he was forced to take a longer route in order to avoid people.

Where should he go? How long could he remain at home until the police would come? Gunilla had recognized him. Of course, he was not registered at the Bergslags' apartment since he was subletting it, but the police would eventually track him down if they started to look for him. Perhaps through the hospital or his former sister-in-law. She was the only one who had visited him since he had moved up to Sävja.

Who would take him in? There was no one to give him shelter, dress his wounds, and let him rest. And who would take care of Julia? He sobbed and stumbled on. He had to get home to her, get there before the police. No one was allowed to touch her. He could hide her in the forest. She would get cold and wet, but it was better than ending up in the fascist hands of the police.

He reached Bergsbrunna farm in a disoriented state. He had taken walks here before and now he recognized where he was. He heard the horses neighing in the barn. He was freezing. It had to be at least fifteen degrees below zero. The cut in his forehead felt stiff. He hesitated in the yard. Should he go into the barn? He didn't have anything against horses. They were noble animals, wise, but there were cats in there too. He had seen them before, one white, one brown.

From the distance came the sound of insistent barking and it struck him that the police must have called in dogs to track him down. They would reach him soon. The barn offered no protection.

He ran on past two fields. The snow was deeper here and harder to trudge through. His energy was starting to wane and he was breathing hard. At the end of the road he saw some light. Someone had erected a Christmas tree in front of their house. He had the feeling that he had been through this before, running for his life in the cold. Without friends, able to rely only on himself. His chest burned.

He came out by the railroad tracks and followed them to the north. He would reach the crossing shortly. He had read about hobos in the United States who jumped onto freight trains and traveled across the entire continent in search of work, but here the trains simply thundered by at high speed.

He came to a stop, indecisive. A car came by across the fields on the other side of the crossing. Vincent ran over and threw himself down on the road.

The car came closer. He could hear from the sound that it had a diesel engine. Suddenly the beams from the headlights illuminated him. He closed his eyes but lifted one arm as if he were in distress at sea. He thought for a moment that the car was simply going to drive past him but then it came to an abrupt stop.

The car door opened and a man came running over.

"Are you hurt?"

Vincent moaned.

"I've been run over."

"Here?"

Vincent raised himself on one arm and nodded.

"A car. It took off. Can you help me?"

"I'll call an ambulance," the man said and got out his cell phone.

"No, just drive me to the hospital instead."

The man crouched down and took a closer look at Vincent.

"That doesn't look too good."

"I'll pay you."

"Don't be silly. Can you walk?"

Vincent slowly got up on all fours. The man helped him to his feet and into the car.

Viro was momentarily distracted by Jupiter's smell. Then he dragged himself away and his officer followed, smiling at the dog's eagerness despite the serious nature of their business.

They reached the railway crossing in fifteen minutes, just as a southbound train rushed by. Here the scent trail ended. Viro looked around, confused, then looked up at his officer and whimpered.

"He either had a car parked here or he was picked up," Sammy Nilsson said. He had followed the canine unit.

They took a look around. Viro followed the scent back a few meters, turned, and again concluded that the tracks stopped abruptly.

"Where could he have gone?"

"The ER," said the officer with the dog. "He's been hurt. There's even blood on the ground here."

"I think Fredriksson called them already, and I think he sent a car over there."

Nilsson took out his cell phone and called Allan Fredriksson, who was still back in Gunilla Karlsson's apartment.

They were sitting in her living room. Detective Inspector Allan Fredriksson blew his nose. Gunilla felt sorry for him. It was the fifth time he had taken out the multicolored handkerchief. He should be at home nursing his cold.

"He ran down toward Bergsbrunna, at which point the trail goes cold," Fredriksson said when he had ended the conversation with Nilsson.

He could still see the terror in Gunilla's eyes.

"We'll station a unit outside your apartment," he said and put the handkerchief away.

His calm expression and voice reassured her. The shivering that had come over her a short while after Vincent disappeared, stopped.

"You knew him, you said?"

"Yes, from school. His name is Vincent, but I don't remember his last name. It's on the tip of my tongue, it sounds German. I can call a friend of mine, she'll know."

"That would be good."

"Hahn," she said suddenly. "That's it."

"Vincent Hahn?"

Gunilla nodded. Fredriksson immediately called the station and gave them the information.

"Have you seen anything of each other since you left school?"

"No. I've seen him in town from time to time, but that's it."

"Were you in the same class?"

"No, he was in another class in my year. But we had a few subjects together."

"Has he ever called you or tried to contact you in any way?"

"No."

"Why do you think he came here?"

"I have no idea. He was always a little strange, even back in school. He was alone a lot and I think he was religious or something. A bit odd."

Fredriksson looked down at the floor.

"He said that he wanted to see your breasts?"

"Yes. And that then he would leave."

"Did you believe him?"

"Of course not. He looked completely wild."

"And you have never had a relationship with him in the past?"

"Never."

"Have you ever met him at work?"

"I'm a preschool teacher."

"He's never had children at your school?"

"I strongly doubt he has children."

Fredriksson looked at her. Was she bluffing? Was this a relationship dispute? Why would she withhold such information? He decided to believe her.

"It must have taken some courage to hit him," he said.

"I thought he was going to die. He was bleeding so much, even though the bottle was in my right hand. I'm left-handed, you know."

"Did he say anything that would explain his actions? Anything at all. Think carefully."

Gunilla shook her head after a moment's thoughtful silence.

"It started with the rabbit," she said. "That's all I can think of. He was the one who killed him."

She told him about Ansgar, how he had been strangled, strung up on the patio, and subsequently disemboweled. How she had reported the crime to the police.

"He didn't think rabbits should be kept in the city?"

"He said they were disgusting."

"And so he killed it," Fredriksson said in a perplexed tone.

Even though he had been in this line of work for a long time he had not ceased to be astounded by his fellow citizens.

Ryde, the forensic specialist, walked in at this point. He said nothing, simply stared at his colleague.

"The kitchen," Fredriksson said, and Ryde left without a word.

Fredriksson knew there was no point in trying polite conversation or conveying unnecessary information when Ryde had that look.

"It was funny—well, I guess *funny* isn't the right word," Gunilla said. "But I've been thinking back on my school days a lot today. That guy who was murdered recently had also gone to school with me. And then this creep."

Ryde, who had overheard her comment, came out of the kitchen.

"You went to school with John Jonsson?"

His voice was abrupt, not modulated for contact with the public. Gunilla looked sternly at him.

"Are you also a police officer?"

Fredriksson couldn't help smiling.

"This is Eskil Ryde," he said. "He's our forensic expert."

"The only one," Ryde added. "But go on about John."

Gunilla sighed heavily, clearly exhausted.

"I know John better," she started. "We've run into each other from time to time over the years. And I know his wife."

"Please excuse my forwardness," Fredriksson said as Ryde snorted, "but have you ever had a relationship with John?"

"No. Why on earth would you say that?"

"You were so quick to put in that bit about knowing his wife."

"That's a perfectly normal thing to say. And it's the truth."

"What did you think when you heard John was murdered?"

"I was horrified, of course. I liked him," Gunilla said, and looked at Fredriksson steadily as if to say: *Don't try to make anything of it.* "He was the quiet type, very sweet. He never made much noise at school. We met some this fall, actually. He seemed really happy, which was unusual for him. I asked him what was going on and he said he was going to go overseas."

"Any particular country?"

"No, but I had the impression it was far away."

"When was he planning to go?"

"I don't know. He didn't say anything about that."

"It's possible sometimes for people to talk about wanting to travel," Fredriksson said, "without having actual plans to do so."

"I know, and he mentioned it in passing like a joke, but I still had the feeling he meant it."

"You didn't get any details?"

"We were both in a hurry and only said a few words."

"Did you see him again after that?"

"No, it was the last time," Gunilla said, and then she started to cry. Fredriksson almost felt relieved.

Sixteen

The bartender gave him a cursory glance and continued to wipe down the counter. Lennart took a drink of his beer and looked around the bar. One of the city's most famous lawyers was sitting by himself at a table by the window. Lennart had met him before in some context he couldn't remember. Now the lawyer was conducting a one-man trial over a glass of whiskey. It was probably not his first drink, because he was talking to himself with his face propped up in his left hand and the glass in his right.

"Well, well," Lennart said and turned back to the man behind the counter. Lennart knew that the man's lack of interest was an act, but right now he had no time for games.

"It was a while since he was here," the bartender said.

"When was it?"

"I can't remember."

"Where is he now?"

The bartender paused, seeming to weigh the bother of keeping up his passive act versus the difficulties he could expect from Mossa if he told

Lennart what he knew. He opted for what seemed the most comfortable option.

"Try him at Kroken," he said, but the comment was more a test to see how knowledgeable his visitor was.

Kroken was an illegal gaming club housed in the basement of a building downtown. It had a handwritten sign on the door with the name POS IMPORT and a dozen crates of plastic weapons arranged along one wall, a business supposedly involved in importing toys from Southeast Asia and textiles from the Baltic states.

"He never goes there," Lennart said.

He returned to his beer in order to give the bartender another chance. If he came up with another idiotic suggestion, he would know.

The lawyer by the window staggered to his feet, threw a five-hundred-kronor note on the table, and walked with assumed nonchalance toward the door. The bartender hurried over to the table, whisked away the money, and cleared the glasses from the table.

Lennart thought about Mossa. Where could he be? He hadn't seen him in weeks. Mossa divided his time between Stockholm, Uppsala, and sometimes Denmark. Lennart suspected that gambling was not the only business Mossa had in Copenhagen. There had been talk of drugs, but Lennart didn't think the Iranian was stupid enough to dabble in narcotics.

Mossa was a gambler known for his carefulness. He had not gotten himself tangled up with the law over the past few years. This was not because he had kept on the right side of the law, but rather it was a mark of his ability. He had the reputation of being beyond the police and prosecution.

Lennart had known him for about ten years. He knew that John had sometimes played with Mossa, who had liked his quiet ways. John rarely gambled large amounts and never in the big leagues, but was good when it came to the middle ranks, the enjoyable small-time games, which were not about the money.

Mossa didn't play at the clubs except very occasionally a game of roulette, but when it came to card games he played only privately.

Lennart had joined him once or twice but had neither the tenacity nor the funds required.

"I heard he was in Stockholm these days," the bartender said. "But he usually comes back to town at Christmas. His mom lives here."

That's more like it, Lennart thought. He knew where Mossa's mom lived but he could hardly pay her a visit to ask her for her son's whereabouts. Mossa would go ballistic. But there were other ways.

"Thanks," he said and laid a hundred-kronor note on the counter.

He stepped out onto Kungsgatan and followed St. Petersgatan east. He stopped outside the Salvation Army and lit a cigarette, looking at the building and thinking back to the one time he had celebrated Easter there as a child, dressed up as a wolf cub. It was one of the neighborhood kids, Bengt-Ove, who had talked him into going. He had eaten a ton of Easter eggs.

One time, in later life, Lennart had stumbled into the Salvation Army drunk out of his mind. Bengt-Ove had been there to greet him. He must have stayed after their wolf-cub days. They had looked at each other for a few seconds and then Lennart had turned on his heel without saying a word.

He had felt shame that time, ashamed of his drunkenness and filth. Every time he walked past, that feeling of shame returned. It wasn't Bengt-Ove's fault. He would probably not have blamed him for his dissolute lifestyle, ratty clothes, stinking breath, or slurred speech. Sometimes Lennart wondered what would have happened if he too had stayed. He had friends who had been saved and left crime and alcohol behind. Would he have managed it? He didn't think so, but the visit had awakened the thought of another life. He didn't want to admit it, but secretly he thought of the hasty, unplanned encounter as a wasted opportunity. It was probably just a thought constructed in hindsight, like so many others, but it was an appealing thought, especially in moments of regret.

He didn't blame anyone. Earlier he would have done so, but now his worldview was clear enough so he understood that only he was responsible. What good did it do to moan about injustice? He had had the chance. He had met Bengt-Ove's gaze and he had seen it there, but had chosen to walk away.

It had been winter then, like today, but the Salvation Army windows were dark and it was quiet. Lennart kept walking.

The list of names was in his coat pocket. Three names had been crossed off; five remained. He was not going to give up until his brother's murderer was checked off. These eight guys were going to help him.

He decided to stop by and see Micke. They hadn't talked since it had happened. He knew the police had been talking to him and maybe he had picked something up.

When Lennart arrived, Micke was about to go to bed. The last few days had wiped him out but he had found it hard to sleep.

"Oh, it's you, is it?"

He didn't like Lennart, but he was John's brother.

"I'm sorry about John," he added.

Lennart walked into the apartment without saying a word, in that presumptuous way that drove Micke crazy.

"Do you have any beer?"

Micke was surprised that he even asked. Usually he just walked over to the fridge and helped himself.

"I hear the pigs have been talking to you," Lennart said and popped open the can that Micke handed him.

Micke nodded and sat down at the kitchen table.

"What did they say?"

"They asked me about John. He came by here on the day he died, you know."

"He did? No one's said anything about that to me."

"He stopped in the late afternoon."

"Why did he do that?"

"For Chrissakes, Lennart."

The fatigue made Micke irritable.

"What did he say?"

"We just talked about normal stuff."

"Like what?"

He knew what Lennart was after, and tried to re-create an image of a living John, not trouble-free exactly, but happy, with bottles of wine and spirits and a family he was eager to get home to.

"He didn't say anything?"

"About what?"

"About some shit going on, you know what I'm talking about."

Micke got up and helped himself to a beer as well.

"He didn't say anything out of the ordinary."

"Think hard now."

"Don't you think I've thought about it? Every damn second since it happened."

Lennart looked at him searchingly, as if weighing his words, and took a drink from the can while continuing to gaze at him.

"Stop staring," Micke said.

"Did you two cook something up?"

"Shut up!"

"Horses and shit," said Lennart, who almost never got involved in the gambling parties that were formed and dissolved on a regular basis—mostly because his ability to pay up was generally doubted.

"Nothing like that," Micke said in a voice steady and assured but in which Lennart sensed a moment's hesitation, a look that flickered unsteadily for a tenth of a second.

"Are you sure? We're talking about my only goddamn brother here."

"My best friend," said Micke.

"Fuck you if you're not telling me the truth."

"Was there anything else? I'd like to turn in."

Lennart changed the subject.

"You coming to the funeral?"

"Of course."

"Do you understand it?"

Lennart's eyes and the gaze he directed straight down into the table—as if the worn Formica surface could offer any explanation for the murder of his brother—revealed the depth of his despair.

Micke stretched out a hand and put it gently on Lennart's arm. Lennart looked up, and where Micke had only ever seen alcohol-induced weepiness he now saw the glimmer of real tears.

"No," Micke said hoarsely. "I don't get it. Not John of all people."

"John of all people," Lennart echoed. "That's what I've been thinking too. When there's so much scum."

"Go home and try to get some sleep. You look like shit."

"I won't stop until I get 'im."

Micke felt torn. He didn't want to hear Lennart's thoughts of revenge, but he also didn't want to be left alone. The fatigue was starting to wear off and he knew it would be a long night. He recognized the symptoms. He had suffered from insomnia for many years. From time to time it got better and he sank into a deep, dreamless sleep that bordered on an unconsciousness that felt like a gift. But then the wakeful nights returned, the open wounds. That's how it felt. Burning sores that ravaged him on the inside.

"What does Aina say?"

"I don't think she really understands," Lennart said. "She's confused as it is and this will break her. John was her favorite ever since Margareta died."

John and Lennart's little sister, Margareta, had died in 1968 when she was run over by a delivery van outside the grocery store on Väderkvarns-gatan. It was a subject that the brothers had never touched on, and her name was never mentioned. Photographs in which she appeared were put away.

There were those who said that Aina and Albin had never fully recovered from losing their daughter. Some even hinted that Albin had taken his own life when he slid off the roof of the Skytteanum that day in April in the early 1970s. Others, especially his fellow workers, maintained that he had been sloppy with the safety ropes and hadn't managed to compensate by gaining a foothold on the slippery roof.

Albin would never have committed suicide, and even if he had entertained the crazy idea it would never have happened during his work hours, on a roof. But the uncertainty hovered over the family like a cloud.

"I haven't talked so much with her," Lennart admitted. He got up and Micke thought he was getting himself another beer but instead he walked over to the window.

"Did you watch him as he was leaving? Did you happen to look out the window, or something?"

"No," Micke said. "I stayed on the couch. *Jeopardy* was on."

"Do you remember Teodor?"

"You mean Teodor from when we were little? Of course."

"I think of him sometimes. He took care of me and John after Dad died. He put us to work."

"Do you remember when we played marbles?" Micke smiled. "He was phenomenal."

"John was his favorite."

"He looked out for all of us."

"But especially John."

"That's because he was the youngest," Micke said.

"Just think if our teachers had been like Teodor."

Clearly, the loss of his little brother was causing Lennart to look back at his Almtuna childhood, and there was no better person than Micke to relive it with. Micke understood Lennart's need to access these comforting memories of early childhood. He didn't have anything against it himself either, reveries of the busy playgrounds, the games, bandy matches on Fålhagen ice rinks, and track-and-field practice on Österängen.

It was the life they'd been given, that's how Micke felt, and he thought it was even more true for Lennart. After those early childhood days, all hell had broken loose, starting with their attendance at Vaksala High School.

Lennart had been placed in a remedial class because he had "trouble following standard instruction," and thus he fell into the hands of Stone Face, whose instruction was not particularly hard to follow since it consisted mainly of playing table tennis. Lennart was good at Ping-Pong from all the matches with Teodor in the boiler room. So good that he creamed Stone Face in match after match.

But where Teodor had figured as a portal to an adult life with as full a register of emotions as the sentimental janitor could muster, Stone Face was merciless about drumming his particular brand of life knowledge into his pupils.

Lennart would have none of it. He cut class, or hit back. From ninth grade on he was absent more and more, which had resulted in his poor reading and writing abilities. He knew nothing of history, math made him uncontrollably enraged, and he even cut shop classes.

The alternatives for Lennart were the pool hall in Sivia, Lucullus restaurant—which made the town's first pizzas—and Kullen. He stole to survive, in order to finance his pool and pinball habit, to buy cigarettes and soda. He stole to impress, and fought in order to frighten others. If he couldn't be loved he would be feared, he seemed to reason.

He didn't accuse anyone, or direct blame at others, but inside he hated his teachers and the rest of the adults. At home, Albin stuttered out his admonitions. Aina became nervous and could oftentimes not take care of herself, let alone her difficult son. Aina found comfort in her youngest, John, whom she nonetheless saw being dragged into his older brother's increasingly wild escapades.

"John was a good guy," Micke said. He heard how inadequate it sounded, how flat.

"There's one thing I've been wondering," Lennart said and sat down at the table again. "Did John have another woman?"

Micke looked at him in disbelief.

"What are you saying? That he was fooling around on the side?"

"I don't know. Maybe he said something to you."

"No, I never heard him talking about another girl. You should know that. He adored Berit."

"Of course he did. He was only unfaithful with his cichlids."

"What's going to happen with those fish?"

"Justus is taking over," Lennart said.

Micke thought about John's son, Daddy's boy. In Justus he could see the teenage John. A man of few words, an easily averted gaze. It was as if the boy saw through whomever he was talking to. Many times Micke had felt inadequate, as if Justus was choosing not to burden his mind with Micke's chatter, much less dignify it with an answer.

Come to think of it, in childhood John too had had that attitude. John could also give the impression of being superior, proud, unwilling to make compromises. That's probably why he and Sagge had never seen eye-to-eye, even though John was a good craftsman.

It had been only in his closest relationships, especially with Berit, that John had revealed himself at all, flipping up the visor to display a thoughtfulness and capacity for dry humor that it took a while to catch on to.

"If anyone should carry on, it's that boy," Micke said.

He wanted another beer but knew that if he had one, Lennart would inevitably join him. And he wouldn't stop at one. Chances were they would clean out his whole supply.

It was close to midnight and Lennart made no motion to leave. Micke got up against his will. He had a hard day to look forward to.

"Don't know when it last snowed this much before Christmas," he said and went to get the beers.

Seventeen

Berglund had been posted at the number 9 bus stop downtown for more than an hour. He had a police ID in one hand and a picture of John Jonsson in the other. It seemed to him that he had asked hundreds of people if they recognized the man in the photograph.

"Is he the one who was murdered?" someone had asked eagerly.

"Do you recognize him?"

"I don't associate with people like that," the woman had said.

She was weighed down by numerous bags and boxes, like most of the others. There was a general air of tension. The people did not look happy, Berglund thought.

He had been a policeman in Uppsala for a long time. This was another routine assignment, one of several thousand, but he never ceased to be amazed by the reactions of his fellow citizens. Here he was, trying to solve a murder, working overtime, freezing his butt off when he should be home helping his wife with the Christmas preparations, and he was met by reserve, if not outright distaste.

He walked up to an older man who had just stopped, put his bags down, and lit a cigarette.

"Hello, my name's Berglund. I'm from the police," he said and held up his ID. "Do you recognize the man in this picture?"

The man inhaled deeply and studied the photo.

"Yup, I've known him for a long time. He's that metalworker's boy."

He looked up and scrutinized Berglund.

"Is he caught up in some trouble?"

Berglund liked the sound of the man's voice. *A little hoarse, he must smoke a great deal,* he thought. The face matched the voice: a lined, friendly face with clear eyes.

"No, quite the opposite, so to speak. He's dead."

The man dropped his cigarette and crushed it under his foot.

"I knew his parents," he said. "Albin and Aina."

Berglund suddenly sensed a great network. It was a diffuse feeling that, strictly speaking, had nothing to do with solving a crime. It was rather that the man's pleasant voice and demeanor fit into a certain context. Sometimes Berglund pursued this instinct, although if he tried to put it into words they felt awkward, insufficient.

He guessed that the man had been some kind of worker, perhaps in the construction business. His weathered skin told of years exposed to sun, wind, and cold. His dialect gave him away, also his way of wearing the overcoat, the slightly moth-eaten but respectable hat, the hands and their hard nails. He looked after himself, somewhat hunched but still tall.

If they talked a while the network and connections would become clear. And surely they would find a number of shared acquaintances, experiences, and reference points, despite their fifteen-some years' age difference.

Solving a crime was a matter of discerning a pattern, Berglund knew, and in that way this man and his context, his part of town, his expressions, gestures, and language were a part of the answer. It was as if nothing was impossible if one only had the ability to put the pieces of the puzzle, the puzzle of the town, together.

"Do you live nearby?"

The man gestured with his head.

"Marielundsgatan," he said. "But right now I'm on my way to see my boy. He lives in Salabackar."

"I'm going to stand here for another hour," Berglund said. "But maybe you could come by later and we could have a cup a coffee together."

The man nodded as if being stopped by a policeman and taken out to coffee was the most natural thing in the world.

"I need to flesh this thing out," Berglund said.

"Yes, I see that," the man said. "My name is Oskar Pettersson. I'm in the phone book so you can call me if you like. I'll be home again around eight. I'm just taking herring and some other things to my boy."

He picked up his bags and stepped on the bus that had just pulled up. Berglund saw him settle in a seat. He didn't look out the window, but then why would he?

Berglund stayed the course until seven. A few passengers seemed to recognize John, but no one had any information to give, no one had seen him at the bus stop.

He walked back to the station. It was cold and he was freezing. He had called home and said he was working late, which had not come as a surprise to his wife.

Berglund did not feel like going into his office. Instead he got a snack from the vending machine and sank down in a worn armchair. A few colleagues in uniform came by. They talked about Christmas. Berglund took his coffee and went to the calling station. Nothing out of the ordinary had been reported, but when he had finished his cup and was about to leave, an emergency call came in. He lingered and heard patrol cars being ordered to Sävja and knew that it meant Fredriksson would be working late.

"Attack on a woman," said the officer manning the phones.

Berglund walked out into the December night.

Oskar Pettersson lived in a two-bedroom apartment on Marielunds-gatan, a short street in the Almtuna district. Berglund declined his offer of coffee. Pettersson took out a beer and two glasses and put them on the kitchen table. A radio was on in the background. Pettersson listened for a few seconds as if he heard something of interest to him, then turned it off with a thoughtful air.

"I only listen to the public radio station nowadays," he said. "My ears can't take anything else."

Berglund poured out the beer, first his own glass and then Pettersson's.

"I knew Albin well," the latter said without further ado. "We were related, and then I'd see him on construction jobs from time to time. And back when we were young I'd see him out and about. The town was smaller back then."

"You worked in construction?"

"Laid concrete mostly," he said and then looked around the kitchen. "I'm a widower now."

"How long?"

"It'll be three years in March. Cancer."

He took a sip of beer.

"It was really through Eugene—Aina's brother, that is, John's uncle—that I came to spend time socially with Albin and Aina. Eugene and I worked together for a long time. First with Quiet Kalle and then at Diös. He was a happy fellow. Aina was more careful. Albin too. But I think they liked each other. It seemed that way anyhow. You never heard them arguing or anything. Albin was one of the best metalworkers you ever saw. He died, you probably know that."

Berglund nodded.

"I would bump into John in town after that, especially after he got his foot in the door at the workshop. I wonder sometimes what it is that makes a man. If it's genetic, there'd be no reason for Lennart and John to get mixed up in crime."

"Upstanding," Berglund recalled Ottosson saying.

"And then there's environment," Pettersson continued in the gentle but forceful voice that Berglund had immediately responded to. "They grew up in this area. There were a few bad eggs of course but mostly responsible folk. Where are you from anyway?"

Berglund laughed at the rapid turn of conversation.

"Born in Eriksberg," he said. "When it was still out in the country. My dad built a house there in the forties. He worked at Ekeby."

Pettersson nodded.

"He handled the furnace out there, and Mom stayed home and took care of the kids. Dad worked a lot of nights and slept during the day."

"There you go. Are you sure you don't want any coffee?"

"No, thanks. Tell me more about John."

"I think he was damned bitter about losing his job. He said something once, something about feeling worthless. It was kind of his thing, welding. He had inherited Albin's attention to detail. A person has to find a place where they fit in, that's all. Don't you think?"

"That's probably right," Berglund said. "Did you see each other regularly?"

"Not really. Sometimes at Obs. I like to go down there and have a bite to eat and talk to the other guys. A few times we met up and had a coffee. I think he liked to talk to me. He liked to talk, period."

That's strange, Berglund thought. *This is the first time I've heard someone describe John as talkative.*

"But I could tell he was sitting on something."

"What was it?"

"Well, he had those fish. You know about that. I got the impression he was cooking something up with those fish, so to speak. He was incredibly active in some kind of organization. Turns out there are organizations for anything you can think of."

"And what can you cook up when it comes to fish? Start up a shop, is that what you mean?"

"I don't know. Just something to do with that fish tank. He must have been nursing a dream."

"But he didn't say anything specifically about what that would be?"

"No, nothing straight out, nothing more than that something was going on."

"When you met, did you ever talk about how things were at home?"

"Not a lot. He was close to the kid. Maybe you know someone called Sandberg who worked at Ekeby. He also worked the furnace, I think. A fat little guy, short-tempered."

Berglund laughed.

"Everyone who worked the furnace was short-tempered. I thought that was part of the job description."

Their eyes met and both men smiled.

"He must have been dead for forty years," Pettersson said. "But he knew my dad."

"What was the state of John's finances?"

"I don't think he was in dire straits. He was always well dressed, and so on."

"Did he drink?"

Pettersson shook his head.

"What a way to go," he said. "Everyone putting your life under the microscope. What if we paid that kind of attention to people while they were alive?"

Berglund stayed until shortly before ten. Pettersson followed him to the door but then turned as Berglund was putting his coat on and went back to the kitchen. Berglund heard the radio come on in the middle of a religious program, a brief evening meditation.

"I like to hear the news rundown before I go to bed."

Pettersson came back out into the hall.

"Then I like to read a little," he said while Berglund was doing up the laces of his boots.

"That's serious footwear," he said approvingly. "I'm a member of Association of Retired Persons and we meet once a month and talk about books."

"What are you reading right now?"

"A book about the black plague, actually. But there's something I've come to think of: How are things with Lennart now, the brother?"

"Well," Berglund said uncertainly. "He is what he is."

"No improvement then. He was always of a different caliber. I remember the grief he caused Albin and Aina though he did work a few years at Diös. It ended with him underneath some prefab material, or perhaps he fell from a scaffolding, I can't remember. He was always poorly after that."

"Albin fell off a roof," Berglund said.

"Typical. It was a job for the rich folk on the other side of the river."

"Thanks for the beer," Berglund said.

"Thank *you*," Pettersson said and shook Berglund's outstretched hand. "Feel free to look me up again. Maybe we can sort out that question of why people who work the furnace get so short-tempered."

Berglund started walking home—barely one kilometer away—rather slowly. *It was here in Almtuna it all started*, he thought. He dallied outside the antique store where a Santa Claus lit up the display window with a small electric lantern. With its frozen expression and waxy red-painted cheeks the Santa looked a little spooky.

Ymergatan—that was named after the giant Ymer of Norse mythology. He was killed and out of his flesh the world was made and out of his blood all the world's water. The heavens were formed from his skull and a wall was constructed out of his eyebrows to help defend people against the giants. Midgard, the human realm. *That's where it started. Our history. I wonder if the people who walk up and down this street and who are descendants of Ask and Embla know this story. Probably not.*

He couldn't remember the legend in its entirety but enough to make him pause before crossing the street. A few other people were out walking around, a Volvo drove by, and Berglund had the distinct impression that it was a colleague in an undercover car.

He let his gaze wander down the length of Ymergatan. John's little sister had died somewhere along this street. "What is it that makes the man?" Oskar Pettersson had asked. The Jonsson family had lived here in Almtuna. The disasters had come one after the other. Now three of them were dead: the little girl, Albin, and his son John. One accident, a possible suicide, and a homicide. As if the collective violence of the street, of the neighborhood, were concentrated upon one family.

Berglund had seen their kind before, the unfortunate ones who seemed to form their own group. Families who appeared destined to suffer accidents, heart attacks, lightning strikes, fires, and other violent deaths rather than draw their last breath peacefully between two sheets. As if they took upon themselves the quota for society as a whole, numerical abnormalities in the predictable world of statistical probability.

One accident led to another, Berglund believed. You could also find the accident-prone in books. Sometimes living, but dead more often than not, talked about, ill-fated, and pitied.

Ymergatan. For half a minute or so Berglund perceived the beauty of the late evening. The snow was blanketed in snow, disturbed only by a few bicycle tracks running down its length like tiny tracks in the land of the giants. Trees were weighed down, resting, waiting, the windows lit up by Christmas stars and candles. The big snowflakes whirled in the streetlights.

My town, Berglund thought. Even though he had grown up on the other side of the river, he knew these streets in Almtuna; they formed the basis for the ideal society that his father, the furnace keeper at Ekeby, had always dreamed of. Berglund was able to thrust the thoughts of John and his family out of his mind only by thinking that Christmas was soon approaching. He had always liked this holiday.

For a moment he wanted to say, *I'm a criminal inspector in the middle of a murder investigation*. But he would remember the sight of Ymergatan enveloped in snow for a long time.

His city. Oskar Pettersson had talked about *skånkarna*, an old slang word for university graduates. It had been a long time since Berglund had heard anyone use this word. But Berglund was certainly aware of the fact that there were two cities, two Uppsalas: Oskar's and the *skånkarna's*, with their academic degrees. You didn't hear people talk about it much anymore, but you still felt the effects of this division. Even at the police station.

Would things have been better if Albin had fallen from any old roof and not one of the buildings of the university? Berglund knew what the old man had been talking about. It was about a class system, the fact that the underclass, Oskar and Albin, always slipped off the roofs of the rich folk. That had been Berglund's father's opinion and he had inherited it. He had always voted for the Social Democrats. You seldom heard political talk along party lines down at the station, but he knew he belonged to a minority there. Ottosson voted for the Folkpartiet, not out of a strong sense of political urgency but out of habit and a lack of imagination. They agreed in their analyses of social developments. Ottosson wanted to be like the people, and that's why he voted for the Liberal Party. Ann Lindell was harder to pin down. She seemed uninterested in politics. Riis belonged to the Conservatives, like Ryde. Sammy Nilsson was for the Center Party, mainly because he had grown up in the country.

Berglund pushed away these thoughts of his colleagues. It was time to get home, but he couldn't help getting out his cell phone and calling Fredriksson.

"Everything's fine," Fredriksson said. "Thanks for asking."

Berglund heard the fatigue. He hoped the man wouldn't hit the wall again like he had a couple of years ago.

"There's a connection between the attack here in Sävja and John's murder," Fredriksson continued. "The attacker went to school with this woman and John Jonsson."

"Has he been apprehended?"

"Still looking."

"What's his name?"

"Vincent Hahn. Lives in Sävja but is not at his home. He's got a nasty blow to the head and is probably quite messed up."

"Physically or emotionally?"

"Both, I think."

"Do you need any assistance?"

Berglund wanted to go home, but he couldn't stop himself from asking.

"Thanks, but we'll manage," Fredriksson said.

He hung up and felt a gnawing sense of anxiety. Were they dealing with a lunatic who was targeting former students of Vaksala High School?

Eighteen

Justus placed his hand on the surface of the water, just like John used to do. The fish were so used to it that it would take only a few seconds before they were there, nibbling at his fingers. But that had been with John. Now they didn't come. *No one can claim they're stupid,* Justus thought.

Why had John done that? Was it to test the temperature or simply to make contact with them? Justus had never asked; there was so much he had never found out. Now it was too late, but he was the one who had taken over the care of the aquarium. Berit had never really been interested, though she thought it was beautiful and her protests against the new tank had been lukewarm. She had known her protests would make no difference to John. Justus thought deep down that she had been pleased with John's passion. There were worse things for a man to be obsessed with.

Justus dropped in the hose and started to drain the water. Berit sat in the kitchen with his grandmother. He could hear their muffled voices, deliberately lowered so he wouldn't hear. They thought he couldn't take it. He knew they were talking about the funeral.

When the bucket was half full he transferred the hose to the next one and carried the first out to the bathroom. Three hundred liters had to go. Thirty buckets, though Justus didn't have the confidence to fill them up as high as John, so he would probably have to empty closer to forty. And then fill it all up again.

This had to be done once a week. How many times would he have to walk to the bathroom and back? He sensed that Berit wanted to sell the fish and the tank but she hadn't said anything.

My Princess of Burundi, John had called her. At first she didn't get it, then she laughed.

"Oh, I'm a fine princess!"

John had exchanged a look with Justus. Only the two of them knew about this. Berit would find out in due time when everything was good and ready, as John had put it. Justus emptied his third bucket. Only thirty-seven to go.

"You are my princess, you know that."

Something in his voice had made her stop laughing, become alert. John, who was normally so perceptive, hadn't noticed this change and kept going.

"I'll get you your very own title and royal domain one day."

Was he drunk that night? Justus wondered.

"Do you think we have to live like this?"

"What are you talking about?"

That had brought him back to reality, and he had wilted like a plant under her gaze.

Justus hadn't liked it. Why couldn't he have said something, not everything certainly, but enough to take away her look? Why couldn't he have his moment of triumph? Now he was dead, and no feeling of triumph would ever light up his face again.

Justus carried bucket after bucket. Only thirty to go. The cichlids swam around nervously. Justus had to take a break and sat down on a chair in front of the aquarium. He let his mind drift in between the rock and stone arrangements. He could imagine the twenty-six-degree water enveloping him. The underwater cliffs in Tanganyika Lake were deceptive and he would have to be careful. The caves were not safe. Were there any crocodiles? John had told him about a German fisherman who had been eaten on the shores of Lake Malawi.

He went to get the atlas out of the bookcase. Malawi was a long way from Burundi.

"What are you doing?"

Berit was in the doorway. Justus heard his grandmother groaning in the hall, the bench creaking as she sat down.

"Just looking at something."

"Is it going okay?"

Justus nodded.

"You won't spill anything, will you?"

He didn't answer. Of course he wouldn't spill anything. Had John ever spilled anything? The Princess of Burundi looked at him.

"Hello, Justus," his grandmother said even though they had said hello when she got there. She had managed to put on one boot.

"Hello," he said and took a bucket out to the bathroom.

"Come here," said the old woman when he came back out. "I'd like to talk to you."

Justus went up to her reluctantly. She had been crying. She cried a lot. She pulled him to her.

"You are my grandchild," she said, and in that moment he wanted to escape. He knew what was coming.

"Take good care of yourself."

He didn't like listening to her voice. When he was younger he had been afraid of her. He wasn't afraid anymore, but the feeling of being ill at ease was still there.

"John was so proud of you. You have to take good care of yourself."

"Of course, Grandma."

He freed himself from her grasp.

"Do you need any help getting home?"

Aina was always afraid of slipping on the ice and John or Justus would often follow her home.

"No, I'll be all right. I have studded boots."

"I have to finish cleaning the aquarium," he said and left. Then he turned. She looked so helpless with her unwashed hair poking out from under the knitted cap and with her other boot in her hand. Berit came by with a full bucket. She smiled. He took it from her and went to empty it.

His arms were starting to hurt. Next time he would take the hose and run it all the way into the bathroom, but this time he wanted to use the bucket.

The fish were swimming around in synchronized, sweeping motions. He watched them. In the wild these flocks could be seen by the thousands with their territories in such close proximity that they sometimes looked like a giant metaflock. Every part of the reef had its own flock, its own species, perhaps closely related to another species but with its own coloring. The sandbanks between the reefs divided them up.

The Princesses were substrate spawners, others in the tank were mouth brooders, but they were all cichlids, John's favorite. He preferred African cichlids even though the South African cichlids were more in vogue these days.

Justus had plowed through just about everything there was to read about cichlids. In the process he had gained an interest in geography and knew the African continent better than anyone else in his class. Once he had even ended up in a fight over Africa. One of his classmates had said something about how Africans should climb back up into the trees, where they belonged.

Justus had reacted instinctively. It was as if the fish had generated an identification with all of black Africa, its lakes and rivers, savannahs, tropical rain forests, and even the people who populated his and John's continent. Africa was good. It was home to the cichlids. Home to their dreams.

He had struck without a second's thought.

"He doesn't know shit about Africa," he had said to the teacher who broke up the fight.

They started calling him "Jungle Boy," but he paid no attention and eventually they lost interest.

"I talked to your teacher," his mother said, interrupting his thoughts. "She sends you her regards. Are you going to go back to school before Christmas?"

"I don't know," Justus said.

"It could be good for you."

"Has Grandma left?"

"Yes, she did. I'm not worried that you'll miss very much work, but don't you think it might feel good to go to school?"

"I have to take care of the aquarium."

Berit looked at him. *He's so like his father*, she thought. *The aquarium*. She glanced at some cichlids circling the hose.

"We'll work on it together," she said. "You know you have to focus on your studies."

He looked down at the floor.

"What do you think Dad was thinking?" he asked in a low voice.

"I don't know," Berit said.

She had identified his body, asked to see all of it. What scared her wasn't the wounds, the grayish cast of his skin, or even the severed finger and the burn marks. It was his face. She had seen the terror etched into his features.

John had been a brave man, never sensitive to pain, never one to complain. That's why his face had been almost unrecognizable. *I didn't know terror could change a person so,* she had thought and taken a step back.

The female police officer at her side, Beatrice was her name, had taken her arm, but Berit had shaken her off. She didn't want to be propped up.

"Give me a few minutes," she had said. Beatrice looked doubtful but did as she was asked.

As Berit stood there, completely still beside the gurney, she felt that she had always known it would end this way. Maybe not known, exactly, but sensed. John's family was no normal family. It was as if they could not escape their fates.

She had walked over to him again, bent over the body, and kissed his brow. The chill spread to her lips.

"Justus," she had mumbled, then turned and left the room.

Beatrice was waiting outside. She didn't say anything, which Berit had appreciated.

"I imagine he was thinking of the Princess," Justus said.

"What, who?"

"The Princess of Burundi."

Then she remembered. That was the evening John had unveiled the new aquarium. He had pointed out the various species to her, among them the Princess. She had heard all the names before—how could she not?—but the Princess was new.

He had been leaning forward with his face close to the glass and pointed them out to the guests with warmth in his voice. Then he had looked at Justus and Berit.

"This is my Princess," he had said, putting his arm around her waist. "My Princess of Burundi."

"Who the hell is Burundi?" Lennart had asked.

Justus had explained that it was a country in Africa, at the northern end of Lake Tanganyika. Berit had heard the eagerness in his voice. John had patted him on the head with his free hand.

"Yes, that's right," she said, recalling everything about that evening, how happy she had been. "It's a beautiful name."

"Burundi is beautiful," Justus said.

"Have you been there?" Berit said, smiling.

"Almost."

And he came close to telling her everything.

Nineteen

The man had certainly been friendly, he thought, offering to follow him into the emergency room. *Maybe he thought I had a concussion and couldn't manage on my own.*

He put his hand on his head and waited until he saw the car drive away. The dizziness came and went. He didn't think it was a result of the blood loss, but rather of the exertion. The wound had stopped bleeding and a sticky scab had formed over it, plastering his hair onto his forehead. He felt gently along the edges of the wound.

After a few minutes he was on Dag Hammarskjöld Way, unsure of what to do next. A light snow was falling. A few cars drove by. He retreated into a park, where a young couple came walking toward him, laughing. They were probably dressed up under their thick down coats. The woman was holding a plastic bag with something Vincent assumed were shoes.

He stepped behind a tree and let them pass before he snuck up behind them. The snow muffled his steps and he took them by complete surprise. He grabbed the man's wool cap and ran into the park. After fifteen meters or so he turned to see if they had followed, but they were still standing in the same spot, staring at him. He knew they wouldn't come after him, but he still ran as he made his way toward Uppsala castle.

He pulled on the cap as he ran, veering down to Lower Slottsgatan and coming out slightly north of the swan pond. There he stopped to rest, rubbing his face clean with a handful of snow and pulling the cap back down over his eyebrows.

A taxi was leaving the restaurant, Flustret. He stopped it in the middle of the street and climbed into the backseat. The driver looked at him in the rearview mirror.

"I'm going to Årsta," Vincent said and was surprised at how collected he sounded. "Årsta center."

The driver punched in some information on his meter before he gathered speed and crossed the Iceland bridge.

Vincent said nothing during the trip, while the thoughts churned in his head. He was a hunted man now, and it was with a certain measure of delight that he thought about how he would elude his would-be captors. So far everything had gone well. The man who had picked him up would no doubt contact the police after he read about this in the morning paper. But all traces would end at the emergency room. The couple with the cap would probably do nothing. The important thing now was that Vincent not do anything stupid. His wound had to be taken care of, that was the priority.

He paid the driver generously, climbed out, and watched until the taxi was gone before he started walking in the direction of Salabackar. Now everything depended on Vivan's being home.

Vivan was his former sister-in-law, who had been divorced from his brother, Wolfgang, for almost fifteen years. She lived in a two-bedroom apartment on Johannesbäcksgatan. She had room enough, but the question was if she would be willing to let him in. They weren't close but sometimes ran into each other in town. A few times they had had coffee together and she had on one or two occasions visited him in Sävja. His brother almost never got in touch with him, and this contact with Vivan was a way of keeping tabs on Wolfgang, who had settled in Tel Aviv.

He threw a snowball at her window and was pleased to see it hit the mark on his first attempt. Vivan's face appeared between the curtains almost immediately, as if she had been waiting for the snowball to strike.

She looked scared. Vincent could see that, even though her window was on the third floor. Maybe she thought it was his brother, her former husband. That first year after their divorce he had harassed her, called her, banged on her door, and waited for her outside the front door when she came out to go to work.

Was that why she smiled when she saw that it was her brother-in-law? Her face left the window and a few seconds later the stairwell light came on. Vincent felt gratitude, a feeling he almost never experienced. *Finally, someone who's there for me,* he thought and walked close to the front door.

Vivan was still smiling, but her expression changed to one of fear when she saw his face.

"What have you done?" she asked.

"Someone attacked me," he said, which seemed to make her even more frightened.

"Attacked you?" she repeated automatically.

He nodded and stepped inside.

Twenty

Mossa lingered outside the restaurant. He took out a cigarette, lit it up, and inhaled, nodding at an acquaintance on his way in. Lennart thought he had aged. The hair was not as dark, nor was his posture as confident. But he still had style. *Composed*, Lennart thought.

As always, Mossa was alone, probably the reason why he had managed as well as he had. He was alone in accepting his defeats, but also his winnings.

He started to walk, and Lennart followed, but not too closely. He imagined that Mossa would begin to sense his presence, as if with built-in radar. Lennart preferred to bide his time. It wouldn't be a good idea to make contact with him on the street. You never knew who was watching. Not that it mattered to Lennart, but Mossa could be sensitive about it.

He followed him down Sysslomansgatan, through the thick snow, and with every step Lennart was reminded of his brother's death at the snow dump and his resolve to avenge John grew stronger.

Mossa's footsteps were small, as was his build. He moved quickly and easily, gliding forth, smoking, his head somewhat bent. Lennart watched him pass St. Olofsgatan and decided to make his move in the narrow, dimly lit alley below the cathedral. He lengthened his stride, the snow muffling his progress.

Suddenly Mossa turned. Lennart was up close now, perhaps only a few meters away.

"What do you want?"

"Hey, Mossa. How's it going?"

"What do you want?" he repeated and let his cigarette fall to the ground.

"I need some help," Lennart said, and immediately regretted it. Mossa helped no one except his mother and his handicapped brother. He looked back at Lennart without any expression.

"Your brother was clumsy. That is that," Mossa said.

Lennart felt a mixture of apprehensive joy and fear. Mossa had recognized him and was going to talk.

"What do you mean?"

"Just what I said. He was clumsy, careless."

"Do you know something?"

Mossa lit another cigarette and Lennart moved closer. The Iranian looked up and pushed one hand into his pocket.

"No."

"You haven't heard anything?"

"Your brother was a good fellow, not like so many of the others. He reminded me of a childhood friend I had in Shiraz."

The Iranian paused, smoked.

"I only know he was up to something. Something big, at least for him, if you know what I mean. I heard something back in the fall, something about a job. John suddenly had a little money, more than he usually put in. He was in a game and wanted to increase the stakes, to try to win more."

Lennart stamped his feet anxiously as he listened. His shoes were letting in moisture. Mossa's talk was making him think.

"And he won."

"How much?"

Mossa smiled. He always did when it came to poker winnings.

"More than you've ever had your hands on. Almost two hundred thou'."

"He won two hundred thousand kronor? What did he say?"

"Not much. He took his money and went home. It was half past four in the morning, I think."

"Where was this?"

"I lost thirty-five thousand myself," Mossa said.

Lennart felt betrayed. John had won a fortune and not said a word about it. It was as if Mossa could read his thoughts.

"As he left he said something about how things were finally coming together for him, that he was close to realizing a dream. And that you would be involved."

"Me?"

"Yes, I assume he only has one brother. He said that his brother would come along."

"Come along?"

"I thought you knew what he was planning."

Lennart shook his head in bewilderment. He was to come along? But what was it? Where? Lennart understood nothing. He hadn't heard so much as the ghost of a hint.

"My friend from Shiraz also died too early. He was burned to death. Your brother died in the snow."

"Did he say anything else?"

Mossa gave Lennart a somewhat gentler look.

"I think John liked you," he said and took out the cigarettes again.

"Who else knew about the money?"

"Ask his friend—Micke."

"Did he know?"

"I don't know, but John mentioned his name."

An older couple walked by.

"I have to go now," Mossa said, turned, passed by the couple, and walked around the corner toward Cathedral bridge.

Lennart remained rooted to his spot, overwhelmed by the information. What was he supposed to think? Had Mossa been deliberately misleading him? But why would he do something like that? Lennart had the feeling that the Iranian had actually been waiting for him, that he had wanted to tell him about John and the poker winnings.

What did Micke know? The damned weasel. He had been so sincere and sobbed about the friendship and not said a word about the money.

Lennart stamped his feet to rid them of the snow and cold. He decided to go to Micke immediately and get him up against the wall. It hit him that he had forgotten to ask Mossa who the other players had been. Maybe one of them had wanted to get back at John for his loss. Mossa had lost thirty-five thousand, but someone else must have lost substantially more.

Mossa would probably never reveal their names. It was against the un-written rules of the game. There were winners and losers, but no one could run off at the mouth about it afterward. On the other hand, losses were hard for people to get off their minds, there was always a desire for revenge, and sometimes this took precedence over the honor code.

John was not the kind to flaunt a win or taunt his opponents. He never took on superior airs, but Lennart knew how money could affect people. Maybe someone had been driven to revenge.

Micke had just finished watching a German crime film on TV when the front door opened. He jumped off of the couch and for a split second he was convinced that John had returned. He was gripped by terror. Instinc-tively he crouched behind an armchair and listened to the intruder close the door behind him.

"Where the hell are you?"

It was Lennart, sounding like he did when he had had a few drinks, an accusing voice full of anger and impatience. Micke got up out of his hiding place as Lennart walked into the room.

"What the hell are you hiding for?"

"Didn't anyone ever teach you to ring the doorbell? And how did you get past the door downstairs?" Micke's terror had turned to rage.

"You can yell and scream all you want," Lennart said, stopping in the middle of the room. "What I want to know is why you've been lying to me."

"What are you talking about?"

"About John. He won a bucketful of cash and you didn't say shit."

"I thought you knew."

"The hell you did. You were lying."

Micke felt very tired suddenly. He sat back down on the sofa and reached for his glass of wine. It was empty.

"Don't sit there and try to defend yourself," Lennart shouted out of nowhere.

"What's got into you? I knew he won big in some poker game, but that's all. He didn't tell me who the other players were."

"Did he tell you how much?"

Micke shook his head.

"You know how he was."

"Don't you talk shit about my brother!"

Lennart took a step closer to the sofa.

"Calm down for God's sake!"

"Don't you tell me what to do, you fucking bastard," said Lennart and grabbed him by his shirt and forced him up off of the sofa. *How strong he is,* Micke had time to think before Lennart banged his head into Micke's nose. The room spun around and his body collapsed onto the coffee table.

When he came to, Lennart was gone. Micke crawled up onto all fours. Blood was pouring from his nose. He felt his face with one hand. *What a fuck-up he is,* he thought and fury coursed through him. *To be disturbed in your own home,* he thought indignantly. And now the rug would be stained with blood.

I'm going to the police for this one, he thought, but immediately thought better of it. It wouldn't help, more likely the opposite. Lennart would never forget or forgive something like that. He would follow him for years. Maybe not attack him physically but keep talking about it. Micke had never been friendly with Lennart, but he had always been there, as brother to John. The sporadic contact would stop now. Just as well. He didn't want any other visits from Lennart.

Best to lie low and hope the bastard never comes back, he thought while he dragged himself to his feet and walked out to the bathroom.

Lennart was sitting in there crying quietly. His face was swollen and red.

"It's okay," Micke said. "Go on, get going. Have a beer and forget all this."

"I miss him," Lennart said. "My little brother."

Micke put a hand on his shoulder.

"Sure you do. John was better than all the rest of us put together."

Twenty-one

Ann Lindell was zipping Erik into his snowsuit. His eyes followed her attentively. She paused for a moment. *Which one of us does he look like?* she wondered. *Me or his father?* The engineer with whom she had spent one night and never seen again. He didn't even know he had become a father— how could he? Perhaps he had seen her around town, at the height of her pregnancy, and figured it out. *But men aren't that smart,* she thought, and smiled. Erik smiled back.

"But you're smart," she said and helped his tiny fingers through the sleeve.

She had made an appointment with the pediatrician. Erik had patches of an itchy rash that had come and gone for about month and she wanted to know what it was. Her parents were coming up for Christmas and her mother would be bound to pester her about it. For this reason alone it would be good to see the doctor.

She took out the stroller and decided to walk. She was heavier now than before the pregnancy. Her breasts and thighs had swelled up and her formerly taut stomach was softly rounded. She wasn't particularly concerned about it but she knew that a woman her age easily puts on a pound here and a pound there, only to end up overweight and immobile.

The weight gain was surely connected to her new lifestyle. She moved around less now, ate more frequently and in larger portions. It had become one of her weaknesses to help herself to a little extra, to indulge in rich food. Her social life had never been very extensive, but now she rarely socialized with anyone. She enjoyed staying at home watching TV, eating a good cheese with crackers, or perhaps ice cream. She was surprised at how quickly she had adjusted to this life. Of course, she missed her work, the stress, chatting with her colleagues, and the excitement of moving among so many people. At the start of her maternity leave she had felt a big relief, but now she was getting restless.

She was no longer in charge of any investigations, did not attend any morning meetings, and was never woken up by calls relating to violence and misery. She felt released from responsibility. Erik was a surprisingly easy baby. If she kept him on a reasonably regular schedule, he was content. He didn't have even a hint of colic. The first real problem, if you could call it that, was this rash.

Ann was in town after twenty minutes. She was sweating inside her coat. Earlier she had rarely worn a coat, preferring a short jacket or just a sweater.

"You're turning into a real lady," Ottosson had said when she last came down to the station for a visit.

"He means a real *old* lady," Sammy Nilsson had added.

They had looked at her in a way they had never done before, or so it seemed to her. She didn't know what she thought of that. She was proud to be a mother. To be caring for a son on her own. It was no grand achievement, she knew, it was something that millions of mothers had done throughout the ages, and most often without the help of a maternity ward and one-year checkups, but in this matter it was she, Ann Lindell, who was the mother. No one else, neither man nor woman, could take this point of pride from her. She knew it was an old-fashioned and ridiculous thought, but in some way she felt she had been judged good enough. She had been taken up in the ranks of all mothers, living and dead. It was an exclusive club, automatically excluding half of humanity and many others besides, those who could not or did not want to give birth.

Was it the same for men? she wondered. She sensed that she knew too little about them to be able to say. Of course she had met fathers pushing baby carriages with that exalted, almost silly expression, but did it feel the same for them? She had no man to ask. Edvard, the man she had been closest to, had been pained by a lack of contact with his two boys. But he was the one who had left them. Would a woman have been able to escape the way he had done? She was getting tired of these quasi-philosophical homemade analyses but couldn't shake them off entirely. She knew they provided her with a way of dealing with her loneliness and frustration. For all her intoxication with the wonders of motherhood, she remained alone.

To give birth to a child and watch him develop was a wonderful experience, but at the same time it was rather boring. This was the word she used to herself. She missed the excitement of police work. She now understood more fully why she had chosen this career. It was not so much for idealistic reasons as for the tension, the anticipation of the unknown, the extraordinary, the feeling of playing a furious game where the stakes were nothing short of life and death.

Shortly after one o'clock she arrived at the children's clinic and was shown into an office to see Katrin, a nurse-practitioner she had met several times before. She liked Katrin, a little woman in gold-colored sandals. She had talked to Ann about mastitis, and about the mixture of emptiness, longing, relief, and freedom that accompanies the absence of menstruation. She and Ann got along.

Ann was still nursing Erik but thinking seriously of weaning him. He refused to nurse on the left breast, which had now gone down to its normal shape, while the one on the right had ballooned up as big as a soccer ball. Ann often felt like a cow. She wanted to retain the closeness of nursing but also wanted her breasts back. Lately Erik had also taking to biting her.

She removed Erik's clothing and showed Katrin the rash on his chest and back. Katrin studied them carefully and then said she thought they were a reaction to something Ann was eating.

"Think carefully about what you're having," she said. "Erik is reacting to something in your diet. If it were summer I would guess strawberries."

"I'm fond of Indian food," Ann said. "Could that be it? There's lots of cumin and ginger in Indian food."

"No, I think spicy food would more likely cause a stomachache."

"And you're sure it's not a virus?" Ann asked, feeling helpless. She had grabbed on to this idea from the woman who ran the drop-in playgroup, a group she sometimes attended not because she really liked it but because she felt it was part of the experience.

"No, I don't think so. Not with you still nursing him."

Ann agreed to keep close track of what she was eating and to watch for any changes in Erik's rash.

They sat and talked for another thirty minutes. Katrin was someone who did not shy away from asking personal questions. She intuited Ann's bafflement in her new role as mother, probably because she had seen it before, but her penetrating questions were posed with such gentle tact that Ann felt completely relaxed. Katrin had an ability to give advice that never felt like criticism.

They said good-bye in the corridor. Ann turned and waved after a few steps, taking Erik's hand and letting him wave too. Katrin looked suddenly shy, but held up her hand.

Ann stepped out into the weak December sun, which was now sinking ever more rapidly into the horizon, and felt a wave of gratitude. She continued on down the street and decided to stop by the station. She checked the time: shortly before two. Ottosson was probably in, and he would likely take the time to have a cup of tea and a chat.

The door was open and Lindell looked in. Ottosson was sitting at his desk, his gaze fixed on a piece of paper in front of him. She heard him humming. Then he turned the page and sighed.

"Is this a bad time?"

Ottosson flinched, looked up, and the momentary confusion gave way to a smile.

"Did I startle you?"

"No, what I was reading startled me."

He didn't say anything else, but he studied her.

"You look blooming with health," he said.

Lindell smiled. He always told her that, even when she felt terrible.

"What are you doing?"

Ottosson ignored the question, instead asking her where Erik was.

"He's sleeping in his stroller just outside your door."

The chief got up and Lindell saw that his back pain had returned.

"It would be a pity to miss an opportunity to complain," he said when he noticed her gaze.

They walked out together and looked at the baby. Another colleague was walking by and he also looked into the stroller. Ottosson started humming again but didn't say anything.

"He'll be one soon," Lindell said. "Well, 'soon' is relative, I guess."

Ottosson nodded.

"My wife sends her regards, by the way. She was talking about you the other day."

Lindell pushed the stroller into Ottosson's office and he shut the door.

"It's your usual festive pre-Christmas season here," he said. "We have a murder in Libro and a lunatic intruder in Sävja, with a possible connection between the two events. Little John, the woman, and the loony—his name is Vincent Hahn—were classmates in high school. I've just been reading through the few items we have on Hahn. He seems remarkable, to say the least. Complains about every little thing. We've recovered five thick folders containing copies of letters he's sent over the years, with the accompanying replies from various companies and state departments."

"Has he had run-ins with us before?"

"No, nothing like that."

"How strong is the connection to John?"

"Not more than their school, which could be mere coincidence. But the murder could also mark the start of some private revenge scheme. We're trying to get our noses in everyone's business. John's widow has never heard of Hahn."

"And what about John's brother?"

"We haven't been able to reach him for a while."

Lindell felt the thrill of suspense. After only a few minutes of talk she was back.

"As I recall, Lennart was a fairly unsympathetic character," she said. "Loudmouthed and arrogant."

"He has his bad sides, to be sure," Ottosson said. "But it's clear he's mourning his brother. He appears to be staying sober and I think he's doing his own investigating. You know Nilsson, Johan Sebastian, the one Sammy is in touch with, he called and told us."

Lindell had always had trouble tolerating informants, but Johan Sebastian Nilsson 'Bach,' as he was called, gave them plenty of tidbits, so it only made sense to overlook his dubious character.

There was a loud thud from the window and both Ottosson and Lindell jumped. A few small downy feathers stuck to the windowpane.

"Poor bastard," Ottosson said. He had walked over to the window and was looking down to see if he could spot the bird.

"It's probably okay," Lindell said.

"It's the third time in just a few weeks," Ottosson said in a worried tone. "I don't understand why they keep flying into my window."

"You're the chief," Lindell said.

"It's as if they're looking for death," Ottosson said.

"Maybe there's something about the window that creates an optical illusion."

"It's hard not to see it as a sign," he said and turned back to the window, where he remained for a moment.

Lindell looked at him and felt a sudden tenderness. She saw that his beard had more gray hairs and the pain in his back had made his posture stooped. He was the best chief she had ever had, but sometimes it was as if he didn't have the energy anymore. Evil was exhausting him. A philosophical tone had sneaked into his argumentation, which in turn ceased to be focused on the crime in question and concentrated more on the underlying social reasons. This was also important, and all police officers pondered these things, but they couldn't let it obscure the concrete tasks at hand.

"What do you think Lennart is up to?" she asked in an attempt to turn the conversation back to the present. Ottosson turned.

"What he's up to? He's probably looking in on a few pals. They were close, you know. There was a connection between them that was stronger than with most siblings, and it doesn't surprise me in the least that he's hunting his brother's killer."

"Tell me about Little John."

Ottosson walked around the desk and sat down.

"Are you sure you don't want some tea?"

Lindell shook her head.

"He wasn't really all that smart," her chief said. "He was a thinker in his own way, but my sense is his perspective was always too narrow. He focused in on one thing and grabbed on to it, as if he had neither the imagination nor courage to drop it, to try other thoughts."

"Stubborn?"

"Very. To the degree that I actually admired him. And he really knew his fish. I think that saved him."

"Or led to his death," Lindell said, but regretted it when she saw his expression.

"It was an arena where he could be the best at something and I think he needed that. He probably suffered from low self-esteem his whole life. Berglund said something about this being about society, his upbringing. He came from a background where you weren't supposed to try to be better than anyone else."

"What do you mean?"

Ottosson got up and walked to the window again, let the blinds down, and adjusted them so that a little light still came in. But the room grew dimmer. A typical December day, Lindell thought. It was as if Ottosson read her thoughts, because before he sat back down he lit the three Advent candles on the windowsill.

"Pretty," she said.

Ottosson smiled a crooked smile, pleased but a little embarrassed.

"You asked me what I mean," he said. "Maybe John realized his environment was too narrow. You know he wanted more."

"Sure, but I didn't think he was dreaming of another life."

Ottosson paused. Lindell sensed it was the first time he was airing these thoughts about Little John.

"What does his wife say?"

"Not much. She walks around in a fog. The boy is more complicated."

Ottosson took no time to elaborate on this last statement but returned to the topic of the two brothers, Lennart and John. Berglund must have been the one who dug up this information, Lindell thought. He was the right one for this kind of job. A little older, native to Uppsala, and with a calm and reassuring demeanor. He was made for it. Sammy would never have been able to do it, nor would Beatrice. Possibly Haver.

And would Lindell have been able to walk around the city gaining the confidence of various members of the working-class population in order to establish a picture of the Jonsson brothers? It was doubtful.

There was a knock on the door and Sammy looked in.

"Hi, Ann," he said quickly, then looked at Ottosson. "We've found something. The murder weapon, no less."

"Little John's?"

"Yes!"

He held up a clear plastic bag with a large knife.

"The youth patrol brought in a young guy. He had it on his person, tucked into the waist of his pants."

"It's big," Lindell said.

"Twenty-one centimeters," Sammy said, smirking. "Made in France."

"Why was he brought in?"

"Some trouble in town. He had threatened a guy with it."

"Is he our man?"

"I know him from before, but I doubt it. He's fifteen and a real trouble-maker but no killer."

"Capable of manslaughter?"

Sammy shook his head.

"Immigrant?"

"No, as Swedish as they come. Mattias Andersson. He lives with his mother in Svartbäcken."

"What makes you think this is the murder weapon?"

"John's blood is on the blade and the handle," Sammy said. "Bohlin was the one who noticed the stains and demanded an analysis."

"Bohlin in the youth patrol?"

"That's the one."

"That was a smart decision," Ottosson. "What does Mattias Andersson have to say?"

"We're bringing him here right now."

He glanced at Lindell and she thought she could see a triumphant expression on his face but told herself it was her imagination. Sammy's cell phone rang at that moment. He answered, listened, and ended the conversation with an "okay."

"They're coming in the door now," he said and took a step out the door. Then he turned and looked at Lindell.

"Do you want to be there?"

"Where?"

"When we question Mattias."

"I have the little one with me," she said and nodded in the direction of the stroller, which Sammy hadn't noticed before.

"Leave him with me," said Ottosson.

Twenty-two

Vincent woke around half past four. Vivan had made up a bed in her sewing room and for a while he lay there looking at the sewing machine. The rows of different colored thread arranged on some shelves, the cutting table she had pushed against one wall, covered in black cloth.

The headache, which had come and gone all night, had finally lifted, but he still felt its weight. His sister-in-law had washed and dressed the wound on his forehead.

"You are the only one who's willing to help me," he told her, and Vivan softened at these words and the sight of him.

He went out into the hall. The newspaper had been partly pushed through the mail slot and he gently pulled it out. He found it on page 3. Vincent Hahn was described as "unpredictable" and "mentally disturbed." The forty-two-year-old woman in Sävja had not been physically hurt but was considerably shaken. The police were urging members of the public with information on the assailant to come forward.

He shoved the paper to the bottom of the kitchen trash. His sister-in-law's bedroom was right next to the kitchen and he had to move with extreme care. He knew from before that she could be grumpy in the morning and assumed that this was still the case, though they had not spent the night under the same roof for over twenty years.

He put on water for tea and tried to order his thoughts. The police would most likely have placed his apartment under surveillance. He could stay with Vivan for one, perhaps two nights at most. Then she would start to grumble. He had to make a plan. Bernt, a man he talked to at the bingo hall, could potentially help him out. But the first thing he had to do was get money.

If Gunilla Karlsson thought she had gotten away, she was sorely mistaken. You could maybe trick Vincent Hahn once, but not two times. She would get a dose of her own medicine, that fucking bitch. The more he reflected on the events of the preceding night, the more determined he was to get revenge. She would be punished ten times over.

At six-thirty Vivan came stumbling into the kitchen. It was as if she had forgotten that he was there, because for a few seconds she stared at him uncomprehendingly. Vincent said nothing, just stared back.

"How is it?" she asked, but didn't wait for an answer. He heard her walk out to the bathroom, pee, and then turn on the shower.

"How long are you staying?" she asked when she came out again, wrapped in a towel.

Vincent was still sitting at the kitchen table. His headache had returned. His sister-in-law was making it easy for him by bringing up the subject herself.

"One or two nights," he said. "I'd rather not be by myself. Only if it's all right with you, of course."

She was clearly surprised at his meekness. She had not heard him be so gentle before.

"That sounds fine," she said, relieved.

She left the kitchen and Vincent relaxed for the first time since yesterday. He heard her pulling and shutting dresser drawers and opening the doors to the closet. He wondered why she didn't have a new man in her life.

"Have you taken the newspaper?" she asked.

"No, I didn't think you had one."

"You can't rely on anything anymore," she said with unexpected sharpness.

"I think I'll go back to bed for a while," he said. "I woke up so early and this headache won't go away."

Vincent felt almost peaceful. It was as if he and Vivan were an old couple, or very good friends, chitchatting in the early morning.

"I can pay my way," he said.

"Don't be ridiculous," Vivan said, walking back into the kitchen. "Go back to bed. I'm having some breakfast."

Vincent went back to the sewing room. Vivan took out some yogurt and cereal. To make up for the absent paper, she fished an old one out of the recycling pile and turned on the radio.

Twenty-three

The search for Vincent Hahn intensified in the early morning hours. His temporary home on Bergslagsresan had quickly been found and Fredriksson had gone in with four men. As expected, it was empty.

The apartment, a one-bedroom, gave an abandoned impression. There were no curtains, only a few pieces of furniture, and very few personal belongings. The phone was not hooked up. There was no computer.

"The most remarkable thing we found," Fredriksson said at the morning meeting, "was a mannequin. It was lying in Hahn's bed dressed in a pair of black panties." Fredriksson blushed slightly as he described the somewhat soiled doll.

"No address book, letters, or anything?" Beatrice asked, hoping to jog her colleague along.

"Well," Fredriksson said, pinching his nose, "there were three binders filled with letters that Hahn has written over the past few years. These were addressed to the local district authorities, to the Uppsala transit authorities, Swedish Public Radio, and God knows who else. He seems to have devoted his time to writing letters of complaint about everything and everyone. He archived their replies. As far as I can tell, most of them were brief and dismissive."

"He must have made quite a name for himself," Ottosson said.

"The question is where he is now," Sammy said.

"We know he was picked up by a car at the train crossing in Bergs-brunna. The driver, a technician from the waterworks, called in this morning when he had read the news. He dropped him off at the ER."

"When was that?"

"Some thirty minutes after the attack," Fredriksson said. "We checked, but no Vincent Hahn was admitted to the hospital yesterday. They'll let us know if he turns up."

"How serious were his wounds?"

"He was bleeding profusely, but it's hard to say how deep the wound was. The man from the waterworks said he had blood all over his face but that he seemed coherent. He was able to walk unassisted."

"Is he German? With a name like Hahn, I mean."

"No, he's a Swedish citizen. His parents have been dead for many years. There was a brother, Wolfgang, but he emigrated to Israel fifteen years ago."

"Is he Jewish?" Lundin asked.

"On his mother's side. His mother came here after the war. This is all according to public records."

Fredriksson stopped talking and looked down at his papers.

"Okay," Ottosson said. "Good work. We will continue surveillance in Sävja, both the apartment and Gunilla Karlsson's place. Fredriksson, you'll continue to look into the matter of whether Hahn has any relatives or friends in the area. He must have gone somewhere. It's unlikely he would have left town, at least not on public transport. With that head wound he has he would only draw attention to himself."

"Does he have a car?" Sammy asked.

"Not even a driver's license," Fredriksson said.

"Okay," Ottosson said again. "Let's hear the part about the knife and the youngster. Sammy, you're up."

"Mattias Andersson was arrested after a fight downtown. He was found to be armed with a knife. Bohlin, from the youth patrol, had heard about Little John's murder, so when he saw the knife he took a closer look at it. It had stains that have been confirmed consistent with Little John's blood."

"Well, I'll be damned," Beatrice said. "How old is he?"

"Fifteen."

The door opened and Berglund stepped in, with the district attorney in tow. They sat down and the briefing continued.

"He claims he pocketed the knife at the Akademiska Hospital parking garage earlier that same day. We've checked, but no car break-ins have been reported. This doesn't necessarily mean anything, because Mattias claims he swiped it from an unlocked pickup truck. Apparently he walked around testing car doors, and when this one opened he found this knife in a black bucket in the back of the truck."

"Do you believe him?"

"Maybe," Sammy said. "The guy's scared shitless. He's been crying mostly. His mother's doing the same thing. The tears are just pouring out of her."

"Did you talk to the security guards?"

"Yes," Sammy said. "They had no incidents that day, no reports of theft or damage. Normally this happens almost daily. We took Mattias down there last night so he could point out the place for us. The guard thought he recognized him but couldn't remember a pickup truck in that spot. It's not unlikely the guard could recognize him, because he regularly patrols the garage."

"A pickup," Ottosson said thoughtfully. "What color, and make?"

"Red," Sammy said, "possibly with a white hood. It could be a Toyota, but he is extremely unsure on this point."

"If we're going to take this story at all seriously we'll have to show this boy some pictures of different models," Beatrice said.

"Does he have an alibi for the evening John was murdered?" Morenius asked. He was surprised that no one else had thought of this.

"It's doubtful," Sammy said. "He says he was hanging out with his friends downtown. We've tried to pinpoint where they were and when, but the friends are all vague. 'That's years ago, man,' as one of them put it. Some of them even think it's cool that Mattias was found with a murder weapon in his possession."

"Last but not least, I can say that Ann made a guest appearance here yesterday," Ottosson said. "She sat in on the questioning of Mattias, and helped calm his mother afterward. I even think they had a cup of coffee together."

"How are things with her?" Beatrice asked.

"She's bored," Sammy said. "She's thinking of selling the baby."

"Give me a break."

"She's already looking through the Yellow Pages," Sammy said and smiled at Beatrice.

The meeting finished an hour later. Ola Haver felt unusually dispirited. The mention of Ann Lindell made him long for Rebecka. He thought about sneaking home to her for an hour or two. He had done this on a few previous occasions, before the children had come along and when she had had a day off.

He smiled at the memory and opened the door to his office. At the same time, the telephone rang. He looked at it, let it ring a few times before answering.

"Hi, it's Westrup. Are you right in the middle of something?" the voice said quickly, then continued, "You're working on the Little John case, am I right? We received a tip this fall about a gambling ring and Little John's name came up."

"Damn," Haver said, and all his low spirits were gone.

"We're keeping our eye out for an Iranian called Mossa, a player, maybe he also deals drugs, what do I know. He's allegedly part of a high-stakes poker ring."

"How did you find this out?"

"One of the participants couldn't keep his mouth shut. Åström took him in for questioning in connection with some forged business invoices. It's a case of suspected money laundering: this guy was sitting on a lot of cash he had trouble explaining how he got his hands on. That's when talk of this poker game came up. He probably exaggerated the whole thing, mostly to get Åström off his back about the invoices, but he dropped a few names."

"Had John won or lost?"

"He won—a lot, as it turns out. There was talk of a couple of hundred thousand."

"Let's talk to this guy. What's his name?"

Haver studied the name in front of him. It meant nothing to him. Ove Reinhold Ljusnemark, forty-six and trained as an airplane mechanic. He had been fired from Arlanda after reports of theft.

He had an in-care-of address out in Tunabackar. Haver immediately had the impression that he would dislike Ove Reinhold. Maybe because he was a snitch who tried to go free by burning his friends. Westrup, a colleague from Skåne who had joined the Uppsala police a year ago, had promised to bring Ljusnemark in.

When the ruddy Ljusnemark was led into Haver's office an hour later, he had a sheepish smile on his face. Haver scrutinized him without saying a word. He gestured for Ljusnemark to sit down and nodded to Westrup. The latter remained in the doorway for a moment and smiled. This was something Haver appreciated in his colleague. His large frame, slightly slow gait, and then his smile. Not always transparent, but friendly.

Haver sat quietly at first. The visitor's smile grew more stiff. Haver pretended to be looking for something, took out a thick binder that concerned a completely different investigation, opened it to a report that he spent a few seconds eyeing, and then gave the snitch a quick look.

"Impressive," he said and closed the binder. "So what will it be? Cooperation or confrontation?"

Ove Reinhold Ljusnemark sat up a little in his chair. The smile had completely disappeared from his face and he cleared his throat. Haver wasn't sure if he understood the words he had just used.

"You knew Little John. There are those who claim you had something to do with his murder."

Ljusnemark swallowed.

"What the hell," he said. "Says who?"

Haver laid his hand on the binder.

"Do you want to tell us, or do we do this the hard way?"

"It's a fucking lie! I played with him a few times, that's all."

"Yes, let's start there. Tell me about your games."

Ljusnemark looked at him as if they were in the middle of a poker game.

"We played cards. I didn't really know him. We were a group of guys who met from time to time. There were no big sums involved, but occasionally the stakes would get higher."

"You're on disability right now?"

Ljusnemark nodded.

"Forty-six years old and physically incapacitated," Haver said.

"I have sciatica."

"But you're strong enough to stay up all night playing poker, it seems. Tell me how much money we're talking about."

"Lately, you mean? Well, we didn't start big. It was small amounts."

"Who was there?"

"People came and went because games went on for a while. The time goes so fast when you're enjoying yourself. We would order pizza, that kind of thing."

Ljusnemark paused and tried to smile.

"Cut to the chase."

"It's a little while ago. I don't remember so well."

"We have information that connects you to the murder weapon used in Little John's case," Haver said curtly.

"What?"

"Who were the people you played with? How much money was involved?"

"What kind of weapon? I've never had a weapon."

Haver waited.

"Give me a break," Ljusnemark said in English, and at that moment Haver was prepared to put him away on bread and water for twenty years. He opened the binder.

"It was me and Little John," Ljusnemark started and then related the whole story with remarkable fluency, including a full account of all the participants. Haver recognized the names of a few of them.

"You lost?"

"Five or six thousand at most. I swear. I was forced to back out and Jerry took my place."

"Jerry Martin?"

Ljusnemark nodded, squirming in his seat. Haver stared at him for a few seconds.

"You can go now," he said.

Eight names. Haver sensed that the answer lay here somewhere. Money and passion, that's where you looked for answers. People came to grief over money and unrequited love.

Haver leaned back in his chair. Was there any society in which money didn't rule? He had heard of some tribe in Africa in which violence and theft almost never occurred and there was no concern over measuring time. He longed to join them, but assumed that the tribe was most likely already extinct, or had been driven into a shantytown where the members were dying from alcohol and AIDS.

Eight names. Haver took the list and went to find Ottosson.

Twenty-four

Vincent Hahn woke with a start. He checked his watch. A little after nine. He had been asleep for only a few minutes and had immediately slipped into a dream. A man's voice was coming from somewhere. It took him a few seconds to understand what it was: the news on the radio.

He found Vivan in the kitchen by the telephone. She looked up at him with a frightened expression and he knew that she knew.

"Put down the phone," he said and took a few steps closer.

"You're just like your brother," she said. "Lying and fighting all the time."

"Shut up. Don't mix him up in this."

"Why did you do it?"

He took the receiver from her and she let him do it. He saw that she was sweating. The piece "Waltz of the Sea-Eagle" by Evert Taube was playing on the radio. He was very close to her. Blood was seeping through the bandage on his forehead.

"She was a whore," Vincent said softly.

"Did you know her?"

He flinched and ripped the phone cord from the wall.

"We went to school together. She was nothing but a shit even then."

"It's such a long time ago. Can't you let bygones be bygones?"

Vivan knew that Vincent had been unhappy at school, been bullied and shunned. Wolfgang had once said that his brother was the perfect victim.

"I remember everything," he said, his voice so low now she could hardly catch his words.

He pulled the phone cord between his hands.

"I won't say anything," she said.

"Who were you calling?"

"Nettan. She's in the middle of a divorce and wants me to go with her to the lawyer's office."

"Who the hell is Nettan?"

His outburst came on so suddenly that she pulled back and would have lost her balance if he hadn't grabbed her arms.

"Who the fucking hell is Nettan?"

"You're hurting me," Vivan moaned in his grip. His disgusting breath nauseated her. "She's my best friend."

"Friend!" he spat.

"Why don't you stay here?" she said. "I need the company."

He let go of her suddenly and she started to collapse, then steadied herself against the kitchen counter and straightened up. *No crying,* she thought to herself. *He hates teary women.*

"What do you mean 'stay here'?"

She swallowed and chose her words carefully. She had a flashback to Wolfgang's rages and her attempts to placate him. After years of practice she had become more adept.

"I'm lonely," she said and looked away.

"Lonely," Vincent repeated.

"I don't care about that woman. She hit you, after all."

"Yes, she hit me."

He paused with a thoughtful look on his face, and Vivan thought she saw the same quality of gentleness that had drawn her to Wolfgang so many years ago. The brothers had both inherited their mother's rounded and slightly childish features, but also their father's heavier ones, a mixture that was reflected in their intense emotional vacillations.

"That blow she gave you could have killed you, if you didn't have such a strong skull."

He sank down onto a chair. She put a hand on his bandaged head. *If only he had died,* she thought, *no one would have missed him.* But then she instantly regretted her thought—it was unfair. He was a human being like anyone else.

"Would you like some tea?"

He shook his head weakly.

"A little juice?"

He nodded. She quickly made up a pitcher of rhubarb juice and poured him a glass. He drained it. The gentle expression returned.

"Wolfgang says hello," she said. "He called me a few days ago."

Despite their divorce and the years of conflict, Vivan and Wolfgang stayed in touch. He called from Tel Aviv three or four times a year.

"You haven't called me."

"I've tried to, but you aren't home very much. Anyway, Wolfgang is fine but he complained about all the trouble they're having."

"It's the fucking Arabs," Vincent said.

Vivan was very careful not to get into the subject of the Israel-Palestine conflict. Instead she relayed gossip from Wolfgang. One of their cousins had had a grandchild, and a few other relatives had taken a trip to Poland. Vincent listened with interest. Vivan had discovered that he liked hearing news even about distant relatives, had memorized names and trivial facts about them to a degree that amazed her.

"I heard that Benjamin got married," he said, and Vivan pretended to be surprised.

"Really? I had no idea. Who did he get married to?"

"Some American girl who bought a house in East Jerusalem."

They continued to talk about people they both knew. Vincent grew calmer, drank more juice. Vivan kept him entertained with questions and comments. She suggested they celebrate Christmas together and his face lit up a bit when she said that.

The attack came out of nowhere. Vivan hardly had time to register what was happening, let alone understand where it had come from. She died unknowing, with a small gurgling sound not unlike that which arises from a plugged drain.

He laid her on the bed and was somewhat reminded of Julia. They had the same beautiful air of peace. The marks on her neck from the phone cord were like the angry red strands of a necklace. The blue-toned tip of her tongue stuck out a few centimeters. Vincent chuckled at it and poked it back into her mouth, then quickly pulled his fingers away, convinced that she was going to bite him.

His chuckles gave way to an unarticulated roar, which died away almost at once, and he sat down on the floor to look at his sister-in-law. *Almost family,* he thought. *As close to family as I can get in Uppsala.* His feeling of loneliness was intensified by the sound of the clock ticking, as if to say, *You are dead, you are dead.*

Vincent reached for the clock, which he remembered Wolfgang had bought on a business trip. He threw it against the wall. An Argentine tango was playing on the radio in the kitchen.

He put his hand on hers. It was still warm, and suddenly he felt dizzy. *The work of a moment and a person is gone,* he thought. He let his hand travel up her arm, he stroked it lovingly. Somewhere in the innermost depths of his confused mind he sensed that he had committed an unforgivable act. Vivan, the one who had smiled at him in the window, the one who had been frightened by his appearance but nonetheless given him shelter, the one who had given him juice. *Almost family.*

He sensed that she had been as lonely as he, even though she always talked about her girlfriends. He thought suddenly that he could take his own life, that he should do it.

He got up, walked into the kitchen, picked up a chair that had been knocked over, and drank some more juice. When he took hold of the pitcher to pour himself yet another glass, he experienced something like an electric shock. A greeting from Vivan. It was her hand that had last held the pitcher. Now she was making her presence known. She would do this as long as he lived, he realized.

He found a laundry line with the cleaning supplies but could not bring himself to tie a noose. Instead he remained sitting with the green plastic-coated line in his hands, unable to kill himself.

After about an hour or so—he was unable to determine how long—he let the line glide from his hands and stood up. He ate some leftovers in the refrigerator, went into the sewing room, and fell asleep.

Allan Fredriksson had traced Vincent Hahn's brother to Tel Aviv and with the help of Israeli police had managed to reach him on the phone.

Wolfgang Hahn, who worked as a computer-science instructor, had not been in Sweden for seven years. During that time he had talked to Vincent on the phone a handful of times, most recently a year or so ago. He even claimed not to know his brother's most recent number. When asked if there was anyone in Uppsala who would be able to provide more information, Wolfgang mentioned his ex-wife, who he knew had sporadic contact with Vincent.

"How are things back in Sweden anyway?" Wolfgang asked. "I hear you'll soon have even more Arabs than we do, and look at the problems they make for us!"

"Maybe that's because you took their land," Fredriksson said calmly. "What was Tel Aviv called fifty years ago?"

Wolfgang Hahn laughed.

"I see they've infiltrated the Swedish police," he said, but with no hostility in his voice.

"Will you have a white Christmas?" was Fredriksson's last question. When he hung up, he realized that Wolfgang Hahn hadn't even asked why the police wanted to find his brother.

He looked up Vivan Molin in the phone book. She was listed as a laboratory assistant, living on Johannesbäcksgatan. According to Wolfgang she had been on disability for a while, he was unsure of the exact reason. They had no children together and she lived alone. A few years ago there had been a boyfriend in the picture, but he hadn't heard anything about him for a while. Vivan Molin did not answer the phone.

Fredriksson called the health agency. She was not listed as being on disability. No employer was registered by her name either. Her last employment seemed to have been a temporary position with the Uppsala Biomedical Center. That position had lasted until August.

How likely was it that Hahn had looked her up? According to his brother, they were not on particularly good terms. Fredriksson sighed. Johansson and Palm were going door to door in Sävja, but so far they it had given them nothing. Most of Hahn's neighbors had not even been able to identify him from the picture. His closest neighbor, a Bosnian from Sarajevo, had only smiled enigmatically when asked if he associated at all with Vincent Hahn.

Fredriksson pushed the papers away. He didn't even want to be working on the Hahn case right now. It was the murder of Little John that concerned him. He was sure they would be able to solve it eventually, not from any concrete knowledge but simply from the years of experience and the sense that a murder in John's circles would eventually be cleared up. The new information about the poker game and John's alleged winnings provided them with a motive. They would search for their perpetrator among the poker players—Fredriksson was 100 percent convinced of this. Now they simply had to uncover the whole story.

Haver and he had discussed potential overlap between Little John and Hahn, but both of them were skeptical. It was most likely a coincidence that they had been classmates. Little John's murder was no work of Hahn's. Even though they knew almost nothing about Hahn's profile, his background and behavior, the fact that Little John's body had been dumped in Libro made Hahn an unlikely suspect. He had neither a car nor a driver's license—how would he have been able to carry it off?

Someone had proposed the idea that Hahn was targeting former classmates with pets. John with his fish, and Gunilla Karlsson with her rabbit. That Hahn saw himself as a freedom fighter for animals. But Fredriksson had dismissed this idea as highly unlikely.

He called Vivan Molin again, with no result. Should he drive out to Johannesbäck and check it out? The fact was that Vivan Molin was the only name he had. And it was possible that she would be able to provide them with additional names.

Fredriksson took off his indoor shoes, tied his boots, put on his fur hat, and left.

December. The sun had barely made it over the horizon that day, but it didn't matter anymore. The clouds lay heavily over Uppsala and there was snow in the air. Fredriksson paused for a second before he turned the ignition. *Christmas party.* The words came out of nowhere. He couldn't remember exactly, but this was probably connected to slumbering childhood memories, boisterous adult voices, the children more quiet, full of anticipation, dressed up, hair slicked down, the Santa Claus with his fake beard.

In the olden days, Fredriksson would let the words roll over his tongue. Even to say it now sounded outdated.

"In the olden days," he said aloud.

That was something people said. Had it really been better in the olden days? He turned the key and the motor answered with a roar. Too many thoughts, too much gas.

Two cars had collided at the corner of Verkmästargatan and Apelgatan. Fredriksson thought about stopping but changed his mind when he caught sight of the face of one of the involved parties. Collisions weren't his thing. When he had worked a beat he had never much liked dealing with traffic accidents, not because of the potential physical injuries and gore but because of the shocking stupidity of the drivers.

Fredriksson rang Vivan Molin's doorbell, waited for a few minutes, then rang again. No response. He peeked in through the mail slot in the door and caught a whiff of stale apartment air. There was no mail or newspaper to be seen on the hall floor. When he let the mail slot swing shut he thought he heard a soft click from inside the apartment, like the sound of someone turning on a lamp. He strained to hear anything else, opened the mail slot again, but now all was quiet. Had he imagined it? He straightened his back.

He took out his cell phone and the slip of paper with Molin's phone number. He let her phone ring six times but didn't hear any sound from the apartment. Either her phone wasn't working or she had turned it off.

Fredriksson thought hard. He turned and looked at the neighbor's door. M. ANDERSSON was inscribed on the mail slot. He rang the bell. A woman opened immediately, as if she had been waiting with her hand on the door handle. She was around seventy years of age, with long white hair, braided and pinned in a knot. The hand on the door handle was thin, with large swollen blue veins.

He introduced himself and said he was looking for Vivan Molin.

"Something's not right," she said immediately.

"How do you mean?"

"There were such strange sounds this morning. And a man came by last night."

"At what time did you hear these sounds?"

"Around eleven. I was finishing the Christmas spare ribs—I'm going to Kristinehamn this afternoon. He was out there shouting on the street."

"What did he look like?"

"I didn't see him so well. He was wearing a hat. Vivan let him in."

"Vivan went down and opened the front door?"

"Yes, it is locked at nine."

"These sounds you were talking about, what did they sound like?"

"Like screams. Something has happened. I almost called the police but I didn't know if I should get involved in other people's business."

"How well do you know Vivan? Does she often have visitors in the evening?"

"No, never. This part of the building is very quiet."

"Does she go to work?"

"No, she's on disability. She was burned out, I think they call it."

Fredriksson thanked her for the information and went down to the street. He made a call to the station and eight minutes later a patrol car pulled up. A van from the locksmith company Pettersson & Barr pulled up right behind them. The locksmith was a young man with Rastafarian braids, hardly more than twenty.

Fredriksson and his colleagues discussed their options. If Vincent Hahn was in the apartment he could very well be armed. It was doubtful that he would have access to firearms, more likely a knife or other object.

The Rastafarian locksmith worked on the lock for about thirty seconds. He whistled as he worked and Fredriksson asked him to be quiet.

"Cool," he said. "Are you Sweden's answer to Carella?"

Fredriksson had no idea what he was talking about, but nodded. Slättbrant, famous among his colleagues for his implacability, opened the door.

"Police!" he shouted before going in. "Anyone home?"

Silence.

"Torsten Slättbrant from the police. I'm coming in."

He forced the door all the way open and stepped into the apartment, his gun in his left hand. He took another step while looking at what Fredriksson assumed was the kitchen door. Then he stood quietly for ten seconds, as if testing the air like a hunting dog.

Slättbrant looked back and shook his head.

"Is anyone home?" he shouted again, and Fredriksson felt impatient.

"Heavy, man," said the Rastafarian, and Fredriksson gestured for him to stay back.

"You're no Carella," the young man said again and walked down half a flight of stairs.

"There's a woman under the bed in the bedroom," said Göthe, the other officer. Fredriksson nodded as if he already knew this.

"Strangled, I think," said Göthe. The young locksmith appeared behind him and craned his head forward.

"Get lost!" Fredriksson shouted.

"Can we strike Hahn from the Little John case?" Ottosson's question hung in the air among the assembled officers for a few seconds. One of the overhead fluorescent lights was flickering and underscored the anxious atmosphere.

"Can't we have that light fixed?" Sammy Nilsson asked.

"I, for one, don't believe in the connection for a second," Fredriksson said. "Hahn's profile is totally different. You've seen his correspondence, a misanthrope with a twisted worldview. I read one letter he wrote to the transit authorities where he proposed a special immigrant bus so that ethnic Swedes wouldn't have to associate with foreign scum, as he put it. I think his being John's former classmate is pure coincidence."

"I'm not so sure," Sammy said. "We can drop the question of motive here. This guy is a nut case and simply did something on impulse. Maybe he bumped into John, recognized him from their school days. Maybe something had happened between them a long time ago and it led to a confrontation."

"But where would such a confrontation have taken place?" Morenius said. "On Vaksalagatan downtown where John waited for the bus? Where did the murder, not to mention the torture, actually occur, and how did Hahn transport the body to Libro?"

Morenius shook his head.

"We know very little about Hahn," Sammy said. "Maybe he had access to another apartment, maybe even to a car. We haven't actually met a single person yet who knew him and could tell us how he spends his days."

Ottosson scratched his head.

"I think we can disregard Hahn for now," he said, but he did not sound entirely convinced.

"Little John's killer is one of these poker players or someone else who keeps to society's fringes," Berglund said.

"We have to proceed with open minds," Ottosson said. "Not lose the tempo. It's very easy to lose one's focus, even unintentionally."

"Okay," Haver said. "Eight guys, excluding John, were there that night. Ljusnemark gave us all the names. Four of them, plus Ljusnemark, have been questioned today. That leaves three remaining. One of them is abroad, possibly in Holland. His mother lives there. One has disappeared from the face of the earth, and the third is Mossa, the Iranian, whom we all know and who appears to be out of town for the moment. We have talked to his brother and mother, who live here."

"Who is the one in Holland?"

"Dick Lindström."

"The one with the teeth?"

Haver nodded.

"And who is the person who has disappeared from the face of the earth, as you put it?"

"One Allan Gustav Rosengren. He has the nickname The Lip. He's been convicted twice of trafficking in stolen goods. The last time was five years ago. He has no permanent address. The last one is in Mälarhöjden two years ago when he was renting a room from an old lady. He moved out and since then he has disappeared from all sources."

"One with teeth, and one with a lip," Riis said.

"Can we rule out Ljusnemark?" Morenius asked.

"I think so," Haver said. "Too much of a coward. I can't see him cutting off a finger."

"You're assuming the motive is money?"

"Gambling debts don't seem likely to me," said Haver. "Everyone so far corroborates the fact that John won. The alleged amounts have varied somewhat but seem to cluster around two hundred thousand. If John had had an outstanding debt he would have paid up."

"Maybe he didn't want to?"

"Well, that's a possibility."

"Maybe it whet his appetite and he went on to play more games in which he accumulated debt?"

"Even more possible," Haver said. "The game took place sometime at the end of October. There was a lot of time for poker between then and the murder."

"I don't agree," Ottosson said. "Little John was smart and cautious by nature. He would never have risked losing so much money."

"But to win in the first place he must already have had a lot. Many of these guys say he was betting freely, almost wildly. No one had seen him play this way before."

"Maybe that's why he won. Everyone was taken by surprise," Fredriksson said.

"Can someone simply have been ticked off?" Morenius asked. He always had a question.

"Not enough to commit murder," Haver said.

He wanted someone to think of something new. Everything that had come out so far were things he had already mulled over in his mind, but at the same time he knew the discussion had to proceed in this way in order to eventually construct a likely scenario.

"If we return to Hahn," Ryde, the forensic expert, said. "It's clear that Vivan Molin was strangled sometime this morning. Hahn had spent the night, we have recovered samples of his hair from the bed in the room he most likely would have used. Today's paper had been crumpled up and shoved to the bottom of the trash, as if he had tried to hide it from her. The phone cord has been torn from the wall. He may have been trying to prevent her from calling, or else it was something he grabbed when he wanted to strangle her. In some way, we think, she found out that he had attacked Karlsson in Sävja."

"Radio or TV," Fredriksson said. "There was a radio in the kitchen."

Ryde nodded. Only Fredriksson could interrupt him without getting a caustic remark.

"True. We'll have to check if the Sävja incident was reported in the morning news. There's no trace of a third person, even if we can't rule it out. Murder, unclear motive, either uncontrolled impulse or to keep someone quiet."

"Excellent," Ottosson said and smiled, a smile that bore witness to great fatigue. He was running a fever and several of them had already suggested he go home to bed, not least Lundin, who refused to get anywhere near him.

"How did he get from Akademiska Hospital to Johannesbäck?" Berglund asked. "He must have had access to a car."

"It's not very likely that he took a bus," Fredriksson agreed. "We'll have to check with the taxi companies."

"The only thing we can do is try to find any acquaintances of Hahn and continue patrolling the areas. Ottosson asserts there's a high probability he'll be drifting around the city. He's the type. Allan, you'll have to research where Hahn would hang out."

"Thanks," Fredriksson said and pinched the top of his nose.

"How will we proceed with John?" Morenius asked.

"We'll grill the poker guys, check their alibis, and find Dick Lindström, 'The Lip' Rosengren, and Mossa," Haver said. "There isn't much else to do. Then there's a thing I've been thinking about. Many individuals have asserted that John was planning something big. What could that have been?"

"An aquarium store, I think," Berglund said. "Pettersson, whom I talked to, said John had alluded to something like that."

"It wouldn't necessarily have had to be a store," Sammy said. "It could have been something big with poker."

"Have we checked with John's wife about the poker playing?"

"Beatrice is there right now," Ottosson said.

They sat in the kitchen, like last time. Justus had lingered outside the doorway but then had gone to his room. The rap music carried all the way to the kitchen.

"I know it's too loud," Berit said, more factually than apologetically, "but I don't have the heart to ask him to turn it down."

"How has it been going for him?" Beatrice asked.

"He doesn't say much. He hasn't been going to school. Mostly he sits in front of the fish tank."

"Were they close?"

Berit nodded.

"Very," she said after a while. "They were always together. If there was anyone who could get John to change his mind, it was Justus."

"How were things financially? You've said before there were hard times."

Berit looked out the window.

"We had a good life," she said.

"And lately?"

"I know where you're going with this. You think John was involved in something illicit, but you're wrong. He was quiet and sometimes unreachable, but he wasn't stupid."

"I'm not implying he was. But I'll get to the point: it seems John won a great deal of money this fall."

"What do you mean 'won'? Horse racing?"

"No, a card game. Poker."

"Well, I know he played cards sometimes, but it was never for high stakes."

"What about two hundred thousand," Beatrice said.

"What? That's not possible."

Berit's surprise seemed genuine. She swallowed and stared at Beatrice in bafflement.

"Not only is it possible, it seems almost certain. We have several witnesses."

Berit lowered her head and hunched over. One hand fumbled along the tablecloth, fingering the embroidery, in this case a sleigh-riding Santa. The music from Justus's room had stopped and the apartment was quiet.

"Why didn't he say anything? Two hundred thousand? That's a fortune! There has to be some mistake. Who says he won that much?"

"Among others, four people who lost a lot of money that night."

"And now they're angry at John and trying to pin this on him."

"You can choose to see it like that, but I think they're telling the truth. It's not to their benefit to lie about being involved in a high-stakes poker game, but they feel pressured now and they're choosing to come clean. Many of them even have trouble accounting for the money they were betting that night."

"Was he murdered for the money, then?"

"That's starting to look like a possibility."

"Where is the money now?"

"We've wondered about that. It may have been stolen in conjunction with the murder or it's in a bank account somewhere, or else . . ."

"Somewhere around here," Berit finished. "But we have no money in this apartment."

"Have you checked?"

"Checked—well, no, not exactly. But I've been putting John's things away and you and your colleagues have turned the place upside down."

"I'm afraid we'll have to do that one more time."

"It'll be Christmas soon. I'm thinking of Justus. He's going to need some peace and quiet."

They kept talking. Beatrice tried to get Berit to reflect back on the fall again, now that she knew he had won so much money. Had he been different in any way? But Berit claimed he had been his usual self.

Beatrice showed her pictures of the men who had participated in the poker game. Berit studied each one carefully but didn't recognize any of them.

"One of these men could be John's killer," she said. Beatrice didn't reply, just gathered up the pictures.

"Do you mind if I have a word with Justus?" she asked.

"I can't stop you," Berit said quietly. "Are you going to show him the pictures as well?"

"Maybe not, but I also want to ask him if he noticed anything different about John in the fall."

"They mostly talked about their fish."

Beatrice stood up.

"Do you think he'll talk to me?"

"You'll have to ask him yourself. One more thing: when did he win the money?"

"In the middle of October," Beatrice said.

Beatrice knocked carefully and cracked open the bedroom door. Justus was sitting on his bed with his legs pulled up. A book lay open next to him.

"Are you reading?"

Justus didn't answer; he closed the book and looked at her with an expression Beatrice didn't quite know how to interpret. She saw distance, not to mention hostility, but also curiosity.

"Can I talk to you for a little bit?"

He nodded and she sat down on his desk chair.

"How are things?"

Justus shrugged.

"Do you know anything that could help to explain why your dad died?"

"Like what?"

"Maybe he said something, something you didn't think was important at the time but that could help explain all this. It could be something as little as the name of an acquaintance he thought was acting crazy."

"He never said anything like that."

"Sometimes grown-ups want to tell you something but they don't manage to get it out, if you know what I mean."

Beatrice waited, giving him time. She got up and closed the door before she continued.

"Did he ever give you money?"

"A monthly allowance."

"How much is that?"

"Five hundred."

"Is that enough? What do you buy?"

"Clothes, records, sometimes a game."

"Did you ever get a little more?"

"Yeah, if I needed something and they could spare it."

"Did you ever get extra money this fall? Did it seem like your dad had more money than usual?"

"I know where you're going with this. You think Dad stole some money, but he worked for it like everybody else."

"He was unemployed."

"I know. Sagge was the one who ruined everything. He didn't get that Dad was the best welder he'd ever had."

"Did you sometimes visit him down in the shop?"

"Sometimes."

"Do you know how to weld?"

"It's really hard," Justus said emphatically.

"You tried it?"

He nodded.

"The part about Sagge ruining everything—how do you mean that?"

"He made Dad unemployed."

"Did it make your father anxious?"

"It made him . . ."

"Angry?"

Justus nodded.

"What did you used to talk about?"

"The fish."

"I know nothing about aquariums and fish—and I've never seen a tank as big as yours."

"It's the biggest one in town. Dad was really good at it. He sold fish to other people and sometimes he was invited to give talks on cichlids."

"Where did he get invited?"

"Meetings, miniconferences. There's a national organization for people who have cichlids."

"Did he travel a lot?"

"He was supposed to go to Malmö next year. Last spring he went to Gothenburg."

"Do you take care of the aquarium now?"

"Dad showed me how to take care of it."

"You're in eighth grade now. What do you plan on doing when you graduate?"

Beatrice realized her mistake as soon as she had mentioned school, judging by Justus's expression. He shrugged.

"Maybe you can work with aquariums," she said.

"Maybe."

"Didn't your dad ever think about working full-time with the fish?"

Justus didn't answer. His initial grumpiness had been replaced by a kind of passive sadness. The thoughts about his father were like logs on their way downstream that were snagging and accumulating in a narrow passage. Beatrice wanted to coax him forward but didn't want the dam to burst. In her experience, it only created more resistance down the line. Right now she wanted to establish a line of communication, establish trust, push those logs along one by one.

"Is it all right if I come to you with questions about aquariums? In my line of work, and as a mom, I get asked a lot of questions. But there's no way I can know everything about everything."

Justus gave her a knowing look that unsettled her as if he saw right through her.

She got up and opened the door.

"One more thing," she said before she left. "You should know that everyone we've talked to had only good things to say about your dad."

His eyes met hers for a millisecond before she closed the door.

Twenty-five

Ola Haver left the station with a sinking feeling. On his way out he had read the police chief's traditional Christmas message. Several other officers were gathered around the notice board. Some of them made bitter, sarcastic comments, others shrugged and kept walking, unreceptive to the latest whims of their superiors. All the phrases about another successful year, despite the serious challenges, rang more hollow than ever. One of the officers, who worked a beat, burst into laughter. Haver walked away. He didn't want to listen to the criticism, even if it was warranted.

Instead of going home he took a route past Ann Lindell's apartment. He hadn't visited her for several months, but suddenly he felt like talking to her. Maybe it was the meaningless Christmas message that had given him the idea, or else he wanted to discuss the Little John case. He didn't think she would have anything against it. As far as he could tell she couldn't wait to get back to work.

She opened the door wearing an apron, with flour sprinkled on her chest and hands.

"Come in, I'm in the middle of baking," she said and didn't seem at all surprised by his unannounced visit. "My parents are coming up for the holidays so now I have to prove my competence in the housewifely arts."

"Quite a sight, in other words," Haver said, and immediately felt the warmth and ease that characterized his relations with Ann.

He watched her while she finished kneading the dough. She had gained a little weight since having Erik, but not much. The extra kilos suited her. She placed a cloth over the bowl.

"There. Now it has to rise for a while," she said. "How are you doing?"

She sat down across from him. He resisted an impulse to touch her, but it knocked him off-kilter.

"You have flour on your cheek," he said.

She looked at him quizzically, then brushed her cheek with her hand, with the result that it became even whiter.

"Better?"

Haver shook his head. He was happy to hear her voice again. Her bare, flour-covered arms were arousing him. She may have noticed, because an expression of confusion crossed her face. Both of their states of confusion created an electrified atmosphere. He had never felt anything like this for Ann before. Where did this desire come from? He had always thought her attractive, but he had never felt this rising warmth and pulsing desire.

Ann, on the other hand, couldn't place his look and expression at all. She knew him so well that she thought she knew all his moods, but this was something new.

"How is the Little John case coming along?"

"We think there's money behind it," he said and told her about questioning the witnesses to John's big poker win.

"Was he an habitual poker player?"

"Seems like it, according to several people he often played, but never for this much money."

"You have to be brave, dumb, or rich—or a combination of all three—to be willing to bet such amounts," Ann said.

Haver had been thinking along the same lines.

"He must have had some money tucked away to play a game like that," Ann continued.

Haver was enjoying hearing her talk. *Colleagues mean so much,* he thought. *Ann is the one who pulls our team together.*

"Yes, he does seem to have accumulated some. He lent ten thousand to a friend in September, for example."

"That's not an exceptional amount."

"It is if you've been unemployed for a while."

"Would you like some coffee?"

"No, thanks. I've had enough coffee today. But something to drink would be nice."

Ann put some Christmas beer on the table. She knew he liked dark beer.

"Do you remember that conference out in Grisslehamn?" he said, then drank some beer straight from the bottle.

"I remember Ryde drinking too much and losing his temper with Ottosson."

"You said something back then, something that stayed in my mind. Something about the limits and conditions love places on us."

Ann was momentarily thrown for a loop, but answered in a light-hearted tone.

"Did I? I must have been tipsy myself."

"You had a glass or two of wine," Haver said, and regretted bringing it up, but he couldn't stop these thoughts that had been threatening to break out the past few weeks.

"I don't remember talking about anything like that," Ann said defensively.

"It was when you met Edvard."

Ann got up, walked over to the kitchen counter, and peeked under the towel.

"It probably needs more time to rise," Haver said.

Ann leaned against the counter and looked at him.

"I was confused then," she said, "and vulnerable. Both in my professional and private life after Rolf had left me."

"You don't have any luck with men, Ann. That's not a criticism, by the way," he hastened to add when he saw her expression. "You probably give too much to your job, and forget yourself."

"Forget myself," she repeated with a snort. She walked over to the pantry and took out a bottle of wine. She poured herself a glass.

"I'm weaning him," she said.

"Still drinking Rioja," Haver stated, relieved in some way.

She sat down and they continued talking about the case. Ann also wanted to hear all the details of the attack in Sävja and the murder on Johannesbäcksgatan. Haver noticed her eagerness and felt his brain—for the first time in this investigation—start to click into gear. Up till now he had been obsessed with doing everything right. He was formally in charge of the case. Only now could his mind move freely, as it had so many times before in conversations with Ann. He suddenly wondered if she felt any sense of competition with him since he had taken her position while she remained absent. He didn't think so. Ann was not concerned with prestige, and she had a natural air of authority that meant she would have no trouble moving back into her former role at the station.

"How are the girls?" she asked when their conversation about Little John was starting to ebb.

"They're doing great. Growing all the time."

"And Rebecka?"

"It's probably the same for her as for you. She wants to go back to work, or at least I think so. She seems so restless, but then the other day she was talking as if she didn't want to return to the hospital. Something about too many budget cuts and bullshit."

"I read an article by Karlsson, from the county council. I can't say I was impressed."

"Rebecka starts getting worked up if she so much as sees his face in the paper."

Ann poured another glass for herself.

"I should probably get going soon," Haver said, but didn't get up.

He knew he should call Rebecka, but felt somehow embarrassed about doing so in front of Ann, to reveal that he needed to call home and say where he was. It was a ridiculous thought, but right now he didn't want to bring his wife into this. He didn't want to think about the standstill their life had come to, an armed truce of sorts, where neither party was willing to get up out of the trenches, nor willing to lay down arms.

"You look worried," Ann said.

He had an impulse to tell her everything, but quelled it and mumbled something about having a lot to do.

"You know how it is. You run around all the time, back and forth, and all the time new shit is coming in. Sammy is completely frustrated. His work with the youth groups has come to a dead end. It started so well but now we don't have the people and the resources to keep it up."

"We should send out a message to all scum: 'Please suspend all criminal activity for the next six months as we are in the middle of a youth project.'"

Haver laughed. He was about to have more beer when he realized that the bottle was empty. Ann set out a new one and he drank without thinking of the fact that he was driving home. *I should call her,* he thought again and put down the bottle.

"You were thirsty," Ann said.

"I have to call someone," he said.

Haver excused himself and walked out to the hall, then returned almost immediately.

"Everything's fine," he said, but Ann read the opposite in his face. Neither of them said anything. Ann sipped her wine and Haver looked at her. Their eyes met. Haver's unexpected feeling of lust returned. He gripped the beer bottle. Ann put her hand on his arm.

"Why don't you tell me about it?" she asked.

"Sometimes I feel like getting a divorce," he said. "Even though I love Rebecka. I play with the idea, like a masochist, to punish myself or her, for I don't know what. Before, I was drawn to her like a magnet. And I think it was that way for her too. Now we're indifferent. She looks at me as if I were a stranger."

"Maybe you are a stranger to her sometimes," Ann said.

"She watches me as if she were waiting for something."

"Or someone. Is she still jealous? You said something about that when we went to Spain."

"I don't know. I don't think she really cares."

Ann saw that he was becoming more and more uncomfortable. She worried that he would start to cry and she couldn't handle that. She had to think of sensible things to say, even if they weren't so sensible. She was afraid of the emotionality, a trap she would willingly fall into. She would become a victim, no doubt about it. Not because she loved him but because her longing for intimacy gnawed at her like hunger, so strongly that she thought her carefully constructed life would collapse altogether. She hadn't been close to a man since last summer. *I'm drying up,* she thought from time to time. Occasionally she stroked herself but it never satisfied her. She thought about Edvard on his island, Gräsö, a thousand miles away. She would have given anything to feel his hand on her body. He was gone for good, had slipped out of her life after one night of drunken sex. Her longing and self-disgust went hand in hand.

Haver took her hand and she let him hold it. The silence was painful, but they couldn't bear to break it with words.

"Maybe I should go," Haver said in an unsteady voice. He cleared his throat and looked at her unhappily.

"What about you?" he continued, and that was a question she absolutely didn't want to hear or answer.

"One day at a time," she said. "Sure it's hard sometimes, but I have Erik, and he's a doll."

That was what was expected of her, and sure, sometimes the baby was enough. But more and more she felt the need for another kind of life.

"It's hard sometimes," she repeated.

"Do you still miss Edvard?"

Stop it, she thought and was suddenly angry at his intrusive questions, but then she forced herself to calm down. He wasn't trying to make her angry.

"Sometimes. I feel like we threw away our chance. We never really managed to get in sync."

He squeezed her hand.

"I'm sure you'll meet a great guy," he said and stood.

Stay, she wanted to say, but stopped herself. They walked out into the hall. Haver stretched an arm out for his coat but then it was as if his arm changed direction on its own and found its way around her shoulders and drew her close. She sighed, or was it a sob? Slowly, she put her arms around his back and hugged him gently. One minute went by. Then she loosened herself from his grip, but remained close. She felt his breath and was enjoying standing so close to him. He stroked her cheek, brushed her ear with the tips of his fingers. She shivered. He leaned over. They looked at each other for a tenth of a second before they kissed. *What did Ola Haver taste like?* she asked herself after he had left.

They didn't look at each other again, gliding apart as in a play, mumbling good-bye. He closed the door behind him with care. Ann put one hand on the door while the other touched her lips. *That was bad,* she thought, but then changed her mind. There had been nothing bad in their short meeting.

A kiss, filled with longing and searching, friendship but also lust that threatened to erupt in a flow of lava and lead who knows where.

She went back into the kitchen. The dough was swelling over the sides of the bowl. She removed the kitchen towel and studied the mass. Suddenly she started to cry and she wished Ola had stayed for a while, just a short while. She imagined he would have liked to see her make the bread. She would have liked that. Her sleeves rolled up, the warm sticky mass of the dough, and his gaze. She would have formed and baked the golden loaves. But instead the dough lay in front of her, a shapeless lump she did not want to touch.

Ola Haver walked slowly down the steps, then quickened his pace. His stomach was churning, his brain was in chaos, and a burning feeling of regret followed him out into the snow. When would it ever stop snowing?

He thought of Rebecka and the children and hurried on. Once he was out in the parking lot he looked up at the building and tried to find Ann's window, but he wasn't sure which one it was. He overcame the impulse to run back. Instead he got into the car but didn't turn on the engine immediately. He shivered with cold and realized that their short meeting would forever change their working relationship. Would they even be able to continue working together? Their kiss had been innocent, but potentially explosive. He had never kissed another woman since he'd met Rebecka. Would she notice anything different? He ran his tongue over his teeth. The outer traces linger for only a moment while the inner ones remain. In a vague way he felt pleased with himself. He had conquered Ann, an attractive woman who wasn't known for being easily wooed. He knew it was a ridiculous thought, but the coldness at home had created a psychological space for this feeling of triumph he clung to like a piece of candy. He toyed with the idea of starting a relationship with Ann. Would she want to? It was doubtful. Would he be able to do it? Even more doubtful.

"What's that white stuff on your clothes?"

Haver looked down at his chest and blushed.

"Ann was baking," he said sheepishly. "I must have brushed against something."

"Oh, she was baking," Rebecka said and disappeared into the bedroom.

He looked around. The kitchen was sparkling clean and everything had been put in its place. The counter gleamed. The only thing that marred the picture was a candle that had burned halfway, and a glass of wine with some dregs left in the bottom. Candle wax had run down in a striking pattern over the verdigris-coated candlestick, an object Haver had inherited from his grandmother. He still remembered how she would light it on family celebrations and special holidays. The wineglass was green and he recalled buying it with Rebecka in Gotland during their first trip together. The wine was a red wine that Haver had bought for New Year's Eve, which they had been planning to celebrate with Sammy Nilsson and his wife.

He heard her moving around in the bedroom. The roller blind was pulled down, a dresser drawer was shut, and the bedside lamp was turned on. He could imagine what she looked like, the tight-lipped attitude and slightly abrupt movements she made when she was upset.

He opened the refrigerator and took out a beer, then sat down at the kitchen table and waited for the storm to break.

Twenty-six

Lennart gave a short laugh and got out of bed. The alarm clock had woken him brutally. He laughed when he imagined how everyone around him would react to seeing the alcoholic, good-for-nothing Lennart Jonsson get dressed, sober, with the coffeemaker going and the Thermos set out, all at a quarter to six in the morning. No beer gripped by shaking hands and no fumbling search for a half-smoked cigarette under piles of dirty dishes. A scene flashed through his mind: a morning he had woken up to see Klasse Nordin drinking from the plastic bags he had earlier vomited wine into. *Fuck those morning-afters,* he thought.

At least he wouldn't be cold. His father would have envied him his Helly Hansen gear. Albin had often complained about the cold when he came back from work. In the summer he had complained about the heat. The temperature was rarely perfect, but on the other hand Albin almost never complained about anything else. Not even during the worst of Lennart's teenage years, when he was the most messed up.

"T-t-try t-to act l-l-l-like a human being," he had sometimes managed to get out. But he had rarely said anything stronger than that.

Lennart wasn't used to it, but it felt good to be getting up at half past five. He was almost able to convince himself that he was a hardworking man going about his daily business on an early December morning, with the snow coming down even heavier than before. The fact that he was setting out to work with something that fell into his father's sphere reinforced the sense of importance. He was going to accomplish something today, point to a sign and say, *We're clearing snow away here, please walk on the other side of the street.* Maybe even add a *please* if it was a civilized-looking person. Most of all he wanted some of his drinking buddies to walk by. Or, on second thought, no. They would just start shooting the breeze and distract him from his work.

He owned a good pair of work boots, snow overalls, and a heavy winter coat. In addition he had the mittens from Fosforos that could handle up to thirty degrees below zero. They lay in the very back of the closet, black, rough, and with matted inner mittens. He was fully equipped.

The vacuum flask—of the brand name Condor, where someone a long time ago had scratched out the final *r* and inserted *m*—was fiery red with a gray mug. Lennart came to think of the tractor driver on Brantings square, the one he had met that night he walked home from talking to Berit. He had been a good guy, that's what Albin would have said. He knew he would remember the warmth inside the tractor and the sweet coffee for a long time.

Was it being sober that had whet his appetite for work? Since John died he had been mostly sober, drinking only a little beer. He paused by the window. Thoughts of John returned in full force, the memories coming thick and fast. How long would this last? Until the murderer was caught, and then for the rest of his life, was his sense. To lose the person who was closest to you, whose life was so completely tied up in yours, that was a lifelong loss. Never to be able to chat with John in that relaxed way, the way he couldn't with anyone else. That was an irreplacable loss.

Pull yourself together, he thought. *You're going out to shovel some snow, and then hunt down a killer. You can drink yourself to death once that's done.* He smiled crookedly. Deep down inside he was nursing the idea that he could maybe make a decent person out of himself. Maybe not a worker who toiled from seven to four. He was too lazy for that, and he had a bad back. But maybe part-time or so, help out in Micke's business from time to time. He knew something about working metal, he was the son of a roofer and welder, for God's sake. And in the winter there was snow. With the Fosforos mittens he was good to go for the whole day. How he wished people would see him directing old ladies to safety under the falling snow, the shovel in his hand, and an enormous, matted, black, and warm mitten resting on the handle.

Trying to figure out what his brother had done after he left Micke's apartment had made Lennart realize how little he really knew John. How was he when he met other people? What role did he play in these tropical-fish organizations? A lot of people listened to him when he talked about fish, they saw the expert in him. They didn't know his story, to them he was just that nice guy who had a passion for African cichlids. In their circle, John was another person interested in fish. In an unarticulated way Lennart now saw this as a betrayal, a betrayal of the life he and John had had together. Earlier he had looked on John's interest as a hobby, no better or worse than anything else. Other people bowled or went to rally races, but it didn't change who they were. He had been proud of his brother's aquarium, of course, gladly accepting part of the glory of having a brother with the largest aquarium in town, but now he realized that John had been the respected expert, the one you called and asked for advice. In short, another man, another role.

And then this poker playing. He would never have guessed that John had won such amounts. Why hadn't he said anything? John wasn't one to volunteer information but he could have told his only brother when he won a small fortune. Why this silence? Not even Berit had been in on it. The only one who knew how much money was involved was Micke, even if he didn't want to say.

What had John been cooking up? This was the question Lennart had been asking himself the past few days. He thought the answer would lead to whoever had murdered John. There was something his brother had been working on, something secret, that had led to his death.

Lennart would have been able to protect his brother. If only John had told him, Lennart would have watched his back like a hawk around the clock. That's what brothers were for. But John had kept Lennart in the dark on this and that was half the heartache.

Micke was already in place on Dragarbrunnsgatan with the company truck pulled up on the sidewalk. He had already unloaded most of the equipment when Lennart arrived.

"It would make more sense to do this on an early Sunday morning," Micke said and brought out some red cones.

Lennart didn't say anything, pitching in to help in silence. It was several years now since he had worn his full winter gear and he felt self-conscious. He concentrated on the work, but it wasn't complicated. The truck had to be fully unloaded, all the warning signs and blockades set up.

Micke was talking to the building manager, who gave them the keys and helped arrange roof access. Lennart looked up. It was high, not worse than he could manage, but Micke would never let him up there.

His fear of heights had come and gone. When his father had taken him up on rooftops he had never been scared. That had come later. On construction sites he had never liked working on high scaffolding but had never said anything.

The first hour went well. The morning traffic grew heavier and Lennart kept an eye out for people who might walk into the restricted area. It was possible to ignore the cold if you walked up and down slapping your arms across your chest for circulation.

The bus drivers nodded at him as they drove past. An older woman complained about the inconvenience. An old acquaintance from Ymergatan walked by but pretended not to recognize him, or else Lennart really was impossible to recognize in his full gear.

Around nine he grew anxious. That was always the time when the usual suspects, a loose-knit group of substance abusers, gathered around the front doors of the state liqour store. Luckily Micke came down from the roof for a snack and Lennart's thoughts were interrupted. They drank coffee in the truck. Steam rose from their cups and their breath fogged up the windows immediately.

"The job's going well," Micke said. "How are the old ladies?"

"It's okay. Most of them are in a good mood today. It's a bit boring is all."

Micke looked at him. Maybe he sensed what was going on in Lennart's head. He poured him another cup.

"Do you miss being up on the roof?" he asked.

"No, I can't say I do."

"Did you ever work together with Albin?"

"No, not really. Occasionally I'd help out. Now no one would let me up there."

They sat in silence for the rest of the break. Lennart felt his anxiety return. He should be hunting down a killer, not standing on a street trying to look busy.

The rest of the morning they moved the barricades a few times and worked their way down the street. Pieces of ice broke off and smashed into the street with a delicate yet hard sound. People paused on their way past, fascinated with the beauty of the sparkling icicles and the glittering clouds of ice thrown up as they smashed onto the pavement.

Lennart shoveled both ice and snow off the sidewalk, as he also kept an eye up and down the road. He stopped and rested for a moment, leaning on the shovel. A familiar face appeared, a woman pushing a stroller. Lennart took a few steps closer. Their eyes met.

The woman nodded and slowed down.

"Hi, Lennart. So you're working out here in the cold?"

"Someone's got to do it."

"How is it going? I heard about John."

Lennart looked up at the building. He walked closer to her.

"Do you know anything?"

"I'm on maternity leave, as you can see."

"But you must have heard something."

Ann Lindell shook her head.

"Do you know he gambled and won a lot of money?"

"I heard about it, but don't know any details."

"I can give you some leads."

"Give them to Ola Haver, he's the one in charge of the investigation. Do you know him?"

Lennart shook his head.

"No, Sammy was the one who came to my place. I don't like him at all."

"Sammy may have his quirks, but he's a good police officer."

"A good police officer," Lennart repeated.

A load of snow came off the roof. Lennart took a few steps out into the street. No pedestrians were around. He returned to the sidewalk and again drew close to Lindell.

"I want to talk to you."

"I'm on leave."

"Can't we talk anyway? Have a cup of coffee? I can't do it right now, I have to make sure no little old ladies get killed."

Lindell smiled. She looked down at Erik bundled up in the stroller. Only the tip of his nose and mouth were visible.

"I'll come by your place at five thirty. Okay?"

He nodded. More snow fell. Lindell knew what she was doing was wrong, but Lennart might have some valuable information. He clearly had no confidence in Sammy, and it was possible that he would tell her something he wasn't willing to share with her colleague. Her desire to work made her willing to bend the rules.

"Are you still at the same address?"

He nodded and returned to the street. Micke's head could be seen high above them. Despite the distance, Lennart could tell he was irritated. Lennart gestured placatingly with his hands and deliberately walked out into the very middle of the street.

Twenty-seven

Ola Haver studied the knife. It was roughly twenty centimeters long with a black shaft and a sharp edge. Who used a knife like this? Haver had checked with a few officers who liked to hunt and they had judged the knife too cumbersome for hunting and fishing. The same verdict had been issued by the riffraff in town: the knife was too big to be easily concealed in clothing. It might be a knife some teenager would use to impress his friends, but it would never become something you carried habitually. Berglund had proposed the idea that it was a weapon someone had bought as a tourist. Maybe the sheath, which they had not recovered, was finely decorated and that was what had tempted the owner to buy it in the first place.

Haver turned it this way and that. He had questioned the young man again, the one who claimed to have stolen it from a pickup truck parked in the hospital garage. Haver was inclined to believe him, because he had seen fear and not lies in his eyes. Mattias was no killer, even if he was a small-time thief and troublemaker. You could only hope he would have second thoughts about the way his life was headed after finding himself dragged into a murder case.

Haver had asked Lundin to check who normally parked in the garage, which turned out to yield a daunting number. Hospital employees parked in a reserved area, and the rest was open to patients, friends, and relatives. Hundreds of people parked in the garage every day. Haver remembered that he himself had parked there one day a few years ago when he had seen the orthopedic surgeon.

They had talked about trying to compile a list of all the people who would have had reason to park there on that day, but finally decided it would take too long. The only thing they had to go on was Mattias's vague recollection of a pickup, maybe red and white. When they had taken him to the parking garage to point out the place where the car had been parked, he had started wavering about whether or not the truck had had a hard or soft tonneau cover. In other words, they were talking about a dozen different possible makes and models. The only thing Mattias had been really sure about was the color red.

Had the killer been wounded and had to go to the hospital? They had checked with the ER and surgery, but that had yielded nothing.

Finding the murder weapon often gave way to more leads, but in this case it seemed like a dead end. The knife would become important only if they fixed on a suspect and could tie the person to the weapon.

Haver put the knife back in the plastic bag and leaned back in his chair, letting his thoughts move alternately from the investigation to Ann Lindell. Their kiss had ballooned into a cloud over his head. A gnawing feeling of uncertainty gripped him. For the first time in his marriage with Rebecka there was real doubt. The squabbles and conflicts of the fall, punctuated by equally wearying periods of silence and unasked questions, had escalated to the level of warfare. Rebecka hadn't said anything else about his visit to Ann Lindell or the flour on his clothes. She had simply given him a cold look, moved quickly and nonchalantly around the house, avoiding him mainly. She had spent most of the morning in the bathroom, showering for an unusually long time, and in the bedroom. They had not had breakfast at the same time, which Haver was grateful for. At least he didn't have to face the reproachful looks.

Now he was dreading going home. Should he tell her the truth? She would be furious. She was the jealous type, he knew that from before, not least when it came to Ann. Haver tried not to mention her at home since he knew that Rebecka was threatened by the fact that they were so close. Up till now there had been no grounds for her jealousy, but if he told her about the kiss, all hell would break loose. Even if she accepted his explanation and tried to erase the whole thing from her mind, the underlying suspicion would always be there.

He decided not to tell. It would stop at a sprinkling of flour on his chest, an embrace, and a kiss, but he could not deny the curious mixture of pride and shame he felt at betraying Rebecka. A soft voice inside encouraged him to get in touch with Ann again, to continue the foray into explosive, dangerous territory.

It had been a long time since he had felt attractive. And now someone had wanted to touch him. He wasn't the one who had taken all the initiative. Ann was just as guilty, if one could call it guilt. Even though they had stopped at an embrace and a single kiss, Haver sensed that Ann would have considered going further, and when he thought about this he was suddenly angry at her. She had tempted him, damn it. She knew very well how jealous Rebecka was—she had used him, his vulnerability had been written in his face. *No, that wasn't how it was,* he told himself and couldn't maintain the anger. They were two adults, both in need of human warmth. Ann was the woman, besides Rebecka, whom he felt closest to. They had been brought close through their work, and apart from their mutual respect for each other's abilities there had always been an undercurrent of sexual attraction.

Now the foundation was trembling. The underground channels were quaking and their hot inner lakes threatened to spill over. Was it love or more a desire for warmth, an expression of friendship where the boundaries had simply become blurred?

So much was broken in his relationship with Rebecka, he could see that now. The passion in Ann's embrace and in the answer of his body was not only a rush of lust but a yearning for intimacy, evidence of the emotional poverty of his life. Rebecka and he were unhappy together, it was that simple, and Haver had needed only one single kiss to see this clearly.

Could he continue to live with Rebecka? He had to. They had two children together and still loved each other. At least he thought they did.

Twenty-eight

Allan Fredriksson read through Ryde's report from Vivan Molin's apartment. There was nothing noteworthy. The place was full of Vincent Hahn's fingerprints.

The only thing they had found in the apartment that made Fredriksson raise his eyebrows was a pair of handcuffs that the technicians had found stuffed away in a closet, together with two porn films and a vibrator. Battery-operated with two speed settings, Ryde had noted.

They were still establishing her network of friends and relatives. Her parents were dead and she had no siblings. There was a note in her address book about an "Aunt Bettan" and a phone number with a 021 area code. They had called it, with no results yet. Fredriksson had asked a cadet, a Julius Sandemar, to contact Hahn's brother again. He seemed to be the only one who would be able to give them more information about possible relatives. He would also need to be informed that Vincent was now wanted for suspected assault and murder.

Someone threw out the idea that Hahn might try to leave the country and look up his brother in Israel, but it turned out that Hahn had never applied for a passport. Nonetheless, officials at Arlanda airport were notified to be on their guard.

Fredriksson had no idea where Hahn might have gone. *Strange,* he thought. *A person without any social network. Where does a person without any contacts go? To a bar?* He had trouble seeing Hahn nursing a drink in a bar. *To the library?* More plausible. Sandemar would have to go down to the public library and show the employees there a photo of Hahn. Was there a branch in Sävja? Fredriksson didn't think so. Many of the smaller branches were being closed down.

They had checked the clinic in Sävja and the Akademiska Hospital, but no patient had ever registered under the name Hahn. He had been treated for depression at Ulleråker mental institution, but that was eight years ago. The doctor who had treated him had moved elsewhere.

The search of his apartment had also yielded almost no clues. Fredriksson suspected that Hahn would eventually turn up somewhere, but sitting around merely waiting for a killer to turn up was not his style. He wanted to track him down, but he was running out of ideas.

A traditional criminal was easier, his hangouts and associates more predictable. A psychically disturbed individual, a loner, was much more difficult to find. On the other hand, in Fredriksson's experience, once the ball was rolling they were easier to catch because they were more likely to be careless and make mistakes.

Fredriksson was convinced that they were looking for two different murderers at this point. It was really only Sammy Nilsson who insisted that Hahn had had something to do with Little John's murder. His theory was that Hahn was taking revenge, maybe even for incidents that happened as long ago as his school days. Sammy didn't think that the connection between John and Hahn was a coincidence and was still searching for a possible explanation. Ottosson let him be for the moment. Sammy had started looking up old classmates of John, Gunilla Karlsson, and Hahn. As it turned out, most of them still lived in Uppsala, and Sammy had already worked through a number of people on the list, but so far nothing had come out that would indicate that Hahn was on a rampage to revenge himself on them. But there could very well be some event in Vincent Hahn's mind that would not seem like a motive for revenge in other people's eyes.

After leaving his former sister-in-law's apartment, Vincent Hahn had walked to Vaksalagatan and taken the bus into town. The hat he had stolen the night before covered his wound. He had found seven hundred kronor in her apartment and that was the extent of his funds. Now there was only one place for him to go.

The smell of people on the bus confused him and made him angry, but thinking about the rattling sound Vivan had made as he pulled the telephone cord tighter around her neck made him feel bigger. He could feel superior to the other people on the bus. They had nothing to do with him, they were small. He was big.

Vivan had assured him she wouldn't tell on him, but he had seen in her eyes that she was lying. He had felt a rush of excitement while her body was convulsing under his. She had tried to scratch his face but hadn't been able to reach. His knees had held her arms down. It was all over in a few minutes. He had pulled her along the floor and in under the bed and left her there to rot. They would find her when she started to stink, but not before. And by that time he'd be long gone.

He smiled. The feeling of satisfaction at having resolved everything so well filled him with an almost painful joy. Painful because he was unable to share it with anyone. But within a week he would get to read about it in the paper. Then people would know that Vincent Hahn was not to be treated lightly.

The headlines of the *Upsala Nya Tidning* at the railway station startled him. UPPSALA MURDER STILL UNSOLVED, it said. He stared at the black letters and tried to understand what it meant. Had Gunilla Karlsson died? But that wasn't possible. Granted, she had collapsed in the yard outside the building, but it was he who had been closer to death. He bought the paper, pushed it down in his pocket, and hurried on. Some event was taking place in the plaza in front of the station. A dozen people or so dressed up as Santa were performing a dance of sorts. The small bells in their hands made tinkling sounds. Suddenly they all threw themselves to the ground and remained there, motionless. Vincent watched them, fascinated. One after another the Santas came back to life and joined hands to form a circle around the thirteenth Santa, who continued to lie on the ground.

"This is the darkness of Christmas," shouted one of the Santas.

Vincent thought it must be a doomsday sect of some kind. He liked it.

The sound of the bells followed him as he walked down Bangårdsgatan.

The bingo hall was unusually empty. He nodded at a few other regulars, but most of them were absorbed in their game. Vincent sat down in his usual spot and unfolded his newspaper. The first thing he saw was a picture of John Jonsson. The reporter summarized what had happened and presented a variety of motives. John's colorful past was emphasized, the fact that he was a serious gambler alongside his burning passion for tropical fish.

A representative from the tropical-fish society had spoken out and declared John's death a tragedy and an irreplaceable loss for the society and all cichlid lovers.

The paper, however, was more interested in John's potential connections with Uppsala's shady underworld and illegal gambling circuit.

Vincent read with great interest. He remembered John very well. He had been a short, quiet boy who inspired respect with his judicious use of words but was also insecure. He had lived not far from Vincent and in middle school they had often walked to school together. Vincent would walk quietly and sense that John appreciated the fact that he wasn't chattering away.

Vincent put down the paper. The headache was coming back. He stared at the picture of his former classmate and wondered when he had died. Had he been included in Vincent's plan for revenge? The bullies had to be punished. He flinched as if being struck. His father leaning over him, his mother's whimpers from the kitchen, the repeated blows.

"No!" he shouted, and the other bingo players looked disapprovingly at him.

The blows rained down on him and he crouched to ward them off. Once he had struck back, but it had only made things worse. Now his father crawled around in his body like a parasite. John's picture in the paper reminded him of his father, the blows meted out without words. Why had it been him? He was the youngest, the most defenseless. Wolfgang received the love, he the blows, the humiliation.

Had he murdered John? Vincent looked at the picture in the paper again. Perhaps the time had come for revenge. No one had cared. Where had his father's rage come from, the rage that drove him to develop increasingly sadistic forms of punishment? In the beginning his fists had been enough, then came the strap, and finally the most horrific, the face forced down into the sink.

Vincent shook. The headache threatened to take over, to transform him into a crawling pile of bone and skin. *You got what was coming to you, John. If it wasn't me it was someone working in my spirit.* He was sweating in the woolen cap. His head itched. He wanted to cry but knew his tear ducts didn't work the way they were supposed to. He had stopped crying at the age of thirteen.

He rested his head in his hands and felt the gaze of others in the room. He should start playing. John was close-by. A neutral picture, without expression or clarity.

"You died," he mumbled. Soon it would be Janne's turn, or someone else. Vincent could no longer remember the rankings of the list he had drawn up. The picture of John in his mind was replaced by his father's. He had woken up too late! When the time came for revenge, his father had disappeared into illness, the worms eating away at him until he was just a skeleton. Vincent remembered the thin hand gripping the hospital bed railing. He had taken it and squeezed it as hard as he could. His father had cried out, looked at him with watery eyes, and understood. Then he had smiled his satanic smile, the smile that seduced the women around him, and charmed the world, but Vincent knew better.

The picture in the paper of his father smiled at him and he tried to hit it. One of the bingo hall employees came over to him.

"You'll have to go," he said. "You're disturbing the others."

The voice was not unkind.

"I'll go," Vincent said submissively. "But my head hurts so much." He pulled off his cap and revealed the makeshift bandage over the wound.

"What did you do?"

"My daddy hit me."

"Your father did this?"

Vincent nodded.

"And my brother too."

He stood up.

"I have to go now."

"You should see a doctor," the employee said.

"My father was a doctor, or something like that. Mommy spoke mainly German. She was Jewish and he a Nazi. Or communist, maybe. No, that can't be. They're red and Daddy was black."

"Your father was black?"

Vincent staggered out onto the street. Bangårdsgatan was like a wind tunnel where the snow was swept along with a howling sound. People steeled themselves against the wind, pulling shawls, scarves, and hats more tightly around them. The sounds of their footsteps were muffled by the snow. An ambulance drove by. Then a series of trucks obscured the view. He wanted to be able to see farther and made his way to the river.

Twenty-nine

Lennart Jonsson was exhausted. It was half past four and dark out-side as well as in the apartment. He let the apartment remain in darkness while he took off his clothes and let them fall in a pile. He was covered in dried sweat but it was not an unpleasant feeling. He brushed his hand over his hairy chest, across his left shoulder and left forearm. Some of his old musculature remained. He scratched his crotch and felt a stirring sensation of lust.

His back ached but he was so used to it that he hardly noticed it. He had some pills for arthritis relief left and decided to take one. On his way to the bathroom he noticed an unfamiliar scent. He stopped and sniffed. Perfume, an unmistakable smell of perfume.

He looked around. Someone had been in his apartment. Was the person still here? He snatched his pants up and started walking to the kitchen with the idea of finding something to defend himself with. Was he mistaken? No, the smell was undeniably here. Was it the scent of a woman or a man? He remained alert for any sounds.

He tiptoed into the kitchen, carefully pulled out a drawer, and took out a bread knife.

"Put it down," he heard a voice say, "or you'll regret it."

The voice came from somewhere in the kitchen and Lennart realized that someone was sitting at the kitchen table. He recognized the voice but couldn't place it in his confused state. He judged the threat as serious and didn't hesitate in throwing down the knife.

"Who the hell are you?"

"I think it's time you turned on the light."

Lennart quickly pulled on his pants, then turned and switched on the light. Mossa was sitting at the table, a pistol laid out in front of him.

"You? What the hell—"

"Sit down. We need to talk."

Lennart did as he was told. He sensed what was coming.

"It wasn't me," he said, and the Iranian smiled mockingly.

"That's what they always say," he said and took up the gun. "Tell me instead who ran straight to the cops."

"Not me, in any case," Lennart said. "Do you think I'm stupid?"

"Yes," Mossa said. "Stupid enough to try to win their favor. You thought the cops would help you. I think you are stupid enough for that. I trusted you. We talked about your brother. I liked your brother, but I don't like you."

"Someone else must have squealed. Someone who played that night."

He didn't want to say what he thought, that Micke had told the police what he knew. But could he have known the names of the players? John might have told him, but it wasn't likely. He kept quiet about such things.

"Stop giving me lies. You don't believe it yourself," Mossa said. "You turned me in. I couldn't care less about the others, but no one runs to the cops with my name, you understand?"

Lennart nodded.

"I get it, I do, but it really wasn't me. I want to do this on my own, you know that. That's why I looked for you."

"In order to have something to barter with."

"You have a brother, Mossa. You love him, you should get it. I'm doing everything I can to find the guy who killed John."

"Don't mix Ali in this."

"He is a brother. John was a brother."

Mossa sat quietly and seemed to weigh his words.

"I think you are *a shit*," he said finally and stood up, the gun still in his hand. "Put on a shirt. I don't want to shoot a man with a bare chest."

"Kill me then, you dumb bastard. Do you think I give a fuck?" Lennart said belligerently and looked at Mossa with defiance.

Mossa smiled.

"You really are stupid, aren't you?"

"Did you kill John?"

The Iranian shook his head and raised the gun so it pointed at Lennart's knees.

"It wasn't me," Lennart said with sweat running down his face.

In a way he felt relieved. He had experienced this sensation before, one night when his drinking had led to an episode of heart palpitations. That time he had been prepared to die, had made peace with his shitty existence. He had gotten up, drunk some water and looked at himself in the mirror, and then gone back to bed with his heart jumping around in his chest.

Mossa raised the gun a few centimeters.

"You remind me of an Armenian I once knew," Mossa said. "He also met his death with courage."

Lennart sank to his knees.

"Plant the bullet in my skull," he said and closed his eyes.

Mossa lowered his gun, kicked Lennart in the mouth, and leaned over him.

"If you want to play the detective, then go talk to his whore for a wife," he hissed and left the apartment. Lennart, who had fallen down when he was kicked, lay still on the floor until he started shivering with cold.

Twenty minutes later, Lennart had managed to take a warm shower and wrap himself up in a sheet. The kick had busted his lip and he had to tape it up to stop the bleeding. He jumped when the front doorbell rang. He had forgotten all about Lindell stopping by.

He opened the door, prepared for anything, until he saw the stroller.

"What the fuck?" he said and backed up into the apartment.

They sat down in the living room.

"What happened to you?"

"I slipped at work," Lennart said. "The shovel caught me right here."

"You don't have any Band-Aids?"

"Tape works fine."

All the air had gone out of him. The early morning, the work in the snow, Mossa's unexpected visit, and the warm shower had so drained him that he could hardly keep his eyes open. If Lindell hadn't been sitting there he would have fallen asleep in a minute.

"You said something about a lead," Lindell said. "Why didn't you say anything to Sammy Nilsson?"

"Like I said, I don't care for him. He's too cocky, comes on too strong."

"You do too, sometimes," Lindell said. "For your information."

Lennart smiled. With his lip taped up it looked like a grimace.

"So now you're the private eye, huh?"

"Not at all. But you did pique my interest."

"Why are the cops not spending any time on trying to catch my brother's killer?"

"I think you're wrong. From what I understand, this case is top priority."

"The fuck it is. You think he's some poor shit who doesn't matter. If he had been a VIP, things would look a lot different."

"All murder cases are treated with the same seriousness," Lindell said calmly. "You know that."

"So what have you found out? He stopped by Micke's apartment and then he disappeared. Have you checked Micke's alibi?"

"I take it for granted."

"You take for granted—I don't take shit for granted. Do you know John gambled?"

Lindell nodded.

"Have you checked with his gambling buddies? They're probably a pack of rats."

"I'm not officially on this case, but clearly every part of John's life will be carefully scrutinized."

"That means you don't have anything. What happened to the money anyway?"

"What money?" Lindell said, aware of the fact that he meant the poker winnings.

"He won at poker, didn't you know that?"

Lindell shook her head.

"You don't fool me," Lennart said evenly. He was used to cops doing this, playing dumb, and he wondered how he could get her to spill what she knew.

Lindell smiled, got up, and went over to the stroller.

"And what about Berit, the hypocritical cow," he said. "She doesn't say shit to me, just talks to Mom and Justus. I'm the one she should be talking to, but no, she's too fucking good for that. She's the one sitting on the money."

Lindell watched him clench his hands.

"I'm his brother and if anyone can sort this out it's me, and damn if she isn't keeping something from me."

He looked up quickly and met Lindell's gaze.

"But she's the widow, probably cries all the time, and you treat her with kid gloves, isn't that right?"

"I'm sure she's been questioned just like anyone else," Lindell said. "And even if you are John's brother, Berit is the one who should be able to give us the most information about John's movements during his last few days. Why would she need to keep something secret, as you were suggesting?"

"She's always . . . ," Lennart began, then stopped. "You can't trust broads." Lindell had trouble determining if he was making a little joke or if there was some substance behind the half-articulated accusations against his sister-in-law.

"I'll get it out of her, whatever it is," he said, his teeth clenched. "I'm going to get the guy who killed my brother and if it takes her down too I couldn't care less. She asked for it."

Lindell sat down again.

"Who hit you?"

"What do you mean?"

"There's blood on the kitchen floor," Lindell said.

"I started bleeding again after I came home."

"In the kitchen?"

"Is it against the law?"

His raised voice woke Erik, who started whimpering in the stroller. Lindell walked over and reassured him, rocking the stroller.

"I think you had a visitor," she said after the whimpering stopped.

"So what?"

"If you want to help us catch your brother's killer you'd better play with open cards."

"You're just like Sammy Nilsson," Lennart said and got to his feet. The sheet trailed on the floor as he walked into the bedroom.

Lindell heard him moving around and assumed he was putting clothes on. She saw that she was right when he came back wearing pants and a T-shirt. The piece of tape on his lip had come off.

"You should have someone look that over," she said. "I think you need stitches."

"I thought you had left already."

Lennart watched her cross the street with the stroller, aiming for the bus stop.

"Fucking bitch," he mumbled.

It was only now that Mossa's final comment fully penetrated his mind. Mossa had used the word *whore,* and that was a strong statement coming from him. He was a tough guy but one who chose his words with care. If he used the word *whore* he meant it, not like how some guys just tossed it out when they were talking about women. Everyone who knew Mossa knew that he was respectful of women, that he worshipped his mother, and that he was always conscientious about sending his greetings to his friends' sisters and wives.

He had called Berit a whore. That could only mean one thing: she had been unfaithful. "Talk to his whore for a wife," he had said. The meaning of the words hit Lennart with an almost physical violence. Had she really had someone else?

His tiredness was gone. He put on socks, boots, and outerwear, and was out on the street within minutes. The route he chose was identical to the one he had walked the night he found out that John had died. Instead of tears this time, he was filled with anger and unanswered questions throbbing in his head as he half ran, half walked.

The snow was as deep as it had been that night. There was no snowplow on Brantings square but instead a group of drunk youngsters singing Christmas carols. He stopped and watched them. He had also been here, making noise in the same way, thrown out of the Brantings community center and a drug-free Christmas party, drunk out of his mind on beer, fourteen years old and already an outsider, literally and figuratively, something that still ached in his body, a mixture of shame and hate. God, how he had hated, breaking a window of the public library and throwing bicycles around. The police had arrested him and Albin had had to pay for the damages.

He walked over to the youngsters.

"Anyone have a cell phone?"

They stared at him.

"I need to make a call."

"Get your own, mister."

"I need one now."

"There's a pay phone over there."

Lennart grabbed one of the boys.

"Give me a phone or I swear I'll fucking smash your head in," he hissed at the terror-stricken boy.

"You can borrow mine," said a girl and stretched it out to him.

"Thanks," Lennart said and dropped the boy. "Two minutes," he said and walked off to the side.

He called Micke, who had just fallen asleep on the sofa and answered incoherently. They talked for a few minutes. Lennart threw the cell phone into the snow and took off half running over Skomakarberget.

Berit had just turned off the TV. For some reason she had become more interested in the news since John's death. Even Justus joined her in front of the television. Maybe it was to measure their misfortune against everything else happening in the world, to feel that they weren't alone. Quite the opposite, as it turned out, violence was doubled and reprised many times over on the TV screen.

She threw the remote control onto the table and put her hand on Justus's shoulder. He was about to get up, but she wanted him to stay on the couch with her a little while longer. He turned his head and looked at her.

"Sit a little longer," she said, and to her surprise he sank back.

"What's a Traveler?" he asked.

"The Travelers? Well," Berit said. "Well, what to say? They were a kind of people who weren't gypsies but not Swedish either. Dark. There were big Traveler families, or clans. Your father used to talk about them. 'They're Travelers,' he might say about people. He said that explained a lot about a person. Why do you ask?"

"A kid I met outside said that."

"About who?"

"About Dad," Justus said and looked at her with that mercilessly direct gaze that would take no half-truths or evasions. "He said Dad was a Traveler."

"That's not true," Berit said. "You know that. Your father was light-haired."

"But Lennart is dark."

"Justus, it's just something kids say. There are no Travelers anymore. Was he mean to you? Who was it?"

"Patrik," Justus said. "But he's screwed up. His dad beats his new wife."

"What are you saying?"

"Everyone knows about it."

She thought about his words. Of course he would be likely to hear a thing or two, but she wasn't worried. He was used to standing up for himself. Justus could look delicate but it was a mistake to think he was soft all the way through. Inside, he was as hard as flint, just like John.

She sniffled involuntarily at the thought of John. Justus stared straight ahead but put his hand in her lap.

"Dad wanted us to move," he said. "I did too."

"Where would we move to? When did he say this?"

"During the fall. He wanted us to move far away."

"He had his dreams, you know that. But I think he was happy here."

"He said he wanted to get away from this shit hole."

"He did?" Berit stared at him in amazement. "He used those words?" Justus nodded and stood up.

"Where are you going?"

"I have to feed the fish."

Berit watched him from the sofa. He moved like John, making the same hand movement over the surface of the water. The cichlids swam up to him in sweeping groups, beautifully synchronized so that they looked like one big body.

Then someone thumped on the door. The person didn't bother with the doorbell, just kept thumping. Justus dropped the can of fish food and stared into the hall. Berit got up but felt as if her shaky legs were not going to carry her. She looked over toward the clock on the sideboard.

"Do you want me to get it?" Justus asked.

"No, I'll go see who it is," she said and walked to the front door.

The thumping had stopped. She put the chain on the door and opened it. Lennart was standing outside.

"Why are you banging on the door?"

She thought about not letting him in, but he would make such a racket in the stairwell that it was just as well to let him in. He came in like a shot.

"Have you been drinking?"

"Don't start that with me, you bitch. I've never been more sober in my life. Bitch!"

"Go away!" Berit said curtly and opened the door again, holding it wide open and boring her eyes into Lennart's.

"Take it easy. I'll leave when I'm good and ready. There's something you need to tell me."

"Justus, go to your room," Berit said with a shrill voice. She placed herself between her son and her brother-in-law.

"Just leave," she hissed. "To think you have the nerve to come here with your dirty mouth."

"I've talked to Mossa and Micke," Lennart said calmly.

Berit threw a quick look over her shoulder. Justus was still there, frozen in place. There was something reminiscent of John in him.

"Go away. Please. We can talk later."

"There's not going to be a later," Lennart said.

A quiet power struggle was going on between them. If only he had been drunk, she thought, it would have been easier. But Lennart looked unusually clearheaded. His cheeks were ruddy and there was no lingering smell of alcohol or sweat on him.

"What happened to your lip?"

"None of your business. We're not here to talk about my lips," he chuckled, pleased with his improvised joke.

Berit lowered her head and drew a deep breath.

"Lennart, for heaven's sake, think of Justus. He has lost his father. He doesn't need this now. It's enough, we . . ."

She sobbed once.

"This is a fine time to cry. You should have thought of it before."

Berit went over to Justus, put a hand on his shoulder, and looked him in the face.

"Justus, please go to your room. He's either drunk or crazy. He's talking bullshit. I don't want you to have to hear this."

"I live here too," Justus said, without looking up.

"Of course you do," Berit said. "But why don't you let us alone for a minute."

"What is he talking about?"

"I don't know," she said in a low voice.

"The hell you don't!" Lennart shouted from the door. "Justus needs to hear a little about his mother. You go putting on some act like you're the grieving widow and crying and shit. Who says you weren't behind it?"

"That's far enough. Even if you've gone stark raving mad, then think of your nephew. Justus, go to your room. I'll take care of this."

"I don't want to," Justus said.

"We'll talk about this later. Go to your room and close the door," Berit said in a firm voice and more or less forced him into his bedroom. Then she turned to Lennart.

"Who sent you here with this disgusting babble?"

"Dick, do you remember him? Sure you do, you probably remember his teeth."

"Stop it!"

The anger made her voice rise an octave.

"Shut the door!" she shouted at Justus.

"You can't scare me by screaming. There are people who say you had something to do with John's death."

She stared at him.

"Fucking idiot," she hissed. "You goddamned fucking idiot."

"Shove it up your ass."

"First you tell me who is spreading these lies about me."

"They aren't lies. Micke told me."

"Micke Andersson? I thought you knew me. And John," she said.

"In the stillest waters," he said, and she slapped him in the face.

"It's time for you to go now."

"Look here, bitch," he said and grabbed her arm as Justus burst out of his room.

"Stop fighting!" he shouted. "Stop!"

Berit embraced her son but he freed himself. Anger convulsed his face, he sniffed and stared helplessly at her.

"Justus, don't listen to him."

"Suit yourself," Lennart said derisively. "Mossa called you a whore and that's a good name for you, the way you carried on with that neighbor of yours."

"You mean Stellan? He's gay! He hugs everyone. You know that, Justus. That's just Stellan."

"And what about Dick Lindström. You've been with him too, haven't you? Did you like the way he bit you?"

"You are not in your right mind," Berit said calmly. "You are a sick man living in a sick world."

"Who's Dick?" Justus asked.

"He's a friend of John, someone Berit has been getting it on with. Going behind John's back with."

"He came on to me once, tried to feel me up, but I fought him off. You were here, for God's sake. I was cooking in the kitchen, while the rest of you sat in here playing cards. I didn't want to say anything because John would have tried to kill him."

"So that's your story now, is it?"

"There's never been a different story. He tried to feel me up, he was disgusting. Do you really think I would . . ."

Berit didn't finish the sentence.

"Don't believe a word he says," she told Justus. "He's sick."

"Don't say stuff like that," Lennart said.

Justus looked at the two of them with a blank expression, then walked into his room and slammed the door.

"Are you happy now, you bastard?" Berit said. "He has enough on his mind without you coming here with your shit. Go now, before I kill you. And don't you ever come here again, or I'm calling the cops."

"If anyone should call it would be me," Lennart said. "Did John know about this? Is that why he died? If it is, you're going to be dead soon."

Berit stared at him.

"You shithead! God, how I hate you. Running around, drinking all the time. John tried to get out and he succeeded, but you still run around like the disgusting wino you are. And you have the nerve to come here and threaten me, you damn scumbag. It's like John said, you never grew up. He despised you, do you know that? He hated all your talk about Ymergatan and pool halls. That was all a hundred years ago. Is it anything to talk about? Pathetic small-time gangsters who terrorized the block. Go drown yourself, pisshead. You think you were really something then, like kings, but purse snatching and thinner sniffing only kills your brain. John had the guts to leave all that behind, but you're still crawling around in the shit. Do you know that John hated all your loose talk but he put up with it because he was your brother—otherwise he would have thrown you out a long time ago."

Berit stopped abruptly, chest heaving. Lennart was smiling tauntingly at her, but she could see fear in his eyes, and for a moment she felt a twinge of guilt. His smile stiffened into a grimace, a macabre mask, behind which a desperate anguish became more and more apparent. He drew back, out of the apartment and into the stairwell, still with lifted head but then the twitch came, the one Berit knew so well. He drew air in through his nose, bent over and sobbed. It was as if her dagger had only now reached his heart. His eyes grew dim and restless, he turned and charged down the stairs with thundering steps.

She heard the door downstairs shut. As if in a fog she shut her own door and sank to the floor. The only noise was the sound of the aquarium pump. There was only silence from Justus's room. Berit looked up. It was as if the boy's anxieties and questions pulsated through the closed door. She should go in and talk to him, but couldn't summon the strength. Her body no longer obeyed her. Lennart's talk and her attack had drained her completely. She had held herself together for so long, spent so much time talking to Justus. They had watched TV in the evenings, ostensibly watched, that is, but really talking. Berit had reminisced about times in her and John's life, tried to create images that Justus would be able to treasure. She had told him about John's youth, leaving out the worst, talked about how skillful and admired he had been at work, his knowledge of cichlids and how much he loved his son. She knew that the dead walked alongside the living. Now the myth of John was born, the image of a man who put his family first, whose goal in life had been to create a secure childhood for Justus.

The night before, she had told Justus that John had opened a bank account when Justus was born and that every month, no matter how hard up they were, he deposited 150 kronor. She had shown him the latest deposit and he had sat with the slip of paper in his hand for a long time.

Now Lennart was threatening to tear this all down, and this double pain knocked her to the ground. How long would she be able to carry on? Her work as a disability attendant did not provide her with enough income, and the possibilities of going to full-time were slim. She had no education, no contacts. Of course she would receive something after John, she didn't know how much yet, but it would be hard. She wanted to spare her son the worst of it, especially now.

She got up with a great effort and stopped outside Justus's door. It was completely quiet in there. She knocked and opened the door. He was sitting on the bed and took no notice of her when she came in.

"You don't believe him, do you? He's full of lies."

Justus stared down into the bed.

"He's confused, Justus. He's heard some rumors and he's looking for someone to blame. Do you understand?"

He nodded.

"As if we don't have enough to deal with," she said with a sigh and sat down at his desk. "I have never been unfaithful or as much as looked at another man. Your father was enough for me, do you understand? We had a good relationship. People are surprised that we stuck together for so many years, but for John and me there was nobody else."

"But there was something," Justus said and gave her a hasty look.

"No, nothing," she said. "Absolutely nothing."

"Then why did Lennart say that stuff?"

Again she tried to explain to him that Lennart was living in another world, one in which there was nothing other than John's death.

"You and I can talk about him, remember him together, and we have each other. Lennart has nothing."

"Daddy liked Lennart," Justus said very quietly. "Why did you say those things to him?"

He didn't say anything else, but in his eyes she saw something she had never seen before. Grief and hate, which aged his face, as if the hate didn't have enough place in his youthfulness. She damned her brother-in-law. She stood up, wanted to say something else, but sighed and left him, walking out into the hall. She heard him close the door behind her.

His words about John having wanted to move worried her. They had talked about it before, but never seriously. They had both been born in Uppsala, and for her part she couldn't see herself living anywhere else. *Shit hole*, he had said to Justus.

She felt let down by the fact that he had talked to Justus—not to her, just the boy. What else had they talked about that she didn't know about?

Ann Lindell looked at the building in front of her. The yellow brick house reminded her of something, probably a building involved in a case from the past. Now she was out on her own, which felt strange. Normally she would have been here as part of a team, with a defined strategy and a definite goal. And although she had had to improvise somewhat before, she now had to question her every step. It was a feeling of freedom mixed with a bad conscience.

She had called Information and received Berit Jonsson's phone number and address. She lived in one of these brightly lit apartments. She took out her cell phone, put it back, and then looked up at the building again. She should call Haver, but it was late and perhaps this impulse was ill-founded. If she had been working she wouldn't have hesitated for a second, but now she would be obliged to explain to Haver why she was out on her own. She sighed heavily, dialed his number, and after a few more seconds of hesitation pressed the Talk button. Rebecka Haver answered after the first ring. Lindell heard in the way she answered that she expected it to be her husband.

"May I speak to Ola Haver?" Lindell asked without introducing herself.

There was a second's pause on the other end before Rebecka answered.

"He's at work," she said.

Silence.

"Who is this?"

"Thank you, I'll call back," Lindell said and hung up. *You idiot,* she thought to herself. *They must have caller ID.*

She was overcome with shame and she cursed her clumsiness. He was at work. She could reach him there but now it felt as if it would simply compound her mistake.

The phone rang and Berit lifted the receiver as if she was expecting news of another death. But the caller was a woman she had read about in the paper and heard John talk about: Ann Lindell, with the police. What surprised Berit was that she sounded so tired, and that even though it was late she wanted to come by and have a few words with her.

Ann Lindell came in a few minutes later. She was carrying a little baby in her arms.

"This is Erik," she said.

"You bring your children to work with you?"

"I'm not officially on duty right now," Lindell said. "But I'm still helping out a little."

"Helping out a little," Berit repeated. "And there's no one else to look after the baby?"

"I'm a single mom," Lindell said and carefully laid Erik on the sofa. He had woken up as soon as they entered Berit's building but fallen asleep again when she took him out of the stroller and carried him up the stairs in her arms. Berit turned off one of the lamps so that it wouldn't shine in his eyes. The two women quietly watched the sleeping baby for a while.

"What do you want?"

There was a note of impatience in her voice, as well as something that Lindell judged to be fear.

"I'm genuinely sorry for what has happened," Lindell said. "John was a good man." She unconsciously used Ottosson's words.

"Yes," Berit said.

"I think he was murdered for money, and I think you're sitting on that money right now."

"Me, sitting on the money?"

Berit shook her head. There were too many questions, impressions. First Lennart, then Justus, and now this off-duty officer.

"It means you may be in danger," Lindell said.

Berit looked at her and tried to understand the full implication of her words.

"Quite honestly I don't care about the money," Lindell said. "It was John's and now it's yours, but a lot of money always brings risk with it."

It was a stab in the dark from Lindell's side. She didn't know for sure if the motive was money or if Berit knew where it was. She wasn't able to judge Berit's expression to determine if she had known about John's poker winnings or not.

"If we assume he won all this money, did he have some friend that he would tell?"

"No," Berit said immediately. She thought about Micke, and Lennart's words came back to her.

"What about Micke?" Lindell said, as if she had been reading her thoughts.

"What do you want?" Berit asked. "It's late, you have a baby with you, you ask a lot of questions but you're not on duty. Who do you think you are?"

Lindell shook her head and glanced at Erik, who was sleeping peacefully.

"I just had an idea," she said. "I was talking with a colleague of mine today and I had the idea to . . . well, I don't know exactly."

She looked at Berit. She had heard her described as beautiful and Lindell could see her beauty, though most of it was gone. The fatigue, grief, and tension had carved into her skin like knives, and her carriage bore witness to enormous emotional and physical exhaustion.

"How is your son?" Lindell asked.

Berit heaved a sob. She stood in front of Lindell with no pretense, looked her in the eyes, and cried. Lindell had seen a great deal, but Berit expressed the deepest despair she had ever seen. Perhaps it was the quiet way in which she was crying that amplified it? A scream of pain, grief, and a collapsed life would have been easier to take, but Berit's steady gaze and quiet tears touched Lindell deeply. Erik shifted uneasily and Lindell felt close to tears herself.

"I think I should go," she said and rubbed her cheek. "It was silly of me to come here. I just had a strange feeling, almost a physical compunction to come by."

Berit nodded. Lindell picked up the baby.

"You can stay longer if you want," Berit said.

"I can't," Lindell said.

Erik's warmth and his tiny movements inside the snowsuit made her determined to leave Berit and the whole case behind. It wasn't her investigation. She was on maternity leave and in a few days her parents would be coming up from Ödeshög.

"Yes, you can," Berit said, and Lindell marveled at her metamorphosis. "I don't know what made you come here, but whatever it was it must have been important."

"I don't know," Lindell said. "It was pretty dumb and unprofessional, actually."

Berit made a gesture as if to say it didn't matter, unprofessional or not, she was here now.

"I'll stay a little longer if I can have something to drink. I'm so thirsty."

While Berit went to get a bottle of Christmas mead, Lindell laid Erik down again, unzipping his snowsuit and pushing his pacifier back in. He slept. She turned to the aquarium. It was certainly enormous. She followed the movement of the fish with fascination.

"They have their own territories," Berit said when she came back. "John was so proud of that. He had created an African lake in miniature."

"Did he ever visit Africa?"

"No, how would we have been able to afford that? We dreamed of it, or rather, John was in charge of the dream department; I made sure everything kept working."

Berit looked away from the fish tank.

"He got to dream," she said, "and he pulled Justus with him. Do you know how it is to be poor?" she asked and looked at Lindell. "It's living on the margins, but still wanting to enjoy things. We spent everything on Justus. We wanted him to have nice clothes. John bought a computer this fall. Sometimes we bought good food for a special occasion. You can't feel poor all the time."

The words fell like gray stones from her mouth. There was no pride in her voice, simply a factual statement that the Jonsson family had tried to create a sphere where they felt real, part of something bigger and more attractive.

"We sometimes played with the idea that we were rich, not outrageously rich, but that we would be able to fly somewhere sometimes, take a plane and see something new. I would like to go to Portugal. I don't know why Portugal exactly, but a long time ago I heard some music from there and it expressed what I felt inside."

She looked around the room as if to size up what she and John had built up over the years. Lindell followed her gaze.

"I think your home is nice," she said.

"Thanks," Berit said flatly.

Lindell stepped out into the wintry landscape an hour later, that familiar sense of weakness in her body. The only sounds were from cars driving by on Vaksalagatan and the hum of a streetlamp. People were inside their homes, boiling hams and wrapping presents. She thought about calling Haver but realized it was too late now. How would he take the fact that she had just blundered into his investigation? What would his wife say about the fact that she had called?

She decided to wait until tomorrow before contacting Haver. Deep inside her mind she was harboring a thought that maybe they could see each other. They had hardly twenty-four hours before her parents came into town. *See each other,* she snorted. *It's his embrace you want. If all you want to do is see him you can walk into his office whenever you want. No, you want him in your home, at the kitchen table as a very intimate friend, one who could give you a hug and maybe a kiss. That's how deprived you are of human closeness.*

She wasn't looking forward to her parents' visit. In fact, she feared it. Right now she couldn't handle her mother's attentions. Her dad would sit quietly in front of the TV, and that was fine, but her mother's well-intentioned expressions of concern about Ann's future would drive her insane. And this time she wouldn't be able to get away, not like her increasingly rare visits to her childhood home.

On top of it all, her mother had started to talk about moving to Uppsala. The house in Ödeshög was becoming too much for them, she said. The ideal scenario according to her mother would be a little apartment close to Ann and Erik.

Had talking to Lennart and Berit been the right thing to do? Lindell stopped in the snow. She didn't know if it was to rest her arms—it was hard work pushing the stroller over the unplowed sidewalk—or because she was struck by the unprofessional nature of her actions, but it didn't matter which. She simply stood there. Snow fell all around her in generous, beautiful, and somehow reassuring proportions.

"I'm certainly not sophisticated," she said quietly to herself. "Not like detectives on TV, the ones who listen to opera, know Greek mythology, and know if a wine is right for fish or a white meat. I just am. A normal gal who happened to become a police officer, the way other people become chefs, gardeners, or bus drivers. I want there to be justice, and I want it so much I forget to live my life."

None of my colleagues are sophisticated either, she thought. *Some of them don't even know what that word means. They just work. What do they talk about? Definitely not about different years of wines from a fantastic vineyard in some unknown part of the world. At most they compare box wines from the state liquor store.*

Sammy Nilsson had subscribed for many years to *Illustrated Science* magazine and regularly—with childish enthusiasm—volunteered small anecdotes from new developments in astronomy, or medical research, delivering these pop-science facts with the authority of a Nobel Prize winner. Fredriksson would fill in with wonderful facts such as the one that the mountain egret spends the winter in Alunda, or explain why wolves don't cross railway tracks. *This is our version of educated culture,* she thought.

Ottosson often appeared absentminded and a little lost. Most likely he would have preferred to be out at his cabin, chopping wood and working in his vegetable garden. Berglund was a reassuring uncle, with a large store of knowledge about the human race and the ability to win people's trust.

Fredriksson was the nature lover who found it hard to keep up with the increasing tempo and the stress of everyday life. He could also offer up evidence of hostility to foreigners, not in conscious harangues about the superiority of the white race—nothing like that—more like an expression of confusion about the state of things, uncomprehending in the face of the rootless kids with immigrant backgrounds that figured more and more often in their cases. Sammy could become furious when Fredriksson made some sweeping generalization, short arguments that always ended with Fredriksson saying, "That wasn't what I meant, you know that."

That's why we're good, Lindell thought and pushed the stroller a few more meters. *If we were cultured in that lofty way, our jobs would suffer.* Maybe that kind of police officer existed in other districts, but in Uppsala, the seat of higher learning, the police were regular people.

Sammy could understand teenagers, not because he was deep—most of the time he wasn't even particularly methodical or sharp-witted—but because he represented something the kids on the street had been looking for. No flakiness, no meaningless social chatter, just the real thing. They could have used him, and a dozen others like him, full-time on the beat in Gottsunda, Uppsala's most populated suburb, where the powers that be had taken the inspired step of shutting down the local police branch. "I guess it's a natural development to increase police visibility by turning us out onto the street," one colleague had commented at the morning meeting. If only they could place Sammy there, all the vandalism, graffiti, theft, fear, and threats to personal security would fall off drastically.

Lindell smiled. She knew that this self-satisfied argumentation was motivated by a desire to justify her current independent police venture. She tried to convince herself that her colleagues would have done the same thing in her stead.

But of course that wasn't true. Her independent investigating was not consistent with good ethics. Ottosson would be deeply concerned about her actions and most of her colleagues would shake their heads. But what should she have done? Lennart wanted to talk to her, and her alone, and wasn't it therefore her duty as a citizen to talk to him? And once she had talked to Lennart, what was the difference in talking with Berit?

Lindell didn't know what she thought about Berit. It was possible that she was concealing something behind the surprised expression in her beautiful but harrowed face. Information she would keep from the police, however intimate the girl talk became. Her priority was to protect her son, then John's memory, two sides of the same coin. Did she know where John had stashed the poker winnings? Had she had an affair with another man? Was there jealousy as well as money at the root of the murderer's motive? Lindell had trouble imagining Berit cooperating in the murder, or even that a rejected lover lay behind the murder. Lindell believed in Berit's fidelity. She wanted to believe in it and she toyed with the idea that they would have occasion to chat again in the future. Berit seemed wise, had a direct way of talking and probably also a good sense of humor.

Lindell folded up the stroller and lifted it into the trunk of the car. Erik woke up when she strapped him into the car seat. He looked at her with his big eyes, and she stroked him gently on the cheek.

Thirty

He knew that in some way John's death had something to do with him. It could not be mere coincidence that two tormentors had been punished. Justice was being served.

Vincent had only vague memories from his first five, six years of school, during which time he had managed pretty well. The problems had started in middle school. He didn't know why he had started to feel like an outsider, but it often had physical manifestations. His classmates avoided touching him. He was left out of the boys' jostling, often gravitating to the girls, but too odd to be accepted fully. After seventh grade his classmates left their childish games behind, the games where boys and girls could play together, in favor of trying out their new gender identities. And then Vincent stood out even more. He was neither cute nor charming, only silent, something the girls often appreciated in contrast to the other boys' loud and noisy behavior, but in the long run he became more and more isolated.

He had tried to approach Gunilla. They sometimes met on their way to school. They weren't friends but Vincent felt comfortable with her, she was someone he could talk to. Their paths diverged once they reached school.

She increased her stride as soon as they rounded the corner by Tripolis and the iron fence of the school yard appeared.

One recess he finally told her about his father, about how his father beat him. The trigger had been a bruise on his neck, below his left ear. Someone said it was a hickey. Most of the others ignored him, but Gunilla had walked over and looked at him, not with the teasing, taunting attention he usually attracted but with genuine interest. She had placed her fingers carefully on the blue-red mark. A light touch, lasting a second.

That was when he said it.

"My dad hits me."

She had pulled her hand back and looked at him with frightened eyes. For a moment he thought he saw something else, but then her expression changed.

"Vincent gets spanked!" she had shouted in the corridors before they gathered to file into the classroom. Everyone had looked at him.

"Vincent's a bad boy!"

"Do you wet your bed?" one of the boys asked.

"Poor Vincent gets spanked on his bottom!"

Gunilla had been smirking, then the teacher had opened the door to the classroom. Vincent recalled they had learned about amoebas that day.

With John it had been different. He was in a different homeroom, but they had a few classes together. It had started in home economics. Neither John nor Vincent said much in this class, and the teachers had to work to get either one to say or try anything. They had been paired one day when the class was learning to bake pound cake. They had followed the instructions uncertainly and mixed the ingredients together. Unfortunately Vincent managed to tip the bowl when they were adding the flour and both boys had watched paralyzed while the gray-white mixture flowed out toward the edge of the table and down onto the floor.

The teacher rushed over and for some reason assumed that John was the one who had caused the accident. Neither boy said anything, least of all Vincent, who assumed he would be beaten for it.

John was assigned to clean it up, Vincent was sent over to work with another group. From that day John had hated Vincent. With his quiet diplomacy he had steered the class to outright bullying. Vincent's status changed from awkward outsider to outright victim. After that the machine was in full swing. Once he had complained to the teacher, but that only escalated the terrorism. He knew that John was behind it, although they never talked to each other and John was never an active participant in the persecutions.

Now he was dead and Vincent was pleased. Gunilla was not dead, but she had been severely frightened and she wouldn't be likely to forget him. The fear would stay with her.

The early-morning confusion gave way to a harmonious, dreamlike state. He knew he was on the right track. The phone cord around Vivan's throat, the terror in her eyes, and that rattling sound had done him good. She had gone quiet so quickly. Her eyes, filled with suspicion and then panic-stricken, had made him laugh. That was the last image she had seen, his laughing, foul-smelling mouth. He had wanted to draw out this laugh. Disappointed, he had kicked her dead body, kicked her in under the bed.

John had been killed by a knife. "Stabbed repeatedly," the paper had said. Vincent suspected that his eyes would have been as full of terror as Gunilla's and Vivan's. Did Vincent have a helper? A quiet avenging force that he was unaware of, or had he been there himself? He was becoming more unsure. He had suffered memory blanks before, especially when he was angry. Maybe he had been there, had stabbed John.

As usual he stopped on Nybro bridge and stared down into the river. Even though it was bitterly cold and in the middle of December, there was a sliver of open water in the middle. Vincent Hahn rested his eyes there for a moment before continuing over the bridge. Again the feeling that he was wandering in a foreign land came over him, a land where no one knew him, where the buildings had been erected by unknown hands, and where even the language had become foreign to him. He became more alert to the people around him, trying to read something in their eyes, but they looked away quickly, or never met his gaze.

He raised his hand and walked straight across the street without paying any attention to the fact that the road was slippery and the cars had trouble braking on the icy surface. Someone shouted at him, words he didn't understand. He could see that they were angry at him. He took out the knife he had picked up at Vivan's apartment. A few teenagers shouted something, turned around, and ran.

Vincent repeated the maneuver, stepping straight out into the road. A car had to slam on the brakes, skidded to the side, and almost crashed into a parked taxi. The taxi driver got out and shouted at him. Vincent waved back with his knife.

He walked toward St. Erik's torg, where people were selling things from stands. An older couple were selling Christmas ornaments. He stopped and looked at all their colorful wares. There were few customers and the couple looked at him expectantly.

"I don't have a real home," he said.

"It doesn't cost anything to have a look," said the woman.

The man, who was wearing an enormous fur hat, pulled off a leather glove, picked up a bag of homemade candy, and held it out to him.

"I have no money," Vincent said.

"Take it, you look like you need a sweet," said the woman. "It's our house blend."

The man nodded. The hand holding the bag shook slightly. Vincent looked at it, at how the blue-black veins made a pattern on the broad back of the hand. The nails were thick, curved, and yellowed.

"He's had a stroke," the woman said. "He can't talk."

Vincent took the bag without saying anything.

"This is the most beautiful present anyone's ever given me," he said finally.

The woman nodded. She had green-blue eyes, with a faint grayish cast over the cornea. Apart from a few liver spots on her cheek her skin was smooth and youthful. Vincent thought she had probably laughed a lot in her life.

A younger couple came over, looking through the collection of wreaths.

"They have wonderful candy," Vincent said.

The young woman glanced at him and smiled.

"We'll take one of these," she said, holding up a lingonberry wreath.

Vincent left the booth and wandered on aimlessly, with a hole inside that was only growing bigger. He had felt it many times before. It was a black hole, indescribably dark and deep, from which thoughts both emerged and were drowned. He felt as if he were caught in a maelstrom and was being sucked down into himself.

He tried to say something and heard an echo in his head. The dizziness came and went. He had another piece of candy and stopped outside a shop window where a tabloid headline promised tips for a better sex life. People walked in and out, relaxed, carrying colorful packages, looking at him briefly, smiling.

Where should he go? His legs could hardly hold him anymore. The candy had given him some energy, but wherever he went there were new challenges. The sidewalk was becoming more crowded. He kept bumping into people and their packages repeatedly, pushed hither and thither.

When he had decided to head to the east side again he was stopped by a man wearing a Santa outfit who tried to interest him in a sleigh ride through the old town. Two hundred and ninety kronor for an hour. Vincent accepted a flyer and walked on. The dizziness was getting worse. He leaned against a wall and anxiety charged over him like a battalion on horseback. He took cover, put his arm over his face, and cried out into the wind.

The police came an hour later. The owner of an art gallery had alerted them. He had observed Vincent for a while before he called, had watched the snow falling around him. It was a striking image, or composition, the dark-clad man, a cap pulled down over his forehead, crouched against the wall as if he was afraid that the people walking by with their Christmas purchases would hit him, the gently falling snow—all this created an image of tangible authenticity. It was happening here and now. The gallery owner stood there in the warmth, with the miniatures on the wall, people came and went, Christmas greetings were exchanged.

This image was also a reminder of the timelessness of need. Through the ages thousands of needy people had wandered past on this street. They had come through the city gates to the north, fleeing hunger and punitive overlords, looking for something better. In times of pestilence they had gone in the opposite direction, driven away from the overcrowded and stinking city.

This could be any city in the Northern Hemisphere. The gallery owner saw the homeless man as a reminder of the limits but also the possibilities of contemporary art. A classic motif of genre painting; a challenge for contemporary video artists.

But these aesthetic ruminations eventually gave way to compassion. The gallery owner called the police and they turned up thirty minutes later. When he saw them he stepped out into the street. The officers seemed oblivious of any aesthetic dimension, seeing this only as a routine task of picking up a drunk, perhaps mentally ill, vagrant.

The cold had penetrated Vincent's clothes. He had tucked his bare hands into his coat and his head had fallen toward his knees. One of the officers shook his shoulder. Vincent woke up, opened his eyes, and saw the uniformed policeman. The other officer was talking to the gallery owner.

Vincent had dreamed that he was in a country where there was snow on the ground all year round. A land of eternal ice where the people couldn't spit at each other and had to make do with stiff grimaces when they wanted to express their displeasure. He had been standing on a street corner, selling lottery tickets that no one wanted to buy. He had gestured in vain. It wasn't possible to speak, then the cold threatened to pierce your heart, and that was the end.

"Hey, buddy, how's it going?" the officer asked kindly. He didn't smell the usual stink of alcohol on this man, he wan't one of their regulars. In a half hour the officer was scheduled to finish his beat and start his holiday. He was going up north to Ångermanland with his family.

Vincent moved his head stiffly, trying to dispel the dream and focus on the officer. Slowly the present overtook his consciousness. He saw the uniformed legs, heard the voice, felt the hand, and with lightning speed he had taken out his knife and thrust it upward in a slicing motion. The bread knife sped toward the neck of Jan-Erik Hollman, born in Lund, christened in Gudmundrå church, where his funeral would be held in a week or so, hit the artery, pierced the neck, and went out the other side.

His colleague, Maria Svensson-Flygt, did all she could to stop the bleeding but it was no good. In a few minutes Jan-Erik Hollman had bled to death on the icy sidewalk of Svartbäcksgatan.

Vincent leaned back against the wall as if he was completely unaware of what had just happened. Maria looked at him. Passersby were standing around in a ring, in complete silence. Traffic had come to a stop. The blood-red puddle on the ground had stopped growing. One of Maria's hands lay on her colleague's chest, the other pulled out her cell phone. After a short call she grabbed the knife that Vincent had either thrown to the ground or simply dropped.

"Look, she has a gun!" a little boy shouted.

Vincent gave Maria a dull look and she saw the insanity in his eyes. Someone down the street laughed and a taxi cab honked, otherwise there was only silence, broken—after a few seconds—by the sound of approaching sirens.

Maria Svensson-Flygt had been very fond of her colleague. They had worked together for two years. She hated the man slumped against the wall and it struck her that if they had been alone, without staring witnesses, she would have shot his head off.

She sensed that the man in front of her was Vincent Hahn, who was wanted for the murder of a woman in Johannesbäck, although he did not really look like the picture she had seen.

Thirty-one

The police were in mourning. Some cried, others were simply tense and quiet. The image of the pool of blood on Svartbäcksgatan returned over and over in their minds. Thoughts of Jan-Erik's wife and his kids were interspersed in people's minds with the most troubling point: *It could have been me.* These words were not actually spoken aloud by anyone—that would have seemed unprofessional and disrespectful—but it was there, strengthening the sense of connection with the deceased. Even the chief of police's words at the brief meeting sounded genuine.

The chief, with his tinder-dry and normally so uninspired voice, earned a new respect from his colleagues. He spoke in a low voice without fuss and left the podium with heavy steps after an unexpectedly short amount of time. A paralyzing silence fell over the assembled group, then a middle-aged man who was familiar to most stood up.

It was the hospital minister who had been at the police station for other reasons when news of the death came in. Liselotte Rask had recognized him and asked him to stay until they had formally appointed a crisis management team.

Ola Haver listened to his words, letting them into his shaken mind. Fredriksson sat next to him with his head bent, as if in prayer.

Because Fredriksson had been the first on the scene at Gunilla Karlsson's apartment, he had informally taken the lead in the hunt for Vincent Hahn. Now Hahn had been captured, but at what price?

Fredriksson had gone down into the holding cell in order to take a look at the two-time murderer. He wanted to see his face, and the sight of him was infuriating. Hahn was drinking a cup of tea and eating a cheese sandwich. It felt wrong, improper, almost indecent. The guard had been standing next to him and Fredriksson had been tempted to upbraid him, but had managed to calm himself.

Did Vincent Hahn have anything to do with John's murder? There was a personal connection between them, in that they had grown up in the same area and gone to school together. Now Fredriksson's thoughts centered on the knife. Could Vincent be tied to the knife they had recovered, the one the youth claimed he had stolen from the hospital parking garage?

Sammy Nilsson had immediately gone to see Vincent and asked him if he knew Little John. Vincent had smirked and admitted it.

"And he died," he added, his smile broadening.

"Did you kill him?"

"He was stabbed," Hahn had said.

After that he had stopped talking, even though Sammy Nilsson had shaken him, pulling him up from the cot and asking him again. The guard had been forced to show him out. Later, the guard told Fredriksson about it.

"He laughs sometimes," the guard says. "I think he's completely nuts."

Fredriksson had asked the guard to tell him the moment Hahn seemed like he was ready to talk.

Haver turned on his cell phone after the meeting. After a few seconds the phone showed that he had received a voice message. It was Rebecka. He heard her straining to sound normal. She asked him to call back.

He dialed the number and Rebecka answered immediately.

"Oh, God," she said. "Thank you, God."

"What is it?"

"I heard it on the radio," she said.

"It was a patrol officer, I don't think you knew him."

"Did he have a family?"

"A wife and two kids. A girl and a boy. Eight and four."

"Shit," she said, although she seldom swore.

"I have to go," he said.

"You'll be careful, won't you, Ola?"

"Of course, you know that."

"I want to—" Rebecka started, but Haver interrupted her.

"I have to go. I'll see you."

He was left with mixed feelings. Her concern touched him but also filled him with irritation. They had had a huge fight when he came back late last night. She had been sitting silently at the kitchen table and given him an ice-cold look, a glass and a half-empty bottle of red wine in front of her. When Haver walked into the kitchen all hell had broken loose. Rebecka told him about Ann Lindell calling without leaving her name, but Haver knew it wasn't the true source of her anger.

It was very late when they finally went to bed and he had lain awake for a long time. Rebecka had tossed and turned, sighed, and shifted pillows around. An oppressive silence had reigned. So much had been said, yet so much remained unsaid. At half past two he had tiptoed out into the kitchen. The bottle of wine was still on the table. That was unlike Rebecka, she was normally so neat. Haver poured himself half a glass. He should sleep. He should love his wife, make love to her, but first he knew they had to talk.

Haver dialed Lindell's home number on his cell phone. The answering machine came on after four rings. He tried her cell phone but had no luck. He left a short message asking her to call.

Why had she tried to phone him, and why wasn't she answering now? It wasn't like her to be unreachable. Her call earlier this evening had to have had something to do with work. She would never have tried him at home to talk about what had happened between them. And what was it that had happened anyway?

Haver kept on thinking, with a growing sense of irritation. The feeling that everything was too late came over him, the same feeling that had been bothering him in the dark, that things had gone too far, both at work and at home. He had fallen into a light sleep. In his dream a woman was bent over him, repeating the words, "Why did my son die?" Over and over. Haver tried to answer but couldn't make a sound because he was gagged and bound to his office chair. He helplessly listened to the grieving woman's mournful cry. Rebecka had fallen asleep. Her breathing had become calm and regular and he wished he could snuggle next to her. He fell back into sleep and into the nightmare.

After the meeting everyone went his own way. Haver was irresolute. Ottosson had set up an investigative session with Fritzén, from the district attorney's office, in ten minutes. Haver called Ann at home again and left a message there too. Then he went into the bathroom and cried.

Ottosson started by talking about Jan-Erik, their collective vulnerability, and also about all the flowers and phone calls from the public that had been pouring in. No doubt people were even more willing to show their compassion because it was so close to Christmas. Liselotte Rask had done an amazing job, Ottosson said. She had stood her ground in the reception area, taking the wind out of the sails of even the most aggressive reporter with a single look, a word.

The chief changed the topic of discussion.

"Now we can start to imagine how Berit Jonsson feels," he said, and at least Fritzén was taken aback at these words, but Ottosson continued calmly.

"Death comes to us all, that is the only thing we can be certain of. It makes no difference whether it is a thief in a garbage dump or a policeman in the line of duty. When someone dies at the hands of another, the pain for the survivors is the same."

Haver wondered about Ottosson's relationship to Little John. He did not mention Vivan Molin, who had been strangled and brutally kicked in under her bed.

"It's true," Berglund interrupted, and all eyes turned to him, surprised because he rarely said anything at the meetings. "We have to do better. All of us. No one should have to die like Jan-Erik, Vivan Molin, or Little John, there we can agree. We need to be part of the solution because we are part of the problem."

His words fell like heavy blows. Ottosson raised his eyebrows and Fritzén looked disgusted.

"What do you mean?" Fritzén said. "I don't think this is the right time to air your homespun theories about the burden of guilt and the inadequacies of our society."

"It's always the right time," said Berglund, now in a calmer tone of voice. "It's our job and our responsibility to continue asking ourselves the question of what we could have done to prevent this."

Fritzén moved as if to interrupt him again, but Lundin jumped in with a cough.

"I want to hear what Berglund has to say," he said.

"I went up to see Oskar Pettersson on Marielundsgatan again. He knew Little John and his parents. He's a wise old man," Berglund said, looking at Fritzén. "We speak the same language. Most of you aren't from around here, even if these things are the same all over Sweden, but you are also all too young. There is a kind of culturedness that exists apart from the kind transmitted by schools and universities, and Oskar Pettersson represents this educated culture. Once upon a time I think this kind of culture flourished in the neighborhood where Little John grew up, and it helped to stem the flow of today's lawlessness. Of course, there were scum in the fifties and sixties, but there was also a social resistance that is lacking today."

"What kind of resistance?" Sammy asked.

"Something upheld by normal people, but also by the authorities."

"Sweden isn't how it was," Riis agreed. "There's a lot of new folk now, that's bound to lead to trouble."

Berglund turned his head and looked at Riis.

"I know you don't like immigrants, but both Little John and Vincent Hahn are products of Swedish social democratic policy, our so-called People's Home. I think it is the isolation of individuals in our country that breaks them. The gap between people's dreams and the potential to get off track is too large. What was it we once dreamed of, what did Oskar Pettersson dream of?"

The silence was overwhelming. These questions were rarely or never aired. The backdrop was dark, a pool of three thousand milliliters of blood on the street, a dead colleague. Berglund did not feel able to articulate the questions he felt deep inside, what he had experienced as he sat at home with the old concrete worker. There was something about the way Pettersson talked about the old furnace workers at the Ekeby mill. That was why he had started thinking about these things, thoughts strengthened during the walk home. During the last visit Pettersson had remembered even more about Little John and his family. With an endless series of anecdotes Pettersson had described a utopia sunk into the mire. Berglund had spent most of the time listening. There was something about his way of talking that made Berglund widen his speculations beyond the usual sphere of things. The discussion went back and forth in time. Slumbering, undiscovered, and yet familiar connections emerged. Berglund wanted to retain these thoughts, deepen and refine them, but realized his limitations.

"And this doesn't have anything to do with *svartskallar*?" Riis said peevishly.

"There's something in what you say," Sammy Nilsson said. "I've felt the same thing. But I don't think it's a question of age or even class."

"I think we're getting off track again," Fritzén said.

"Look here," Ottosson said, "we have to be able to talk this through. We're police officers, not hung over army reservists guarding a completely unnecessary stockpile of military goods in the forest."

Where Ottosson had gotten this image was not clear, but most of them thought it funny. Even Riis smiled.

"Take the kids in Gottsunda or Stenhagen," Sammy continued. "They're so lost. I'm starting to doubt my work more and more, maybe I should become a boxing coach or something. Get close to the kids like that UIF guy who does such a great job and has a name no one can spell. That would be better economically too. All the politicians talk about unemployment and segregation but they don't do anything, they stay in their world."

"That's right," Berglund said. "They don't live there, they don't know any immigrants, and they're afraid. Then they send us out when things get out of hand."

Fritzén made an effort to get up but ended up sinking back onto his chair.

"This is beginning to sound like a leftist consciousness-raising group from the seventies," he said.

"So you were involved back then?" Ottosson asked innocently.

"I prefer to wash my hands of all that," he said, and suddenly an emotional divide appeared in the room that they knew would be hard to bridge. They had all had good experiences working with Fritzén, but now a new factor came into the picture: politics. Not the shallow question of party adherence but the underlying convictions.

"We should talk more about this," Ottosson said in an attempt to curb the discussion in an elegant way, "but now we have to turn to the matters at hand. I suggest Haver and Beatrice take care of questioning Hahn. He appears to be in bad shape and we probably need to bring in a physician. Can you arrange that, Ola?"

Haver nodded.

"I'll talk with Liselotte," Ottosson continued. "We have a press conference tomorrow at nine. She'll handle that with the boss. I know what you're thinking but he volunteered to be there. The question now is if Hahn had anything to do with Little John. Personally I find this hard to believe. I think it's merely a coincidence that they went to school together."

"He said he knew Little John," Sammy Nilsson said. "And he knew that John had been stabbed."

"He could have read it in the paper."

"Sure, but the way he said it . . . it was like he was gloating or something."

"Do we have anything new on the knife they found at the hospital garage?" Ottosson asked, turning to a new detail.

"No, we have been trying to trace where it was bought," Sammy said. "So far we haven't determined anything. It probably came from abroad."

Riis smirked and Sammy looked up but did not allow himself to be provoked. Instead, he continued. "I believe Mattias when he says he stole it from a parked car, from someone who was at the hospital."

"Isn't there a construction site next door?" Berglund asked. "If we're still talking about a pickup."

"Yes, but those guys have their own parking area."

Haver made a motion with his hand, almost a reflex, but lowered it immediately. Ottosson, who caught it, looked inquiringly at him.

"No, it was nothing. I just had a kind of flashback," he said.

"To the hospital?"

"I don't know. Maybe something about a construction site. You know how these things are."

He sank back onto the chair, trying to shut out his environment and recapture his train of thought. Hospital, parking garage, construction, pickup, knife, he arranged the words in front of him, but it was only the set images that flashed past, everything that they had already discussed and considered.

"The questioning of the poker players should be regarded as finished," Bea said. " 'The Lip' was admitted to a rehab in November and he seems to have stayed put since then. Now Dick Lindström is the only one left. We've asked the Dutch authorities for help in locating him. There's really nothing that binds any one of them to John. Everyone has an alibi for the evening John disappeared, even if these were difficult to extract in some cases."

"It could have been a hired killer," Fritzén said. "Murder by mail."

"It's possible," Bea agreed, "but we have nothing to indicate anything like that right now."

"Okay," Ottosson said. "We'll see what Vincent Hahn has to say. We have no problems placing him with Gunilla in Sävja and Vivan in Johannesbäck. It remains to see what he has to say about Little John."

Thirty-two

"Justice has been served," Vincent Hahn said in a clear voice.

His firmness surprised Beatrice. She had expected the hesitant speech of a confused mind.

"I take it you realize that you have been arrested for two murders, unlawful entering, sexual harassment, and threat of violence?"

Vincent didn't answer and Beatrice repeated her question.

"Yes," he said at last.

"What do you mean by saying, 'Justice has been served'?"

"You don't understand? Now I can be at peace."

"Did you know John Jonsson?"

"Yes." The answer came quickly. "He belonged to the legion."

"Which legion?"

"The legion of evildoers."

"What do you have to say about his death?"

"It's a good thing."

Haver and Beatrice exchanged a look.

"Did you murder John Jonsson?"

"I stabbed him with a knife."

Vincent made a stabbing motion with his hand, and a chill ran through both of the officers.

"Could you describe the knife?"

"A knife. A long knife. He did not get away. I stabbed him again and again."

"Could you describe it in greater detail?"

"A knife that kills."

"Do you still have it?"

Hahn fumbled in his right pants pocket.

"No," he said. "I . . . It . . ."

"Did you throw it somewhere?"

"I don't know. I had it in my coat."

"Tell me how you met John."

"I saw him on Vaksala torg, outside the school. He was close to me. I stabbed him."

"Right there in the square?"

"I don't know. Not that square."

A note of insecurity sneaked into his voice again. He hesitated, looked away from the police officers, and rocked back and forth before continuing.

"He laughed, he laughed at me. He pointed. He was angry. Everyone was angry that day."

"When was it?"

"It was . . . He was holding a Christmas tree."

"A Christmas tree? He was buying a Christmas tree in Vaksala torg?"

"Did you talk?"

Beatrice's and Haver's questions overlapped.

"John never said anything to me. He was making fun of me."

"You said you stabbed him with a knife. Where did you do this?"

"I stabbed him many times."

"But where? On the square?"

"He chased me there once."

"When you went to school, you mean?"

"He wasn't a good man. The other one wasn't good either."

"Which other one?"

"The one with the cap. He was talking so loud. I don't like it when people raise their voice."

"Was he also there on the square?"

Hahn nodded.

"What did the man look like?"

Ola Haver was so impatient that he felt as if worms were crawling under his skin. Beatrice took a deep breath that afterward, when the tape was replayed, sounded like a desperate attempt to get air.

"He looked like a military man. I stood close to him in case John was going to make fun of him too."

Here, Hahn paused.

"Could you describe his clothing?"

Silence.

"You wanted to protect him against John, is that what you mean?"

"Now I know I was right."

"Right about what?"

"To take revenge. Justice."

"What happened with the man and John?"

"They walked away with the Christmas tree."

"Where?"

Hahn's face now took on a pained expression. He slumped down in the chair and shut his eyes. Haver looked at the time. They had talked for fifteen minutes. How long would Hahn have the energy to keep going?

"Would you like some juice?"

"They walked up to the school, under the arch," Hahn continued unexpectedly. "It echoed under there if you shouted."

Haver had been to the Vaksala school to give a talk about drugs and had a clear memory of what it had looked like. The entrance to the school facing the square was a large archway leading to the school yard. On the other side was the cafeteria, which was being rebuilt. *Another construction site*, he thought, and the glimmer of something he had had felt during the meeting returned. There was something he had seen or heard. Was it all about construction sites? Construction at the hospital, and now construction at the school.

"Did you follow them through the arch?"

"Sometimes it smells like shit in there," Hahn said. "Then I don't like to go."

"But this time you did?"

A new nod.

"John threw one at me."

"A what?"

"A stink bomb."

"But this time it didn't smell, so you could walk through?"

"They put the tree in the car and I ran over to catch up."

"And did you?"

Hahn raised his head and stared at Beatrice.

"Did you catch up to them?"

She was trying to sound friendly. He didn't answer. The piercing gaze scared her. *That swine murdered one of my colleagues*, she thought. She repeated the word *swine* to herself again and again, steeled herself, and stared back.

Hahn's head sank down.

"I want to go home," he said.

Haver stood up, turned off the tape recorder, and nodded to the guard, who came over and grabbed Hahn's arm. He let himself be led away. Haver put on the tape recorder again and quickly recorded a few words stating the end of the session.

"What do you think?" he asked Bea when he was done.

"I think he's certifiably crazy, but I believe he really saw John in the square, maybe even on the day he was murdered. It could work. John leaves Micke Andersson, who lives right next to the square, decides to pick up a Christmas tree, or at least to look at them, bumps into someone who offers to drive him and the tree home. The car could very well have been parked in the school yard—is it possible to exit from the school yard in the evening?"

"I think so. There are exits both on Salagatan and Väderkvarnsgatan."

"Who was the man who looked like he was in the military?"

"That's the question. A military man, what does that mean? Was it his manner or his clothing, perhaps, that gave that impression?"

"What military presence is there in Uppsala?"

"We have the F-16 and F-20 Air Force squadrons," Haver said. "But how many of them walk around in their uniforms when they're off duty?"

"Maybe we should bring in some of their uniforms to show Hahn?"

"It could also be another kind of uniform, something that he thought was from the military."

"Bus driver, parking police, there could be a number of uniforms he could have mistakenly identified as military."

Haver rewound the tape and listened. Hahn's voice sounded metallic on the tape, as if the recording had erased all emotion.

"What should we think?" Haver asked.

Beatrice stared at the wall. Haver was struck by the thought that for a short moment he felt like he was talking with Lindell. There was a discreet knock on the door. Fredriksson, Haver thought, but it was Sammy who gently pushed open the door and looked in.

"You've sent him back down," he stated and walked in.

Haver played the tape one more time.

"It's got to be him," Sammy said when Haver turned it off.

"I'll grant you a motive of sorts, but opportunity?" Haver said in a detached voice.

Beatrice glanced at him from the side. *He takes on too much*, she thought. *It's as if he thinks the outcome of the whole case rests on him. Maybe it's Hollman's death that's pressing him further into exhaustion.*

"And transporting the body to Libro—how did he manage that?" Beatrice asked.

"Those severed fingers," Sammy said. "That was done by a sicko like Hahn."

"But the transport," Beatrice repeated.

"If he stabbed Little John in the school yard—he did say something about not that square, and the school yard works as a kind of square—maybe he was aided by the military man."

"You're reaching," Beatrice said. "Why would a witness to the murder help Hahn transport the body to Libro?"

"They may have known each other."

Beatrice shook her head.

"Perhaps he was forced," Haver said. "Maybe Hahn threatened him."

"Exactly," Sammy said and got up. "He was threatened."

"Why . . . Do you mean he was also murdered?"

Sammy nodded.

"Yes. There's another dead body out there somewhere."

They sat quietly for a while, trying to think through this scenario. It did not strike any of them as completely implausible.

"We need to question him again," Sammy said.

"Of course we do," Haver snapped. "What did you think? I'll go talk to Ottosson." Haver left the room before his colleagues had a chance to react.

"What got into him?" Sammy asked.

"He's completely exhausted," Beatrice said.

"He misses Rebecka," Sammy stated in a tone that Beatrice didn't like.

"He's been crying," she said, then closed her notebook, and left the room without saying anything else.

Thirty-three

Ann Lindell had just finished nursing Erik. She had gone about her morning routine in an apathetic way. Fat headlines in the morning paper had announced Jan-Erik Hollman's murder. Stunned, she had read about yesterday's events. She remembered him as one of the nice guys, a northerner, good at badminton and apparently a father of two.

Ann lingered at the kitchen window, ignoring the pot on the stove. Her mother had offered to cook the ham but Ann had refused. A faint scent of spices and broth rose from the pot. Her father was fond of dipping bread in the broth so she had to remember to buy the traditional herb bread.

She spread out the first page of the paper again. It carried a photograph of the dark pool of blood on Svartbäcksgatan, which reminded her of pictures that often accompanied articles about the murder of Prime Minister Olaf Palme. The same image of spilled blood in the street.

The sight of the large ham she was cooking made her feel sick. That gray-white flesh and then the fat that rose to the surface. She skimmed some away with a ladle. This was the first ham she had cooked in a long time. *Meaningless,* she thought. The thought of her parents with their gestures of concern and worried expressions depressed her. A guilty conscience mixed with anger.

The meat thermometer showed barely forty degrees Celsius. *At least an hour left,* she thought. She turned the heat up but then immediately turned it back down. You couldn't hurry a ham.

Ola had called but she hadn't answered the phone. Maybe he wanted to talk about Hollman's murder, maybe their brief interaction. An imperceptible shudder ran through her lower body. She felt desire for him and her self-disgust grew. Her attraction to him was so unexpected, so confusing. She hadn't desired any man since Edvard. Well, maybe, but not in the same way. Ola was married. She would never allow herself to take another step in that direction. At first she had toyed with the idea that maybe they could flirt a little more, even start a secret and shameless affair. But then she had pushed these thoughts away, reproaching herself by focusing on the unrealistic and immoral aspects of such a relationship. How low had she sunk? Not only was he a married man, a father, he was a colleague she saw on an almost daily basis.

Berit Jonsson called at half past nine to say that Justus had disappeared. After breakfast he had packed his school backpack—full of she didn't know exactly what, but it was an ample bag—and left. He hadn't told her where he was going, but he rarely did.

It wasn't the fact that he hadn't said much that concerned her; it was his expression. He had eaten his yogurt and cereal grimly, cleaned up after himself, walked into his room, and emerged fifteen minutes later with his bag on his back, said good-bye, and left the apartment. It had been shortly after eight.

"He's been sitting in there keeping to himself for days," Berit said. "Then he suddenly takes off likes this. Something's wrong."

"Does he like to do any sports?" Lindell asked. "Maybe he had sports gear in the bag?"

"No."

"He'll turn up soon, you'll see."

"He didn't feed the fish. He didn't even look in their direction."

"Has Lennart been in touch again?"

"No, thank goodness. If he tries I'll throw him out on his ear."

"Justus will turn up again. Try not to worry."

Berit agreed to call her if Justus didn't come home in the next few hours. Justus had the cell phone with him but didn't pick up when Berit called.

Ann's parents were coming in a few hours. The temperature of the ham had inched up to forty-eight degrees. Ann stared dully into the broth and watched a few peppercorns swirl around in circles, like the planets in their unchanging orbits.

She walked away from the stove, suddenly nauseated, reminded of the sensations she had felt when she first discovered she was pregnant. Katrin at the health clinic had told her the most likely reason for her pregnancy: she had been taking Saint-John's-wort and this had neutralized the effect of the pill.

Why this feeling of self-contempt? Was it because she was cooking a ham solely for the benefit of her parents? She wouldn't have bothered with Christmas otherwise, not hung any decorations. Her desire to see them again was deflated by this sense of duty to perform the role of good daughter and mother.

She feared her mother's gaze and comments. Ann couldn't remember her mother being this way while she was growing up. It was her father's ill health and passivity that had set off a process where controlling her daughter became her dominating focus. Ann had been judged an unsatisfactory mother. It was as if she were fully incapable of taking care of Erik. *And perhaps I really can't do it,* she thought. *Maybe I'm not fit to raise a son by myself.*

"Because I'm destined to stay single," she said aloud.

She went into Erik's room, stood by his bed, and looked at him. He was healthy and developmentally on track. Why was she a worse mother than anyone else? Ann knew it was her own insecurity and low self-esteem that was the source of all this self-doubt.

The phone buzzed. She had turned the ringer off so as not to disturb Erik. It was Berit.

"He's cut up some of the fish," she said.

"What are you talking about?"

"He's taken up some of the fish out of the tank and cut their heads off."

Berit drew air into her lungs as if to stop a scream from escaping.

"This morning?"

"Yes. I thought he had ignored them and not fed them, which is true. But he took out all the Princesses and beheaded them. I don't get it."

"The Princesses?"

"That's the name of the fish. The Princess of Burundi. The other ones are untouched."

"Why these particular fish, do you think?"

Berit burst out into loud sobs that developed into desperate wails. Lindell tried to regain contact with her but had the impression that Berit had walked away from the phone, perhaps collapsing into a chair or onto the floor. Her crying became more distant.

"I'll be right over," Lindell said and hung up.

She looked at the time, ran into Erik's room, put a cap on his head and wrapped him up in a blanket, and left the apartment.

The meat thermometer rose to sixty degrees.

Thirty-four

Karolina Wittåker's handshake was limp and clammy.

"But appearances can be deceptive," Haver later said to Berglund. "She took the lead immediately. I felt like a little boy. She lectured me about personality disorders and—"

"What was her verdict?" Berglund interrupted.

"We're free to question him, but she would like to be present."

"I see," Berglund said curtly and walked off down the corridor.

Haver stared after him, then shrugged and went into Ottosson's office. The latter sat hunched over a crossword puzzle from the *Aftonbladet* newspaper.

"I need to clear my brain," he said apologetically and pushed the paper away.

"The psychologist wants to be present when we interrogate Hahn," Haver said.

"That's fine by me. Did he make a good impression?"

"It's a she. She's thirty-five, attractive, and extremely determined."

"One of those," Ottosson said, and smiled. "That'll be good."

"What's up with Berglund?"

"Is something up with him? Are you thinking of what he said in the meeting?"

"He just seems so damned on edge," Haver said.

"All of us are right now. And it's almost Christmas, and for Berglund that's a sacred time. He gathers his clan, eats rich food, lays puzzles, and God knows what. I've never met anyone so fond of family and traditions. He wants nothing more than to be at home, making Christmas candy and hanging up ornaments."

Haver had to laugh. Ottosson looked at him kindly.

"I have every confidence in you and your expertise," he said. "Just remember that Hahn is sick. He stabbed one of us but he's a wounded person. Wounded and a human being."

Ola Haver warmed to Ottosson's support and belief in him, but he was also angered by his chief's understanding attitude toward this murderer. Ottosson was like that, understanding and mild, and it was something that made him a good boss, but right now the station was engulfed by grief and anger. Yes, Hahn was a human being, but despicable and hateful.

"Janne had a wife and two kids," Haver said.

"I know that," Ottosson said calmly. "But we're not here to judge."

Where does he get off talking like a goddamn minister? Haver thought.

"I know what you're thinking, but once upon a time Little John and Vincent Hahn were children. You know, little kids, like the ones you see in the street. I thought about that in the fall, when school started. I saw the little boys running down the streets with their backpacks and shorts and thought: *There goes a thief, a wife beater, a drug addict, or a dealer.* Do you see what I'm saying?"

"Not really," Haver said.

"They were on their way to school, on their way out into life. What do we do with them?"

"You mean somehow it's already been determined which ones become pimps and murderers?"

"Quite the opposite," Ottosson said with unexpected sharpness.

"Everyone has a responsibility," Haver said.

"Yes, we can't escape that, but I just want you to keep it in mind as you question Hahn. Your task, our task, is to investigate and tell the DA as well as the public what has happened, but we also have to keep an eye out for all the little boys on their way to school."

Ottosson stroked his beard, looked at Haver, and nodded. Haver nodded back and left the office.

"Can you describe the man you thought was from the military?"

Vincent Hahn sighed. Karolina Wittåker sat to one side, her legs spread as wide as the narrow skirt of her suit allowed. Haver couldn't help glancing in her direction. She was looking at Hahn.

"He was angry," Hahn said suddenly.

"He was shouting?"

"Yes, he shouted and carried on. It looked unpleasant."

Beatrice and Lundin had been down to Vaksala square and talked to the Christmas-tree sellers. No one recalled seeing either John Jonsson or an older military man.

"Why did you call him 'military'?"

"He looked that way."

"Do you mean his clothing?"

Hahn didn't answer right away. He turned to the psychologist and stared at her legs. She looked back at him calmly.

"Who are you?" he asked, although they had been introduced just a few minutes ago.

"Karolina," she said, smiling. "I'm listening to you and trying to imagine how it felt for you on Vaksala square, when that man shouted and you became frightened."

Hahn lowered his gaze. An expectant silence fell over the room.

"He looked like Hitler," Hahn said.

The words came out as if he were spitting.

"Did he have a mustache?" Beatrice asked.

Hahn nodded. Haver felt a rising excitement.

"Tell us more," he said and leaned over. He was trying to meet Hahn's eyes.

"I ran over to them."

"How old was the other one?" Haver asked.

"Sixty-three," Hahn said quickly.

"Tell me about his clothing."

Hahn didn't answer. Thirty seconds went by, then one minute. Haver's impatience grew. He exchanged a look with Beatrice.

"How did you feel when you were running up to them?" Wittåker asked. "Did you get short of breath?"

Hahn looked at her and shook his head.

"You knew you had to follow them?"

She received a nod in the affirmative.

"Do you think John was afraid?"

"He was never afraid. Not even when the truck ran into the wall and the teacher screamed. He just laughed."

"Maybe he was scared even though he was laughing," Wittåker said.

Haver realized that the session was going to take a long time. He wasn't sure how he felt about the psychologist's interjections. He had assumed she would be play the role of passive listener, but now she was actively steering the conversation. But she was also getting Hahn to talk. He glanced at Beatrice and she nodded.

"It was a pepper truck. A lot of cans fell out. Cans with little red peppers. Everyone took the cans. I did too. Two cans. My father thought I had stolen them, but I said everyone took them. They were just lying in the street."

"Did he get angry?"

"Yes."

"Like the man in the square."

Hahn nodded.

"What did your father do?"

"He was a Nazi."

"What sort of work did he do?"

"He was nothing. He screamed into my ears."

"You didn't want to be a Nazi."

"I'm a Taliban," Hahn said.

Haver burst out laughing and Wittåker shot him an icy look. Suddenly Hahn stood up, and Haver shot out of his chair but sat back down when Hahn started to talk.

"He walked quickly. It wasn't even a pretty tree. Why do people need those? It just costs money. Think about all the glitter, and those balls. That's what I said to John. He just laughed. He laughed at everything. The other one laughed too, even though he was angry."

"Was that in the school yard?" Beatrice asked.

"You shouldn't keep trees inside."

"Did the angry one talk to you?"

"He talked to me. I said trees don't like to be cut down. Then they drove away and I screamed, even though you're not allowed to scream."

"What did you scream?"

"I screamed that the trees want to be left alone. Don't you think they want to be left alone?"

"Yes, I do," Haver said.

He hadn't bought a Christmas tree yet. That usually happened the day before Christmas.

"We have to find the angry man," Beatrice said. "I'm sure you understand that. He may have hurt someone. We have to talk to him."

It felt silly to speak in such an infantile way but she realized that Hahn was still partially a child. The psychologist would no doubt talk at length about this, but she didn't care about the medical explanations. Beatrice felt instinctively that it was best to address him in this childish way.

"How was he dressed?" she continued. "Did he have nice clothes?"

"No, no nice clothes. He was wearing ones like on the TV, with pockets."

"A military uniform?"

"They shoot."

"A hunter?"

Haver heard from Wittåker's voice that she was as tense as he was.

"A hunter," Hahn repeated. "They hunt."

He sank down on the chair. His inner suffering was etched on his face. He shuddered and touched the wound on his head. Haver sensed that he was reliving yesterday's events in Sävja. Hahn mumbled something inaudible. Haver leaned over the desk and Hahn raised his head to look at him. It was a remarkable moment, Haver thought, a few seconds as a sudden insight came to the killer: *Why am I sitting here? Have I killed someone?* Haver sensed that Hahn was searching for answers, support, and perhaps understanding in those few seconds. Then the expression disappeared from Hahn's face and was replaced by the absent gaze that they had seen all morning.

The contact was broken and for the remainder of the session he answered their questions in nonsensical fragments. Wittåker made a few more attempts to break through to him but Hahn remained unreachable.

Thirty-five

Justus Jonsson was on his way. Where, he wasn't sure, but he couldn't stay at home any longer. The idea he had had this morning no longer seemed as sensible and justified as it had. There was a person John had trusted. Justus knew where he lived because John and Justus had been there many times. Erki had been like a second father to John. John, who was normally so self-sufficient and sure of himself, softened when he talked to the old Finn. The closed quality in John disappeared. Sometimes Justus had heard John repeat things in conversation that he had picked up from Erki.

Justus had seen them together at work and almost felt jealous at how smoothly they cooperated, as if they were one. Over the noise, the sharp sounds of sheet metal and steel and the scream of the machines, through the smoke, their wordless work had bound them together, the whole shop in fact. It looked so easy when Erki and John worked. A brief moment of thought, then action. Justus had observed, fascinated, that momentary pause before the action was carried out. It wasn't because they had to sort out what they were doing, but rather it seemed as if they were coming to an agreement with the material in their hands. A look was followed by the smallest of gestures to lower the visor and then the crackling glow of the welding tool. Or the flicker of a finger on the green button and the blade that eagerly cut into the sheet of metal.

Erki would understand. Maybe he had known about John's plan?

Lennart's accusations had cut a hole into his heart. Why had Berit, his mom, said John hated Lennart? It wasn't true! In fact, Lennart was included in the plan. John had said that many times. Together they would make a new life for themselves. John, Berit, and Justus, and Lennart would be there too. John had been evasive only when it came to his mother.

"We'll see," he had said, and Justus had heard from his voice that he wasn't sure what to do about her. "She's old," he had added. Maybe John was going to wait until she had died?

Justus passed Erki Karjalainen's house a second time. An old car was parked in the driveway. There was a decal of the Finnish flag in the back window. He glimpsed a woman in the window, behind some Christmas stars. She looked out and Justus picked up the pace. The street ended about one hundred meters away and beyond that lay a patch of forest. Justus stopped where the trees started. The snow-laden spruce trees reminded him of a walk he had taken with John a few years ago. He felt empty and tired, but the memory of his father's happiness made him smile briefly. Then came the tears. They had set out to find their own Christmas tree. "We'll save a couple of hundred, at least," John said. Justus didn't know if it was the cheap Christmas tree or the fun of being with his son in the forest that made John so elated, but it didn't matter. Not then and not now. He had laughed, taken Justus by the hand, and together they had examined more than twenty spruce trees before they found the one they wanted.

A car came by and Justus drew into the side of the road. The car skidded a little on the ice as it turned around. It had a Finnish license plate and it turned into the Karjalainens' garage.

Justus walked straight into the forest. Snow was falling and even though it was the middle of the day it was already getting dark. At the edge of the forest there were footprints, but after only ten meters the surface of the snow lay undisturbed. He trudged on. The backpack bounced up and down on his back. He was aware of its weight but it didn't bother him. When he had been walking for a few minutes he came to a clearing and saw an old-fashioned red cottage. There was a light on inside and in the garden there was a straw goat, a traditional Christmas ornament. He walked up to the goat. It was bound with red satin ribbon. He patted it, dusting off some of the snow that had gathered on its back. He started to cry again, although he tried hard to keep the tears back.

The cottage looked like it was straight out of a fairy tale. He thought how strange it was that a cottage like this could be so close to town. *Who lives here?* he had time to think before an older woman opened the door and put her head out.

"Merry Christmas," she said, and if it hadn't been for the weight on his chest he would have laughed.

"Merry Christmas," he mumbled. "I think I took a wrong turn," he added, hastening to explain why he was standing in her garden.

"That depends on where you were headed," she said and stepped out onto the little porch.

"You have a fairy-tale house," he said. His hand was still touching the goat's head.

"Yes, it's nice, isn't it?" she said. "Are you on your way to the Christmas meeting?"

He nodded although he had no idea what she was talking about.

"Go out to the road and take a right," she said. "After a while you'll get to a sign that says UKS. Go in there. It won't take you long."

Justus started walking in the direction she had indicated.

"Merry Christmas," she said again.

He walked a few meters, then turned. The woman was still there.

"You're not on your way to the meeting, are you?"

He shook his head. For a few seconds all was still. The snow had stopped.

"You're welcome to come in, if you want to," she said. "Maybe you'd like something warm to drink."

Justus looked at her and after a second's thought he shook his head.

"I have to keep going," he said.

"It looks like you've been crying."

He almost broke down and told her everything. Her kind voice, the cottage tucked into the snow, a toy house with cotton wool on the roof, and his longing for warmth made him hesitate.

"I thought I was lost," he said and swallowed.

"Come in and warm yourself for a while."

He shook his head, managed to get out a "thank you," and turned. He walked with a long, determined stride. After a while he started to run. The backpack jumped all around. After a hundred meters he went past the sign the woman had been talking about. A car was driving down the badly plowed road. Another car was in the distance. He ran faster and faster until his breath was like a cloud around him and his tears were frozen on his cheeks. Then he stopped abruptly, wiped his cheeks with his glove, and decided never to return to the apartment in Gränby. He kept going at a calmer pace and tried to look carefree, but his despair tightened his muscles like cables. His heart was pounding in his chest like a fist beating on a door.

A third car went by. The driver stared at him in curiosity. Justus gave him the finger and kept walking. When the noise of the car had died away he looked around. He saw a spiral of smoke from the cottage rise over the treetops. Then the road turned.

He knew that all the bad stuff had started when John was fired from the shop. Until then they had been happy. He had never before heard his parents quarrel in earnest, but that was when it started: the night talk that they thought he couldn't hear. Their low, grinding voices from the kitchen or living room. Sometimes he couldn't even tell who was talking. But he knew it was about money. He had sneaked up and listened. Once, they had been talking about him.

Justus walked on and quickened his step unconsciously. With every step his longing for his father intensified. How far would he have to go before the pain went away?

He reached an intersection where he came to a stop, not sure of what to do next. One thought he had had was to destroy that which had destroyed John. But suddenly he wondered if everything was Berit's fault. What if it was true that she had met someone else? Justus collapsed as if a knife had been driven into his body. He sobbed as he thought about the shadow that had turned up in his doorway, when she thought he was sleeping. How she had simply stood there looking at him. Had she betrayed John? Was that why he had died?

He didn't want to believe it, but the thought pestered him, rearing up like an ice floe inside. Was she the one who deserved to be punished? Had he been right to kill the Princesses? Loneliness drove him down into the pile of snow at the side of the road. The cold crept into his body as he pulled up his knees and leaned his head against them. A car drove by and slowed down, but Justus didn't have the energy to pay any attention to it.

The car stopped, a door opened, and the sound of a radio streamed out. The driver's footsteps were muffled by the snow but still audible.

This is how Dad died, Justus thought. *He died in the snow.* Justus wanted to fall back into it. Then he felt a hand on his shoulder.

Thirty-six

Ann Lindell called Haver from Berit's apartment and told him that Justus had left the apartment early in the morning and not been heard from since. Berit had convinced Lindell that this wasn't like him. The sight of the butchered fish was enough. Berit had picked up some twenty Princesses of Burundi from the floor and laid them out on a plate.

Ola had not asked her anything about the other night. Lindell didn't know if he was angry. He had sounded normal. He had agreed to come by and talk to Berit.

Lindell thought about leaving before he arrived but didn't want to leave Berit alone. Deep down she also wanted to see Ola again. She felt guilty about what had happened and wanted to at least explain why she had jumped into the investigation.

He arrived after fifteen minutes, nodded to Ann, and shook Berit's hand. They sat down in the kitchen and Berit related what had happened. The plate of fish was on the kitchen counter and Lindell thought it was already starting to smell.

She looked at Ola Haver. He looked tired. The lines in his face, which she normally didn't notice, stood out more than usual. She couldn't help gazing at him in a new way, as if he were someone she didn't know, and she thought how handsome he was. Well, *handsome* was perhaps not the right word. *Nice-looking* was better. His hands were on the kitchen table, his eyes kind and directed at Berit, who was talking. At one point he glanced at her before again redirecting his whole attention to Berit.

He's ignoring me, she thought. *He's upset and angry, but he's keeping it under wraps. He's probably had a fight with Rebecka and I'm the reason.* It evoked conflicting feelings in her. She regretted what had happened, but it also generated a thrill that ran down her body. *Forbidden love,* she thought, and smiled when she realized how melodramatic it sounded. Berit finished talking and Lindell suddenly realized that both she and Ola were looking at her.

"I'm sorry," she said. "I was lost in thought."

Ola raised his eyebrows.

"Could you write down the names of his friends and anyone else he might go see?" he said to Berit.

"I've already called everyone," she said. "He isn't with any of them."

"Do you think he knows anything about the murder?"

Lindell caught the subtext of Haver's question: *Did Justus feel threatened?* But Berit didn't seem to understand.

"No, what would he know?"

"Maybe he's seen or heard something?"

Berit shook her head.

"I don't think so," she said, but the tone of her voice revealed she was weighing this new possibility.

"Why did he behead the fish?"

Lindell had asked the same question, and it had driven Berit to tears. Now she hesitated before answering.

"John sometimes called me his Princess of Burundi," she said in a low voice. "When he was happy he had a habit of calling me special names."

She looked uncomfortable, ashamed, but also genuinely perplexed. Ann Lindell took her hand, which was cold. Berit met her eyes and slowly the words started to come out. She told them about Lennart's visit and his accusations.

When she finished, Lindell saw that Haver was trying to decide how to proceed. A few seconds went by.

"Are there any grounds for these accusations?"

Berit looked at him with empty eyes. *She's tired to death,* Lindell thought. *She'll collapse soon.* She had seen it before, how the tension grew, only to be released in screams. But Berit appeared to have some strength left.

"We loved each other," she said with a quiet but firm voice.

She simply let the four words hang in the air without elaborating, as if there were nothing else to say. Lindell had the impression that she didn't care if they believed her or not, that it was enough for her that she knew the truth and that John had known it.

Haver swallowed.

"Could John have been interested in anyone else?" he said, and Lindell knew he felt bad about continuing in this vein.

Berit shook her head.

"I knew John," she said and took a deep breath. Haver shot Lindell a look.

"You don't understand," Berit said. "We only had each other."

Haver swallowed again, but had to keep going.

"Justus seems to have believed Lennart," he said in a dry, strangely mechanical voice, as if he were trying to neutralize his own presence. "What reasons could he have for doing this if your marriage was as happy as you describe?"

"He's a boy who has lost his father," Berit said.

"You mean he's searching for answers."

Berit nodded.

"Can he have seen or heard anything that would give him an idea of who the murderer is?"

"No, I don't think so." Her voice was as thin as ice after the first frost.

"Many people have said that John seemed to be planning something, a heist or some such thing. Do you have any idea what it could have been?"

Berit stared into the table.

"I don't know," she said, barely audible. "Apparently he talked to Justus about us moving somewhere, but that wasn't anything he discussed with me."

"Move where?"

"I don't know. I don't understand any of this."

"Okay," Haver said. "We'll put out an alert for Justus, but I don't think he's in any danger. He's probably out walking around the town."

Berit looked drained of energy. Lindell got up and went to check on

Erik, who was sleeping in his stroller in the hall. He would be waking up soon. Haver and Berit talked in the kitchen.

Suddenly Lindell came to think of the ham still on the stove at home. She hurried out to the others and said she had to go home immediately. Haver gave her a quick look but didn't say anything. She went up to Berit in order to say something comforting but couldn't find the right words. Berit looked at her without expression. *May the boy be safe,* was all that went through Lindell's head.

She ran over to the car with Erik whimpering in the stroller. There was a parking ticket on her windshield. She tossed it into the backseat.

Her parents would be arriving in a few hours. *I'll have to buy a new ham,* she thought and turned onto Vaksalagatan. At the same time the cell phone rang. She picked it up, convinced that it would be Ola.

"I know, I know," she said, "but the ham is going to be ruined."

"Hi," said a familiar voice, and she almost rammed the car in front of her as she braked for a red light at the intersection of highway E4.

Thirty-seven

Justus knew where to go. There was a hole in the fence. The construction site nearby made it even easier since the scaffolding shielded him from the street.

A feeling of power surged through him. No one saw him, no one heard him, no one knew what he was about to do. He stopped by a puddle of oil that shone with metallic darkness against the white ground, and looked back. He had left tracks in the snow but he didn't care. He was planning to take the same route back and he could erase his tracks then.

A piece of sheet metal sticking out of a container vibrated in the wind and the sound made him stop one more time. He looked up at the familiar building but it was only now that he saw how worn down the place was. When he was little, this had been a palace and John had been king. This was the place of the good sounds and smells. This was where his father grew to a giant in the shower of sparks, handling the black, heavy steel plate with ease. When struck, the metal resonated at a deep pitch and left a distinct smell that stayed on your fingers for days, just like the stainless steel burnished as fine as a mirror and that reflected light all over the blackened shop ceiling.

When John and the other workers took a break in the back room, the shop seemed to rest. Justus would walk around in the silence and touch the welded seams that ran like scars across the metal. He heard voices and laughter from the back room. Often they called his name and he would sample the hawthorn juice from the Finnish archipelago and eat sandwiches with black fingerprints on the cheese.

A car drove by on the street and Justus sneaked in behind the container, continuing on to the back of the building where there were a few windows closer to the ground. He smashed one of these with an iron pipe. He wasn't particularly afraid of being discovered because a high fence ran along the back of the property and no one was working on the construction site.

He cleared glass and debris from the window and hoisted himself up with the help of a pile of crates. The back room looked like it always did. There was a newspaper on the table where John usually sat. He pushed it to the ground. Where Erki sat there was a book of matches, which he picked up. Now there was no hesitation in his movements. It was as if the sight of the old lunchroom strengthened his resolve. He opened the makeshift plywood door of a storage area and dragged out a few containers of gasoline and oil. There were also jars and bottles filled with various chemicals. He carried the containers to assorted places in the shop. In Sagander's office he poured out five liters of ligroin.

He did a final walk-through of the shop floor, looking around John's old workplace. He was getting dizzy from all the smells. He poured out a whole container of gasoline in and all around the lunchroom, squirting some on the table and chairs, and then crawling out the back window.

The wind was picking up. He waited outside the window for a while before he took out the matches. The first match went out immediately, as did the second. He counted the ones that were left and worried that there wouldn't be enough. He crawled in again and grabbed some newspaper, soaking a corner in the gasoline before he crawled out again.

Before he lit the newspaper and threw it in he thought about John. What was it he had said about dreams?

He heard a *whoosh* from inside and then came something like an explosion. The remaining window was blown out and Justus was almost hit by the glass projectiles flying through the air. In awe he watched as a pillar of fire shot out from the window. Then he ran. As he was crawling out through the fence, he suddenly remembered about erasing his footprints. He hesitated before crawling back through it and looked around for something he could use to sweep the snow clean.

Many small explosions came from inside the building and he thought about the gas. There were a number of gas bottles inside and he knew how dangerous they were. John had talked about that. He grabbed a piece of metal and ran to the back of the building. It was impossible for him to get all the way to the window, but he wiped the snow as far as he could, then ran dragging the piece behind him until he reached the street. Then he tossed the piece of metal onto a heap of scraps and ran off, laughing.

He ran westward, into the city, but stopped himself after fifty meters. John would have walked calmly. That was smarter.

He worried about the tracks outside the window but suddenly realized that the intense heat would melt all the snow around the building. He had been wearing gloves, so there would be no fingerprints. The man who had put his hand on Justus's shoulder, the one who had compelled him to get up from the snowbank and who had given him a ride into town, would never connect him with the fire. He had dropped him off on Kungsgatan, probably a kilometer from the shop. Justus had told him that he wanted to go see a friend, had tried to take a shortcut through the forest, and had gotten lost.

The emergency call came at 2:46 P.M. from someone who happened to be driving past the shop. A fire truck was on the scene in seven minutes. Two patrol cars arrived a few minutes later. They immediately cordoned off the area with yellow tape.

"A machine workshop," the commanding fireman explained succinctly to the police officer who walked over. "Sorry to hear about your colleague, by the way. We lit a candle at the station when we heard the news."

For a moment the uniformed policeman stood completely still before he picked up his phone and called in to work. The first thing he had seen was a sign saying SAGANDER'S MECHANICAL WORKSHOP. He knew that was where John Jonsson had worked.

"I have an aquarium," he later explained to Haver.

Ola Haver got the call when he was on his way back from Berit's, and he arrived on the scene some five minutes later. He had had to negotiate the blockades on Björkgatan.

"It's burning like hell," the uniformed policeman had said.

Haver, who was looking at the smoke and sparks rising into the sky, became unexpectedly irritated for some reason and snapped at his colleague that he could damn well see that. The latter had only stared back at him and mumbled something to himself.

The wind was blowing from the east and drove the flames toward the building that was being constructed. A pile of lumber under a tarp caught fire but was immediately extinguished by the firefighters.

Haver stared at the building. The fire had broken through the roof and yellow-orange flames were shooting up. It was a hauntingly beautiful sight. Haver saw the stress and focus in the firefighters' faces. Haver was unable to do anything to help them and it bothered him. He grabbed the fire commander's shoulder.

"What do you think? Arson?"

"Hard to say. It appears to have started in the back, but has spread rapidly to the rest of the building."

"By a series of explosions," Haver said.

"I think you could safely call them that. Come over here and let me show you something."

The fireman walked off with Haver hurrying behind. The heat emitted by the burning building was even more intense. Haver was forced to shield his face with his hand.

They stopped at the hole in the fence. The fire commander pointed silently to the swept tracks on either side of the fence. Haver got down on his knee and scrutinized the snow.

"Someone has been here and tried to sweep away their tracks," he said and got up again.

The sound of another explosion made him jump.

"You'd better go back now," the fireman said. "There's gas in there."

Haver shot him a look.

"What can you do about that?"

"Try to cool it down," the other one said curtly, and now all of his attention was directed at his colleagues' efforts to contain the violent blaze.

Haver slowly walked back to the street, went over to the construction site, and placed himself behind a tall steel container. *This thing can stand up to a lot of punishment,* he thought and fished out his cell phone. Ryde answered right away. Haver started to explain where he was but was interrupted and informed by his colleague that he was already on his way.

Before Haver had time to put the phone back again it rang. It was Ann Lindell, and for a moment Haver felt that everything was back to normal. Ann wanted to explain why she had left Berit's apartment so suddenly. She told him about the ham and her parents.

"Sagander's workshop is burning," he interrupted. "It could be arson."

He heard her catch her breath.

"Has the boy turned up?"

He sensed what she was thinking.

"What do you think?" he asked.

"It could be coincidence," she said slowly. Haver heard in her voice that she was on edge.

"We have to make sure he's safe."

Haver peeked around the corner of the container. A new explosion shook the building, but Haver didn't think it was from the gas, because then it would have been more violent.

"It's burning like hell."

"Where is the workshop? Does it pose a risk to the surrounding area?" Lindell wondered.

"The wind is pretty strong," Haver said and explained where the workshop was.

"Where do you think Justus is?" Lindell asked. "It's getting dark now. He's probably beside himself. I think we should take Berit's concern seriously."

"Sure," Haver said.

He saw Ryde walking in the distance with a firefighter at his heels who was gesticulating and from the looks of it arguing vehemently, but Ryde gave him only a cursory glance and walked on. Haver smiled and told Lindell he had to go.

"One last question," she said. "Have you checked out Lennart? Justus might have gone to see him."

"Ryde's here. See you," Haver said and hung up.

He waved to Ryde, who looked energized.

"They talk too damned much," he said, and Haver understood that he meant the firefighters.

"There's gas in there," he said.

"Did someone start it?"

Haver told him about the tracks around the fence, and before he was finished, Ryde walked around the side of the container.

"Idiot," Haver said to himself.

He stuck his head out and saw Ryde kneeling by the hole. He took a camera out of his bag and started to work. Snow started to fall. Ryde worked quickly. Haver sympathized with his eagerness, his energy perhaps bolstered by the fear of a gas explosion.

The phone rang again, but before he managed to answer the signal cut out. He didn't bother checking to see who had called. At that moment there was an incredible bang and Haver saw how Ryde instinctively threw himself to the ground. One end of the building collapsed completely. Haver watched in fascination as part of the roof hesitated for a moment before it started to sink as if in slow motion, sending off a shower of sparks that transformed the sky into a sparkling show.

"Jesus, Ryde!" Haver shouted as the latter crawled through the hole in the fence and ran hunched over toward the contruction site. *Thank God,* Haver thought, but was then struck by the thought that several of the firefighters had been close to the explosion. He saw how one of the firefighters' cranes swung around and a powerful stream of water was directed into the gaping hole. Clouds of steam rose and shrouded the other end of the building completely for a few seconds. Then another fire truck with a sky lift pulled up and Haver saw two men in the cage.

"Amazing," he mumbled at this display of bravery, and listened to the orders shouted over the din.

Ryde came walking down the street. He stopped under a streetlight and checked his camera. He was bleeding on one cheek but seemed completely oblivious to the fact. Haver ran over to him.

"That was a hell of an explosion," Ryde said. "But the camera made it."

"You're bleeding," Haver said and made an attempt to check his wound.

"I fell," Ryde said. "Someone has crawled in and out of that hole, that's for sure. Hard to say if it's one person or several, but it's clear the guy tried to sweep away his own tracks. There's a strange look about it."

"Any prints?"

Ryde shook his head.

"Looks like someone dragged a two-by-four behind them. I'll try to do a more thorough check. Do you think it's going to blow?"

Haver shrugged. In spite of all the dramatics, he felt calm. He knew the anxiety and shock would make themselves felt later.

The ham was a lost cause, Ann realized as soon as she got into the kitchen. The temperature had reached almost ninety degrees. She turned off the burner and pulled the pot to the side. She resisted the impulse to throw the whole thing away. It was still food. Maybe she could fry it up.

She sighed, sat down at the kitchen table, checked the time, and thought about Justus. Where was he? Berit had called everyone she could think of, even Lennart, but the latter hadn't answered. Berit knew he had caller ID and perhaps he was deliberately not answering. If Justus was there, he would know that she was worried and he wouldn't have anything against letting her stew.

Ann got up, checked the time again, and went to Erik. He had been fed and was now sleeping in his bed. The apartment was quiet. It was too quiet for her tastes. The anxiety drove her to the window and she looked out into the late-afternoon dark. A car drove into the parking lot, a man got out, took a number of grocery bags from the trunk, and went to the front door of number 8.

She thought about Edvard, who had called to wish her a Merry Christmas. It was the first time they had spoken since they had said good-bye to each other at the hospital in Östhammar that fateful evening last summer.

She had been forced to pull off onto the side of the motorway, although she knew it was dangerous, but she was unable to talk to Edvard and continue to drive safely. What more had he said? She couldn't remember. His words were obscured by fog, as if the conversation had taken place decades ago. She had asked him how he was and how his teenage boys were doing. Had he asked about Erik? She couldn't remember, but she had at least sensed a question about how things were going for her and the baby.

They had ended the conversation after a few minutes, stressed as she was by cars honking as they drove by. He had sounded like himself, thoughtful and warm, the way he did when they had felt so much for each other.

Soon her parents would be here and Ann thought about rushing down to the nearest store to pick up a new ham, but suddenly she didn't care what they thought. Her parents could eat dry ham. There was enough broth to please her father.

The doorbell rang shortly before four.

"Here we are," her mother said cheerily when Ann opened the door.

And she was unexpectedly happy to see them. Her mother was carrying several large grocery bags with Christmas presents. Her father was carrying the food.

"And there's more in the car," her mother said when she saw her daughter's look. "Is he sleeping?"

They hung up their coats and looked around. Ann felt a rising sense of unease. It was only now that she realized she would be a captive for the next four days. She wouldn't be able to get away. But then she felt guilty. They were, after all, her parents, and they had been looking forward to this visit for months. They immediately walked into Erik's room. Her mother teared up at the sight of the little one in his bed.

"What a darling child," she said and gently stroked his thin locks.

Her father didn't say anything but was humming, something that Ann interpreted as approval.

"I cooked the ham too long," she said, breaking the spell. It was best to get it out of the way.

"How many degrees?" her mother asked.

"Ninety," Ann said and left Erik's bedroom.

"Is there any broth?" her father asked.

Ann turned around and smiled at him.

"Lots," she said.

"In that case," he said, satisfied.

"Ninety," her mother echoed.

"Erik was crying and I forgot to check it. I think he has colic."

"Does he cry a lot?"

"Yes," Ann said. "But mostly at night."

She walked out into the kitchen and everything felt wrong. She stared at the ham, which had contracted into a grayish lump. The smell made her step back. She heard her mother still making cooing noises in Erik's bedroom. She knew she should start to unpack the food they had brought and exclaim delightedly over their spare ribs, herring salad, homemade pâté, cured herring, but she couldn't bring herself to.

"I'm going out for a while," she shouted and walked to the front door.

Her mother immediately left Erik's room, stopped in the doorway, and stared at her with bafflement.

"Going out?"

"There's something I have to do. If Erik wakes up just give him a little baby porridge. There's a box on the kitchen counter."

"But we only just got here."

"I won't be gone long, I promise. Maybe I can get a new ham. Is there anything else we need?"

Her mother was hurt but also concerned.

"Is it your job?"

She knew her daughter.

"Not exactly," Ann said evasively and put her coat on. She pretended to think it over, trying to smooth over her escape by reaching out to her mother in some way, but she couldn't think of anything to say. Instead she gave her mother a halfhearted smile and opened the door.

"Only give him one bottle," she said, her body already turning away. "If he has more he gets a tummy ache. He likes a little mashed banana too," she added and slipped out.

Lindell immediately called Haver, but he didn't answer. She checked the time and decided to go to Sagander's workshop. Maybe he was still there.

When she arrived there wasn't much left of the building. The oldest part, which had been made out of wood, was completely devoured. The two masonry ends and a gable remained as sooty ruins. The snow that had not melted on the ground was no longer white but covered in sooty particles. The firefighting operation was still in process but no open flames were visible.

She looked around for Ola Haver and was beginning to think he had left the scene when she spotted him.

She walked over and stood close to him. He hadn't seen her. He was talking to the fire chief, whom she recognized. He nodded to her over Ola's shoulder and Ola turned. He laughed when he saw her.

"Couldn't stay away, I see."

"My mom and dad are looking after Erik. Have you heard anything about Justus?"

Haver shook his head. He ended the conversation with the fire chief, who gave Lindell an amused look.

"We've called Sagander. We thought he would want to come down but it turns out he's on bed rest."

"Bed rest?"

"He had an operation recently and has developed an infection," Haver said, and his expression shifted so perceptibly that Lindell thought he was wincing in pain.

"What is it?" she asked and touched his arm.

"The crutch," he said. "I knew there was something. The hospital," he added, as if that explained everything.

"Tell me more," Lindell said.

She had seen that look before and knew it must be something important. He drew her aside and she liked the feeling of his hand on her arm.

"Sagander has recently had an operation, probably at Akademiska Hospital. The knife was stolen from a car in the hospital parking garage. Maybe Sagander has a pickup truck. Maybe he's the 'angry man' from Vaksala square?"

"That's a lot of maybes," Lindell said.

"I should have thought of it before. When I came down here to question Sagander he was sitting the whole time, zooming around on his office chair. A crutch was leaned up against the wall by the door."

It was all falling into place. The vague feeling he had around construction sites now had its explanation. The construction site at the hospital and the neighboring site here. He recalled how he had watched the workers for a while and how one of them had waved to him. As the son of a construction worker he had always liked the sight of pits, work sites, and temporary barracks. Construction had been the key word, but his love of construction in general had masked the connection for a while.

"Who is the angry man?" Lindell asked.

Haver gave an succinct account of what Hahn had told them.

"If we accept your line of reasoning for now," Lindell said, "do you think Justus could have suspected that Sagander was responsible for the murder?"

Haver looked at her thoughtfully. Lindell assumed he was trying to make more connections now that the first pieces of the puzzle had fallen into place.

"I don't know," he said quietly and looked around.

Nearby, a fireman was rubbing his face with snow, spitting and grumbling. He straightened his back and turned to look at the burned building as if he fully expected it to burst into flame and smoke again.

"They're doing a fantastic job," Lindell said and nodded to the firefighter.

Haver didn't answer. He had his cell phone in his hand.

"Maybe we should call Berglund," he said. "And a patrol car."

Lindell knew what he was thinking: *Drive out to Sagander's house.*

"Where does he live?"

"On a farm in the Börje area, I think. I'll have Berglund check it out."

He dialed a number and Lindell walked away. She took out her phone and called Berit. The phone rang several times before she picked up. Her voice was muted, as if she was expecting bad news.

"Did Justus know Sagander very well?" Lindell asked.

"Sagge? Why do you ask?"

Lindell thought about telling her that the workshop had just burned to the ground but decided not to.

"I thought that . . ."

"I can tell you that Sagander was hated in our family. Justus would never have gone out to see him. Why would you think that?"

Lindell told her about the fire and heard Berit draw her breath. She had said it herself: Sagander was hated. Sometimes the step from hate to arson was not so big.

"Do you think Justus did it?"

"No, I'm just asking," Lindell said.

"Are you at the shop? What does Sagge say?"

"He's not here. He can't walk right now. We're driving out to see him."

"You too? Where's the baby?"

"He's with my mother."

Lindell left her car at the scene. They picked up Berglund at the station and a patrol car with three officers followed behind.

"You shouldn't be here," Berglund said as soon as he got into the car.

"I know," Lindell said curtly. "But I am."

"And the baby?"

"Mom and Dad are visiting."

"And you run out on them? What are you thinking? It's almost Christmas!"

"That's why," Lindell said. "I knew it would drive them nuts."

Berglund sighed in the backseat.

"I never really believed that Hahn killed Little John," said Haver, who had paid no attention to the squabble between Berglund and Lindell.

"Sammy was the only one who put his money on Hahn," Berglund said.

"He always wants to go against the pack," Lindell said to him. It felt good to be back among her colleagues.

"Does Ottosson know you're here?" Berglund asked sternly. She shook her head.

"Not even my mother knows I'm here," she said and gave him her sweetest smile. Haver turned on the car radio, and the Pointer Sisters' "I'm So Excited" came through the speakers. Lindell gave Berglund a meaningful look and sang along. ". . . I'm about to lose control . . ."

"You're impossible," Berglund said, but smiled. "Turn it down."

"I like this song," Haver said.

"I promise I'll be completely calm," Lindell said.

"I'll believe that when I see it," Haver said. He chuckled, but both Berglund and Lindell knew it was from nervous tension.

Thirty-eight

Sagander's house sat on a small hill. If the circumstances for their visit had been different, Lindell would have commented on how idyllic it looked. It was a traditional red-and-white-painted house in two levels with a covered porch that also functioned as a balcony to the upper story. Two small Christmas trees had been put out on the balcony, covered in a string of lights just like the tall one out in the yard that was eight meters or more. A few smaller buildings on either side with cozy lights in the windows completed the look of a well-established farm on the Uppland plains.

"Is it for real?" Haver asked as they drove up the small road to the house.

"He probably owns just the farmhouse, and not the farm proper," Berglund said.

On either side of the road someone had placed ornamental arrangements of juniper twigs. Small Santas peeked out from between the branches.

"Isn't it a little out of control?" Haver snorted.

"I think it looks nice," Berglund said.

Lindell didn't say anything, keeping an eye out for a red pickup truck.

"No car," she said.

They understood what she meant although three cars were parked in front of the house. Haver parked behind a run-down Nissan and the patrol car stopped behind Haver. Everyone got out at the same time. Six police officers, of which five were in uniform and armed. Even Haver was carrying his gun, which surprised Lindell.

The three patrol officers waited outside. A ragged dog ran over and sniffed their legs but disappeared as quickly as it had come. Lindell wondered if she should hang behind too, but an almost imperceptible gesture from Berglund told her it was all right to come along.

A woman in her sixties opened the door. She tried hard to appear relaxed and friendly but her eyes betrayed her. They fluttered between the three police officers, resting for a few seconds on Lindell as if hoping to find a show of support, woman-to-woman.

"Mrs. Sagander?"

Berglund's gentle voice, in contrast to his somewhat grumpy demeanor, made her attempt a weak smile as well as a nod.

"You must be looking for Agne," she said and stepped aside.

Lindell smiled at her as she crossed the threshold.

"Ann Lindell," she said and put out her hand.

"Gunnel," said the woman and smiled back.

The large hall was filled with the rich scent of Christmas baking. Lindell looked around. The door to the kitchen was open and inside Lindell could see a whole wall covered with copper wares, but above all it was the floor of the hall that drew one's gaze. It consisted of broad pine planks that shone from varnish and daily polishing. A gigantic bureau in the Swedish country style and a pair of antique Östervåla chairs, as well as homemade rugs in bold colors, underscored the rustic character of the home.

In one of the windows Lindell saw a glowing small-scale Advent church surrounded by cotton wool and a few Santas. Mrs. Sagander followed her gaze and told her that her father had made the model church and the gnomes sometime in the 1940s. This talk about everyday things enlivened her.

"Christmas is such a festive time," Lindell said.

Agne Sagander received them from his easy chair, one leg supported by an ottoman. Haver, who had first met him at the metalwork shop, thought he looked ill at ease in the comfortable room. It was evident that he did not like his current state. He sighed heavily as they came into the room.

"Here I am sitting like a goddamn cripple," he said, dispensing entirely with the polite formality of introductions.

"Agne, please," his wife said, submissive and tired.

"What the hell does it matter?" he asked.

"Pity about the shop," Berglund said.

"This is quite a delegation," Sagander said and looked at Lindell. "I know you from the papers. Murder and mayhem, is it really all that fun?"

Lindell walked up to him, stretched out her hand, and introduced herself. Sagander squeezed her hand forcefully. Lindell smiled.

Berglund also walked up and introduced himself.

"Do you hunt?" he asked.

"Yes, I bagged that one in Jämtland," Sagander said and looked up at the enormous elk head above the fireplace. "Eighteen points, as you can see. Ström's valley. There's an abundance of elk there. Or was," he added with a satisfied smile. "What about you, do you hunt?"

"I used to," Berglund said.

"Well, what do you have to say for yourselves? Do you have any leads? It feels like ape shit to be sitting here, I can tell you that much."

"Agne is in a great deal of pain," his wife inserted. "They operated on his back and now something seems to have gone wrong."

"It's those damned butchers at Akademiska," Sagander said. "Butchers."

"I think you have an infection," Gunnel Sagander said in a firmer voice. "You should go in."

"And be stuck there over Christmas? Not if I can help it."

"If it's an infection they'll give you antibiotics," she said. "Would you like some coffee?" she said, changing the topic and turning to Lindell.

"Thanks, that would be nice," she said. Mrs. Sagander left the room. Her husband gazed after her thoughtfully.

"The shop has burned to the ground," Haver said ruthlessly. "It's a fucking wasteland." He seemed to have adjusted his language to Sagander's own.

"So I've been told."

"Are you upset?" Lindell asked.

"Upset? What the hell kind of question is that?"

"We think someone put a match to it," Berglund said.

"Can't you sit down? From down here it feels as if you've come to pay your final respects."

The three officers sat down. Lindell felt like she was paying a visit to a sick, bad-tempered relative.

"Put a match to it," Sagander said. "Who would do that?"

"Are you on bad terms with anyone?"

"That would be the tax authorities, but I don't think they resort to arson. Hardly Ringholm, minister of finance, either, that yellow-bellied sap."

"We've been thinking," Haver said and leaned forward. "Recently one of your former employees was murdered and now your shop has burned down. Is there a connection?"

Sagander shook his head.

"What did you do on the seventeenth of December?" Berglund asked.

Sagander looked at him for a second before answering. Lindell thought she saw a brief look of disappointment on his face, as if Sagander thought that Berglund was letting down a fellow hunter.

"I can tell you that. That was the day I lay under the knife," he said and gestured to his back.

"You recovered quickly," Haver said. "When I met you in your office on the nineteenth you seemed very fit."

"I was operated on for a slipped disk and they send you home as quick as the devil."

"When did you come home?"

"The afternoon of the eighteenth, my birthday."

"What kind of car do you drive?" Berglund asked.

"The Volvo out there," Sagander said quickly. It was obvious that he was in pain and that he hated it, not for the pain itself, Lindell sensed, but because of the inactivity it imposed.

"How did you get home?"

"My wife picked me up."

"In the Volvo?"

"Yes, how else? In a limousine?"

Mrs. Sagander came into the room with a tray covered with cups and plates, buns and cakes.

"Let's see," she said and turned to Lindell. "Maybe you could push those newspapers aside?"

The cups rattled. Lindell helped to set them out.

"This is beautiful china," she said, and Gunnel Sagander looked at her as if she were drowning at sea and was being thrown a lifesaver.

"I hope you aren't sick of gingerbread yet," she said.

I would be enjoying this if it weren't for Agne Sagander, Lindell thought.

"The coffee is brewing," Mrs. Sagander said.

"I saw some pretty copper pots in your kitchen on the way in. Do you mind letting me have a closer look?"

"Of course not. Come with me."

They walked out to the kitchen and Lindell felt Agne Sagander's eyes in her back.

"He gets a little brusque," Mrs. Sagander said when they were in the kitchen. "It's the pain."

"I can see that," Lindell said. "He seems like the kind of person who thrives on being up and about."

Together they viewed the pans and pots. Gunnel told her that she had inherited most of it but also bought some things at auctions.

"He goes crazy when I come home with more stuff, but then he thinks I make the house look nice."

"That's so like a man," Lindell said. "You picked him up at the hospital, I heard."

"Yes, that's right," Gunnel said, and her eyes lost some of their spark.

"That was the eighteenth?"

"Yes; it was his birthday, but there wasn't much in the way of a celebration. He was in a bad mood mostly and wanted to get back to work."

"I can't believe they send people home so soon. He had been operated on the day before."

"It must be the budget cuts, but he wanted to come home. It's worse for those who are alone."

"The ones who don't have ground service, you mean?"

Gunnel smiled.

"Ground service," she said slowly. "I don't think of my role in that way. I like making things nice around the house, and he's not as impossible as he seems."

Lindell thought that Gunnel Sagander had aged attractively, and there was a warmth in her voice that indicated that she had seen and heard a great deal but forgiven and made her peace with that which hadn't gone her way. Was she happy? Or was she simply making the best of her role of home-maker and wife to that grumpy old man?

Lindell had seen too many of these women who subordinated them-selves, but could also feel the temptation of giving in to a more traditional woman's role. It would be so easy to be like her mother. So seemingly se-cure. She wanted to talk to Gunnel Sagander about this but realized that it wasn't the right time and would probably never be right either.

The coffee in the percolator gurgled a last time. Gunnel gave Lindell a hasty glance as if she had read her thoughts.

"Are you married?" she asked and poured the coffee into a big Thermos.

"No, single with a little Erik."

Gunnel nodded and they walked back out into the living room.

Lindell could see from his face that Haver was disappointed—or was it the exhaustion? He sat slouched back in his seat and looked at his hands. He glanced at Gunnel Sagander and Lindell when they walked back in. Agne Sagander was talking. Berglund was listening attentively.

"Little John was good at his work. A singular man," Sagander said. "It was too bad I had to let him go."

"You fired him," Berglund corrected him.

"I had no choice," Sagander said. "I have a business to run. Employees—such as yourself, I might add—never understand."

"Of course," Berglund said and smiled.

"Another cup?" Gunnel asked and held the Thermos aloft.

"Thank you, I've had enough," Berglund said and got to his feet.

Haver looked up at the sky. The clouds pulled back like a curtain at the theater and revealed a starry sky. He moved his mouth as if to say something but changed his mind.

"Thank you for the coffee," he said to Gunnel Sagander. She didn't say anything in reply, just nodded. Berglund shook her hand. Lindell lingered for a moment.

"You must have known John," she said.

"Of course. He worked at the shop for years. I always liked him."

"His son, Justus, has run away. Do you have any idea where he might have gone?"

Gunnel shook her head.

"He ran away? The poor boy."

A car engine started up. It was the patrol car. Lindell shook Gunnel's hand and thanked her. Haver and Berglund were about to get into Haver's car when he stiffened, as if his back suddenly hurt. Lindell saw him leave the car and walk a few meters to the side, crouch down, and shout something to Berglund. The latter reached into the car for something.

"What is it?" Gunnel Sagander said anxiously.

"I don't know," said Lindell.

"I just thought of something, where Justus may have gone. John and Erki Karjalainen, his former coworker, were very good friends."

Lindell had trouble concentrating on what Mrs. Sagander was saying. The outside lights only weakly illuminated the spot where Haver and Berglund were crouched. Berglund turned on his flashlight. She saw Haver's excitement in the way he turned to Berglund. The latter shook his head, looked up at the house, stood up, and took out his phone.

"Erki was almost like a father to John, especially in the beginning," Gunnel Sagander was saying. "When John needed advice. He could be a little impetuous but that never had an effect on Erki."

Lindell craned her neck.

"What are they doing down there? Have they dropped something?"

"Maybe they found something," Lindell said. "What were you saying about Erki?"

"Maybe Justus has gone to Erki. I know he likes him."

"Do you know where he lives?"

"He lived in Årsta before, but now I think he's moved out to Bälinge."

Haver straightened up, put a hand to his lower back, and said something to Berglund.

"I can ask Agne. We could call Erki."

"Yes, ask Agne. I'll call," Lindell said.

Gunnel went in and Lindell hurried over to her colleagues. The temperature had fallen noticeably and it was sparklingly cold. She tightened the scarf around her. Their breath formed puffs of smoke.

"What is it?" she asked.

Haver looked at her and all trace of tiredness had left his eyes.

"Tracks," he said and pointed to the ground by his feet. Lindell thought she could see a smile on his face.

"Explain," she said.

Haver told her about the snow dump in Libro where they had found John.

"Do you think it's the same car?"

Haver nodded.

"Eskil is on his way," he said, and now Lindell saw how nervous he was.

"Should we ask Mrs. Sagander which visitors they've had lately?" Lindell asked. At the same time her cell phone rang. It was her mother, wondering where she was. Erik had woken up once and they had given him the baby porridge, he had fallen asleep again, but now he had woken up again.

"Is he crying?" Lindell asked and walked away from her colleagues.

"No, not exactly," her mother said, and Ann wondered what she meant.

"I'll be home soon. Give him some banana, he likes that."

"He doesn't need a banana. He needs his mother."

"He has a grandmother," Ann said, but she regretted her words at the moment she said them.

There was silence on the other end.

"Just come home," her mother said and hung up.

Ann Lindell stood there with the phone in her hand, looked at Haver and Berglund, pretended to end the conversation in a normal way, and then returned to their midst.

"The baby-sitter?" Berglund said. Lindell nodded and she saw him give Haver a quick look. Then Ryde's old car came up the driveway. He braked and seemed to hesitate before driving up all the way to the house.

Lindell walked over to Gunnel Sagander, who was standing out on the porch. She was shivering.

"Should we go in?" Lindell asked.

Gunnel shook her head.

"What is it?" she asked again and looked intently at Lindell.

"Car tracks," Lindell said. "I have to ask you who has visited you today."

Gunnel looked away.

"Agne's brother Ruben," she said tersely. "He stopped by a few hours ago. He was going off to hunt hare and wanted to borrow a box of ammunition for his rifle."

"Did he have the rifle with him?"

"He usually does," Gunnel said. "He is . . ."

She fell silent. Both of the women watched as Ryde got out of his car, walked over to the other two, and crouched down. Berglund turned the flashlight back on.

"Where does Ruben live?"

"Up the hill," Gunnel said and pointed to a pair of houses a couple of hundred meters away.

"Where the lights are on, the house with the two chimneys?"

Gunnel nodded.

Lindell walked back to the car tracks. Ryde gave her a disapproving look but didn't say anything. He took out a folding ruler and measured the tracks.

"Same width," he said.

Then he took out a camera and quickly took half a dozen pictures. The flash lit up the snow. Haver shivered. Lindell told him that it was most likely Sagander's brother's car, that he was armed and lived close by.

Ola Haver looked at her but Lindell sensed that he was far away in his thoughts.

"The knife that Mattias stole was in the car. The car that made the tracks in Libro and now here," Haver said. "Ruben visited his brother in the hospital the day after the murder."

"Fucking amateur," Ryde said.

"Ruben Sagander," Lindell said, and all four turned north to look at the house with the two chimneys.

"He's armed," Haver said.

As if on a given signal they all started walking to Agne Sagander's house. Gunnel sensed what was going on; they all saw it. She drew the scarf tight around her neck, straightened up, and steeled herself.

"Do you know if Ruben visited his brother in the hospital on the day after the operation?" Lindell asked.

"Yes, we went there together."

"In Ruben's car?"

Gunnel nodded.

"Does he have a red-and-white pickup?"

A new nod.

"What's happened?" she asked, but Lindell sensed that Gunnel Sagander already knew.

"Did Ruben know John?" Berglund asked.

"Yes, certainly."

They went into the house. Haver made a call. Berglund talked to Agne Sagander, who was sitting where they had left him. Even Ryde took out his phone and made a call. Lindell was left in the hall with Gunnel.

"Could you get Erki's phone number now?" Lindell asked.

She knew she should go home. In some way she felt that this case no longer interested her. Perhaps it was because she hadn't taken part in much of the investigation. Was it thoughts of Justus that kept her here?

Haver finished his call and was about to say something when Berglund stepped out of the living room and carefully closed the door behind him.

"We'll have to send for an ambulance and some patrol officers," he said. "Sagander refuses to budge an inch. He says he can't be moved."

Berglund shared none of Haver's excitement. The soon-to-be retired police officer wanted to get home to his wife, children, grandchildren, and Christmas tree, but Lindell knew that he would work all through Christmas without complaining, if needed. He was still standing with his hand on the door handle and looked at Gunnel as if to commiserate with her or perhaps hear her comment on her husband's claimed immovability.

"He's stubborn," was all she said.

"How is his brother?" Haver asked.

They saw how she hesitated, choosing her words with care.

"He's like his brother in many ways—they're twins—but he's more hot-blooded, I have to say."

"Would you describe him as violent?"

"He has a wonderful wife," Gunnel said, as if this were an answer to his question.

Haver's phone rang and he picked up after the first ring. Lindell saw that he was sweating. She started thinking about Edvard. She felt a twinge in her stomach as she thought about how they had made love in their wooden palace at Gräsö, sapping the force of the north wind. One night she had tip-toed out of bed before sunrise, walked to the open window, detached the mosquito screen, and leaned out. The birds were singing at their greatest intensity. The sea lay still as a mirror and the temperature was already close to twenty degrees Celsius. When she turned to look at Edvard in the bed she had thought to herself that no person could be happier than this. During the night he had pulled the sheet off and a few beads of sweat glistened on his stomach.

"I guess we'll go up and see Ruben," Haver said, interrupting her stream of thought. "Two cars will be here soon. I told them to hurry."

"Can I borrow your car, Eskil?"

Ryde turned to Lindell and looked at her as if he didn't understand her question.

"I have to get into town," she said, as embarrassed as if she had asked to borrow his pants.

"Take mine," Haver said to save her, tossing the keys over.

"Thanks, Ola," she said and smiled. "I think you've got it sewn up," she added, using one of Edvard's expressions.

She stepped out onto the porch, unfolded the note with the phone number, and dialed it. It took five or six rings for Erki to answer. In the background she heard Christmas music and the rattle of plates.

She presented herself, but before she had time to explain why she was calling, Erki Karjalainen broke in.

"He's here," he said, and Lindell thought his accent was just like that of the Mumins.

She laughed with relief.

"Have you called Berit?"

"No," Erki said. "The boy won't let me."

"Can I come over?"

"Wait," Erki said, and Lindell heard how he walked away from the phone.

She tried to imagine how he lived, what he looked like, and how he was talking to the boy. It took a while, and she looked out over the fields in front of Sagander's house, the road with the juniper decorations and the brother's house a few hundred meters away. Would Agne call and warn his brother? She didn't think so. It would be hard for him to get to the regular phone, and even if he had a cell phone nearby he would probably let it stay where it was. It was a feeling based on Gunnel's reaction. She knew what was going on, even that her husband might be accused of accomplice to murder, but Lindell saw that deep inside she was relieved that the police were taking over. Maybe even Agne in all his grumpiness felt the same. *Twin brothers can be tricky*, Lindell thought, and recalled a case where one twin had raped a woman in Engelska park and where the other twin, although he abhorred the crime, nonetheless hesitated to testify against this brother.

Karjalainen returned to the phone. Lindell was allowed to come by, he reported, but she was not allowed to call Berit.

"I promise," she said.

Karjalainen lived twenty minutes away, if the shortcut through the forest was passable. She had taken that road with Edvard a few times. It was in those forests that they had made some of their best mushroom finds.

As she was walking to Haver's car she dialed Berit's number. She imagined her anxiously pacing around the apartment.

"We've found him," Lindell said right away.

Berit started to cry and Lindell had to wait before she could speak again.

"It will be a while before he comes home," Lindell said, "but he's in good hands, I promise."

Thirty-nine

Ruben Sagander kicked at a piece of sheet metal hard enough to send it flying. *Lucky the old man is dead,* he thought. He tried to keep himself calm by breathing in through his nose, filling his lungs and chest. Most of all he wanted to scream out his rage over the remains of the building in front of him.

Built in 1951, burned to the ground fifty years later. The sign with the text SAGANDER'S MECHANICAL WORKSHOP lay on the ground, still visible. One of the legs of a mobile crane used to fight the blaze had been positioned over it so that only the letters SAGA were visible.

Fury, as black as the soot on the only remaining wall, coursed through his body. He had talked briefly to one of the firefighters, telling him who he was and that he and his brother had started working in the shop for their father during the fifties. The firefighter had taken his anger for grief and tried to console him. It was clear that someone was responsible for starting the blaze. A full forensic investigation would be launched into the matter but the police had already found traces in the remains that indicated arson. It appeared that someone had systematically poured out flammable liquids in the building and then set it on fire.

"Who?" Ruben asked.

"The police will have to look into it," the firefighter said.

Now the very last stage of the fire operation remained. Ruben spotted the safe under a few collapsed beams. There was no money in it. Six months ago there had been almost a half a million there. His money. Agne knew it was black money from Ruben's entrepreneurial firm and had wavered when Ruben asked him to keep the money in the safe.

Someone had subsequently emptied the safe of the money and it was someone who knew the code. Ruben had never thought for a moment that it was Agne. Together they had tried to figure out who it was. They hadn't told any of the guys in the shop about the theft or noticed anything unusual in their behavior. They had returned from their vacation and started work as usual.

Their suspicions had fallen on John almost immediately. When Mattzon had mentioned in passing that he had seen John outside the shop one Sunday in August, they had been convinced. John was the one who had stolen Ruben's hard-earned money. A half million that was supposed to fix up the house in Spain where he and Maj-Britt were planning to retire.

Ruben's phone rang and he checked the caller ID, but didn't answer. He didn't have the energy to talk to his brother again. Instead he sat in the car and wondered what to do next. Half a million gone and the shop in ruins. He wanted to flee. Even from Maj-Britt.

He felt no remorse for John's fate. He was a thief and he had admitted as much, laughing Ruben right in the face. "Try to prove it," John had said and laughed even more. What he regretted was having gone about it with so much vehemence. He should have let John go, watched him, maybe threaten to hurt his son, and in one way or another forced John to give back the money. Now it was too late. There was only one avenue of recourse and that was confronting Berit. She would no doubt deny knowing anything about the theft, but he could still use the threat against Justus.

He looked over the ruins of the shop one last time. The spotlights that had been erected around the scene gave off a spooky light. A few of the firefighters were laughing. They were probably pleased at finally having contained the blaze.

He turned the key in the ignition and suddenly felt as if John were sitting in the backseat taunting him. He had to turn around but saw only the rifle and the hunting bag. He let off the parking brake and rolled off toward Gränby.

He felt that he was at a crossroads. This moment was going to determine the rest of his life. He knew he didn't have so much time left, five or maybe ten years. The doctors had given him some reason to hope, but that was with the qualifications of taking it easy, cutting out all tobacco and alcohol. He had sold his business and stopped smoking but still had a cognac from time to time. He wanted to end his life in Spain. He had slaved for forty years, first in the shop, then as a crane operator and driver on construction jobs, and finally owning his own business with a stable of around twenty machines for hire.

He was proud of what he had built up. It was none of anyone's business if he had managed to put away some money on the side. He had worked for every last penny. Little John had laughed at him, but who was laughing now? He must have stashed it somewhere. The only sensible course of action was to go to Berit and get it back.

Forty

The revolver on the table drew his gaze like a magnet. Lennart walked out into the kitchen again and again just to look at it. He had never owned a firearm of any kind, though he had often had a knife. The idea of going around with a revolver or pistol had never appealed to him. You could never be sure what it would lead to if the going got tough. The courts always looked more harshly on firearms, and they automatically carried higher sentences. A gun in your pocket made you a hard-core criminal, but with a knife you were just another drunk bum in a brawl.

The Belarusian dealer showed no surprise. He had heard what happened to Little John and completely understood Lennart's need. He even sold it to Lennart on an installment plan, which he normally never did. "Do me a favor and make sure you survive," the Russian had said laconically, "so you can pay me back my money."

Sergei had lived in Uppsala for four years. He had had come to Sweden via Estonia and demanded political asylum. If someone like Lennart had been in charge he would have been sent packing, but now he had to admit that he felt a certain gratitude toward him.

Lennart had never wanted to kill anyone, but he needed a powerful weapon. With a revolver in his hand people would know he meant business.

He couldn't help fingering the weapon. It was beautiful and frightening, threateningly metallic, and it filled him with anticipation, as if his own importance had grown. He wanted to keep it out so he could get used to the idea that he was armed.

Lennart had not had a drop of alcohol, not even a light beer, for thirty-six hours. He couldn't remember the last time he had been this sober. Maybe when he had been taken into custody by the police that time. But then he had been on the verge of confessing just so he could have a beer.

He felt like a new man, as if the old Lennart had stepped out of his body and was looking at his old shell. He saw himself walk around the apartment, stand in the window, look out at the snow, pick up the gun, and get dressed.

Tonight he wanted to get to the bottom of this. That's how he felt. He was sure that Berit was involved in some way, and now the truth was going to come out. He didn't want to hurt her, he couldn't hurt her. She was after all John's wife and mother to Justus.

He wanted so desperately to believe the assurances that she had been faithful, but Mossa's words kept ringing in his ears: *His whore for a wife.* Strong words. He had always trusted Mossa, and why would he lie about this?

Was it Dick? He hadn't seen him for a long time. Someone had said he was in Holland. *That may be as it is,* Lennart thought. *I can go there. If he thinks he can get out of this he's wrong. I will track him down to the ends of the world if need be.*

He stepped out onto the snowy street, sober as a god and cleansed from his past life. He felt a great calm and strangely enough thought of his father. Was it the short interlude of working with Micke that had brought back these more frequent thoughts of his father? Albin had been good, not only as a welder but as a father. This conviction had grown in Lennart over the years, not least when he saw John with Justus.

He sighed heavily. He was back on Brantings square again. No tractor, no noisy teenagers, just mounds of snow and him. His need for alcohol made his innards contract as if he had a steel wire rigged up inside, a steel wire that was slowly being turned tighter, a fragile center of despair. It could break at any moment. He could run home and have a swig of something, but that would essentially mean giving up on the search for John's killer forever.

He tramped on with gritted teeth. Christmas stars and blinking colored lights on the balconies lit up his way over Skomakar hill. "Albin and John," he mumbled quietly. He felt as if Albin were with him, as if his father had stepped down from his roof and his heaven in order to support him. His father walked beside him in wordless sympathy. Occasionally he pointed up and Lennart understood that Albin had once been up there on those rooftops.

Forty-one

Lindell drove slowly, in part because she was not used to the car, in part because the driving conditions were less than ideal. The wind had driven snow from the fields into tightly packed drifts, and when she made it into the forest the road was deceptively slippery underneath this white cover.

When she spotted the bell tower of Bälinge church she knew that she had made it. She had marked on Haver's map the street where Erki Karjalainen lived. After winding her way down small roads in the densely built suburb she eventually came to a dead end. She had to turn the car around and realized that despite the map she had taken a wrong turn.

A rising sense of irritation increased her nervousness. She recognized these symptoms. It was the feeling of creeping danger. Admittedly Justus was in safety, but something else was casting a dark shadow over her. She guessed it was the fact that a murderer was on the loose. It suddenly hit her that it was her concern for her colleagues that made her extra jumpy. Ruben Sagander could be out there somewhere in the dark December night. He had borrowed ammunition from Agne and perhaps he was still armed.

Haver and Berglund would wait until their backup arrived, then they would put on bulletproof vests and approach Sagander's house with the greatest care. She knew all this, but she also knew that violence and perpetrators of violence had their own logic.

When she finally arrived at Karjalainen's house and stepped out of the car she paused and pricked up her ears, as if she would have been able to hear any resulting noise from the Börje area, over ten kilometers away. Haver hated weapons, not least after the events at Biskops Arnö when he—without acceptable provocation—had opened fire against a serial killer whom he erroneously believed to be threatening Lindell with a pistol. Lindell had reacted by also opening fire and the man had died.

Haver and Lindell had never talked seriously about that event. Now Haver found himself in the presence of another assumed murderer. Before she left the house, Lindell had asked Haver if he had his gun. He had nodded but not said anything. Lindell was certain that he was thinking of the fateful chain of events at the hut that summer night not so long ago but shoved away into a distant corner in both their minds.

She took out her cell phone and called home. This time her father answered, which surprised but pleased her. Erik had been up for an hour and his grandmother was with him.

"He's a plucky little boy," her father said.

Lindell smiled and they ended the conversation soon after.

Erki Karjalainen opened the door, a slight smile on his face. He let her in without a word, something she appreciated. She didn't have the stomach for empty Christmas phrases.

Justus was in the kitchen. A woman was at the stove stirring something in a pot. She looked up and smiled. There was a sweet scent in the air. The boy gave her a quick look, then cast down his eyes. On the table in front of him there was a plate and a glass of milk. Lindell sat down across from him. Erki lingered in the doorway for a moment before he also sat down at the table. The woman pulled the pot to one side, turned the heat off, and left the kitchen. Erki followed her with his gaze.

"My sister," he said.

Lindell nodded and looked at Justus, who met her eyes.

"How is it going?" she asked.

"Fine."

"I'm glad you're all right. We've been worried about you."

"I just went out for a while," Justus said defiantly.

"Your mother didn't know where you were."

Lindell found it hard to talk to teenagers. They were neither children nor adults. She always had the feeling that she was pitching her words at the wrong level, either too childish or too advanced. She needed Sammy's innate ability to reason with them.

Justus scratched the plate with a knife. He looked absentminded but Lindell sensed he was boiling inside.

"Did you hear that Sagander's workshop burned down?" she asked quietly and leaned closer to him.

He shook his head.

"You know," Erki said.

Justus looked at him hastily and for a moment Lindell saw the terror in his eyes, as if he was afraid of Erki but conscious of the folly of denying what he had probably just confided to him. Justus nodded.

"Tell me about it," Lindell said.

Justus began awkwardly, but after a while his words started to flow. He stopped in the middle of a sentence and looked at Lindell.

"Sagge is an idiot," he said.

"He has only praise for your father."

"He fired him," Justus said. "What good is his praise?"

"You have a point there, Justus," Lindell said with a smile.

When Justus had finished his story he appeared to realize for the first time that the fire had cost Erki his job. The terror returned to his eyes and he sucked in his breath.

"Take it easy," Erki said, as if he had read the boy's mind.

"What do you want to do now?" Lindell asked.

"I don't know."

"Shouldn't you call Berit and tell her where you are?"

"Am I going to jail?"

"You're under fifteen," Lindell said. "You can't be tried as an adult. There will be consequences, of course, but we'll keep in mind that your father has just died and that you've been extremely upset."

"One more thing," Erki said calmly, and Lindell's appreciation of him grew even more. "Justus has some money. Do you want me to tell her?"

The boy said nothing. Erki waited, then started to talk.

"He came here by taxi and I wondered where he got the money," Erki said and stretched his hand out for a backpack leaning against the wall. Lindell sensed what it contained but drew her breath when Erki unzipped it and revealed thick wads of five-hundred-kronor notes.

"How much is it?"

"I don't know," Erki said and put the backpack down. "I haven't counted it, but it must be a couple of thousand."

"I didn't take it all," Justus said almost inaudibly.

"Where did the money come from?" Lindell asked.

"It was Dad's."

"From the start?"

"We were planning to go to Africa," Justus said defiantly. "He had saved it up so we could start a fish farm. Maybe in Burundi."

"Do you know where the money came from?"

The boy shook his head.

"I know," Erki said. "It came from the shop."

"Tell me," Lindell said.

Erki and Justus looked at each other. Justus's expression changed. The mixture of aggression and passivity slowly gave way to a gentler expression and Lindell saw that Justus had inherited Little John's delicate features. The inner defenses gave way. He looked pleadingly at Erki, who took the boy's hand in his, enveloping it completely. Half a finger was missing from Erki's hand. Lindell and Erki exchanged a look. Lindell saw that he was touched.

"You may not know this but he was an expert in tropical fish," Erki said. "We all have our dreams, don't we? Our lives . . ."

Lindell waited for a continuation but it never came.

"How do you know the money came from the shop?"

"I've worked there a long time," Erki said. "I see a lot. I know."

Lindell left the subject. She would get the details in due course.

"Did Berit know about the backpack?"

Justus shook his head.

"I didn't take it all. I left half."

"Where is it?"

"At home in the closet."

"And she doesn't know?"

"Only Dad and I knew."

"Okay," Lindell said. "I get it."

She turned to Erki and asked if she could use the bathroom. He pointed to the hall. Lindell left the kitchen and closed the door after her. Two children sat on the floor. They had arranged all the shoes by the door into a big pile. Lindell caught sight of her boots near the bottom. From another room came the sound of music and loud peals of laughter. Lindell felt as if she were making an educational visit to a Normal Home.

In the bathroom she picked up her cell phone and called Haver. He told her that Ruben Sagander wasn't home. His wife had been waiting for a few hours and had tried his cell phone but had been unable to reach him.

"What are you doing?" Lindell asked.

"We've sent out an alert," Haver said. "We're trying to figure out where he may have gone."

"He's armed," Lindell said.

"We know," Haver said.

"Is he the one?"

"We can't say for sure, but the tracks in the snow appear to match up. He has a red-and-white pickup and he was at Akademiska Hospital on the same day the knife was stolen."

"Have you asked about the knife?"

"His wife says he has a large number of knives," Haver said. "The whole house is full of weapons and trophies."

"Motive?"

"Money, most likely," Haver said.

A short pause reigned before Lindell got the words out.

"I'm sorry for what happened."

"It's okay," Haver said, but Lindell could hear that it wasn't.

"I have to get home to Erik," she said. "Justus is here with Erki Karjalainen and doesn't want to go home yet. I think he should be able to stay awhile longer."

Finally she told him about the money stolen from the shop and the cash in Justus's backpack. She hadn't been sure she wanted to tell Haver about this. She knew she had to, but it felt like a betrayal of Erki and Justus.

"Money," Haver repeated.

"Ola, be careful."

Lindell ended the call and blew her nose with a little piece of toilet paper. The children in the hall were singing a Finnish Christmas song in shrill tones. She dialed Berit's number. When she answered, Lindell had to fight to keep the emotion out of her voice. She knew what a relief it would be for Berit to hear that Justus was fine.

"Thank God," she whispered.

Lindell could imagine her expression. She swallowed and continued.

"One more thing. In the closet in Justus's room there's a lot of money. It's John's money. I'll tell you later how he got it. It's not just from poker, I can tell you. I'll be over in a while so we can talk, then my colleagues will come down."

"What about Justus?"

"He's safe here. Give him a few hours. I promise you he's fine."

"Tell me more about the money. Where did it come from?"

"I'll be over soon. Okay?"

She went back to the kitchen. Justus looked up.

"I was treated to a Finnish concert out there," Lindell said lightly and tried to smile.

"It's the grandkids," Erki said.

"Can Justus stay with you a bit longer?" she asked.

Erki and Justus looked at each other.

"Of course. We'll call Berit later. I'll bring him back."

Lindell nodded.

"I'm going home now," she said, but paused. "Good-bye, Justus. I'll see you."

She gave Erki a look. He got to his feet slowly and when Lindell left the room he followed.

"There's one thing," she said as she searched for her boots in the pile of shoes.

Erki closed the door to the kitchen.

"I want . . . I know this is wrong, but there's one thing."

Lindell fished out one boot. She turned to Erki.

"This thing about dreams," she said. "Aren't children the most important?"

Erki nodded.

"I was thinking . . . Justus dreams of Africa."

Erki glanced at the kitchen door and took a step closer.

"Africa isn't what he thinks it is, but it's the dream he shared with John. What happens to him now?"

A group of kids ran giggling out of the living room, stopping short when they saw Lindell. They looked at the boot in her hand and the pile of shoes. Erki said something in Finnish and they immediately drew back into the living room and closed the door behind them.

When Lindell continued to speak it was with greater assurance.

"I want you to count out one hundred thousand from the backpack and put it aside. Hide it, and when everything has calmed down I want you to make sure Berit and the boy get to Africa. Do you understand what I'm saying?"

Erki nodded.

"He has to see the place, even if it's only for a week," Lindell said.

"Isn't this wrong?" Erki said.

Lindell shook her head.

"I would be fired on the spot if this came to light, but you like the boy, don't you?"

Erki Karjalainen smiled. Lindell thought she caught a whiff of mulled wine on his breath.

"Treat yourself to a taxi to Berit's and back," she said.

"But stealing?" Erki said. "What will the boy think?"

"Tell him it's what John would have wanted."

Erki leaned forward and for a second she thought he was going to hug her, but he only gave her an intent look, as if he wanted to check the sincerity in her expression.

"Are you alone with your baby over Christmas?"

Lindell shook her head, bent over, and fished out her other boot.

"We're having Berit and Justus over," Erki said. "If you want to come."

Lindell looked around, sat down on a chair, and pulled her boots on with concentration. She wanted to run away but also stay there. She sighed heavily and pulled up the zipper of her boot.

"My parents are in town," she said and managed to give him a smile. "But it's very nice of you to invite me. Thank you."

Lindell stepped out into the cold with a sense of longing. She turned. A nose was pressed against the glass and she waved. The nose disappeared.

She let the engine run for a while, like she always did. When she finally put it in gear she realized where this habit came from: it's what her father had always done with the delivery truck. He would go out a few minutes before he wanted to leave, turn on the engine, then go back in and have the last drop of his morning coffee before setting out on his rounds.

She called home. This time her mother's voice was commanding.

"You are coming home this instant," she said.

"There's a boy here who needed attention," Ann said.

"You have a boy yourself."

"He's hardly suffering," Ann said, but she felt a twinge of guilty conscience.

"Where are you?"

"Don't you hear what I'm saying? I'll be home soon! I'm just going to stop by and see someone on the way back."

Her mother hung up, and Ann was not surprised. She knew her mother was incapable of having a discussion of any length with her daughter. The distance between them was too great.

She pushed away all thoughts of her parents in the way she had always done, by thinking of her work. Had it been right to ask Erki to put away a hundred thousand? He had raised the issue of morality, but the fact was that it was John's money. Even if the starting sum had been stolen, then surely the poker winnings were his? If the money from the workshop was subtracted perhaps there would be even more than a hundred thousand, and this money would go to Berit and Justus in any case. This was how she was going to construct her inner moral defense.

She smiled to herself. After a while she turned on the radio. The calm music that flooded the interior took her back to another car ride on a summer's day several years ago when she had been on her way to visit her parents. The music combined with her own sense of being lost had caused her to turn the car around and drive to Gräsö and Edvard for the first time.

It had been summer. She had had Edvard. Now it was raw winter. She turned off the radio, suddenly exasperated at herself and her depressing fate, her inability to look after herself.

Forty-two

Ruben Sagander was sweating and as the sweat froze it felt as if it were forming into armor. He looked up at Berit Jonsson's illuminated windows. He walked in the front door to the building but did not turn on the light. He took a deep breath and started to walk up. The stairwell was full of Christmas smells. He walked past door after door. He heard music and laughter. Now he was sweating copiously, just like he always did on an elk hunt when the animal turned up in his viewfinder and he slowly, silently raised the barrel.

One flight of stairs left and in his mind he saw the damaged sign to the shop and recalled the sign of the first one they had erected in the shop. Sagander paused. A door opened on the floor below and he heard the sound of footsteps going down.

"Take the boxes with you too!" a woman shouted. The footsteps stopped. A man muttered something and returned to the apartment. There was a brief exchange and then the footsteps went down again. Ruben Sagander stood completely still and was relieved that the man hadn't turned on the light either. The front door opened. Sagander waited and fingered the knife in the pocket of his hunting jacket. A few minutes later the man returned, tiptoed up the stairs, a door opened, music streamed out, and the door closed again. Sagander breathed again and kept going.

Outside Berit's door he stopped and took out a hood. He drew the knife from its sheath and cut two slits in the fabric, pulled the hood over his head, and felt the door handle. The door was unlocked.

Berit was sitting at the kitchen table staring blankly at the carton of bills in front of her. Thousands of kronor. She had never even seen this much money before. She stuck her hand down and put a bunch of five-hundred-kronor notes on the table. Suddenly she started to cry.

"Why, John?" she sniffed and pushed some notes off the table.

Mechanically she started to count, putting twenty five-hundred-kronor notes in each pile. Anger overcame her when she had counted to fifty thousand. He had let her down. God, how she had scrimped and saved all fall, worrying about their finances and their future. She had even wondered if they would be forced to sell the apartment and start renting. This while John had been sitting on hundreds of thousands of kronor the whole time. Justus had clearly taken some money too. He had also known. John and the boy had been planning something together. A double betrayal.

There was a sound from the hall. She reached out and turned down the volume on the radio.

"Justus," she called out. "Is that you?"

Lennart watched the man looking up at Berit's windows. The yard was badly lighted and in the heavy snowfall it was hard to pick out any detail, but the figure looked familiar. Could it be Dick Lindström? He wasn't quite as large, but winter clothes could be misleading. Was he back from Holland and horny as a tomcat? Lennart swore under his breath. *I'll fucking catch you in the act*, he thought. *He's got some nerve showing his face around here. And Justus, the poor bastard, has to stand by and watch his mother being mounted by a scumbag with buck teeth a week after his father has died.*

Lennart drew closer to the entrance but pulled back after he caught sight of a man carrying garbage bags and a large box. He walked toward the garbage shed where Lennart was hiding. He heard the man come closer, how he mumbled something, cleared his throat, and spat into the snow.

He threw open the door to the garbage shed and Lennart more saw than smelled the stink waft out into the winter night. The man shut the door, cleared his throat again, and walked back to the apartment building. Lennart waited a minute or so before following him.

Ruben Sagander stared transfixed at the money in front of him. Piles of money were laid out on the floor and table. His money. He had been right. He gave a harsh laugh.

Berit automatically drew the money toward her as she stared at the masked man. She started putting the money back into the box.

"Don't touch me!" she said and looked around for something to defend herself with.

The man laughed again, bent down, and picked up a note. Berit lunged for a bread knife on the counter but was immediately caught in an iron grip. She felt the intense sweat smell and the hands like a vise around her arms. The man didn't say anything but he was panting. The mask made him unrecognizable but nonetheless there was something familiar about him. She tried to free herself but her attempt resulted only in a tighter grip and another laugh. She kicked him on the leg but it didn't seem to affect him.

I don't want to die, she thought with increasing desperation and remembered the expression of terror on John's face when she had said good-bye to him at the morgue. She made a new attempt to escape by throwing herself to the side as she also knocked him with her head. Her forehead met its mark. For a moment the grip around her arms loosened. She threw herself over the counter but the man was immediately on top of her again. She was thrown to the floor but managed to get one hand up and scratch him in the face. Her hand touched something wet and she understood it was blood seeping out through the mask. He howled with pain and aimed a blow at her body. It hit her on the shoulder and Berit was spun around by the incredible power of the blow.

Then he was on top of her. It had been a silent struggle, but now Berit screamed. He let go of her with one hand and tried to cover her mouth, and that gave her the opportunity to push her knee into his crotch. He cringed with pain, rose halfway to his feet, fumbled inside his coat, and pulled out the knife.

I'm going to die, she had time to think when she saw the raised knife above her head. At that moment there was a violent explosion and she felt the masked man flinch. Then there was another explosion and she saw the mask torn asunder and a terrible wound was revealed in his head before he was thrown forward on top of her.

The man's limbs jerked before everything was still. The weight and sharp smell of his body fueled her panic and she fought to get him off her. Blood dripped down onto her face and chest.

When she had managed to free herself she saw a figure standing in the doorway. She saw the weapon in his hand and realized that he had saved her life. She managed to crawl over, then pulled herself up to her knees and wiped the blood from her face with her sleeve. Then she saw it was Lennart. He was pale as a ghost. The hand with the gun was shaking and his body twitched once as if from an electric shock. She drew her breath and tried to say something.

"Lennart," she whispered.

He shook more violently and started to cry.

"Lennart," she repeated.

He turned around and left the apartment on wobbly legs. She looked at him leaving, stretched out her hand as if to stop him, but where he had stood only the gun remained. Berit leaned her head against the kitchen cabinet as heaving sobs racked her body. She stared, sickened, at the wound where the bullet had entered the man's head and retched violently.

Lennart was running. A door opened to the apartment directly below Berit's as he passed and he fell against it with full force, got back on his feet, and kept going.

He had shot a person, killed a person. Who was it? It was clear that it wasn't Dick. For a moment he had thought about walking over and peering under the mask but he hadn't dared. Now all that mattered was getting away. Had he been wrong about Berit? That was no lover coming for a visit, but a robber. Lennart had seen the money on the table and knew it was the poker winnings. Berit had been lying when she said she didn't know anything about the game.

He stopped by the front door, took some deep breaths, patted his jacket over the pocket to check that the gun was still there, but then remembered he had dropped it onto the floor in the apartment. He realized that it was all over, because even if Berit kept quiet his fingerprints would be found on the gun.

He opened the door. The cold blew over him and in the whirlwind of snow he saw a woman coming toward him. Ann Lindell. She was close but had probably not seen him. He turned on his heel and ran back up the stairs. Several doors were open and anxious neighbors peeked out. He paid no attention and kept going.

He was caught in a trap. Lindell was not likely to be alone. The whole area was probably crawling with police. On his way up the stairs he realized that he wouldn't be able to get to the attic without a key. For a while he paused in front of Berit's open door, not sure of what to do next, then ran back into the apartment.

He looked into the kitchen. Berit was still sitting next to the dead man. Her gaze was empty. She saw him, but not really. Lennart had a sudden impulse to go into the kitchen and sit down next to her on the floor. He wanted to say something to her, something that would explain everything. She had been good for John and because of that he liked her a lot. The words were there but Lennart hesitated.

He realized with an increasingly paralyzing clarity that his own life was over, that his words had no more power. He ran into the living room, glanced at the fish tank, and in his mind he saw John there, smiling, just like he had on the evening of the inauguration. Lennart stretched out his hand to touch his brother but there was no one there.

He could barely open the balcony door because of the amount of snow that had fallen. Nonetheless he managed to squeeze out onto the balcony, and suddenly he remembered the day with Micke, shoveling snow and the feeling of doing a good day's work. He looked out over the railing and felt dizzy. There was no one down in the yard, but he heard sirens in the distance.

With a strength he hadn't believed himself capable of he jumped up, dug his toes into the brick wall, managed to get one leg onto the laundry line, and heaved his body over the gutter. His legs kicked into thin air and he was panting hard.

"I can do it, I can do it," he said quietly. He was faintly aware of the sirens drawing closer. He rested his head against the roof and felt his strength ebbing away. He started to slip down, He turned his head and saw the police lights reflecting against the building opposite.

He turned his head back and looked at the ridge, catching sight of the oversnowed safety railing about a half meter from the edge of the roof.

"I'm the oldest son of a roofing man," he mumbled. "I'm the roofer's boy." He kicked with his legs, conscious of the fact that this was his last chance, threw out his right hand, and managed to reach the railing. He stretched out his left hand and connected even with that. Slowly, slowly he pulled himself up. He mumbled, chewed snow, felt the taste of blood in his mouth, but he conquered the roof, reached the safety of the railing, and could breathe a sigh of relief.

"The roofer's boy!" he shouted triumphantly. One of his legs was cramping up, he was shaking with cold, but he had managed to get up here on his own. He thought about his father, how he would have been proud. He looked up at the sky, which was covered in clouds.

"Albin," he said and smiled. "Dad."

He looked down and his fear of heights came back over him like a wave. The ground started to spin around and he lay flat against the roof on his stomach. His knees, propped up against the railing, were aching. A powerful puff of wind sent clouds of snow whirling over the roof. But it was as if the wind also brought calm with it. Lennart turned his head again and looked out at the city lights. The snow was no longer falling as thickly and he could pick out both the castle and the cathedral spires.

"That's where you died, old man," he said.

When he turned his head toward the south he could see out to his childhood neighborhood in Almtuna. House after house, roof after roof. People preparing for Christmas.

His fear of heights was slowly sinking away, replaced by a sense of being above all this, all the confusion and noise. He found himself here, and there were worse places to be. It felt silly to be lying on his stomach, as if he were afraid, submissive, as if someone could come over and put his foot on his neck at any time. He turned, straightened his back, and sat up. He laughed.

"I'm up on a roof!" he shouted to the wind.

He stood up with a wide stance secured by the railing, trying to parry the gusts of wind and shouting out his hate at the city that had witnessed his birth, but suddenly he calmed down. *Stop shouting*, he thought.

He should have said those things to Berit. She was the one who could transmit something, tell Justus that John and Lennart were the roofer's kids, that they had laughed together and that there had been moments of happiness. She would be able to talk about the hard things, tell Justus about their little sister, maybe show photographs.

He had killed an unknown man and now there would always be a price on his head, he would always be on the run. He had managed to botch even the simplest thing, his revenge. But he had killed the guy who had threatened Berit. The cold made him shake harder. Shouldn't he go back down to Berit and talk about something important for once?

The wind threw itself over the ridge, squirming past the chimney, howling down seams and tiles.

"Little brother," he said, took a wobbling step, and fell forward. He hit the tile roof violently, felt something break in his face, and then somersaulted off the edge.

Ola Haver, who was on the street, saw him fall. He heard the scream and instinctively held out his hands to stop the man's free fall. But in the next moment the body hit the frozen ground.

The lights from the police cars whirled around, and on the other side of the street, peeking out from between their amaryllises and poinsettias, people were watching.

The ground was white and Lennart's blood was red. For a few moments everything on the street grew still. Berglund took a step closer to the body, which had come to rest in an unnatural position, and removed his hat.